DIG TWO GRAVES
USS BULL SHARK NAVAL THRILLER SERIES
BOOK NINE

SCOTT W. COOK

SPINDRIFT PRESS

Dig Two Graves
USS Bull Shark Naval Thriller Series, Book 9

Copyright © 2024 by Scott W. Cook

All rights reserved.

Formatting and book cover provided by Trisha Fuentes

No part of this book may be reproduced in any form or by any electronic or mechanical means, including information storage and retrieval systems, without written permission from the author, except for the use of brief quotations in a book review.

A WORD FROM THE AUTHOR

Hello, dedicated reader. Thank you for joining our brave crew on yet another WWII adventure. Before we begin this tale, there is something I'd like to address.

This book does not include the conclusion to the Pat Jarvis story from *Blood Warm Waters*. As this book grew much larger in scale than intended, I've decided to separate the two stories in order that you might enjoy this one a little sooner. Rest assured, though, I'm working on Pat's tale and hope to have it to you not long after this yarn.

CONTENTS

1. Fremantle, Australia	1
Chapter 2	11
Chapter 3	23
Chapter 4	35
5. TIMOR SEA Off the southeastern Coast of Timor - 10°38"S, 125°30"E -	45
6. Off Timor	57
7. Timor, Beach Able	67
8. East Timor	79
Chapter 9	89
10. BANDA SEA December 23, 1942 - 0630 ship's time	101
Chapter 11	113
12. Aboard light cruiser Agano	123
13. East Timor	133
Chapter 14	143
Chapter 15	153
16. Light cruiser Agano	163
17. Light cruiser Agano	173
18. East Timor	183
Chapter 19	197
Chapter 20	205
21. Light cruiser Agano	215
22. Light cruiser Agano	225
23. VILLAGE OF MINDELO December 24, 1942	239
Chapter 24	251
Chapter 25	261
Chapter 26	271
Before You Go	279
Other Books by this Author…	281

1

FREMANTLE, AUSTRALIA
DECEMBER 17, 1942

"So how's that hat feelin', Chief?" Paul "Buck" Rogers asked his companion as they and two more men stepped out of the PX and into the bright Western Australian sunshine.

"Well…" newly-promoted Chief Petty Officer Danny Pentakkus mused as he settled his new hat on his close-cropped black hair. "Feels pretty damned good, I guess. Course… I'm still in chahge of my room, same as yesdee. Cont rightly tell ya' that it feels a whole lot different."

"Oh, but it is, pally," Mike Duncan, a fellow chief grinned. "The dames love it."

"Especially in this town," added Chief Clancy Weiss.

Rogers laughed and led his men down the narrow sidewalk back toward the waterfront, "In this town, the dames love any guy in a sailor suit and with an American accent. Hope we work outta here more… like friggin' Shangri-la."

As if perfectly stage-managed, a slightly dusty thirty-six Ford pulled over and idled to a stop at the curb. A pretty redhead who looked as if she might have a fully inflated Mae West beneath her sundress smiled out the open window. She gave the four men the once over and settled on Pentakkus. The new chief had worn his good whites that day and they'd apparently drawn her eye.

"Hey, sailors," she said in a mellifluous Aussie accent. She aimed her high-wattage smile at Pentakkus. "You have a home cooked meal lately, Chief?"

"Uhm…" Pentakkus prevaricated. "I guess not…"

The woman cocked an eyebrow, but her smile never wavered. Rogers rolled his eyes but jumped in to save his friend, "Excuse me, ma'am, my friend here is just a bit shy, is all. Lemme just speak to him a minute and he's all yours."

Weiss and Duncan tried their hardest not to laugh at Pentakkus's bewildered expression. Rogers shook his head and pulled the new chief aside.

"Danny… it's like this," explained the chief of the boat. "So many ladies on this side of the country lost their men to the war. There's a huge disparity here and they're lonely… *real* lonely, you read me? When a woman asks if you had a home cooked meal lately… it means she wants to take you home, cook one for you… and then screw you up one side and down the next!"

Pentakkus's eyes bulged, "Ayuh?"

"Yeah," Duncan cut in, "and if you don't take this pretty lady up on it… we ain't friends no more."

"You've heard of a broad with a heat wave?" Weiss added sotto voce. "Down here they got a hot front."

Pentakkus smiled genially at the woman and saluted, "Ma'am, I ain't had a home cooked meal in ova a yeya. It sounds lovely."

This was a lie, at least the part about the meal. However, the lady's smile grew as bright as the sun and she waved to the passenger side, "Well then, love, climb on in. I'm Gloria, and I don't live but a few kilometers down Sterling Road."

"Bye Danny," Duncan waved. "Been nice knowin' ya."

The lady laughed and drove away, leaving the three men in civilian clothing to amble on their way. As they moved back toward the harbor, they occasionally passed other American sailors, a few of whom they knew. The streets of Fremantle were bustling now that Uncle Charlie had come to oversee the submarine base and the continual work to both expand and reinforce the large square harbor.

"Wonder how many of our guys got waylaid like that?" Duncan asked.

"Much as we've seen them lately, I'd say all of them," Weiss replied with a chuckle. "Got me a cute little dolly over the river in Perth myself. She's pickin' me up tonight, in fact."

Rogers raised his brows, "You, Clance? But you're a married man!"

Weiss shrugged, "True. And I love Mildred to death… but I'm halfway around the world and she isn't around. I'm not made of stone, y'know. What… I'm not human?"

Rogers clucked, "Wicked sinner."

Duncan laughed, "Ain't we all. Say… anybody seen the skipper lately?"

A clouded look settled over Rogers's face, and he sighed softly, "Nah… he did one of them outback treks last week. Supposed to be back today, I think."

Duncan looked pensive, "Hope it helped. He ain't been himself since… since that day we tried helpin' that Nip plane."

"Yeah… sort of cold and impatient with everybody, even me," Weiss said. "About bit my head off day we came in because there was a little smudge on the statement of condition report I typed up."

Duncan snorted, "Hell, everybody on the boat's got a story like that, Clance. He had me and mine scrubbin' and polishin' the rock crushers so's you'd think they never got used. He likes a clean ship, but…"

Rogers looked off into the distance at nothing, "He's takin' what happened hard, fellas. Feels responsible, y'know. Especially over Mr. Hazard. After what happened on The Canal and all…"

Duncan frowned and nodded, "Yeah… Mr. Hazard had it rough. Japs worked him over pretty good. Awful thing… way they hung him up…"

"Plus, poor Hadley… kid finds out his mom goes into remission and now *he's* a gold star in *her* window… that's hard," Rogers said.

"Be good to get out there and sink a few Japs," Weiss added. "Get a little revenge."

Rogers grunted, "Be even better somebody ended this damned

war. Or at least gave us a break. Scuttlebutt is we'll be shippin' out soon. Sooner than the usual two weeks off, as usual."

"We gettin' a new torpedo officer?" Duncan asked. "Plus a new boatswain?"

Rogers shrugged, "Dunno. Far as the boatswain goes, I'd rather promote somebody from within. If I had my druthers—"

"*Druthers!*" Duncan guffawed. "When did you become an egghead, Buck?"

"Michael," Rogers sniffed, "just because I'm a hard-workin' blue collar guy, that don't mean I ain't got a brain in my noggin. If the good lord had seen fit to give you one, maybe you'd put it to use doin' something other than smokin', drinkin' and chasin' broads."

Weiss chortled and slapped his knees. Duncan flapped a hand in Roger's direction, "Says the guy who claims he can outdrink anybody on the boat and who has two, three frills in every port.

"All true," said Rogers haughtily, "but I manage to do some readin' in between. Now, as I was sayin'… if I had my druthers… *Mike*… I'd always promote from within. Like it when the higher ratings come up in their own boats. Means they know the ship and the men. But I'm just a lowly CPO, so I do what the papers tell me to do."

"How about this joint?" Weiss suggested, pointing at a tavern with a hand-carved wooden sign swinging on a pole over the door. Intricate carvings of a swooping whale shark and a monstrous prawn were surrounded by etched letters painted in gold.

"The Shark and Prawn," Duncan read. "Clever."

"They got AC," Weiss said, pointing to a hand-lettered sign covering one of the large windows stating that very fact.

"It's December," Rogers chuckled. "Can't be more'n ninety-three today."

"Cold beer," Weiss declared. "Foster's on tap."

"Well then… how can we resist?" asked the COB.

The three chiefs' eyes had hardly adjusted to the interior when a ruckus broke out in a dark corner on the other side of a small dance floor. At first, the *Bull Shark* sailors couldn't tell what was happening. Half a dozen couples gyrated to a waltz being played on an old phonograph and their meanderings through the multi-colored bulbs blocked the chiefs' view.

However, the curses, shouts, and the heavy thump of something impacting wood drew their attention. The dancers parted, revealing several shadowy forms beyond flailing like somebody had tossed a live wire into their midst.

A tall cocktail waitress with big blonde hair, legs that might've given a giraffe a complex and who appeared to be smuggling cantaloupes under her checked blouse hurried over to them, "You blokes from the *Bull Shark?*"

"Yes, ma'am…" Rogers replied uncertainly.

"Well, I think a couple of your boys are startin' trouble… and I don't need any trouble in my place," said the waitress or perhaps the owner, her dark blue eyes wide and filled with an intensity that captured Roger's own gaze.

"We'll go have a look-see," said Duncan.

The lady smiled at Rogers, "Don't get me wrong, Chief… I like you Yanks. But I don't like the shore patrol."

"We'll handle it, ma'am," said Rogers.

"Sheila," she grinned and tossed him a wink.

Weiss chuckled, "Sheila?"

"Yeah… I know. *Never* gets old," said.

Rogers led his friends into the dark corner and recognized four of their sailors gathered around a table. One of them was standing… although it looked like it took character… and shouting, pounding the flat of his hand on the tabletop, making the glasses and pitcher rattle and bounce.

"It ain't right! Wilbur Dockerty was shouting, his words muddy from too much beer. "It ain't right what they done to old Joey! Ain't he had it rough enough on account of his mom gettin' the cancer? Now he's taking the big dirt nap, too? Nah… nah… not the dirt nap… the fuckin' wet nap! Dumped him right into the drink like yesterday's fuckin' *trash!*"

"Willy, take it easy!" Doug Ingram was saying, holding out a hand to his friend.

"Yeah, you're gettin' all steamed up, buddy!" Fred Swooping Hawk implored.

"We all miss Joey," Bobby Barrett added. "But it ain't worth gettin' sore now. C'mon, Willy, sit down and take a breath, huh?"

"Sit down? Take a breath?" Dockerty shouted. "What for? What for? So's we can go back out and get dead, too? They done got Wendel and Marty and Joey and poor Mr. Hazard… fuckin' slant-eyed sons of bitches! We tried helpin' them out and they pumped our boys fulla lead! They ain't worth *shit!* This war is *shit!* And bein' in these goddamned pipes is *shit!* I'm done! Done, ya' hear me? Gonna go out there right now… go out there and find me a nice Aussie broad and run off into the bush! We're gonna eat crocs and raise kangaroos and fuck all day and night! And you know what? You know what else, chums? If'n I ever see a squint again in my whole fuckin' life… I'll choke him to death! *Death*, ya' hear me?"

"All right, Dockerty," Rogers boomed, stepping up close to the drunken and distraught sailor. "That's enough. Time to go."

"Go?" Dockerty wheeled on the chief, over-compensated and teetered on one foot, his pale face a mask of pained confusion. "I ain't goin' anywhere near that damned boat again… whoever you are."

"It's the COB, Dockerty," Duncan said, stepping up to the other side. "C'mon, now… let's get you some fresh air."

"You freshen this air… ya' somfunnuhbish!" Dockerty swung his fist through nothing, spinning himself around and crumpling unceremoniously into a heap at the two chiefs' feet. The sailor belched, rippled out a watery fart and, without further ceremony… began to snore. Weiss started to laugh and shook his head.

"What the hell's this, fellas?" Rogers asked the other three.

"Sorry, Chief," Ingram sighed. "We didn't realize how much he was drinkin' until it were too late."

"Must be this winter heat," Swooping Hawk said and hid his grin with his beer glass.

"Jesus…" Duncan said, reaching down with one of his long, powerful arms and hauling the limp dish rag of Dockerty to his feet and then supporting him. "All I need is for Mr. Nichols or the XO… or God-forbid the Old Man, seeing my macs like this… Christ."

"You should know better, Doug," Rogers said. "You too, Freddy. You two are almost ready for PO."

"We was just blowin' off steam, COB," Barrett protested. "Will don't mean nothin'… he's just sore about Joe and Wendel. Like the rest of us."

"I know, but it ain't an excuse to cut up in a nice place like this," Rogers said. "Okay, fellas. You think you can get him back to the EQ and into his rack?"

"Sure we can, Chief," Swooping Hawk said.

"Good," said Weiss, "if Hoffman's around, have him give Dockerty an alcohol bath. If he's not, you guys can do it for him. At least get him into the shower, okay?"

"Aye-aye," said Barrett, rising and taking the load of the unconscious Dockerty from Duncan. Swooping Hawk stepped up to do the same.

"You fellas go ahead," said Ingram, pulling a battered Lord Buxton from his front pocket. "I'll take care of the tab."

"Good man," said Rogers and followed Ingram to the bar. The electrician paid the bill, smiled apologetically at the tall blonde who was now back behind it, and hurried to catch up with his friends. Rogers and his two friends found empty stools and perched on them.

"Sorry about that, Sheila," he said to the blonde.

"I couldn't help but overhear," said the pretty bartender. "A cryin' shame about their mates. All too common a story in Freo, though. How long until you ship out?"

"Can't blame ya' for wantin' to get rid of us, ma'am," Weiss smiled.

Sheila laughed, "Oh, it's not that… just curious, is all."

"Well… could be as many as five days or as few as two," Rogers sighed. "Way things have been… no way to tell."

"Hardly seems enough time," said Sheila, meeting Rogers's gaze and running her tongue slowly over full lips. "But it's a start."

* * *

"Captain! Captain Turner, sir! There you are… sir? Sir!"

Art Turner made a gallant attempt to ignore the insistent female voice that called out. He was nearly across the wide expanse of the freight lot near the Naval warehouses along the harbor. Far enough to get away with it?

He was dirty, tired, and still had five days of leave left. He'd be damned if he got pulled into another hairbrained scheme before his well-deserved and too-short R and R was up.

However, the voice persisted and was reinforced by the frantic and rapid tap, tap, tap of heels clicking across concrete. Groaning and wondering how in hell anybody recognized him in his boots, dungarees, chambray shirt, and dusty straw hat he couldn't imagine. If anything, he should be taken for a civilian interloper or a frumpy sailor rather than a ship's commander.

"Sir! I need to speak with you, please!"

Turner growled something dark under his breath and stopped, turning and settling his duffel on his shoulder with practiced ease. He regarded the WAVE who was doing her best to hustle toward him in heels without taking a nasty spill. She was a pretty thing, of medium height and with a well-shaped figure. Although brunette rather than blonde, she reminded him vaguely of his wife Joan, and that only served to foul his mood further.

"Can I *help* you, Lieutenant?" Turner snapped as the lady officer came to attention and saluted. "I'm on *leave*, for Chrissakes. Why I'm dressed like this. Just because I'm headed out to my boat for *five* minutes doesn't mean I'm available, dammit."

The WAVE flushed, "I'm sorry, sir… I hate to be the bearer of bad news and all… but Admiral Lockwood gave me a directive to find you, sir. Said it was vital and that I'd better not come back without you."

Turner snorted, "Well, for the love… I'm headed over to *Pelias* now, anyway. He could've just intercepted me there."

"Well, sir… the admiral's not aboard the tender, sir."

Turner sighed, "What's your name, Lieutenant?"

"Marsha Owens, sir," she said and smiled. "It's a pleasure to meet you. Admiral Lockwood has a great deal of fine things to say about you, Captain."

Turner harrumphed, "I'll bet. Like how ole Anvil Art and his men never need to get a full two weeks of leave no matter how much they've earned it? How ole Anvil Art is just rarin' to go at the drop of a goddamned *hat?* Exactly how *urgent* is this, Lieutenant Owens?"

"I'm sorry, sir…"

Turner rolled his eyes skyward, "Stop apologizing… it's not your fault, Lieutenant. You're doing your duty. But since your duty is taking me prisoner… I'm gonna call you Marsha. So where are you taking me, Marsha?"

"Over into Perth, sir," she replied. "The admiral has a house there. It being a Friday and all… he works out there over the weekend, sir."

Turner sighed, "Do I have time to crumb up first? I'm not exactly at my best, here."

She smiled, "The admiral said I was to bring you as soon as I found you, sir. Whatever your condition."

Turner groaned, "Figures… all right, Marsha… take me to your leader."

2

Marsha led Turner to a black and chromium Packard complete with running boards and white wall tires. The car twinkled in the sunshine and looked vaguely out of place amid the industrial concrete and steel of the port facilities.

As they drove out onto Sterling Road and over the long bridge that spanned the mouth of the Swan River, Turner looked out over the harbor. Fremantle was already a thriving port and was growing still. Aside from the military industrial complex, there were freighters and tankers from the far east moored along the Victoria Quay, freight trains being worked in the Fremantle railyard, and much more to come. It was truly an impressive sight, especially when one considered how remote Western Australia was from the more populous cities of Sydney, Melbourne, and Brisbane.

"How do you like our little corner of the world, Captain?" Lieutenant Owens asked as they rumbled over the bridge.

"Very impressive," Turner said politely, not really wishing to talk. Not that he was much in the mood for conversation lately in any case.

"Which one is yours, sir?"

It didn't take long. Turner could still see the half dozen submarines nested alongside the tender like a pack of juvenile whales jockeying for position at their mother's breast. The boats were tied one to another with gangways leading across so that men from each could make their way along and up onto *Pelias*. From a distance, most of them looked alike. There were two S-boats, which were visibly smaller than the newer fleet submarines, of course. But his *Bull Shark* stood out from her sisters.

She had the sweeping, slightly up-turning deck, the bulging conning tower made angular by its fairings and the same towering radar, radio and periscope masts. However, *Bull Shark* was unique, at least so far in the war, in that she featured two 5x25 caliber deck guns, one forward of the conning tower and one aft. She also sported a quad-barrel Pompom, that too was unusual. Combined with her twin-barreled 20mm Oerlikon abaft the masts, the new *Balao*-class submarine had a surface-action armament nearly as impressive as some destroyers.

"On the end," said Turner.

Owens whistled, "Blimey! She's got some teeth, eh? Bet there are plenty of Japs who wish they'd minded their own when she pops round I'll bet."

Turner snorted, "They don't usually live long enough to regret their folly."

Owens fell silent for a time. She could tell that Turner wasn't in a talkative mood and finally allowed him to simply sit back and enjoy the ride. He wished that he could. Wished that he could appreciate the scenery, the growing city, and the natural areas they were careful to preserve. Even when they neared the beach, the submarine captain was unable to truly savor all of the new sights and experiences… as he hadn't for nearly two weeks.

He was hard-pressed to explain it, even to himself. He'd lost men in battle before. Hell, he had to count himself lucky in that regard.

Submarine duty was the most hazardous in the Navy. So far in *Bull Shark's* short eight months of official life, she'd gone out on no less than eight patrols. Not full sixty-five day runs, but still… and he could count the number of men he'd lost without having to slip off his shoes. Or almost.

On one occasion, he'd lost a pair of officers. They'd turned out to be scheming assholes who'd nearly caused the death of his entire crew. In the end, they'd gotten what they'd deserved. But Porter Hazard's death... and the death of Janslotter, Freeman, and Hadley... was a jagged, aching wound in his soul. A wound continually salted by merciless technicolor memory.

Why? Why had it affected him so badly this time? It had been pointed out to him that he might want to talk to the base shrink about it. Turner had dismissed this out of hand, however. For one thing, he doubted that one or two sessions with a psychologist would give him the answer. Second, if he revealed too much or appeared overly distraught... doubts would be cast. And a captain that'd gone soft in wartime might even be relieved of his command.

In spite of the fact that the thought secretly pleased him... it would mean extended leave and more time with his wife and kids... the idea of giving up his boat was an anathema to his soul. His gold oak leaves weren't even a year old yet, nor was his command pin, and he wasn't about to have them snatched away. At least... not until he got his revenge.

Perhaps what bothered Turner most was the stink of that last incident with the Japs. How a damaged aircraft had landed and how the men aboard had opened up with automatic weapons when Turner and his ship had tried to render assistance.

There had been something... wrong with the whole thing. It smelled of a setup right from the start. A deliberate action that had *targeted* him and his boat. With each passing day, Turner's incessant ruminations and his hindsight had convinced him of that.

He knew that he and *Bull Shark* had gained a reputation among the enemy. He'd faced one of their most brilliant ASW commanders. He'd tangled with and been aided by a pair of well-placed Japanese officers who secretly wanted to end the war early. He'd had something of a duel with a semi-psychotic carrier commander as well. It took no stretch of the imagination... and Turner didn't think he was being at all paranoids... to think that a plot had been hatched against him. That this plot was still underway, and that more danger lurked out in the Indian Ocean and the China Sea for him.

Therefore, Turner knew that no matter how much he might want to simply sail back to Pearl and hold Joanie in his arms again... he had to get back out there. He had to overcome that little voice that whispered to him that maybe it was time to hang up his dolphins... even if for a while. He *could*, if he so desired, easily request a posting at admin. Hell, he was somewhat surprised that he hadn't been sent stateside on a war bonds tour. But no... no... he had to get out there and see this thing through. To discover what trapped Yamata and Lanser and whoever else had set for him. Find it and then turn it back on them.

He wanted his pound of flesh and he'd be goddamned if anybody... even himself... would rob him of his due.

"We're here, sir," Owens said, breaking his reverie and causing Turner to look around in surprise.

They'd pulled into a long, curving drive at an expansive, elegantly groomed beachfront home. Turner whistled at the sight of the two-story palatial residence. He began to wonder just how much an admiral, even a *rear*-admiral, got paid anyway?

"If you'll follow me, sir," Owens said.

Turner could sense the slight chill in her voice. His standoffishness had finally broken through her pleasant demeanor, and he realized he may have offended her. That hadn't been his intention, of course, and yet he couldn't muster up a great deal of sympathy.

"Lieutenant," he said, making the necessary effort. "I've had... a rough few weeks. Please don't take my introspection as a reflection on you."

There was the briefest flash of something in her dark eyes and a slight smile played at her lips when she nodded and said: "Of course, sir. This way, please."

Owens led Turner into the house and past a sunken front living room. Turner took note that no less than a dozen officers sat there, dressed in a variety of khakis and olive-green class-As. One man, standing off by himself and staring out the bay window beside the fireplace wore what Turner now recognized to be a British Army uniform. He couldn't see the rank, as the man's back was turned, but for some reason, the tall, lean figure with the closely cropped black hair stood out among the rest.

"All waiting appointments with the admiral," Owens explained when she saw where Turner was looking. "A bit like the old days, isn't it, sir?"

"Old days?" Turner asked as he followed her down a wide hallway and toward the rear of the house.

"Yes, sir… when men like Nelson or Cochrane or Pellew would go to White Hall and wait for an audience," Owens smiled. "Even happened to Horatio Hornblower."

Turner smiled, "I very much doubt Lord Viscount Nelsen had to wait long… or Admiral Pellew. Exmouth Gulf is named for him, isn't that so?"

Owens's large brown eyes widened, "A student of royal Navy history are you, sir?"

Turner nodded, "Occupational hazard."

Owens led him to a corner room with its door standing open. Inside, a great sweep of windows overlooked a swimming pool and wide, golden-sanded beach beyond. From that angle, Turner couldn't see the port off to the right, just a wide swath of the Indian Ocean gently rolling ashore.

"Ah! The great hero cometh at last!" a familiar voice boomed out.

Turner drew his attention away from the view and saw Admiral Charles "Uncle Charlie" Lockwood emerge from a side door and stride up. The commander submarine southwest Pacific extended a hand and turner took it. The handshake was warm and vigorous.

"How the hell are ya', Art?" Lockwood asked. "Haven't seen you since Brisbane!"

"Fine, sir, thank you, sir."

Lockwood smiled, "Bullshit! But I appreciate the effort. Marsha, honey, would you be a doll and fetch my other guest? Thanks… fine girl, that Marsha. Crackerjack clerk. Sorry for interrupting your leave, Art… but I figured if I had to do it, then sending a pretty WAVE would at least soften the blow."

"Yessir."

Lockwood's gaze locked onto Turner's for a long moment and some of the jocularity ebbed from his tone, "Been rough, has it, Art? Since that last encounter with the Nip floater?"

"It was… unexpected, sir," Turner said neutrally.

Lockwood nodded and moved behind his desk, "Take a seat, Captain. I've got a few things for you… including a question. A hard question… but we'll get to that in a minute. First, let me say you had a helluva trip out here. Wake, Ulithi, Palau… smacking those Japs around and then sinking a couple of tankers off Balikpapan just to wipe old Tojo's eye. Love it. Hell, if I had a squadron full of Anvil Art Turners, we'd have pushed the fuckin' Jap all the way back to Mount Fuji by now… ah well… but that last little thing… damned bad business. I was sorry to hear about Hazard. Good man."

"They're all good men, sir."

Lockwood nodded, "I know. Why I work so hard to get my submariners the best of everything. My opinion, Art, these boats and men like us… true submariners… are every bit as vital to this war as the carriers."

"I agree, sir."

Lockwood steepled his fingers on his desk blotter and studied Turner for a moment, "You're probably still a bit confused about this mission, I'd guess? The slant money you were given in the orders and all?"

"That I am, sir… The real reason for us coming all the way out, I take it?"

Lockwood nodded, "What we want, and I'm sure Bob English already touched on this, is for you to make the rounds behind the lines, as it were. To head up through Indonesia and into the South China Sea, the Sea of Japan, and come out between the Jap islands and sink as many ships as you can along the way. We want to put Hirohito, Tojo, and even Mr. Moto on notice that nowhere is safe. That there is no place they can send their ships without facing the teeth of the fucking for Christ sakes Allied *Navy*!"

Turner nodded, "Ambitious and somewhat dangerous, sir."

Lockwood snorted, "Damned near crazy is what it is… and that's why I need the best, Art. Why we're sending men like Mush Morton and Slade Cutter out there… and why I need Anvil Art most of all."

Turner frowned and grunted something non-committal, "I do my job, sir."

Lockwood chuckled, "And how… but there's a new wrinkle, Art. Well, hell… a couple of them. Intel has come across from Station Hypo that there may be Jap elements gunning for you. Specifically, for you."

"I think that's obvious, sir."

Lockwood sighed, "Yeah… but we've received nothing from Shadow in several weeks. We don't know his disposition or even if he's still alive… or on our side."

Turner raised his eyebrows at that, "I've *met* Commander Osaka, sir… looked into his eyes. I think his goals are genuine."

Lockwood fluttered his lips, "You'd think so… but that last ambush… it stinks, Art. It was a setup. A setup specifically aimed at you and *Bull Shark*."

"I've already made that determination, sir," Turner said. "I suspect that pretend Aussie flyer, Gus Pageant aka Friedrich Lanser, is behind it."

Lockwood nodded, "Yeah… yeah… but the whole thing stinks because it was a perfect setup. They *knew* you'd render aid. They sent that bird *right* at you, Art… almost as if they knew where you'd be."

"Can't see how that's possible, sir… but I can assure you… such a mistake will not be repeated," Turner's words grated like shards of glass. His cheeks burned with fury. He leaned forward and his eyes blazed. "That's the last time I reach out a hand to a fucking Jap. *Sir*."

Lockwood appeared to study his officer for another long stretch before nodding slowly, "Can't say as I blame you, there… though it has paid off in the past."

Turner grunted.

Lockwood sighed, "Before we go further, and I tell you the new portion of your patrol orders… I need to know something, Art. And I need an honest answer. Are you fit to command?"

Turner stiffened and sat bolt upright in his chair, "Admiral… do you believe otherwise?"

"Answer me, goddammit. No bravado, no bullshit. Straight goods, Captain."

Turner's jaw worked and he struggled to suppress the surge of anger that welled up inside him. He was rather surprised at the strength and acidic tang of his rage. It was hardly new, but it seemed to come more easily over the past few weeks.

Turner inhaled, centered himself and said, "I am ready to go, sir."

Lockwood leaned back in his chair and picked up a pen. Absently, he twirled the implement in his fingers, letting it occasionally tap the blotter. All the while, he stared at Turner… into him… as if trying to peel back the layers of the man to see what was really inside.

"Honestly, Art… I'm not so sure," Lockwood admitted finally. He smiled faintly. "Oh, I know you've got the skills, no question there. I'm just… worried about your mental state. I've watched you. I've spoken to your officers… I've sensed the change aboard your boat, even in port. Since that day in the Indian Ocean… you've been a different man."

Turner frowned, wondering who among his officers or enlisted had squealed. Lockwood grinned, almost as if reading his mind.

"Nobody's said anything derogatory or even directly about your mental fitness, Art," said the admiral. "I'll bet that if I asked that directly, even polite Elmer Williams would tell me to go to hell."

Turner smiled thinly.

"No… it's just a sense that I get," Lockwood went on. "Remember, I'm a submariner, too."

Turner sighed, "Admiral… I won't lie to you. I'm pissed off. I want a chance to go out and punish the Jap for what they did."

"I know… I understand. The trouble is that such vengeful emotions can lead to rashness, Art. And for what I have in mind, I need to know that my man is as stable and cool as possible."

"Sir, I am perfectly capable of performing whatever mission you have in mind," Turner declared, making an effort to remain calm. "My officers, my men, and my boat are ready. *I'm* ready, sir."

Lockwood's eyes drilled into Turner once more. When the junior officer didn't crack under the scrutiny, the admiral smiled and nodded, "Good. All I needed to hear, Captain."

As if that were the cue she'd been waiting for… and perhaps it had been… Owens rapped her knuckles on the door and swung it inward. She held it open to allow the tall, lean British officer to enter. Turner could now see his insignia and saw that he was a lieutenant colonel.

"Colonel Archer, please come in and have a seat," Lockwood said. "Thank you, Marsha."

"Can I bring coffee or anything else?" the admiral's aide asked.

"That sounds nice," Lockwood said. "Colonel?"

"Spot of tea wouldn't go amiss," said Archer in a crisp, no nonsense English accent. Turner, although he was no judge, thought it sounded a bit Oxonian. A bit high bred as it were. "But a hot cup of joe should do in a pinch."

Marsha smiled and exited, closing the door behind her. Lockwood sat behind his desk and folded his hands atop the blotter again, "Colonel, this is the man I've been telling you about. Lieutenant Commander Arthur Turner, USS *Bull Shark*."

Archer held out his hand. The hand was, like the rest of him, lean but strong, "Lieutenant Colonel Percival Archer, sir. Your servant. I understand you're the fellow tasked with giving me and mine a lift, what?"

Turner's earlier impression was reinforced. As a student of history, Turner remembered how in the old colonial days, British army officers would purchase their commissions. Usually this was done by well-placed and well-monied sons of parliamentary members or those who held peerage. Lords and sons of Lords. The man even pronounced his rank with the traditional Lefteneant.

"A pleasure, Colonel," Turner replied neutrally. "British Army?"

"Commandos," said Archer, his nose rising ever so slightly. "Was with my unit in Timor until the end of the summer. Had a spot of bother up that way... and I'm seeking to correct a rather inconvenient oversight. Believe yourself up to the challenge, Old Boy?"

Turner cocked an eyebrow, "I don't know what the challenge is yet, Colonel... but my boat and I have faced our fair share."

"Splendid," said Archer, just a hint of a smile pushing up the points of his Errol Flynn mustachios.

"Bad business in Timor, Art," Lockwood said. "Aussie and British units held the island until the beginning of the summer. Japs pushed in from Kupang and Dili and pushed the allies back to the southern coast. The RAN has a plan to get them out... but it could be well into next year before it comes to fruition."

"So what's my role in all of this?" Turner asked.

"What remains of my unit is hiding behind enemy lines in East Timor," Archer explained. "Not far from Dili. My executive officer and master sergeant, along with a few others. Hardly a few dozen men out of an entire bloody battalion… three hundred men wiped out over the course of a month, by God… those who were able fled into the hills and have been running one step ahead of the goddamned Nip since August. We *must* get them out."

Turner frowned. He stood and began to pace, "My crew and I faced a similar situation in new Ireland back toward the end of October, Colonel. Group of refugees… I took in a squad of Marines along with a few of my crew… it was a trap. An intelligence ploy to trap them and us. So with all due respect… are we certain that your people are still there?"

"I'll stake my life on it, Old boy," Archer said sternly.

"You'll be staking *my* men's lives on it, Colonel," Turner replied stonily. "Getting men ashore in such a place is no picnic. Let alone getting even more men off. Who're you taking with you?"

Archer smiled and it held no warmth, "Just me, Captain. Of course… I'd be obliged if you send in a few of yours as a bit of a bolster, eh? Your admiral says you have several men aboard who have engaged in shore operations."

Turner nodded, "Me included… but surely, Colonel, Australia or her majesty can spare their own men… men trained for this… rather than sending in a pack of bubble heads."

"No dice," Lockwood said. "This is a hit and run, get in and get out fast op, Art. It's precisely *because* of New Ireland that I want you on this. You'll put the colonel ashore, give him a bit of time to make contact, and get back to the extraction point and pull him off."

Turner frowned, "Pull him off? Aren't we taking his men off, sir?"

"Not this round, old chap," Archer answered. "I'll be delivering some equipment… mainly a radio… so that proper arrangements can be made. That and with intelligence from the mainland… more might be done on Timor."

Lockwood nodded, "If it works, we can use the same trick when it comes time to extract more men. Then you continue on with the rest of your mission. Colonel Archer may be of some help, there."

Turner frowned and eyed the hard-faced commando for a long moment and then asked: "One question, Colonel… how'd you get out?"

"Pure bad luck, Old Boy," Archer said genially, but again his dark eyes could've chilled a bowl of soup. "Had taken a jaunt down this way to report in… when the Japs invaded and cut off any reinforcement. Been doing all I could ever since to put things right."

Turner nodded. He could understand that. Yet there was something else he could understand as well. The effect such circumstances could have on a man. How guilt and rage could combine into a dangerous cocktail of over-zealousness. He knew the feeling all too well, in fact.

"*Bull Shark* and I will do our best, Colonel," Turner said. "However… I don't know about sending in any of my men. I'd prefer Army volunteers. I'm shorthanded already."

"I'm afraid that's not an option, Old Boy," Archer said, "and as for your lads… I'll have to insist on it."

Turner's face darkened and he cast his gaze over to Lockwood. The admiral drew in a breath and nodded, "Just a few men, Art. Two, three tops. I'll include more information in your sealed orders… and I'll owe you one."

Turner stood and eyed Lockwood and then Archer. He held out a hand to the Brit and offered a duelist's cool smile, "You both will."

3

"Say, Henrie, you're from the bayou, right?" Peter Griggs asked as he and Eugene Parker hefted a heavy crate over the brow from *Gudgeon* and onto *Bull Shark's* deck.

Henrie Martin stood by, watching as the last of his stores came aboard. He studied the stacks of crates lined up beside the hatch into the crew's mess and smiled.

"That's for true," he said. "Now you be careful wit' dem egg, you hear? Any of dem broke, it be taken outta your ration."

"We got it, we got it…" Parker huffed as the two men toted the hundred-pound crate aft. "We're used to handlin' pickles, Henrie. This ain't nothin'."

Martin rolled his cigar from one side of his mouth to the other and smiled, "You break my eggs, you won't be handlin' any pickle but you own. Why you wanna know 'bout the bayou, Pete?"

Griggs and Parker carefully set the crate down beside the others. Griggs withdrew a handkerchief from his back pocket and wiped his brow, "Well, we was wonderin' if there was a way to tell if there were crocs around here, Henrie."

"Dem crocodile? Hoooo! They all around us right now, you hear?" emoted Martin.

From up on the after end of the cigarette deck, Elmer Williams appeared smoking a cigarette that was introduced before or during the war, "Henrie, are you trying to scare my sailors?"

"Oh, no, sir, Mr. Williams, sir!" Martin said, snapping off a quick salute. "Jus 'bout to explain to these boys how you can tell if them crocs is in them water."

"Oh, yeah?" asked Williams, clearly interested. "Is there a special Cajun trick to it?"

"Cajun and Creole is old Henrie," Martin said. "And yessir, there is."

"How can you tell, Henrie?" Parker asked eagerly.

"Well now," began Martin, hitching up his dungarees and flicking an ash over the side. "The first thing you gon do, is brought you self down to a body of water. Any body will do round here. Now… you take you hand, and you scoop dem water up. Do this four or tree time, so you sure… then you rub your hand in that water like this… rub it good… Now, if them water wet… them croc down in there, I ga-run-tee!"

Williams laughed so hard his smoke went sailing out over the railing, bounced off the deck, and sizzled into the harbor. He, like the other men on deck who'd heard were bent over, clutching at or slapping knees.

"I see you men are getting a lot of work done," came a stern voice from the vicinity of the brow.

Everyone jerked up and turned to see the captain standing at the edge of the brow. A man in an Army uniform complete with a green beret stood beside him. The laughter quickly died, and the men all saluted and contrived to look busy. Williams smiled thinly and moved to the nearest companion to meet Turner down on deck.

"Welcome back, sir," said the XO, flushing a little. "Henrie was just explaining how to detect crocodiles in the water around here."

"I see," said Turner neutrally. "Elmer, this is Lieutenant Colonel Percival Archer, British Army Commandos. He'll be joining us. Please find him suitable quarters, find a man to help him below with his gear, and show him around the boat."

"Aye-aye, sir... pleasure to meet you, Colonel," said Williams, extending a hand. "Lieutenant Elmer Williams, executive officer."

"Pleasure, Old Chap," said Archer, shaking. "Fine ship you've got here. Aside from my dunnage, I've got a special crate of supplies to be brought across. Perhaps a couple of your lads would be good enough to see to it?"

"Certainly, Colonel," said Williams. "I'll assign a detail immediately. Where is the crate, sir?"

"Aboard the tender," Turner said, "the supply chief knows where. How soon can we get underway, Elmer?"

Williams pulled a notebook from his blouse pocket, "We've got most everything aboard, sir. All torpedoes loaded, replenished deck and small arms ammunition... last of the commissary stores are being stowed as we speak. All we're waiting for now is the fuel to be topped off."

"And when is that due?" Turner asked, frowning slightly.

"Not until tomorrow morning, sir."

Turner's frown deepened, "Very well. You can give the men the night off, Elmer, but see that word is sent that shore leave... as usual... is being cut short. I'd like to get out of harbor by sunset tomorrow."

"Yes, sir..." Williams appeared somewhat discomfited. "Captain... something else came in this afternoon from HQ. A couple of promotions."

Williams pulled a slip of paper from his pocket and handed it over to Turner. The captain unfolded it and read aloud, "Mug, Eckhart, and Griggs... Ingram and Swooping Hawk moved up to third-class petty... okay. Let them know ASAP, Elmer. The new petties are gonna need time to get some chevrons."

"Uhm... Art... Captain..." Williams appeared pained. "You usually do the promotion announcements."

Turner glanced down at his somewhat worse for wear civilian clothes, "I'm hardly in a position to do that now, am I XO? See to it, if you please. I'll be back aboard in the morning. Colonel, welcome aboard. My XO will see to your needs."

With that, Turner spun on his heel and strode across the brow to the next boat, and then on to the next. Williams stared after him, a scowl painted on his lips.

"Is he usually so abrupt, Old Boy?" Archer asked.

Williams had nearly forgotten about the new arrival, "Uhm... he's a busy man, sir. Hey, Griggsy, give our guest a hand with his duffel, will you? If you'll follow me, Colonel."

"We're going to be working rather closely together, Lieutenant," Archer said amiably. "Let's drop the formalities, eh? Percy will do fine. May I call you Elmer?"

"Certainly, Percy... right this way, we'll go down the forward torpedo hatch. Easier to get to officer's country. Have you ever been aboard a submarine before?"

"First time, Old Boy. Rather looking forward to the experience, really."

Williams led Archer down the ladder and into the forward torpedo room. With all weapons loaded and properly stowed, the room was strangely quiet. All the men who worked there were still on leave and staying in base quarters or with girlfriends.

Archer took a moment to admire the brightly shined brass torpedo tubes... the small bit that stuck out into the room... and their inner doors. To either side were the long, deadly shapes of the mark XIV torpedoes all painted a dull green. The racks of the men who lived in the room were neat and there wasn't a speck of dust to be seen.

"Quite orderly," Archer commented approvingly. "Your skipper keeps a tight ship, I see."

"As do I, Percy," Williams noted. "Bit of a spit and polish man, as they say in your Navy. But the men like it this way, too. You'll find that your submariner is generally an orderly sort. Professional requirement, really... although not all boats adhere to the same standard."

Archer smiled. He was beginning to like Williams. The younger man had an easy-going manner, but the seasoned commando sensed a stout toughness below the surface, "Indeed. Your captain... he seems a bit... stern, perhaps? Bit of a hard-horse tarter as they used to say. Now, don't misunderstand me... I don't mean to criticize. What CO isn't prone to his moods, what? I'm known for them myself."

Williams sighed, "Truth to tell, sir… Percy… Art hasn't been himself of late. He's generally a friendly and kind soul. Slow to anger and quick to forgive an honest mistake. But ever since we ran into a Japanese aircraft a few weeks ago…"

"The blighters that feigned helplessness and opened fire on you?" Archer asked. "I've heard the tale. Hard luck… bloody bastards…"

"Yes, sir," Williams said coldly. "They killed several popular men, including our torpedo officer. Damndest thing. I'm sorry to say that ever since, the captain's been… well, not my place to say."

Archer patted him on the shoulder, "Mum's the word… less said soonest mended and all that. I quite understand, Elmer Old Chap."

"Speaking of keeping things on the QC," Williams said, showing Archer into a small stateroom with two bunks mounted to one bulkhead. "Can you tell me anything about our mission?"

Archer looked around, spotting his duffel on the upper bunk, "Good Lord… is this my cabin?"

Williams grinned, "Our cabin, sir. Yours and mine. Sorry… we don't have special accommodations for VIPs. In fact, that there's only the two of us in here is considered a bit of a privilege. Executive officer and all. Only the skipper gets his own."

"How the devil do we both unbutton ourselves in this cupboard?" Archer asked, bewildered by the cramped space but also showing mild amusement.

"One at a time, sir," said the XO." Again… my apologies."

"Oh, rot!" Archer laughed. "No worse than a foxhole on a dark night, eh? Smells better, too. By the by… where does one… uhm… where's the loo?"

Williams smiled, "We have our own showers in this compartment. They're forward, just before the hatch to the torpedo room. However, our head is up there, and we share it with the crew who bunk forward."

"Indeed?"

"On some ships, that head is restricted, but the captain has always maintained that there's no reason for the guys to go all the way back to the after battery compartment to pinch one off. Especially during battle, it wouldn't do. You'll find, Percy, that aboard a submarine… the lines between the officers and ratings are somewhat blurred."

"I see…" Archer mused, clearly put off by the concept. However, he shrugged and said: "I suppose it's out of necessity, then? Well, Elmer, as they say… improvise, adapt and overcome, eh? Oh… and as to your question… I'd prefer to wait until the captain is ready to brief you. All things considered and my superior rank notwithstanding… he *is* the captain after all. Sovereign under God and all that. Best to be discreet, you know."

Williams nodded. Although he was curious, he was pleased to see that the guest wasn't prone to throwing his weight around. Technically, he did outrank Turner… but the man seemed to understand what was due a ship's captain, "Very good, Percy. I can wait. Well then… why don't I show you the rest of the palace."

Archer smiled, "By George… there's more? I was beginning to feel a bit hemmed in, what?"

"Oh, you'll find that the American fleet submarine is a vast and luxurious appointment, Colonel," Williams explained loftily. "We've got air conditioning, good food, and even ice cream. A wonderful place for eighty-odd men to get cozy."

"Good *Lord*…"

* * *

"Phone, water, and power lines detached, Captain," the chief of the boat said, turning his face up to the group of officers and men clustered around the bridge and on the cigarette deck. "Permission to throw off the brow?"

"Granted," replied Turner. "Signalman, permission to raise the colors. Officer of the deck, sound departure blast."

As the Stars and Stripes rose up the mast, Tony Skaggs pressed the horn control and *Bull Shark*'s horn gave a long, throaty five-second blat, indicating to all in earshot that she was about to get underway. Aboard *Gudgeon*, the special detail hauled in on the gangplank and carried it aft and out of the way. Four men stood by on the boat's starboard side, ready to take in on the departing submarine's mooring lines.

"Good hunting, Art!" *Gudgeon's* captain, Elton "Joe" Grenfell called from his bridge, waving his cap. "Save some Japs for the rest of us, huh?"

"You can have my scraps, Joe," Turner called, smiling for form's sake but not feeling particularly convivial. "Tony, let's get this show on the road."

"Fine day for a cruise, eh?" Archer commented genially as he took up station between Williams and Turner just aft of the bridge.

"It is, Colonel," Turner stated. "But we observe silence on deck until we're clear, please."

"Aye-aye," said Archer, unbowed by Turner's stiffness.

"COB, permission to cast off," Skaggs ordered. "Quartermaster, give us a little port bump and then all back one-third."

Richard "Mug" Vigliano, still beaming from the news that he'd gotten a second chevron, cleared his throat and tapped the bridge transmitter button.

"Helm, bridge, port engine back one-third."

A burst of foam puffed out from the submarine's portside aft quarter and the stern began to slowly creep to the right. After a few seconds, Vigliano pressed the button once more.

"Helm, all back one-third… full left rudder… stop port engine… rudder amidships… all ahead one-third."

The orders were given and acknowledged crisply, and the 312-foot submarine backed neatly away from her sister, hauled her stern and bow around, and then began to slowly accelerate forward, headed straight for the lighthouse on the south mole, marking the extent of the harbor. It was done neatly and smoothly with no mistakes. A fact that secretly made Tony Skaggs, the most junior officer aboard, immensely proud. It was a necessary skill, being able to conn a ship out of and into a dock, and the evolution still made him a bit nervous.

"Chief, you can dismiss the special sea detail," Skaggs said. "Maintain maneuvering watch."

Williams patted the younger man on the shoulder, "Nicely done, Tony. I'll call up shortly."

Williams then disappeared below the hatch on his way down to the control room. As the XO, he was also the navigator and was responsible for marking the chart and coordinating the harbor maneuvers with Skaggs.

Skaggs frowned as *Bull Shark* moved through the rectangular harbor, maintaining a more or less two-hundred-yard separation from Victoria Quay, which she was paralleling. Skaggs turned aft, looking to the northeast and at the two tall, red-painted range markers, still frowning.

"Is it all right to speak now, sir?" Archer whispered to Turner.

The captain glanced sidelong and smiled thinly, "Certainly, Colonel. I apologize if I was abrupt earlier."

"Not a 'tall," dismissed Archer. "Every service has its rules and regulations. Doubtless if I were handling this beast, I'd want quiet as well. But... why is the young fellow looking back where we came from?"

Turner pointed, "See those two poles up there in the hills? Those are range markers. You line them up, one behind the other, and you know that you're right in the center of the channel."

"Ah... quite! I say... this is rather exciting."

Skaggs turned forward again, "Mug, give a little nudge to port."

Vigliano thumbed the button, "Helm, five degree left rudder."

The distant lighthouse swung just a bit to starboard. Skaggs looked aft again, and then nodded to Vigliano. The quartermaster ordered a ten-degree right until the lighthouse was dead-ahead.

"Steady as she goes," ordered Skaggs.

"*Bridge, XO... starboard turn for harbor exit approaching in one-hundred yards. Standby to mark the turn,*" William's voice filtered up through the speaker.

"Bridge, aye," said Skaggs and glanced over his shoulder at Turner. He then thumbed the button himself. "Helm, reduce speed to four knots."

Archer saw Turner nod ever so slightly. The ship's way decreased and Skaggs nodded to himself.

"*Bridge, XO... turn... mark.*"

Skaggs nodded to Vigliano who thumbed the speaker, "Helm, bridge… hard right rudder. Steady up on two-six-five."

Slowly, ponderously, the long, lean ship began to turn to starboard. Turner watched carefully. The turn was close to forty-five degrees, and it took a light touch on the helm and a careful eye from the quartermaster and OOD to check the ship's turn so she wouldn't over-correct. Turner was just about to say something when Skaggs spoke.

"Now, Mug."

"Helm, bridge… meet her," Vigliano said.

The helm was centered but the submarine still swung a little more to starboard. When her bow steadied, however, she was headed straight down the channel and toward the little net tender, already hauling the submarine nets out of the approaching ship's path.

"Perfect," said Skaggs and grinned.

"Well done, Tony," Turner said.

"Good show, lad," Archer enthused. "Couldn't have done it better myself."

Ahead and a bit to port, the lower curve of the sun was just beginning to touch the fuzzy horizon. A crimson blush filled the evening sky, and a smattering of cottony, golden-edged sailing ships ghosted placidly on the light breeze. Archer grinned and held up a camera on its neck strap and snapped a couple of photos.

"Hope you don't mind, Old Boy," said the commando. "Bit of a shutter bug, really. Such a sight can't be allowed to slip past, eh?"

Turner nodded, "We get some lovely sunsets at sea."

The men on deck, Skaggs, Mug, Rogers and his maneuvering watch, along with Joe Dutch who was aft shooting the bull with Andy Post, experienced an odd mixture of emotion. The evening was warm and comfortable, the sky ahead glorious and the darkening sky astern pleasingly tranquil. Archer's enthusiasm and almost child-like delight in the whole evolution of putting to sea was infectious. Yet Turner's reserve was infectious, too… and it somewhat dampened the mood aboard. A small part of him was aware of it, and even felt a little bad… but a larger part ignored it and remained steadfast.

Above and behind the bridge, the search periscope turned in the shears. Williams was no doubt using it to take bearings and double-check their progress.

"*Bridge, XO… right on the money, Tony. Good to go.*"

Skaggs thumbed the button, "Aye-aye, XO. Helm… increase to all ahead two-thirds."

The ship's four big GM diesels revved a little, still not running at full power. However, as more electricity was called upon to drive the boat's four GE electric motors… which actually turned the two propeller shafts… the diesels were sped up to match. Since the batteries were charged, there was no reason yet to run on full power and generate an excess of juice.

"*Bridge, helm… Bendix log indicates ten knots.*"

"Very well," Skaggs said and plucked a Camel from his blouse. He offered one to Vigliano and turned and held out the pack to the two officers behind him, "Sirs?"

"Right kind in you, Lieutenant," said Archer, accepting a smoke. Turner shook his head and continued to stare forward, his eyes distant and his heart far away.

The men got the smokes going against the apparent wind and settled in. Soon, they passed by the little motor launch used to drag the nets across the harbor mouth and the submarine met the first of the long Indian Ocean rollers. They were only three to four footers, yet their wavelengths were dozens of yards long, having rolled across the sea from nearly as far away as the west coast of Africa.

"There's our dance partner, sir," Skaggs pointed off to starboard as the destroyer escort assigned to them began a long, leisurely turn to match the submarine's course.

"My compliments, Tony," Turner said. "And let's put the pedal down."

Skaggs thumbed the button, "Control, bridge… hail the escort with captain's compliment. Advise we're going to all ahead full and going to make one-five knots at a course of three-four-zero."

After the order was acknowledged, Vigliano spoke, "Helm, bridge… all ahead full. Make turns for fifteen knots. Eighty-ninety split on all four."

"And there you are, Colonel," Turner said. "We're free and clear to navigate."

"Capital!" Archer smiled. "Well done, sir… well done. Not that I'm any judge, but you appear to have a well-drilled and disciplined crew. They certainly know what they're about."

Turner nodded, "Yes, they do. Hard won knowledge. Now then, Colonel… what do you say to supper?"

"I thought you'd never ask!" chuckled Archer, flicking his dead butt over the rail. "My bloody bellybutton is sticking to my backbone, what?"

4

"Attention on deck!" The COB's voice boomed out in the mess and every man there, be he sitting, waiting in the chow line, or behind the serving stations, snapped to.

"As you were, fellas," Elmer Williams held up a hand and then a sheet of paper in his other. "Got a couple of announcements I thought you'd be interested in."

"Rita Hayworth comin' aboard, sir?" Sherman "Tank" Broderick called out to a chorus of whistles and laughter.

"Shut your pie holes," Rogers growled, "or maybe I recommend to the XO here that he *don't* deliver his news."

Williams grinned, rather enjoying the fun, "No wonder everybody says we submariners are a bunch of loud, big-mouthed, foul-tempered arrogant sons of biscuits."

That drew another laugh, even from the COB.

"Okay, guys, I've got a couple of promotions to announce," Williams said. He noticed several frowns and quizzical looks. He sighed. "Yeah, I know the skipper usually does these… but he's got a lot on his mind, what with our guest and the mission and all. So he's asked me to dole these out. Hope nobody minds."

"Glad to have you, sir!" Bill Borshowski, the burly Polish kid from Chicago enthused.

"Swell... cuz I'm what you got," said the XO and grinned. "Now, I know everybody already knows what they've got. But still... some Naval traditions we always honor. So... Quartermaster's Mate Third-class Richard Vigliano is hereby promoted to QM2."

A round of applause and cat calls and Mug smiled broadly and waved, "Thanks, sir."

"You earned it, Mug," Williams said. "You keep up the good work and you'll be wearing a chief's hat in ten... fifteen years! On that note, Fireman Fred Swooping Hawk and electrician Doug Ingram are hereto elevated to the lofty ranks of the petty officer. Congrats, Fireman's Mate Swooping Hawk and Electrician's Mate Ingram."

"Good job, Freddy!" Mike Duncan roared over the claps.

"Proud a' ya', Dougie," Pentakkus shouted.

"And last but not least, Peter Griggs is now torpedoman one," said the XO. "And may God have mercy on your souls!"

Raucous applause and cheers rose up in the confined space, now filled with far more men than were usually present. Williams drew himself a cup of coffee from the urn and waved as he ducked through the hatchway to the control room.

"Good for you, Pete," Ingram said as Griggs settled in at the table with him and Swooping Hawk.

"Didn't think I'd make it so soon," Griggs said, flushing slightly. "Y'know... after that thing with the pills a while back."

Ingram sighed, "Yeah... and because of me..."

"C'mon, fellas," Swooping Hawk said. "Just a bump in the road. Lucky for the whole boat the COB and skipper let it go. Hey! Hey, new guy, c'mon over and take a seat here."

A tall, lean E2 who'd come aboard at Fremantle turned and looked over his shoulder at the voice. He smiled nervously and sidled over with his full serving tray. He slid into the seat at the end beside Griggs, still smiling shyly.

"Thanks," he said and flushed. "I'm Lee. Lee Wayts. Steersman. Hoping to strike for quartermaster."

The young man, who was probably no more than nineteen, spoke in a smooth, neutral tone that left no indication as to his origin. He seemed friendly enough, but no one aboard knew much about him. However, the new petties were determined to break that streak.

"Nice to meecha," Ingram said, holding out a hand. "I'm Doug and this here is Pete. Our Navajo guide here is Fred."

"Howe," said Swooping Hawk with a twinkle in his eye.

Hands were shaken and introductions made. Wayts began salting his roast beef, "You guys are kind of legends around here. Heard a lot about you even before I signed aboard."

"First time in the boats?" Griggs asked.

"Yeah, I done a hitch on a tin can and then did my sub school bit," said the new man. "Gotta say I didn't like that simulator."

Swooping Hawk chuckled, "The flooding tester? Yeah, that's a real bear. You got through it, though, or you wouldn't be here."

"So where you from, Lee?" Ingram asked.

"Boise," Wayts said. "That's in Idaho."

"Yeah, we know," said Griggs, but not unkindly.

Wayts flushed. "Sorry… sometimes I feel Idaho is one of those places people never think much about unless they're pickin' out taters at the market."

The three men laughed, and Swooping Hawk said, "So I bet you never even saw an ocean before joining, huh? Me either. From Arizona myself."

Wayts smiled, "Yeah… been a shock. Love it, though. So much different from home."

"Well, listen, Lee," said Ingram after swallowing a bite of au gratin potatoes liberally seasoned with Martin's secret Cajun spice blend. "The fella you replaced was a friend of ours. Good guy. So you ever need anything… need to know where anything is or want help with your studies or anything… our door's always open."

"You got a door?" Wayts asked, appearing surprised.

Griggs laughed, "Nah, pally. Just an expression. Not even petty officers actually get an *office* on a boat!"

* * *

"Roast beef... cheesy potatoes and broccoli?" Archer asked with pleased surprise as he gently probed his food with his fork. "I say... a regimental commander wouldn't eat so well."

"We take good care of you aboard *Bull Shark,* sir," Eddie Carlson, the officer's steward said as he poured out the coffee. "Navy wants us submariners well fed and happy when the GQ alarm goes off."

"Yes... quite..." Archer acknowledged distractedly.

"We live and work in relative discomfort as compared to surface ships," Turner explained. "Spending a good deal of time trapped underwater in challenging conditions, Colonel. The Navy does its best to compensate us."

Archer smiled thinly, "Try sleeping in a foxhole sometime, Old Boy."

"We have, Colonel," said Joe Dutch, trying to hide his mild annoyance at their guest's dismissive comments. "Both the captain and myself were on Guadalcanal when the Marines landed."

Archer glanced up and his brows rose, "Indeed? I knew Captain Turner had gone ashore... but you too as well, Lieutenant?"

Archer's British pronunciation of Dutch's rank brought amused smiles to Frank Nichols's and Andy Post's faces. However, the two made no comment otherwise. As the junior most officer in the wardroom, Post was content to let the others engage, if they did.

"Yes, as did several of our men," Turner said. "In fact, not long ago, several more went ashore on New Ireland. Including our pharmacist's mate... what you might call our field medic as it were."

"I had no idea submarine life was so... diverse," Archer commented and ate some roast beef. He smiled approvingly.

"If y'all don't need anything else for a moment, sir," Carlson said. "I'll go aft and reload my servers for you."

"We're good, thank you, Eddie," Turner said.

"By the way, Colonel... I got a stash of good tea aboard," Carlson said. "Can have a pot of hot water and a quick brew for you, if you prefer."

"Oh, indeed?" Archer looked pleased. "Why, that'd be just the thing, Carlson."

The steward slipped through the green baize curtain and his soft footfalls vanished aft. Archer smiled and cocked an eyebrow.

"I must say, Skipper…a caffer working in your wardroom? And so familiar… rather… untoward, is it not?"

Post frowned but maintained his silence. He knew that someone would jump on it, and he was not disappointed. Frank Nichols, usually quiet and mild-mannered, flushed with genuine anger.

"And I'm surprised to hear that sort of sentiment from a Brit, Colonel," said the handsome engineer. "Considering who it was among the 'civilized' nations who first abolished slavery."

"Well… slavery is one thing, Lieutenant," Archer expounded. "But propriety is another, eh? I'm all for a man of any color serving his nation… but there still ought to be some decorum due one's station, what?"

"We disagree aboard this ship, Colonel," Turner said mildly but with an edge behind his tone. "The traditional lines between men and ratings are blurred here. Necessity. And every man aboard has to qualify eventually. We have three Black men serving on this boat. None of them will ever be anything but stewards or cooks. Yet they're *all* completely sub-qualified. They all have their silver dolphins. That means they can work every piece of equipment on board. That *caffer*, as you so blithely call him, is the best damned gunner aboard. He can hand, reef, and steer, as we used to say in the old days. He could even take command should the need arise. We respect and like these men… and expect our guests to do the same. I hope that's clear."

Archer didn't seem to have been affected in even the slightest way by Turner's rebuke. He simply nodded, smiled politely, and replied, "It is, sir. Do forgive me… I come from a bit of a traditional school; you know. Perhaps I overstated my inquiry. I beg your pardon."

"These things can happen, Colonel," said Dutch, smiling and trying to smooth out the tension. "If you have any questions or anything seems… odd to you. Some things will, I'm sure, then feel free to ask."

"You'll find we're a very fraternal ship, sir," added Post. "We'll adjust to one another, don't you worry."

Archer smiled at the young man, "I'm afraid it's I who must adjust, lad. I'm the guest and this is your house, after all. Now then... I know that in the Royal Navy, it's considered bad form to discuss shop at the supper table... but perhaps..."

"Generally, that's true," Turner said. "But when it's just a run of the mill meal and not a dining in, we often talk work. In fact, it's often the only time when so many of us are in one place at the same time. Perhaps you'd like to fill us in on your mission, Colonel?"

Archer smiled, "Certainly, sir. And my earlier bad manners notwithstanding, Captain... I do wish you'd take to calling me Percy. As you say, we're living and working closely, and it might be for the best."

"In time, I'm sure," Turner said coldly but not unkindly. "I'm afraid that I'm... well, it takes me a bit of time, that's all. Please don't take offense."

"Not at all," said Archer, munching a bite of potato. "Jolly good this... well, then... by the by, you don't think... that is... our steward overhearing and all..."

Dutch laughed, "No secrets on a submarine, Percy. Better that the betting pool doesn't have to wait too long anyway."

Archer laughed, "No doubt Carlson makes a rather tidy bundle of chink from his information pipeline. Very well then... are any of you familiar with the situation on Timor?"

"I know that Australia sent a group of men, called Sparrow Force back in December," Post spoke up. "And that they also sent in the Second Independents. A commando unit like yours, Colonel?"

Archer smiled, "Good show, lad. Yes, indeed... the Second Independent Commandos or 2ICs as I call them, were my special purview. Worked closely to train them along with their CO, major Spence."

Post nodded, "They reinforced Kupang and the Peleliu airfield and eventually went into Portuguese Timor as well if I don't mistake."

"Portuguese Timor?" Nichols asked.

"Well done, Andrew..." Archer nodded. "Yes, Frank. You see, Timor was split between the Dutch and the Portuguese. The Dutch had their capital in the west, southwest in Kupang. The Portuguese in the east in Dili. The Porties are *neutral*, you understand… bloody neutrals, same in every blasted war… they claim neutrality simply to save their own cowardly hides, in my opinion. Then can operate with the blessing of both sides until they see an advantage to one or the other."

"As the Spanish did against France during the Napoleonic wars," Turner mused.

"Well told, sir… until 1808 when the bloody Degos finally saw reason, eh," Archer mused. He cleared his throat. "Now then… Spence went in and occupied the eastern side of Timor. When the Nips invaded, there was considerable fighting. Sparrow force and the 2ICs were left mostly to fend for themselves. Most of 2IC was caught behind enemy lines and worked in conjunction with Colonel Leggatt. Until he surrendered, that is. Can't say I blame him, really… many men killed, more wounded, running low on stores… still in all… it did the war effort no great service."

"So you're going in to make contact with some of the 2ICs and get them out, Colonel?" Nichols asked.

Archer nodded, "Not precisely. My job here is to make contact and deliver a bit of kit… preparation for the actual evacuation, you understand. We've had a devil of a time maintaining contact. No radio gear, you understand. And the bloody slopes cut the telegraph line to Lisbon, so our chaps can't even sneak into Dili and make use of *that*. Damned bad business all around, really."

"And the Allied command won't send in the amphibs to take Timor back," Turner said flatly. "What with their plans for the Solomons and new Guinea."

"Just so," Archer said bitterly. "But however… I can't concern myself with such broad strokes. It's my job… and with the help of your lads, Arthur… to go in, make contact with my lads, and gather as well as provide intelligence."

"What's in that crate in the forward torpedo room… if I may ask?" Dutch asked.

Archer shrugged, "Certainly, Joseph. Radio gear mostly. Along with a few odds and ends I was able to throw together."

"How large of a force do you require, Percy?" Turner asked. "I'm forced to point out that this is a submarine. Full of sailors, not ground soldiers."

"This isn't a raid, Old Boy," Archer said, holding up a hand. "I'm asking only for a few men. Security and to take a turn at lugging that bloody crate about. Five men should be more than adequate. Three would do in a pinch, however."

Turner sighed, "Yeah... I've got a few in mind. Not the least of which is an Indian we have serving with us. A Navajo. Excellent back country man and tracker. In fact, I believe he's been working with Joe and Andy and tony to come up with a special code system. Based on the Navajo language."

Archer's brows rose, "Indeed? I've heard of such a project on a grander scale. Some of your lads from the States, I believe. Ought to give Tojo a run for his money, what?"

"Art... what about the rest of our mission?" Dutch asked. "I mean, we came out here, hitting various Japanese positions along the way... but what was our original mission? Has it been put on hold?"

"No," Turner said. "That part is still underway. We're to put the Colonel ashore and then continue with our patrol. With any luck, we'll be able to pick him, our men and any rescues he's gathered up on the way back. Couple of weeks at most, from what I understand. Elmer and I have to review my sealed orders yet. That's after we top up at Exmouth. But I do know it's got something to do with the South China Sea. Maybe even the East China Sea and Formosa... or Taiwan, whatever they're calling it now."

"Getting pretty close to Hirohito's backyard," Nichols noted.

"Bloody close... although nipping round to the Sea of Japan would be a lark, wouldn't it?" Archer mused. "Bit of a run, though... from Fremantle, eh?"

Turner grunted, "From what I know thus far, we're to make contact with local merchantmen and fishermen. I've been given a supply of coinage for the purpose of bribery. To what end... other than gaining intelligence, I suppose, I'm not sure yet. However, I imagine that after dropping off in Timor, we'll be headed up into the Makassar Strait again. The overriding order of the day is to sink Japanese merchant shipping. Hit them where they live, apparently."

"Well, speaking as the torpedo officer pro tem yet again…" Joe Dutch said with a predatory gleam in his eye. "I'd be quite content to hove back into Fremantle Harbor with a broom strapped to the shears, Captain."

"Hear, hear," said Post.

"You submariners are a rather bloodthirsty lot, I see," said Archer somberly and then broke into a grin. "I say… well met!"

Turner observed the smiles and laughs and even joined in when Archer held up his mug of coffee to be clinked. He appreciated the sentiment… yet found it difficult to raise within himself the same gusto as the other officers.

A gusto he no longer seemed to share.

5

TIMOR SEA

DECEMBER 21, 1942

OFF THE SOUTHEASTERN COAST OF TIMOR - 10°38"S, 125°30"E -

"Twenty hundred position report, Captain," Elmer Williams said after coming up through the red-lit bridge hatch.

Turner glanced at the slip of paper, using the moonlight to make out the coordinates. He nodded and handed it to the quartermaster of the watch. Ralph "Hotrod" Hernandez noted the information down on his maneuvering board and folded the slip of paper into his blouse pocket.

"Very well," Turner said quietly.

"Hard to believe that just ten miles to our west is the island of Timor," Williams mused.

"Wonder if this is how Captain Bly felt," Hotrod said quietly.

Turner looked at the man, "You know about that story, Hotrod?"

"Yes, sir," said Hernandez. "The *Mutiny on the Bounty* story is one of my favorites. I've read the books."

"How about the movie with Charles Laughton and Clarke Gable?" Williams asked. "That Bly was a real hard case…"

"Maybe he had his reasons," Turner said, smiling slightly.

"Actually," noted Hotrod. "There are a lot of differing accounts. That movie did Bly no good and painted Fletcher Christian as a sympathetic hero… but in reality, things weren't quite so black and white."

"Glad to see you don't identify with the mutineers, Hotrod," said Turner. Although the conversation was casual, there was something heavy lying beneath that Williams didn't like. When Turner asked, "How about you, Elmer? Who do you feel the most for? Bly or Christian?"

Williams chuckled, "Well, all I know is that it'd be pretty hard to have to leave Tahiti and all those gorgeous women. On the other hand… Bly was one of Cook's own. A master seaman… so it's hard to say. But it does seem like he was far too strict."

Turner harrumphed, "What's a little flogging now and then."

"That's another myth, sir," Hernandez said. "Lieutenant Bly only flogged someone once during that whole voyage."

Williams grinned, "You're pretty smart for a humble Long Beach villager, Hotrod."

"Yes, sir," said Hotrod quietly.

Williams frowned. The atmosphere of the ship was all wrong. It'd gone south after that attack by the downed Japanese airmen, and he was hard-pressed to know how to fix it. The men were somewhat subdued. Even Hotrod, whose ebullience and gregarious nature was almost irrepressible, felt it and was evidently weighed down by it.

Williams knew the source of the problem… he simply didn't know how to approach it. If negative emotions were a magnetic field, then Turner was the core.

Williams found himself stuck between a rock and a hard place. As the executive officer, he had many duties and occupied a unique position in the crew. The exec was, in a real sense, the bridge between the captain and the crew and other officers. It was Williams's job to both watch over the crew as well as be the captain's right hand.

It was a very fine line, and not an easy one to walk. The XO was directly responsible for crew management as well as to backstop the captain. Turner made policy and Williams saw that it was carried out.

On the other hand, he was also responsible for the crew's well-being. He did most of the clerical work so that the captain was free to command and make important decisions. That meant that Williams was something of a caretaker, working closely with the chief of the boat to ensure that the crew remained both disciplined and that their morale was stable. This was a job Williams was good at and generally found enjoyable… until now.

For on top of all of this, Elmer Williams also had to think of his own career. He'd been the first officer aboard *Bull Shark* since the beginning, with just a few absences out of necessity. He'd completed prospective executive officer training at New London and had racked up considerable experience as well as combat decorations. It was not unreasonable to expect that soon, perhaps even at the end of this patrol should it be successful, that Williams would be leaving again. This time to attend prospective commanding officer training and then to be assigned to skipper his own boat. Possibly even one of the new boats currently slated for construction.

With his experience, Williams could probably even expect to skip the usual PCO rider stage. He'd been in command of *Bull Shark* independently before, and with the war only getting hotter, it was likely he'd be hustled into a command very shortly.

Yet that still hinged on the recommendation of his current captain. Arthur Turner's opinion would weigh heavily in both the promotions' board as well as the command selection committee. If he pissed Turner off or let him down… that might ruin or at least delay his own chances for advancement.

The concern that won out, as would have surprised no one aboard, was Williams's concern for his crew and his ship. To that end, he made his decision and cleared his throat.

"Art… can I have a private word?" asked the XO.

Turner's silhouetted head turned toward Williams. With the moon still low in the east and behind him, the captain's features were invisible in the darkness. Williams couldn't read the expression but the chill in the tone was all he needed to know about Turner's current mood.

"Very well, XO," said the captain softly. "Join me by the after TBT. Hotrod, keep your eyes peeled."

The two men moved aft along the cigarette deck and took up positions at the rail beside the pelorus that housed the after target bearing transmitter circuitry. Here, with the apparent wind of a fifteen-knot speed slightly buffered by the periscope shears and Oerlikon gun mount, it was quieter and yet the two men's words wouldn't float forward to either the lookouts or the man on the bridge.

"Something bothering you, Elmer?"

Williams drew in a breath and steeled himself, "Well, sir… that's what I'd like to ask you. Although I think I already know the answer."

"Got me pegged, have ya', Elmer?" Turner asked, his voice taut. "And I take it you have an issue with me?"

Williams shifted uncomfortably. This was not the Art Turner he knew. The Art Turner who'd coached him through his own feelings of self-doubt. Something had shifted inside Turner. Something fundamental and deep and Wiliams wondered if it hadn't taken permanent root.

The XO sighed and plunged ahead, "Ever since that floater opened up on us, Art… Captain… you've been… different."

Turner scoffed, "And why the hell not? We got ambushed by those fuckin' slants and lost four good men, Elmer. Aren't you different? Doesn't it piss you off?"

"You're damned right it does," Williams hissed. "Port was a good friend. We all loved him… the *men* all loved him. Not to mention Marty and Wendel and Joe… but we're at war. It's hardly the first time we've lost men and won't be the last, God help me."

"So what's your point?" Turner asked. "I'm not allowed to be a bit out of sorts over it, Elmer? Gotta be happy go lucky every goddamned minute?"

"You're not a *bit* out of sorts, Art… you've been affected by it and your entire personality seems to have changed."

"You're out of line, *Lieutenant*," Turner growled, the danger in his tone bright and hot.

Williams didn't miss it, but he pressed on anyway, "I'm doing my job, Captain. My concern is for the ship and the man… and you, too."

"I don't need to stand here and be psychoanalyzed by my exec. So I'm not my usual jolly self… so goddamned *what*? I'm a ship's captain, Elmer. I'm not supposed to be everybody's *pal*. Not a luxury a captain can afford, frankly. Why those guys aboard the carriers and battleships and all are so high and mighty. There's a reason for it. You get too close with your men... too cozy... too casual... and it can get men killed. Maybe if... well, I'm not gonna justify myself to anyone, XO. If you or the other officers or the men feel I'm different, then you're just going to have to adjust. Now, I've got a watch to stand, Mr. Williams."

"Art—"

"Dismissed, Lieutenant," Turner snapped and stalked forward.

Williams stood near the taffrail for a long moment. He suddenly felt small and alone. Adrift with no compass to guide him back to shore.

Sighing, *Bull Shark's* executive officer moved forward, unobtrusively sliding down the hatch and into the control room. Turner never even looked back at him. A moment later, Williams was in the control room and waggling a finger at Paul Rogers. He pointed down into the pump room and the COB nodded and followed him down.

Nestled between the trim and drain pump housings, Rogers smiled thinly at Williams and asked, "Can I take it by your expression, sir, that you had no luck?"

Williams sighed and withdrew a cigarette from his blouse and rogers lit it for him, "If we were looking for bad luck, then yeah, I had plenty. Geez, Buck... he ate my butt off. He's... he's really down."

Rogers sighed and sparked his own Camel to life, "It was worth a shot, sir. Figured you of all people would be able to speak to him... y'know... man to man."

Williams puffed out a stream of grey smoke and frowned, "I might have just made it worse, Buck. Pressed too far... intruded too far. I dunno..."

Rogers thought for a moment, "I've known Art Turner a long time, sir. Lot longer'n anybody else aboard, even Mr. Dutch. This ain't him. This closed-off, stiff-necked thing... it's not who he is at his core."

"Well... I wouldn't have thought so either, a month or two ago. But as he rightly pointed out to me just now... he's the captain. We adjust to him. Still, though... I think he's questioning himself. Maybe feels guilty and thinks that if he was more rigid instead of the approachable, friendly Art we all know... that maybe those men... y'know..."

Rogers harrumphed, "With all due respect, sir... that's bullshit. This boat has been successful *because* of his personality, not in spite of it. There was nothing that anybody could've done that day, and it certainly wasn't because Art Turner is a good guy."

"Try telling him that," Williams said with a rueful little smile. "Anyways... my shot went wide, COB."

Any further conversation was cut off by the resounding fourteen-tone gong of the general quarters alarm. The two men locked gazes for a moment and then Rogers followed the XO up the ladder and onto the platform deck. Williams looked at Frank Nichols, who was standing his watch at his usual place.

"Radar contact, sir," said the engineer. "Don't know anything else, yet. Captain called for BS gun action, though."

From the forward hatch, Joe Dutch half-stepped, half-leapt through the hatchway with Colonel Archer hot on his heels, "What's on, Elmer?"

"No idea!" Williams shouted over the alarm. Once it stopped, he picked up the handset from the overhead above the master gyro compass table, "Bridge, XO... standing by on plot, Captain."

"*Very well, XO,*" Turner said tersely. "*Start the plot and then you and Joe get up here.*"

Williams nodded to Rogers, who took the handset and switched to the 1MC circuit. At the same time, Clancy Weiss, Mug Vigliano, and the new kid, Wayts, appeared from the hatch to the after battery compartment and moved to the chart on the gyro table.

"*This is the COB,*" Rogers's voice thundered through the ship, echoing from both forward and aft. "*Battle stations gun action. Pompom, Oerlikon, and Ma Deuce crews to stations. Permission to open gun access and service hatches.*"

With that and seeing that Mike Duncan had also come forward to take Rogers's place at the manifolds beside Nichols, Rogers led the way up the ladders to the tower and the bridge with Dutch and Williams in hot pursuit.

As he entered the conning tower, Williams paused to look over Ted Balkley's shoulder, "What've we got, Teddy?"

"Surface contact bearing three-four-zero, range twenty-thousand yards, sir… single contact, moving at ten knots more or less paralleling the coast. Not very large, I should say."

Williams scanned the scope and saw the spike on the horizon display as well as the blurp on the sweep. He nodded and continued out into the cool night air. As he transitioned from the hellish light of the conning tower and into the moonlit night, Williams was aware of another man below him. He cringed thinking that this was probably not the time for Archer to come on deck and observe.

"Captain," Williams said, casting a glance at Dutch who moved to his command position by the anti-aircraft cannon behind the masts.

"You spoke with radar, I presume, XO?" Turner asked stonily.

"Yes, sir… small surface contact ahead and closer in?" Williams asked. "Any visual?"

"Negative," Turner said and held up a pair of binoculars to his eyes. "Wouldn't expect that yet. Hotrod, bring me to a due west, maintain speed. I want to get inside his course and put the moon offshore of us."

Hernandez acknowledged and thumbed the button, "Helm, bridge, left full rudder. Steady up on two-seven-zero. Maintain speed."

All around, men were coming up on deck through the forward torpedo room hatch as well as the tater hatch from the galley. In this way, they could take their stations without disrupting the men in the control room, conning tower, and distracting the captain. Williams watched approvingly as dark shapes moved along the decks and began quietly but quickly opening watertight shot lockers and readying weapons.

"I say… quite the hubbub," Archer commented as he leaned against the periscope shears behind the bridge hatch. The man had actually withdrawn a cigarette case and slid one into his mouth before Turner noticed.

"Colonel!" the captain snapped. "Belay that! No smoking on deck during night ops, for Chrissakes. You want the slants to see your lighter flickering?"

Archer paused in his movements, "Oh... oh bloody hell... my apologies, Captain."

Turner cursed under his breath and then in a more even tone said, "It might seem paranoid, Percy, but even a small point of light can be seen by a sharp-eyed lookout. And in spite of what you may have heard... the Japs have sharp eyes."

"I beg your pardon, sir... shall I go below then?"

Elmer could almost feel the desire for his captain to answer in the affirmative radiating off him. However, Turner shook his head, "No... but please stay out of the way and quietly observe. We should've briefed you ahead of time... had plenty of damned time to do so in the past three days..."

Williams wasn't sure if that was a rebuke aimed at him or not, but he took it as one anyway and remained silent. By then, the moon as astern and *Bull Shark* was carving a ghostly furrow of foam through the black sea that melded into the silver finger that flared upon its calm surface.

Turner thumbed the speaker, "Radar, bridge. Report."

"*Bridge, radar... target now bears zero-eight-zero. Range is seventeen thousand yards.*"

"Very well," said the captain. "Joe?"

"All weapons manned and ready, Captain," said the torpedo and gunnery officer from astern. "Shall we load any star shells?"

"Let's see what we're up against first, Joe," Turner said.

Williams cringed when he heard a throat being cleared behind him. He just knew that it would be Archer. In a way, he was grateful that it was the guest posing the question that he did... because Williams himself desperately wished to ask it.

"Skipper... would it not give the game away should we attack this close to land?" Archer asked. "Far be it from me to tell you your business, of course... yet..."

"I'll make that determination when I can identify the target, Colonel," Turner's response was a blast of arctic wind. "We're at *war*, in case you've forgotten. It is the job of this submarine to *sink* enemy shipping."

Williams could almost hear Archer bristling. When the

Englishman spoke, his own voice held enough edge to split firewood, "I'm well aware of that, Commander. However, I'm also aware that we're on a special mission. A mission that relies heavily on stealth. Great thundering gunfire and a few bloody explosions within *sight* of the coast would rather ruin that effect, wouldn't you say?"

"Ay…" Hernandez was barely overheard to groan.

Turner rounded on the man, "I'll decide that, Colonel. When I want your opinion, I'll ask for it."

Archer drew in a deep breath but held his tongue. Williams let out a slight sigh of his own, not aware he'd been holding his breath until he did so.

Turner smacked the bridge transmitter button, "Radar, bridge… let me know when that target bears one-one-zero."

Time seemed to ground to a halt as *Bull Shark* made her way inland. No one spoke. If it weren't for the constant growl of the diesels and the frothing hiss of water along the boat's flanks, Elmer Williams could've fooled himself into believing that time itself had been replaced with a steady, thick tension.

"*Bridge, radar… target is at marked bearing, sir.*"

"Put us back on our previous course, Hotrod," said Turner. "And then come to an all stop. Radar, bridge, what's the range now?"

"*Twelve thousand yards, Captain.*"

"Helm, bridge, full right rudder. Steady up on triple zero and then all stop," Hotrod said into the speaker.

Bull Shark came about, carving a neat arc of foam through the dark water. Once she was on her new heading, the diesels growl softened, and the ship's way came off quickly.

"Lookouts?" Turner inquired.

"Contact!" the forward starboard lookout called down excitedly. "Surface contact bearing zero-three-five horizon! Low profile… can't quite tell what it is yet, sir!"

"Submarine, Radcliff?" Turner asked.

The new electrician held up his Bausch and Lomb 7x50 binoculars and studied the faint silhouette for a long moment, "Uhm… I don't think so, sir. Shape is all wrong. I'd say more like a torpedo boat or trawler or something."

OFF THE SOUTHEASTERN COAST OF TIMOR - 10°38"S, 125°30"E -

"Civilian?" Williams asked, mostly to himself but loud enough to be heard.

Turner harrumphed, "With no lights? I doubt it. Joe, point your guns to starboard. I want to give her a broadside as she passes."

"Aye-aye, Captain," said Dutch, not wishing to receive the same response Williams had gotten a few moments earlier. "Guns one and two, aim for a zero-seven-zero relative and prepare to track aft."

Turner nodded in approval at that. Dutch was going to be ready to hit *before* the target was abeam so that he could get the range and send in multiple rounds. Williams crossed his fingers and watched as the big five-inch deck guns rotated on their turntables and pointed just forward of the starboard beam.

"Can't you dissuade him, Elmer?" Archer whispered into the XO's ear. "As I understand it, we're less than two hundred miles from our landing zone... this is a terrible mistake!"

"He's in command here, Colonel," Williams whispered back, stepping a few yards away on the cigarette deck and drawing Archer with him. "It's his decision. You see what happened when you tried?"

"But I'm just a passenger, Old Boy," Archer persisted. "All this for a bloody trawler? He's jeopardizing the entire *mission*, by Jove!"

"Secure the engines," the two men heard Turner say and a moment later, even the low, throaty grumble of the boat's four diesels went silent.

"What's the bloody *point...?*" Archer cranked under his breath.

"I've got him now," Turner said as Williams stood pensively by Archer's side and watched. Even he could see a dark lump off the ship's starboard bow.

"*Bridge, radar... range closing to six-zero-zero-zero yards.*"

Williams felt the hairs on the back of his neck rising. The tension aboard was like an infection that had invaded everyone. He'd even heard it in Balkley's voice.

It wasn't the excitement of impending battle nor the fear that their target would fire back. Based on what they knew, *Bull Shark's* admirable deck armament would doubtless make short work of it.

No, the tension was born from the fact that by this time, every man aboard knew what the boat's mission was. At least this part of it.

They'd been through it before, putting men ashore and retrieving them. They all knew the vital importance of stealth and not giving the enemy even a hint of their presence. They also knew that their captain was about to metaphorically unzip his fly and wave his pecker at the Japs.

And what would happen at sunset the next day when the boat was to sneak into a secluded little cove and launch a raft? Would the Japs be waiting for them?

"He's almost in line, deck!" Radcliff called down again, more quietly this time.

"Permission to find the range, Captain?" Dutch asked.

The rubber band of anticipation had been yanked back to maximum strain. In the next second or two, Turner would either release it or it would snap. Every man on deck, no less than twenty including the lookouts, held their breath and worked their jaws.

Williams heard a puff of air. For an instant, he thought that maybe one of the guns was being cleared with its compressed air system. Then he realized that it'd been his captain blowing out his breath.

"Stand down," he growled. "Secure the guns… clear the decks."

"Thank God…" Archer was overheard to mumble.

"Sir?" Dutch asked.

"You heard me, Joe… this target isn't significant enough to reveal ourselves…" Turner sighed. "Let's get the men below and button her up. Quartermaster, maintain status until the target passes astern. Then we'll fire the rock crushers back up and get underway."

The gun crews re-centered their pieces and put their ammunition away. The weapons were secured, and the men filed down the ladders. By the time they were done, a small, blocky vessel was passing off *Bull Shark's* beam, highlighted perfectly against the silvery slash of moonlight upon the sea. The remaining men on deck watched it slide past, blissfully unaware of how narrow it'd avoided its fate.

"Thank you, Skipper," Archer attempted. "I think that was—"

"My decision to make, Colonel," Turner said flatly. "Do not presume to question my authority on my deck again."

Archer tensed, about to say something but Williams laid a hand on his shoulder and squeezed, "Let's go below and get a cup of coffee, Percy. Little chilly out tonight."

"Yes… quite…" said the Army officer quietly.

In fact, the temperature only a few hundred miles from the equator was a comfortable eighty degrees, but no one corrected Wiliams. The hint was obvious and taken for what it was worth.

As he followed Archer down the hatchway into the control room, Williams experienced a disquiet he'd never felt before aboard *Bull Shark*. He felt at odds with his captain and friend. He wondered where the old Art Turner had gone and if he'd ever come back.

6

OFF TIMOR
DECEMBER 22, 1942

"Captain, may I join you?" Archer asked as he slid through the curtain and into the wardroom.

Turner looked up from his paperwork, "You're a bit early for supper, Colonel. Just me and the excitement of command."

Archer smiled thinly and poured a cup of hot water from Carlson's little pantry alcove. The steward was elsewhere, but as promised, kept a kettle warm for Archer. He'd also shown Archer where he kept the loose tea and tea ball.

"Indeed… and I thought this might be a fine time for a bit of a chin wag, if you'll permit me a few moments?" Archer slid into a chair and placed the ball into the steaming mug.

Turner laid down his pen, sipped from his own mug and leaned back, cracking his back, "I could do with a short break. What's on your mind, Colonel?"

"Well, sir…" the British Army officer began. "Bit of a delicate subject, this… but I thought that we might discuss my upcoming mission a trifle. Discuss who's going with me unto breech, as it were. I've been reviewing the personnel files provided me by Elmer and have selected a few names I thought would do well. However… I would like to get your thoughts on the matter, of course. I know that you and I have had a bit of a clash here and again…"

Turner sighed, "Not at all, Colonel. If you're referring to last night's aborted attack… well, you had a point, after all."

Archer smiled genially, "Thank you, Captain. Then again, I might've handled my suggestion with a bit more… discretion. I know how I'd have felt in your shoes, what?"

Turner waved it off, "Let's not dwell on it, Colonel. Who have you selected?"

Archer removed a notebook from his blouse pocket and thumbed through it until he came to what he was looking for, "Ah… here we are… naturally, I first looked into those of your lads who've actually engaged in a shore action. Quite a number for a submarine, I should think. I immediately disregarded Joe Dutch, of course. You need your officers. Your COB stands out first, as you might expect. Seasoned man, good headpiece, and experienced. There's another fellow, the bloke everyone calls Tank. He seems a good fit as well, what with his brawn and experience on Guadalcanal and another shore action. The Indian fellow seems an obvious choice. There are a handful of others as well, but since I'm only looking for three or four men, I must be selective. I would, if possible, greatly appreciate Petty Officer Hoffman. I have very little idea of what I'll be facing ashore… and a qualified and experienced medico… one with shore experience into the bargain… would be the very thing. No doubt my lads could use a dose of physic, as we used to say. Your thoughts, sir?"

Turner frowned and considered, "I'm afraid Buck Rogers is out. I need him here. His experience and his ability to mesh between the officers and crew is vital and will be needed aboard. I think Hoffman is a sound choice… although I'm loath to leave the boat without her pharmacist's mate. Yet his assistants, specifically Henrie Martin and Eddie Carlson are remarkably skilled."

"The Black cooks?" Archer blurted before catching himself. "No disrespect intended… just a bit taken aback, I suppose."

Turner frowned but nodded, "Yes… Hank Hoffman has been training them in field medicine at every opportunity. I also agree that you'll need a tough guy for security, which Tank Broderick is more than qualified for. Further, I'd like you to have men versed in electrical as well as mechanical skills. Seems those are always handy ashore."

"Indeed," said Archer. "Would that I had a company at my back… but, however…"

"Fred Swooping Hawk fills many roles," Turner went on. "He's a top-notch tracker, has worked with Joe to craft the Navajo code and is both a helluva marksman and a fully qualified motor machinist."

"Good show," Archer agreed.

Turner frowned, "Doug Ingram is my choice for a fourth man. Although Tank is an electrician, Doug has shore experience, too. Unfortunately… he's down with a touch of the flu at the moment. Also, two electricians are a bit redundant."

"What about the new lad… Wayts?" Archer asked. "I know he's a bit green, but as I understand it, he grew up in your Idaho and was a rookie sheriff's deputy before the war broke out. Might be good for him to get a bit of experience and put some of his to work, eh?"

Turner frowned, "Yes… it's just that he's so *young*…"

Archer nodded and sighed, "Aren't they all, Captain? War is a young man's game, I'm sorry to say, and has ground many of them between its wheels over the span of time."

Turner's eyes grew hard, and he stared at the bulkhead for a long moment before whispering, "And how, Colonel… and how… all right, I'll consider Wayts."

"Of course, that's four men in addition to myself." Archer said. "I was planning on only three."

"You'll have five," said Turner, glancing back at Archer and locking gazes with him. "I'm coming with you."

Archer stared, incredulous, "You… bloody *what!?* You can't come, Arthur!"

"The hell I can't," Turner said flatly. "My ship, my mission, my decision, Colonel."

"Once I go ashore, it's *my* goddamned mission, Captain," Archer felt constrained to point out vehemently.

"And you won't ever reach it without agreeing to my terms," said Turner. "You're taking my men into an unknown situation with long-reaching ramifications for the war. I would be remiss if I didn't evaluate the situation for myself, my service, and our combined Allied effort, Colonel. I'm coming, and I'm damned if I send any of my men in with you while I sit back. Not this time."

Archer worked his jaw, evidently vacillating between shock and frustration. He drew in a deep breath and said, "I suppose that is your prerogative... and I know you too have considerable shore combat experience. I won't lie and say that wouldn't be appreciated. However... would not your superiors balk at such an endeavor? After all, Arthur, you're a bloody ship *captain*... a valuable commodity to any nation. It hardly seems fitting that you should risk your value on what is, essentially, a short jaunt of assessment."

Turner shrugged, "Nevertheless. I'm coming. I've made up my mind and I have my reasons, Colonel."

Archer ran his hands through his hair and then drew a long pull from his mug. Settling back into his chair, he levelled a stern look in Turner's direction, "Then you'll understand, Lieutenant Commander, that I outrank you. Further, once ashore, it becomes *my* mission and *my* command. I want that made plain and understood. How do you feel about this?"

Turner actually permitted a thin smile, "You've done all right subordinating yourself to me while aboard, in spite of our difference in rank. I suppose I can do the same."

"Well..." Archer appeared resigned but still mildly flustered. "Quite an unexpected turn, this. On the other hand... five sailors are better than three. Welcome aboard, as you lot say. I have but one request, Arthur."

"What's that?"

"I insist on being there when you tell Elmer."

* * *

"Fucking *what!?*" Elmer Williams exploded in a most uncharacteristic display of shock, anger, and profanity.

What was even more unusual was that the XO let fly, if not exactly in public, then in the presence of all of the ship's officers and then some. For the part of the chiefs... Rogers, Duncan, Pentakkus, and

Weiss… they unsuccessfully tried to mask amused smirks through a combination of coughs, throat clears, and painful cheek and tongue bites. All of the officers, including Archer, looked on with bemusement, amusement, and carefully controlled facial expressions.

The wardroom was filled beyond capacity, and the four chiefs and Archer had to stand and crowd part way into Carlson's pantry. The ship's four other officers outside Turner and Williams sat at their customary positions and waited to see what would happen next.

"You heard me, XO," Turner said sternly. "I'm going ashore with the Colonel."

"No," said Williams, shaking his head emphatically. "I forbid it."

Turner's mouth flickered upward ever so slightly, "Sorry, Elmer… but you can't forbid it. I've got more shiny things on my uniform."

"That's not the damned *point*, Art!" Williams stood behind his chair, one hand resting on the tabletop and the other balled into a fist which he used to emphasize his objections. "You're the *captain*. You simply can't run off on some hairbrained jaunt. We have a mission to accomplish!"

"I feel it's my duty," said Turner. "This isn't a debate, First Officer, this is an *announcement*."

"Like hell it is!" Williams seethed. "Dammit, Art, this is the most… ridiculous… asinine…"

"As you were, Lieutenant!" Turner's brow was dark with impending thunder. "Don't step over the line into insubordination."

"I am doing my job as executive officer," Williams said with barely contained fury. "It's my job to point out when the captain is behaving like an *ass!* In a way that endangers the ship. Going ashore with Colonel Archer is *not* within our mission parameters and not within your prerogative as captain… *sir*."

"I'm not letting my boys go alone," Turner said flatly.

"Art…" Joe Dutch, who could presume at least as much as Williams due to his long friendship with Turner began hesitantly. "Elmer is right. This isn't your job. And our mission requires you here."

"Elmer can handle the patrol for a week or two," Turner said.

For their part, Nichols, Post, and Skaggs appeared visibly

uncomfortable. It was plain to all that they wanted to object but knew that if the captain's two closest friends couldn't get through, they would probably be rebuffed as well.

"Art… Captain… we're headed right up into the South China Sea!" Williams pressed. "It's Indian country and then some. That's a job for *Bull Shark's captain*."

"Or prospective captain," Turner said. "Either way, I'm going in. We're done here."

Turner's declaration thudded to the table and steamed. Everyone knew the tone and knew that once Art Turner's mind was made up, it was made up. There was no point in arguing it any further.

"Orders, Captain?" Frank Nichols and the rest stood and the engineer, who had the watch, looked on passively. There was little to be gleaned from the eyes that stared at Turner through his gold-rimmed cheaters.

"Continue on to drop point Able," Turner said. "I want to be ashore by twenty hundred. That is all."

It wasn't ten minutes later when a series of rapid knocks echoed on the frame outside Turner's stateroom. He sat on his bunk, doing some last-minute writing. Paperwork, a brief after-action report about the trawler they failed to attack the night before, and a letter to Joan. He sighed and leaned back against the bulkhead.

"Enter."

Paul Rogers slipped through the curtain and stood at attention, "Sir, can I have a minute?"

"Certainly, COB," Turner said. "What's on your mind? Problem with the crew? Take a seat."

"As a matter of fact… yeah," Rogers said as he sat at Turner's small desk. "I've got a rather unusual but worrisome disciplinary case."

Turner cocked an eyebrow, "Oh?"

Rogers nodded, "Man's belligerent, closed-off, and irritable. He's doin' a damned fine job of crushing unit cohesion, if you want to know the truth."

"Uh-huh," said Turner dryly. "And his name is A. Turner, right?"

Rogers smiled thinly, "As it happens… yes, sir."

"Well, Buck, he's leaving the ship, so your problem is solved."

Rogers scowled, "Captain, I've known you since you was hardly more than a ninety-day wonder. And the man I'm talking to now is hardly recognizable as the one I've known over ten years. What gives?"

"You presume much, Chief."

"This is one of them times when I need to talk to you as Art and Paul."

"Permission denied."

"Bullshit. The fact is, Art, you've been behaving like an asshole ever since we got to Fremantle. You're biting everybody's head off, casting a gloomy shadow wherever you go and worst of all is this goddamned shore mission! What the hell are you *thinking?*"

"Thinking of my duty, Paul," Turner's voice was harp-string taut.

"Like hell," Rogers leaned in and speared his old friend with a heated glare. "You're thinking about Mr. Hazard and the others. You're pissed off and want to get up and personal with the Jap. To pay them back for what they done."

Turner flung his papers aside and leaned forward, fists balled on his thighs, "And what the hell's wrong with that? We're at war, aren't we? Kill the Jap, right?"

Rogers said nothing for a long moment and then very evenly said, "You ever hear the expression that a man seeking revenge should dig *two* graves?"

Turner scoffed, "Oh, please... I want to make sure my men are okay, Buck. I don't feel right trusting them to Archer."

Rogers nodded, "I get that. Hell, I can't disagree. He's got his mission and his agenda and doesn't care a lick for our boys. So then you send *me* to look after them, Art. You don't send the boat's fuckin' *skipper* in on something like this."

"I've got my reasons."

"Oh, yeah? What are they? Lay 'em out for me."

Turner scowled, "Great thing about being the captain, Buck... I don't have to."

Rogers snorted and pointed his finger at the pile of papers on the bunk, "That a letter to Joanie you're writing? You may not have to explain yourself to me... but that lady damn sure is owed one. Why don't you explain to *her* why you're doing this?"

"I *have* to do this."

Rogers sighed, "No you don't. You just want to get your hands around some yellow man's throat and squeeze the life outta him."

"So what if I do!?" Turner thundered. "Those slanty-eyed bastards *murdered* my men! Freeman and Marty were good guys. Hadley just found out his mom wasn't dying for Christ! And Port… Jesus, Buck… you know what they did to him on The Canal? It's not *right*, goddammit!"

"And you're gonna put it right," Rogers said. "Art Turner's gonna go in there and murder him a couple dozen slopes so's he feels better… and washes away his guilt."

"It's war… not murder."

"Like hell it ain't," Rogers retorted. "You want not just to attack the enemy… you want to *hurt* them. You want to see the life drain out of their eyes up close and personal. Well let me tell you somethin', Art… you can strangle or knife a *hundred* Nips on Timor and it won't bring those guys back from the dead. But what it can do… what it *will* do… is taint and twist the soul of a good man until maybe, just maybe, what comes back… *if* you come back… will be even more unrecognizable than you are now. A man your wife and kids don't deserve."

Turner's fury was a red-hot mist over his eyes. He shook with rage and could barely find his voice.

"Get the hell out of here, Chief…" he growled. "Consider yourself on report."

Rogers stood and had the curtain pulled half aside when he turned back and levelled a finger at Turner, "Fuck your report, Captain. And you had better keep one fucking thing in mind… that you're there to watch out for our men. Not to use them in pursuit of your own obsessions. Because if any of them are lost that way… then you and me are gonna tangle and them fuckin' oak leaves ain't gonna save your ass."

Turner shot to his feet and stepped close to Rogers, meeting the man's steely gaze with his own. The two men stood toe to toe for a moment of time that might've been no longer than a handful of heartbeats. The tension between them twisted it into an hour, or so it seemed.

Finally, Turner drew in a breath and said, not without effort: "You're a good man, Buck Rogers. I'll keep it all in mind."

Rogers nodded and a ghost of a smile appeared on his lips, "You do that. I don't want to lose any more good men... especially my skipper."

The COB was gone, leaving Turner alone in a room that was suddenly claustrophobic and hot. He tried to blow off what his friend had said and went back to his writing.

He wasn't going ashore for revenge. Not really. Sure, if he had a chance to take down a few Japs then so be it. He wouldn't shed any tears for them. But he was going ashore because he was tired of trusting his men to someone else.

He was going to make sure that those men's lives were preserved and not thrown away on some foolish errand for strangers. That they didn't pay the price for doing a good deed.

As Porter Hazard and the others had done just a few weeks earlier.

This wasn't about revenge... it was about duty. It was about loyalty.

That's all.

When Turner went back to his letter to his wife, however, he found that no words would come from the tip of his pen. He didn't know what to say to her... to them... All he'd managed was Dear Joan... I love you and the kiddos. But the rest of the page remained stubbornly blank.

"Damn you, Buck..."

7
TIMOR, BEACH ABLE
DECEMBER 22, 1942

"Sun's down," Turner said as he slowly spun the periscope. "No visual contacts. Quartermaster, note the time and our position. Officer of the deck, begin event timer."

The conning tower and control room were hushed. Usually, even during an active hunt, there was conversation and certainly information being passed back and forth, up and down. However, the mood in the central areas of the boat was somber, almost as if the entire crew felt compelled to be quiet. As if the Japanese who must be out there somewhere could hear even soft whispers over distance and the incompatible sound mediums of air and water.

"Noted," said Hernandez from the chart desk.

"Eighteen-zero-seven," Elmer Williams said from below.

"Down scope," Turner ordered. "Sound, give me a complete double sweep. Diving officer, give me a sounding."

"JP and JK sweeps, aye," said Chet Rivers with Leroy Potts, the baker, at his side.

A low but audible ping reverberated through the quiet ship and Frank Nichols reported: "Three-seven fathoms, Captain. Two hundred and twenty-two feet below the keel."

"Very well," Turner said.

"No contacts on either head, Captain," Rivers reported after consulting with his assistant.

"Very well," Turner repeated. "XO, the deck is yours. Phone talker, please have landing party assignees and Colonel Archer report to forward torpedo."

Turner slid down the ladder and stepped aside to allow Williams to ascend. Before the first officer did so, Turner put a hand on his shoulder.

"Wait until mark plus fifteen and begin your approach to the LZ, Elmer," Turner said. "I want to surface by nineteen hundred and get the raft off the deck within ten minutes and have you back out and in deep water twenty minutes after that."

Williams nodded. All of that had been discussed in the mission briefing before he'd come on watch, "Aye, Captain."

Turner met the slightly younger man's gaze and held it for a long moment, "She's yours, Elmer. Carry out our mission and take care of her and my men."

Williams nodded solemnly and drew in a breath, "I guess I'll have to, won't I, Art?"

Turner frowned but let the rebuke pass. He simply nodded and turned to go forward.

"I don't like it, Elmer," Joe Dutch said from the chart table.

Williams attempted a weak smile, "That you're now my XO, Joe? Them's the breaks, pally."

Nichols snorted but said nothing. Dutch frowned, "You know damned well what I mean. I don't like this whole business. It stinks. And I'm worried about Art."

"Yeah…" Williams sighed and met Nichols's gaze as well. "We all are, Joe. But what the heck can we do about it?"

"Our best, which is all we can ever do," Nichols offered with a half-hearted shrug.

In the forward torpedo room, the majority of the gang had been moved out. The exceptions were Tommy Perkins, room leader pro tem until Sparky Sparks returned from leave, and Perry Wilkes, his assistant. Aside from them, Colonel Archer was already there, sitting on his trunk of goodies and casting an eye over his men.

Tank, Hoffman, Swooping Hawk, and Wayts stood by, lined up and dressed in olive-green utilities and ball caps. Each man's backpack was set before them and each man also had a Thompson sub-machine gun slung over his shoulder. Turner also noted that all five men had standard-issue Colt 1911 .45 semi-automatics hung at their hips. And like him, they had the new Marine Corps KA-bar strapped to their thigh.

"Welcome to the dressing room, Skipper," Archer said amiably. "I see you've got your piece with you. Your heavy weapon is lying on that bunk there along with your pack. Be a good fellow and line up with the other chaps, will you? Like to check our load out before going topside, what?"

Turner did as instructed, standing beside Tank who appeared as if a smile were trying to wrestle its way onto his lips. At Turner's sidelong glance, however, the big electrician kept his face carefully neutral.

"Now then, lads," Archer began, getting to his feet and adjusting his own weapons. "I'm fully aware that this is not, as you Yanks have it, your first rodeo."

He pronounced it row-day-o.

"I'm glad to have you with me," Archer continued. "Your prior experience will no doubt prove invaluable. Each of you has a long gun and a sidearm, of course, as do your captain and I. There are extra magazines for both… but I want to state here and now that I sincerely hope we shan't have need for any of them. At least for the interim. Our goal is to seek out and connect with my lads in the Second Independent Commandos, the 2ICs. I have important intelligence to deliver and hope to gain some as well. They have set up a network with the indigenous population, so they may be of help in this regard. However, at least on this side of Timor, the inhabitants are mostly Portuguese and mixtures of Malay and Portuguese. They are *purported* to be neutral… but we've already seen how the bloody Jap deals with that. As such, we must be on guard at all times. We move quickly, quietly, and the watchword for the foreseeable future is silent as the grave, eh? Now then… in this package I have here are radio parts and a few bits for the lads ashore. It's vital we get it to them. Once a communication link is established with HQ in Australia, the Timor campaign can begin in earnest. With me so far?"

All of the sailors, including Turner, piped up with affirmatives. Archer smiled and quickly cast a glance at Turner.

"Here's where things become a bit… muddy, lads," Archer said. "We're landing approximately thirty miles southeast of Dili, the capital of Portuguese Timor. It's fairly heavily wooded, as it were, and rough. However, I'm somewhat familiar with the territory and believe that we may find assistance rather promptly. Each of us carries rations for three days, appropriate kit that should last us a bit longer yet. We can stretch this, of course, yet the goal here is to live off the land, to acquire native resources and assistance and get the job done. With any luck, we'll have completed our job and will be ready to depart long before your Mr. Williams can return for us."

"And if luck isn't with us, sir?" Wayts asked.

Archer frowned, "Then we'll be enjoying extended shore leave, Wayts. And by the by… there is no talking when at attention."

Wayts flushed and said nothing. Archer nodded and opened his pack, "Let's go through our checklist then…"

This chore taken care of, the men donned their packs and waited for the announcement that the boat had surfaced. Wilkes opened the torpedo loading hatch and pulled down the collapsible ladder.

"Okay, Marines," Tommy Perkins said in his California surfer drawl. "Time to hit the curl."

"You're a funny guy, Tommy," Turner harrumphed as he went up on deck.

Perkins and Wilkes followed, muscling the heavy crate up the steep steps and onto the damp wooden planks of *Bull Shark's* main deck. Turner was pleased to see that Williams already had a party on deck breaking out the rubber raft and laying it out just forward of the five-inch.

Ahead of the ship, a dark line of blackness separated the sea from the starry night. Great snaggle toothed mountains poked up from the tree line and bit at the night sky.

The submarine was idling in, her diesels grumbling low in their throats as if they too understood the need for quiet. All about them, the small bay was silent and still, without even a ripple upon the glassy water, save the curling arabesque peeling off from the ship's hull and spreading out behind them.

"Beach Able, Captain," Williams said from the bridge.

Turner strode aft past where Eddie Carlson and Horris Eckhart were attaching the CO_2 canister to the raft and looked up at Williams, "Very well, XO. You understand your orders."

Williams nodded, "A looping patrol up into the Makassar Strait and back to Timor's north coast. Regular radio monitoring for messages either from you or Fremantle"

Turner nodded, "My orders are in the safe. We were supposed to go further... but I guess this takes precedence."

Williams licked dry lips and said, "It doesn't have to, Art..."

"One way or another, it does, Elmer," Turner stated. "Eight days and you come back here for a pickup. Whether I went or not... I wouldn't leave my boys here for love or money. So the South China sea and whatever command has in mind is going to have to wait a bit."

Williams nodded gravely, "I guess so. Good luck, Captain."

Turner offered a bleak smile, "And to you... Captain."

Presently, the ship was brought to a stop a few hundred yards from shore. With just over twenty feet under her keel, the bow was flooded down, and dark water crawled up the planks almost to the mount of the forward gun. Turner, Archer, and their four sailors were crowded into the eight-man raft with the crate of supplies crowding their feet.

"We're afloat, Colonel," Turner said from his position in the stern.

"Good show... let us be on our way then," Archer said.

"Cast off," Turner ordered. "Oarsmen, easy all."

The stern line was untied from the gun mount and Turner handed it in as Swooping Hawk and Wayts began to paddle gently. Buck Rogers stood on the bridge beside Williams and Hotrod, waving and saying nothing. Eckhart and Carlson did the same, their expressions unreadable in the dark. Turner cast an eye back, seeing his submarine silhouetted against the moon.

For an instant, he nearly relented. Nearly ordered the boat to return. Hell, he nearly ordered *everyone* to go back, Archer's missions be damned. If the man wanted to go ashore, then he was welcome to it, but Turner would be damned if...

The dark shape of *Bull Shark* began to snort and blow as her forward ballast tanks were cleared and she came level again. The dark, angular shape began to lengthen, seeming to Turner's eye as if by magic. Soon, though, she was beam on as she reversed and turned about. Presently, the distinct shape foreshortened again and began to diminish into the moon's Eldridge shine.

"Still with us, Art?" Archer asked quietly.

Turner focused his attention forward once more, "I'm here, Colonel. All right, fellas, make way. Little more to port... that's it. Colonel, any particular spot?"

Archer, who sat atop the crate Indian style turned and shrugged, "No idea, mate. Any place that looks acceptable, I suppose. Sadly, we couldn't arrange a guide... part and parcel of why we're here in fact."

Turner nodded., "We'll find something... there, to port... looks like a strand of beach and a partially clear area."

"Smashing," Archer said.

"Yeah... swell..." Turner muttered to himself.

* * *

"Control, bridge... sounding," Williams said through the bridge speaker.

A moment's pause and then Nichols replied, "*Bridge, control... two-eight fathoms.*"

"Very well," Williams said. "What's the state of the battery charge, Frank?"

"*Pretty low after today, Elmer. Twenty percent or so.*"

"Okay then, we'll stay on top for the rest of the night," Williams replied. "One and two on charge duty, Frank."

"Thought you were gonna dunk, Elmer," Joe Dutch noted from just behind the bridge.

Williams sighed, "No point unless we detect enemy units. We'll run offshore a bit before we turn north to skirt around Timor."

For several minutes, the only sounds on deck were the constant passage of the apparent wind rolling from bow to stern at eight knots, the shoosh of seawater as the submarine knifed through the mild swell and the monotonous rumble and clatter of the four diesels at nearly full power. The moon slowly climbed the eastern sky, her soft silvery finger reaching from the horizon to gently caress *Bull Shark's* starboard bow.

"They'll be all right, sir," Buck Rogers finally said.

"Yeah, what he said, Elmer," Dutch agreed.

Williams drew in a breath and let it flutter away, "I hope so, fellas. These clandestine missions never seem to go as planned. And I just don't like… well…"

"Art's got a good head on his shoulders," Dutch said.

"He'll take care of them boys, Mr. Williams," Rogers added.

"Better than that British Colonel," said Hotrod.

"I wasn't inviting a discussion," Williams snapped. After a moment, he sighed, "Sorry, guys… I'm just worried."

"We should be ready to make our turn north, Skipper," Hotrod said, not missing a beat or sounding the least bit flushed.

"Yeah… okay, quartermaster, let's—"

"*Bridge, radar! Distant contact bearing three-zero-zero. Range twenty-two thousand yards. Repeat two-two thousand. Bearing remains fairly constant, range decreasing by… ten knots or so,*" Ted Balkley sounded mildly excited.

"Well, well," mused Dutch, "think it's our pal from last night?"

Williams pondered for a long moment. Now that the shore party had gone, there was really no more reason to remain unnoticed. This close to Australia, the Japs would expect to come under attack from Allied submarines.

"Not sure, XO," Williams said and smiled. "But why don't we find out. Hotrod, same play as last night. Put him between us and the moon." Buck, go and get the gun crews ready. If it turns out to be something other than a trawler, we'll get him with torpedoes. Otherwise, the fellas could use a little gunnery practice, I'd say."

Rogers grinned and dropped down through the hatch. Hotrod consulted his notes and then pressed the transmit button.

"Helm, come left to course three-five-five. Maintain speed."

The ship was running at a modest speed while two of her engines charged the battery banks. At the angles projected, it would be a good twenty or thirty minutes until the two vessels came within visual range of one another.

"*Bridge, radar, target bearing coming starboard,*" Balkley reported. "*Estimate bandit heading to be two-zero-zero degrees. Range decreasing rapidly. Range now one-eight-five-zero-zero yards.*"

As with the previous night, two dozen men flooded onto the dark decks of the submarine. They quickly and quietly went about readying their pieces for battle. Even though the target was about nine miles away, they moved with spectral swiftness and spoke in hushed tones. Williams had to admit that they were a well-oiled machine. A submarine crew to be proud of.

When the target was nearly abeam, the acting captain ordered the ship to come to zero-two-zero. A parallel course that should bring the two vessels to within a mile or less of one another. Already, a distinct black shape could be seen by the lookouts in the periscope shears.

"*Bridge, radar... target appears to be same size as last night,*" Balkley reported. "*They don't... oh, shit! Bridge! Broad-spectrum scatter! Assess omni-direction radar beam!*"

Williams narrowed his eyes, "So... the Japs are finally starting to get with the program, huh? Okay, here's what we do, Hotrod... you keep us pointed right at him. Joe, have your gun crews aim to starboard. We're gonna run up on him, presenting the narrowest possible target, then we'll swing to port and give him a broadside. Lookouts, come down on deck. And have Teddy secure the sugar jig, Hotrod."

The quartermaster quickly gave his helm orders and turned to Williams, "There is an ancient piece of Aztec wisdom often touted in the humble land of my rearing, Captain."

Dutch snorted.

"What's that, Hotrod?" Williams asked, trying to remain stoic.

"That a man who waves his huevos about is likely to have them kicked, *señor*."

Dutch and the lookouts guffawed. Ahead of the bridge on its

elevated blister, the Pompom crew, including the COB, laughed as well.

"Well, we have a saying where I'm from too, Hotrod," said Williams. "The man who first gets off his keister is the man who suffers the leaster."

Hernandez bowed, "Very profound, my liege."

"Measure once, cut twice I always say," Rogers opined from forward.

Dutch shook his head, "Art is right… this *is* the smart-assin'est boat in the Navy."

"Hey!" someone called from the forward five-inch. "Them slants are takin' potshots at us!"

The men on the bridge could see it. From the angular dark shape racing toward them, tiny pinpricks of light appeared. Nothing else happened, and from the two miles or so that separated the ships, no sound echoed to them.

"Small arms?" Dutch asked.

Then two slightly brighter flashes flared and a moment later, two dull pops floated to their ears.

"AA guns," Williams surmised. "They appear to be slightly miffed. Get ready, Joe."

"Gun crews, stand ready!" Dutch shouted. "Zero elevation… make your shots count!"

The range was decreasing quickly now, more than ten yards per second. Although the range was long, the Japs's aim would improve as they drew closer.

Williams thumbed the speaker, "Maneuvering, bridge put number three on propulsion. Helm, give me fifteen knots. Begin zigzagging. Hard-over helm each way for thirty seconds."

Orders were acknowledged and the ship surged ahead, gaining speed. The helm was put over to starboard and the approaching black shape of the enemy ship slipped slowly and slightly to port. Then the helm was put over and it moved back the other way. *Bull Shark* wouldn't turn much in such a short time, but Williams hoped it'd be enough to avoid direct fire. So far, it was working.

"*Bridge, radar. Range now one-six-zero-zero yards!*"

"Now, Hotrod!" Williams ordered.

The quartermaster smashed the button, "Helm, bridge! Hard left rudder! Maneuvering, stop port engine!"

The combination of uneven thrust and the rudder angle brought the submarine's bow around with admirable swiftness… for a 312-foot ship traveling at fifteen knots at any rate.

"Get ready, boys!" Dutch hollered, watching the dark shape of the trawler crawl to the right and elongate as it neared the silvery line of moonlight. "Wait for it… *FIRE!*"

Both ships opened up in earnest then. The trawler had little to offer in the way of heavy firepower, however. A few men with machine guns and a twin-barreled AA cannon forward seemed pitiful against the tremendous thunder offered in return.

Bull Shark let loose with two five-inch guns, a quad-barrel 40mm AA cannon, a twin barreled 20mm Oerlikon and a single .50 caliber Browning M2 machine gun mounted on the starboard rail. The submarine's fire was deadly accurate and immediately told.

Bright roses of fire erupted along the small enemy ship's hull. The screams of men being gouged by rounds, shrapnel, and flame pierced the distance between the two combatants and made everyone cringe as much as the sound of rounds peppering the water, zipping by overhead and striking the steel of the hull with gongs and whining ricochets.

"Helm, bridge!" Hernandez roared into the speaker. "Hard right rudder! Maneuvering, start port engine, reverse starboard!"

Diesels growled and weapons clattered as the long submarine muscled her way back to starboard. She had to stop her port momentum and crank her stern around, but the maneuver was working and allowed Dutch to keep his guns pointed in the right direction.

"Fire for effect!" he shouted.

The order was entirely superfluous. The men had their blood up and were pouring it on. The big deck gun crews were rapidly reloading and had already fired another round before their gunnery officer spoke. The two five inchers bellowed, spitting lances of flame as long as they were into the night. The Pompom and Oerlikon popped, and the machine gun clattered and then…

One moment the Japanese trawler was there, and in the next heartbeat, a roiling oily cloud of bright plasma and thick smoke replaced her. Something vital had been hit and the interaction consumed the small vessel in fiery death.

The gunfire from *Bull Shark* ceased and for several taffied moments, no one spoke. They all gawked at the horrifying sight of a ship and men being eaten alive by a writhing incandescent monster. Certainly, they were the enemy… but they were men. Sailors like themselves and even in the heat of battle with fighting madness seizing their souls… they could offer a brief moment of empathy and mourning for their foe.

"Poor devils…" Williams sighed. "All right, Hotrod, get us back on course and on charge. Joe, secure your crews. Good work, men. COB, get me a damage report asap."

The submarine slowed and turned north, racing away from the scene and into the night. No men were killed, although several had minor lacerations from a few bits of flying shrapnel caused by impacting rounds. The DC team found no less than a dozen holes in the outer hull where bullets had punctured the starboard ballast tanks, but that was all. A few quick plugs and all was well.

Imbued with victory and elated by success, the men of *Bull Shark* felt that their patrol was off to a good start.

8

EAST TIMOR

2045 LOCAL TIME

"There's a path, sir," Fred Swooping Hawk said after gulping down a little water. "It's a bit rough and goes inland about fifty yards. Then there's a sort of road, I guess. Rutted and muddy in places, but it seems to go for a while paralleling the coast. Across it is some kind of farm. Lot of open land bordered by trees, and I thought I saw a house or something on the northside."

"Some of these trees *stink*, sir," Lee Wayts said, wrinkling his nose. "Like… skunky."

"That's the Skunk Tree," Archer said with a smile. "Along with the Candlenut, Australian Pine, and pepper tree, they abound here. Unlike the Solomons, which is about the same distance from the equator, the foliage is a bit drier, but still tropical. And the farm you likely saw, lad, is a coffee plantation."

"That's something anyway," Tank Broderick said. "Least we can wake up with a nice cup of joe."

"Yeah, Tank… long as you got time to pick it, process it, dry it, and grind it up," Hoffman chuckled.

"How about the fauna, Colonel," Turner asked, "anything dangerous on this island?"

Archer smiled again, "Oh, indeed, Captain. Saltwater crocodiles are to be found here about. Nasty buggers. In the wooded areas, somewhat inland but not strictly limited to those areas are reticulated pythons. Then there are the usual pests, of course."

"Oh, swell…" Hoffman grumped.

"Don't worry about the snakes, lads," Archer said. "They don't *usually* attack humans… although they can get over twenty feet, even on Timor. Best watch out for them in the brush, eh?"

"Why I joined the boats," Tank grumbled. "Cuz I didn't want this jungle shit… and yet here I am… snakes… crocs…"

"Let's focus, people," Turner said.

"Indeed," said Archer. "Our first order of business is to secure the raft and then move out. There are several villages not far and our priority is to make contact with one of them. I know some locals in the area, and they ought to be able to put us in touch with the 2ICs."

"What about the crate?" Turner asked, indicating the heavy box still sitting in the raft.

Archer frowned, "I'm loath to leave it behind… this spot may be difficult to find again, providing we're even able. We'll have to tote it along, I'm afraid. There are six of us. Two men at each end, hefting it upon their shoulders… the weight is hardly more than eighty pounds."

"In addition to the packs," Turner said. "That's a lot of humping in this climate, Colonel."

"No choice, I'm afraid," said Archer, withdrawing a pack of Viceroys from his blouse and lighting one. "Once we make contact, we won't have to lug the bloody thing about anymore. Have yourselves a fag, lads… then we move out. Want to make proper use of this darkness, what?"

Turner frowned and sat on the sponson of the boat, lighting a Lucky and listening intently to the sounds of Timor night around him. They'd come ashore on a narrow strand surrounded by Mangroves that quickly gave way to tropical jungle. From the scouting report, it wasn't as wet and malodorous as Guadalcanal, at least. Yet there were dangers here, just as in the Solomons.

The men would have to be mindful of insects and spiders as well as snakes and crocodiles. Then, of course, there was the Jap. Turner was also concerned that they were in the middle of East Timor, where the

Portuguese settlers and natives had declared themselves neutral. Neutrality was often purchased at a heavy price, and Art Turner didn't want his men footing that bill with their lives.

"Penny for your thoughts, Art," said Archer as he sat down beside Turner.

Turner grunted, "I'd like to hear your plan, Percy. I get the sense that you don't exactly have one."

Archer sighed, "Very perceptive. The fact of the matter is… I don't. The nature of the mission and the lack of contact with our target makes that a bit difficult to say the least. However, as I say, we'll make local contact and proceed from there."

"Aren't you worried about being betrayed?" Turner asked.

"The people on this side *are* neutral, Art."

Turner harrumphed, "And they'll remain in the Jap's good graces by turning in any Allies they find, I'm sure. You intimated as much back on the boat."

Archer frowned and shook his head, "Perhaps… but they've claimed neutrality simply as a way of preserving themselves. The people of East Timor don't like your Jap any better than do the Dutch in West Timor, to be sure. I'm not suggesting we be reckless… deed there will be turncoats… always are with bloody neutrals… but I've found that somewhat less prevalent here. Remember, I know some of these people. Spent some time here myself, in course."

"I certainly hope you're right."

Archer flicked his dead butt to the damp sand at his feet and met Turner's gaze. There was just enough moonlight for the men to be able to make one another out in the dark, "By the by, Captain… as discussed, we're ashore now and this is *my* operation. I expect you to follow my orders just as any good exec. Would do. Please do not contradict me in front of the men again."

Turner nodded, "Very well, Colonel. But let me remind *you*… these are *my* men. There safety is my primary concern."

"With respect, Old Boy," Archer said coolly. "They're *my* men now. Now that we're here, your only hope is to stick with me and mine. Unless you plan on camping here for the next fortnight."

Archer had a point, and Turner couldn't avoid it nor could he deny it. Without Archer and without making contact with the people he'd come to find; they didn't have enough food to survive without foraging. They had no means of communication, save the radio set in the crate which still needed an external power source.

Turner and his men were, in a very real sense, stranded on Timor. The only person they could rely on was Archer, who was also relying on them. In Turner's current frame of mind, however, this did not sit well.

"No, Colonel, I don't intend to do that," Turner said. "But mark my words… these men's lives are not to be thrown away nor are they to be treated as slaves."

"Of course not," said Archer kindly, patting Turner on his shoulder. "We need one another. However, I do expect you and them to respect the chain of command. As I'm sure you would were the situation reversed."

Turner pitched his butt and stood, "Very well, Colonel. Orders?"

"Right. We move out," said Archer, getting to his feet. "Swooping Hawk, on point. Broderick in the rear. Hoffman, Wayts, you're on crate duty for the nonce. Shouldn't be more than a few hours to our next destination, lads."

Hoffman and Wayts exchanged a brief glance but hefted the metal crate, setting it on their shoulders. That was the best way to carry a heavy load, freeing up the legs to move without being bumped. Upon seeing this, Archer tapped Swooping Hawk's shoulder, and the Navajo began leading the procession into the underbrush.

The mangroves and their heavy scent of salt and wet decay changed to a more pleasant green smell as the team left the shoreline. Although being only 300 miles from the equator meant that there was never anything like winter, the late-December temperature at night was routinely in the seventies and the going was more comfortable than would be the same job on Guadalcanal, 2,000 miles to the east.

There were the usual tropical scents and sounds, of course. Night birds cheeped and hooted, small primates occasionally chittered and insects of all varieties screed and buzzed. A light mist had gathered above the ground and the thick, cloying air was redolent with the sweet tang of jasmine, honeysuckle, and chlorophyll. Every now and then, however, a sharp, bitter odor would waft in, souring the pleasantness and bringing with it the reminder that they were alone in wild, untamed nature. And that danger could be found just about anywhere.

Presently, Swooping Hawk led the team out of a line of pepper trees and Candlenuts and the sailors were surprised to see a wide swath of open land before them. Beyond it and the dark line of trees on the other side, great jagged peaks rose into the night, their granite fangs blotting out the stars in irregular patterns.

The men stood at the edge of a muddy track that looked barely wide enough for a Jeep to pass along. To either side, knee-high grass swayed gently in the evening breeze. Beyond the road, with a translucent blanket of mist hanging low over the fields, were rows and rows of some sort of large bush or small tree, about five feet tall. Interlaced among these were much taller trees with small leaves that drooped and might contain some sort of flower.

Off to the right was a ramshackle house of a single-story design with what might be a storage hut behind. The house appeared to be a hybrid of a wood-frame structure and a thatched roof hut, as did the higher storage facility.

"Coffee plantation," Archer explained. "Those are Candlenut trees mixed in with the arabica plant. They give a good deal of shade, and their nuts are cultivated for their oil, as the name suggests."

"Maybe they won't mind we pick some?" Tank asked wryly.

Archer chuckled, "Quite a process before the beans become coffee, Petty Officer. As I don't know the owners, I believe we shall—"

From off to the right, to the north, a low but insistent hum began to grow. It took only a few seconds for the men to recognize the sound of an engine whining as it was driven in low gear over rough terrain. Turner cursed and waved Wayts and Hoffman back into the trees.

"Put the crate down and arm yourselves," said the captain.

Archer stared up the road, "Yes... odds that this is a friendly vehicle are low, I'm afraid. Certainly, at this time of night. Good show, Art."

The rutted track led north along the plantation for half a mile before widening slightly and climbing up a low hill. Near the top of the hill, the road vanished into more varied trees. Already, the light ground mist was beginning to glow with an eerie, diffuse light.

"Japs?" Turner asked.

"Likely," said Archer and snapped his fingers. "Art, you stay with the two lads and the crate. Broderick, Swooping Hawk, you're with me. We'll settle in across the way and set up a crossfire. Remember, lads, do not fire straight across. We only fire at an angle north or south, at the approach or retreat of the vehicle. No one fires until I do, clear?"

A chorus of yessirs peppered the night as the six men divided and found cover in the darkness of the foliage. Already, the faint glow up on the ridge had solidified into a pair of headlights punching iridescent cones through the mist and onto the gray road as something angled down the hill.

Whatever the vehicle was, Turner could only see a boxy shape behind the lights, it wasn't coming very fast. No doubt the condition of the road was making things difficult. From the uneven whirr of the engine, Turner guessed the driver was having to apply more or less accelerator to get over and through ruts and potholes without bottoming the vehicle out. Based on the moderate pitch of the engine's whine, Turner thought it must be the Jap equivalent to a Jeep or small truck.

Just as attacking the Japanese trawler the night before would have alerted the enemy to their position, so too did Turner wonder about the wisdom of attacking the vehicle. Should they take it out and kill the crew, it would eventually alert their command that *somebody* was out there with ill intent.

On the other hand, that was already established. There would be no proof of who attacked the vehicle, and it probably didn't much matter. At least then the team would have transportation. If only for a short while before having to ditch it.

"Bollox!" Archer cursed out loud.

Turner understood. The colonel had the same thought as did Turner. However, at the bottom of the rise, the vehicle turned off the road and drove toward the farmhouse. A moment later, the engine died, and ghostly voices floated over the fields and tickled at the men's ears.

"That sound like Jap, sir?" Wayts asked.

"Yeah…" Turner said. "Maybe they've set up a command post at that farmhouse?"

"We're going to bloody find out," Archer said tightly. "I want that truck… I assume it's a truck. Be a fair sight better than hoofing it through the lettuce, eh?"

"Yeah," Turner agreed, "but we don't have any knowledge of what's at that house."

"Probably a joy house for the slants," Tank quipped. "Neutrals supplementing their income."

Archer snorted, "Just so. Let's find out, shall we? Broderick, Wayts, Swooping Hawk, with me. Art you and the medico stay here and guard the package. If all goes well, we'll have that vehicle liberated in two shakes. But however… if you hear shooting… make haste to join us, what?"

Turner balked at being left to cool his heels. He nearly protested but managed to curb his reaction to: "We can mark the position and reinforce you, Colonel."

Archer frowned, "While I'd appreciate the additional firepower, Captain… those supplies, and your medic are far too valuable to risk just yet. There seems to be little activity over there… four of us with these coffee grinders should do."

"Very well," said Turner and moved to lean up against a tree. Hoffman joined him and the two men watched as Archer led his three amateur commandos into the coffee fields. Soon, the men crouched low and were swallowed by the dark foliage. Soon enough, all that remained was the whispering breeze, the occasional call of a night bird and the ceaseless chorus of crickets. A placid, island night.

"Think they'll be all right, sir?" Hoffman asked.

Turner sighed, "I hope so, Doc. Here… let's break off a branch and mark the spot. I want to be ready in case we need to move."

* * *

Tank Broderick was bothered by a gnawing worry he couldn't quite pin down. He supposed that it'd begun when this crazy patrol had started way back in Fremantle. Although when he thought hard on the matter, his vague worry probably had its roots in that terrible day the Japs had bushwhacked them.

Something had happened to the skipper the day Porter Hazard and the rest were gunned down by those damned slants pretending to be in trouble. Something had broken inside him... set off a bonfire of anger that was apparently eating away at him somehow. Turner had been prickly, stand-offish, and generally cold ever since. Both with the men and even his officers.

The fact of the captain's insistence on coming ashore with them had not diminished Tank's concerns. In fact, it probably made them worse. Because the electrician was no longer certain of Turner's motives.

Whereas before, they'd gone to Guadalcanal with Major Decker on a specific mission. The captain had come along for a specific reason, too. Yet on this little jaunt, his presence wasn't necessary. Sure, he could fight and for that reason alone, they were better off. And yet...

Turner said it was because he wanted to make sure that Tank and the others were safe and treated right. Tank believed him... yet there was more to it. Had to be. Tank suspected that Turner was out for blood. That the captain wanted to get up close and personal with the Japs and pay them back for what they'd done. To pay them back in a way that firing torpedoes from the conning tower, or the bridge simply couldn't satisfy.

Colonel Archer, on the other hand, was on Timor for possibly similar reasons. Yes, he was trying to make contact with men he'd trained so as to get them a line of communication back to Australian HQ. Fair enough. Yet in this man, too, there was more going on. A deeper reason... perhaps anger as well at having left his men to their fates.

Tank was in the rear of the line, watching as Fred Swooping Hawk wove through the coffee fields. The Indian picked his way through gaps and across rows so quickly and proficiently, Tank could almost believe he'd been there before. The man had a knack for this kind of work... an almost innate sense of the wild that he'd proven not long ago on New Ireland.

Directly behind him was Archer, trotting along in the Navajo's wake, head up just enough to see over the tops of the coffee plants but with no hesitation evident at all in his movements. Like Swooping Hawk, Archer was at home in the brush. Where Freddy's experience was that of growing up in and around the wilderness, Archer's was the confidence of many armed campaigns in the field.

Behind the Colonel was Wayts. While the young man, new to the sub and still getting his bearings, held his weapon with the confidence of a man who knew how to use it... there was hesitation in his movements and in his bearing. He was nervous, out of place and unsure of himself. At least in terms of how he fit into this crazy situation that he couldn't possibly have foreseen.

And what of Tank himself? He'd gone ashore on Guadalcanal just before the invasion. He'd fought a guerilla campaign and had attacked a Jap gun emplacement. He'd gone ashore on New Ireland to find Decker and his men, too. He was confident in his abilities, although he'd hardly call himself a qualified ground-pounder.

Yet there was a fracture in the ranks. Archer had his agenda and Turner had his. And unless Tank was completely off his mark, they didn't quite jive. And perhaps that was at the root of his worry. Two officers working together but with different goals. Could that... *would* that... blow up in all of their faces?

Swooping Hawk raised a fist, and the line came to a dead stop. Tank could see that they were near the edge of the fields and no more than thirty or forty yards from the house. Archer waved and the four men came together, shoulder to shoulder, crouching low behind the last line of coffee plants.

The house up close was less modern than it appeared from a quarter mile away. The structure was perhaps fifty feet long and built on short pilings three feet off the ground. That was fairly common in the tropics, Tank knew. It kept heavy rain flooding from invading the house itself.

The walls were a mixture of rough-hewn planks, logs, and other native materials nailed, tied, or glued in a hodgepodge offering three shuttered windows that looked out onto the fields. The roof was a layered palmetto frond affair but with a decent pitch. In front, the Jap vehicle, a flatbed truck, was parked near a covered front porch. Out back, a deck of logs and bamboo trunks looked out over the plantation and the storage building a bit more to the north. That building was constructed as the house was, and looked like a taller version without windows.

"Blimey," Archer hissed, pointing through the leaves to the back deck where a pair of Nips sat on wooden folding chairs smoking and talking in low voices. "Like a bloody holiday cottage."

"Think they're the same ones what drove up, sir?" Wayts asked.

"No idea, lad," said Archer. "But listen... you hear that?"

"Yeah... from inside," said Swooping Hawk.

Tank didn't hear it for a moment, and then he did. A faint pattern of musical notes drifting atop the mist as if played by a spectral orchestra some distance off.

"Phonograph?" asked the electrician.

Archer nodded, "Bit of a to-do going on inside, eh? Perhaps we should inquire within, lads."

"Wish we knew how many Japs there were, sir..." Wayts said uncertainly. "Dangerous going into a dwelling without information."

"Fewer than the number of rounds we carry, I make no doubt," Archer said in a tone that was low and whose darkness tickled uncomfortably along Tank's spine. "Sling your SMGs. Sidearms and combat knives only. Swooping Hawk, you and I will go in the front door... Broderick, you take Wayts round back, eliminate those two bastards back there and come in the rear entrance. We'll sweep the house and see what's what. Count sixty and then move, lads. Ready now... set... mark!"

9

"Is he serious, sir?" Wayts whispered to Broderick as he crouched beside the big electrician.

"As a heart attack, Lee," Tank said coldly. "And don't call me sir. I work for a livin'. You all right?"

Wayts was sweating profusely. So much so that Tank could clearly see the sheen on his face even in the dim moonlight filtering through the trees. He laid his hand on the young man's shoulder and gave it a gentle shake.

"Hey… you okay, kid?"

Wayts swallowed and something clicked in his throat, "Yeah, I… it's just…"

Tank smiled, "Thought you were a deputy and a hunter, kid."

Wayts snorted, "Deer and duck and shit… not fuckin' *people*, Tank… And the most dangerous thing I had to contend with back in Idaho was speeders, tossin' drunks in the tank, or an occasional domestic thing… I never even had to draw my weapon!"

Tank frowned. He didn't like the look or sound of the kid. He understood. Understood from his own experience as well as from long discussions with Al Decker's men. Your first time in combat was the hardest.

It was one thing to fire a deck gun at a distant ship or launch a torpedo. It was one thing to drop a bomb from thousands of feet up. But for any normal, rational human being brought up with the Judeo-Christian value of the sanctity of life… coming face to face with taking it was a hard pill for many men to swallow.

When it was up close and personal, without even the buffer of a few hundred yards between firing lines, the concept took on a level of horror few could truly comprehend until experiencing it. For Tank's part, he wondered what was worse. The fact that you could lose your life or that you might take another's life from him.

"It's gonna be okay, kid… just think of this as goin' in to roust a bunch of drunks," Tank patted his shoulder.

Wayts harrumphed and then managed a small chuckle, "'Cept these drunks got rifles… I'll be okay, Tank."

"Time to go," Tank whispered. "You hang back and come runnin' if I get into trouble."

Wayt's hazel eyes were great glowing saucers, the light from the low moon illuminating their terror, "What!? I can't let you go up against two Japs on your own!"

Tank held a finger to his lips and smiled, "Don't worry about it, pal. They're just sittin' there suckin' on a pill. Probably not even armed."

Tank slung his Thompson and yanked his KA-bar from its sheath, brandishing the black blade and moving through the last line of coffee plants. Wayts was frozen in place, part fear and part astonishment, Tank thought. But at least he was doing as he was told.

Tank crossed the thirty feet between the field and the side of the house in eight quick, long strides. He pressed up against the wall and began to slide toward the rear, his eyes darting back and forth, and his ears pricked, or so it felt. He'd nearly reached the rear corner and the start of the deck when a shout arose from the front of the house.

Tank cursed. It wasn't very loud, not near the rear, but when the low, calm Japanese voices on the deck stopped in mid-sentence, he knew they must've heard something. He swallowed and slid closer, risking a peek around the corner.

One man had risen and was moving toward an open door. The

other still sat, his cigarette dangling negligently from his lips, its tip glowing cherry-red in the dark and emitting a faint wisp of smoke that was quickly swallowed by the light mist.

Tank said a quick prayer and plunged in.

The deck was only about waist-high, and Tank was able to leap up, using his free hand to boost his jump so that he got his foot on the rough planks and arced up and onto the platform. The man in the chair coughed, yelped something, and his smoke went sailing off into the night.

He was too late, though. Far too late. The last thing the wide-eyed Japanese soldier saw before being struck was a hulking figure lunging at him out of the darkness and the faintly glowing mist.

Then the sharp point of the eight-inch combat blade slid into his flesh below the chin, sliding up and through his tongue, soft pallet and lodging into his brain. The man was dead even before Tank was able to yank the blade free.

Maybe it was instinct, maybe just dumb luck, but as he withdrew his knife, the electrician heard something from inside. Voices, scuffling of shoes, perhaps. He threw himself down and rolled even as a heavy-caliber weapon thundered, spoiling the silence he'd tried to preserve.

Tank found himself on his back and looking at the open door of the house. A man stood in it. Maybe the same one who'd just gone in. The man held a rifle and was searching the darkness for a target.

Coming back with one of the long-barreled Arisakas was his first mistake. His second was standing in a lit doorway, the light from within casting the soldier in perfect relief.

As if sensing his error and perhaps now seeing Tank as his eyes adjusted, the man took two steps forward and brought the barrel around. He chuckled and said something in his native language. Tank didn't know what it was, but when the barrel leveled on him, he could guess.

That's when a heavy, automatic weapon rattled. Half a dozen throaty cracks as heavy .45 caliber slugs tore into the Jap's body, turning him into some grotesque marionette as he danced and spun, dropping his weapon and crying out a gurgling death scream.

The body crumpled to the deck with a heavy, wettish thud even as another shadowy shape materialized out of the darkness and clambered onto the deck.

"You okay, sir?" Wayts gasped, his voice quavering with emotion.

Tank got to his feet and grinned, "Four-oh, kid. And don't call me sir, for Christ! You got him… thanks! Made a racket, though."

Wayts's breath came in short gasps as he said, "Well… told him to freeze."

"No, you didn't."

"Oops."

The electrician laughed and slapped Wayts on the back, "Let's go!"

* * *

Without a word between them, Archer and Swooping Hawk had slung their Tommy guns and withdrew their Colt .45s. Safeties off and rounds jacked into the chamber, they mounted the front steps with quick, silent movements born from long practice. Each took a position at either side of the front door and waited a moment.

There was music coming from within and muffled voices. After a few seconds of listening, though, the voices didn't change in pitch or timbre. The men met one another's gaze and Archer nodded.

The handle of the wooden door was on his side, but that meant it had to open in the Navajo's direction. Swooping Hawk slid sideways, took hold of the handle and jumped sideways again, yanking the door open in an instant.

The sounds from within swelled. Some tune or other played gayly on an old victrola, which meant that there was power here in one form or another. The muffled voices swelled too, taking on clarity and became that of several men and women.

Archer drove in first, plunging into the stuffy air and swirling smoke that filled the front parlor. Swooping Hawk whirled in after him, moving to the left of the door, leading with his weapon.

The sight that greeted the two men gave them a moment's stunned pause. Sitting on a pair of rattan chesterfields were two Jap soldiers wearing only their trousers and two dark-haired women wearing the sheerest of nighties. The four were hunched over a decorative pot-like thing in the center with several long, tapering stems arching up and away. Each of these stems ended in a mouthpiece that was being lovingly sucked on by all four. From the mouths and the pot, streamers of thick smoke wafted toward the ceiling, emitting an aromatic perfume of sweetness and flowers with something bitter underlying it.

"Opium den," Archer sneered.

Swooping Hawk nodded. As part of his Navajo upbringing, he was familiar with rituals surrounding the use of peyote. He had on one occasion participated in a spiritual journey and had endured the psychotropic effects along with three others in the sacred tipi one night. He had not enjoyed the experience and found that those who engaged in it regularly often changed. They became addicted to the ceremonies and often neglected their day-to-day life.

The young motor machinist was just about to ask what they should do when Archer's Colt roared out in the confined space, breaking the seeming euphoria of the smokers.

The two Jap men toppled over, their chests a bloody ruin. The women looked up, blinked dully, and only offered the two men vapid smiles.

"God almighty…" Archer barked and shouted at them in broken Portuguese.

"What…?" Swooping Hawk was momentarily stunned by Archer's cold brutality.

The colonel huffed and moved past the doped-up women, moving toward a hallway that led deeper into the long, narrow house, "What'd you expect, lad? We take them prisoner?"

Swooping Hawk had no answer, but he was still shaken by the calculated viciousness of the Royal Army soldier. What bothered him more was the grim smile and hateful glint he'd seen in the man's eyes when he'd pulled his trigger.

However, Swooping Hawk knew his duty and followed the Brit into the hallway. They passed by a kitchen and eating area and moved into a row of bedrooms. From behind two of these closed doors, a variety of unearthly sounds seeped into the hall. Squeaks, moans, and grunts from both sexes quickly informed the men of what *else* this place must be. Archer had explained that many of the locals were forced to become comfort women for the Jap soldiers. Their homes and their women practically forced into sexual servitude.

"Bloody *bastards*..." Archer's hate was now a living thing that twisted his face and painted it bright red in the faint light of a bare bulb halfway down the hall. "Take the right, lad."

The Brit kicked open one door and leapt inside, his weapon at the ready. Swooping Hawk hesitated for only a second, the idea of walking in on a screwing couple tweaking his conscience. However, when Archer's gun cracked twice more, the Navajo gritted his teeth and shoved the door before him open.

Immediately, a heady fog of incense and musky sex reached out and slapped his face. The room had only a chest of drawers on which a couple of sticks of incense burned and a bed beside the shuttered window. On this bed, a shapely, dark-haired island woman had her rump in the air and her arms and face stretched out on the bed before her. Kneeling behind her and pounding happily away with his sweaty face angled up toward the ceiling was a naked Japanese man. The soldier, lost in the ecstasy of the moment, held a pungent cigar between his teeth in a flagrant display of excess.

Swooping Hawk's modest upbringing froze him in place, as if he'd just walked in on his parents. To his ingrained values, he was interrupting something extremely private and was overcome with red-faced shame.

However, he couldn't look away. The vulgar display of the lean yellow body of the Japanese man, slick with sweat gyrating and grinding its pelvis into the shapely roundness of the woman's backside and her little gasps and squeaks transfixed the young Navajo. But when the ash from the cigar fell and splattered in the woman's firm backside and caused her to flinch, it broke the spell.

She let out a little cry of pain that the soldier completely ignored as he went on, increasing his thrusts as he began to moan louder, nearing his climax.

Swooping Hawk shot him twice in the head.

The body jerked, fell back, and crumpled in a heap at the foot of the bed, the soldier's slick, still erect penis pointing toward the ceiling like some horrid sundial.

"Blimey," Archer said from over the Indian's shoulder.

The woman jerked, performed an almost acrobatic curl, roll, and pivot whereupon she ended up sitting on the bed with her knees drawn up to her chin and gawking pie-eyed at the two large men.

"It's all right, ma'am," Swooping Hawk lamely tried to soothe.

The woman… no, hardly even that… shook her head and said something in what sounded like Spanish but wasn't. Archer patted the younger man on the shoulder and moved into the room.

"Portuguese, lad," said the colonel and spoke to her in a tone so soft and gentle that it caught Swooping Hawk by surprise. He simply stood there, half in and half out of the door as another woman from the room across the hall slipped past him, still naked, and smiled as she did so. She then went to her friend and sat beside her on the bed.

"Comfort women," Archer said with a sad sigh. "Fucking yellow buggers…"

"Sir!" Tank's voice rumbled down the hall. "Colonel? Freddy? You all right?"

"Tank?" Swooping Hawk asked dazedly.

"Yeah, pal," Tank said, coming up with Wayts at his side. "You two okay? What the hell *is* this place?"

"A house of ill repute, Broderick," said Archer, coming out of the room where two naked women were huddled on a bed together.

"They don't look Japanese…" Wayts muttered.

"They're not," Archer snapped, his blue eyes flashing. "They're natives. A mixture of Malay and White Portuguese, most of them. Enslaved by the bloody Nip. Come, let's vacate this damned place."

Tank met Swooping Hawk's gaze and something unspoken passed between the two men. Neither one quite knew what it was, nor did they have time to ponder it, but it was there, nonetheless.

"Come on, kid," Tank said, mustering a little cheerfulness for the frazzled sailor. "I think they're closed for the night."

* * *

"Sir!" Hoffman suddenly hissed and perked up, pointing up the road to the north. "There's another vehicle coming over the hill!"

Turner had been pacing near the tree line utterly failing to be patient. He'd heard the faint and muffled shots from the house and knew that Archer and Turner's men had engaged.

His men. His men who were out of sight and out from under his protection. His men who were being directed by a man that Turner didn't exactly trust and whose motives the submarine captain wasn't entirely sure of.

Hoffman was right. Another vehicle, this one a little larger from the sound and shape of it, was just cresting the rise and coming down the hill. Its twin eyes bore smokey holes through the mist as the mechanical beast rumbled and growled its way toward the house. The movement was unhurried, but Turner would swear that the vehicle bore some ethereal menace.

"Mark our spot," Turner said. "We're going in."

Hoffman had already selected a loose branch and dragged it near the road. The long, leafy branch made a sort of arrow for those who knew what to look for. Hoffman then moved his and Turner's packs behind a tree and unslung his Thompson.

"What about the colonel's orders, sir?"

Turner hefted his own weapon and glanced at the pharmacist's mate, "Fuck 'em. Besides… he said come running if we heard shots. We heard shots."

Hoffman grinned and the two men darted across the road just as the headlights swept to their left and pointed at the other vehicle in what must be the driveway of the farmhouse. As the medic moved toward the field, Turner reached out and tapped his shoulder.

"To hell with that. It's faster straight up the road. Let's move, Hank. Double time it."

Turner broke into a run, pounding up the road and toward the farmhouse. As the two men ran silently toward the enemy, they saw that the vehicle that had pulled in near the flatbed was a covered troop transport truck. The Japanese version of a Deuce and a half. Two men climbed out of the cab and another six or eight tumbled out from the covered bed.

"Jesus…" Hoffman tried to whisper through his puffing. "Special delivery…"

Turner said nothing. He had neither the time nor the inclination to be amused by a truckload of horny slants crowding toward the local knocking shop. His blood was up, and his thoughts were cold, dark, and deadly.

One of the Japs called out. He called out again. When he received no answer, two of the men, Hoffman thought the one's that had been in the cab, appeared to draw something from their belts and move forward.

Several more shots thundered through the heavy night air, followed quickly by blood curdling screams as the two approaching Japanese soldiers were hurled backward.

The men who'd clambered out of the back of the covered two-and-a-half-ton truck took to shouting, gesticulating, and running for cover. Several of them rounded the rear of the truck and began tossing dark somethings out into the night, where a few of their comrades had enough of their wits about them to catch and ready the weapons.

"Hey! Hey, you squinty-eyed bastards!" Turner roared as the two running men neared the drive.

Hoffman gawked at his CO as Turner stopped, shouldered his Thompson and began spraying the Japanese with heavy rounds. Seeing no alternative, Hoffman brought up his own weapon and tried to sight in on targets… but his hands were shaking.

The pharmacist's mate had been in a shore action before. Not long before on New Ireland. Yet the experience had been a jarring one. He'd been captured and nearly killed until one of the Japs turned on his officer and saved him. Once more coming face to face with the enemy with only a few dozen yards of separation had brought up a mix of emotions that the medic, alas, was having trouble dealing with.

It didn't seem to matter, though. Turner simply stood beside Hoffman, emptying his magazine into the gaggle of shocked Japanese. One by one, the soldiers fell, crying out in their death agonies or simply snuffed out of existence as a .45 slug blew apart their skulls.

When Turner's bolt came down on an empty chamber, there were still two or three Japs left. Hoffman sighted in, having regained some composure, but never got the chance to fire.

Turner flung his Tommy gun to the ground and lunged in,

barreling into the nearest soldier who was levelling an Arisaka at the mad American bull rushing for him.

In his haste, however, the soldier had failed to charge the weapon, and his finger simply yanked repeatedly on the trigger only to have it click ineffectively. It would be his final error.

Turner's greater mass slammed into the man and the two of them hurtled back against the truck. With a mindless cry of rage and anguish roaring through his windpipe, the larger American smashed his fists into the man's face before wrapping his hands around the soldier's throat. Grimacing and growling like a wild animal, Turner clamped down with desperate, hate-fueled strength.

Turner was completely unaware of anything but the man in his grasp. He didn't hear Archer or his men shouting. He didn't hear the screams of the women inside or the terrified shouts of the remaining Japanese as they scrambled for cover. He didn't even notice Hoffman's weapon as it chattered, mowing down the last two Japs near the rear of the truck.

All Turner knew for those few seconds was his hate, rage, and despair. He hauled on the Asian man, repeatedly slamming the back of his head against the frame of the flatbed even as he crushed his windpipe. For a few seconds, the dying soldier clawed at Turner's hands, desperately trying to break their iron grasp, but to no avail.

"Art! Captain! Turner, for God's sake!" a man with an English accent shouted almost into the mad submariner's ear. "He's dead, for all love! He's dead!"

Roughly, several pairs of hands dragged at the iron-bound muscles of Turner's shoulders and hauled him back. As they did, the captain's hands released and the dead soldier, crumpled to the dirt, his eyes bulging and the back of his head a pulpy, bloody mess.

"God *help* us…" Archer breathed. "Have you taken leave of your senses, man? I told you to wait!"

Turner turned and the eyes he locked onto the other man's face blazed with demoniac fury. Even Archer, a seasoned soldier with his own inner demons, took half a step backward at the sight of the madness that threatened to spill over the rim of Turner's eyes.

"Sir!" Tank came up and shook Turner. "You all right?"

The red mist began to dissolve from before Turner's eyes and he managed to nod, "You all?"

"Oh, we're crickets, Old Boy," Archer said, sounding cavalier but with steel in his eyes. "Are you with us once more?"

"Yeah," said Turner. "Now we got two trucks. Yay for the visitors."

"Jesus Christ, Tank…" Hoffman whispered to his friend as the Japanese bodies were dragged out of sight. "You see that shit?"

Tank nodded grimly, "Yeah, Hank… yeah…"

"Skipper damn near went berserk…"

Tank harrumphed, "Wasn't nothin' *near* about that, pal. That *was* berserk."

10

BANDA SEA

6°S, 122°E

DECEMBER 23, 1942 - 0630 SHIP'S TIME

"Mind if I ask you somethin', Mr. Post?" Richard "Mug" Vigliano asked, hunkering down in his slicker as best he could.

Andy Post stood beside him on the bridge, his own oilskins and sou'wester doing an inadequate job of keeping him dry underneath. Ahead, both sea and sky were black and the only indication of the state of the sea itself was when a frothing roller crashed over the bow and plowed aft along the deck to explode in a sheet of spray against the conning tower fairing. Off the ship's starboard quarter, however, the blackness was beginning to bleed into a deep, charcoal gray. The sun was nearly up, but low, thick storm clouds muted its effect.

"If you're gonna ask if you can have a smoke, Mug... knock yourself out," Post said and flashed a sodden grin in the quartermaster's direction.

"You gotta remind me to laugh at that one on my day off, sir."

Post laughed and then coughed out a mouthful of spray, "What's on your mind, quartermaster?"

"Well, sir... couple things, I guess. Wonderin' how the skipper and our guys are doin', naturally. But my thinkin' now is wonderin' if we'll

DECEMBER 23, 1942 - 0630 SHIP'S TIME

dunk soon, or if the skipper... that is, Mr. Williams... will keep us on top."

Post considered this as another black hillock of sea rose up and rolled across the deck. He glanced over his shoulder at the lookouts harnessed into their three perches around the periscope shears.

Usually, he felt sorry for the lookouts when the weather was rough. They were higher up, which meant they were subject to more lateral forces. They were exposed to the elements, too. And yet... they weren't being splattered with seawater every thirty seconds either.

"Couldn't tell ya', Mug," Post finally replied. "Dirty weather keeps us from being spotted and probably keeps the Jap birds on the ground... but it'd be nice for us as well as our poor lookouts to get below, get dry and get a hot cup of joe."

Mug smiled, "Can't argue that, sir... but I was just thinkin' about the captain, I guess. He likes to run on top more'n most skippers do. Not sure that our Mr. Williams is quite that bold, though."

Post frowned at that. *Bull Shark*, at least until the past couple of weeks, had always been a ship that ran very loosely on naval etiquette. Most boats did, simply due to the close quarters. Yet Art Turner had never stood much on ceremony and made it clear that so long as everyone was respectful, the great divide between the officers and ratings could be closed.

However, with what had happened recently and the obvious effect it'd taken on Turner's outlook, there were some lines that shouldn't be crossed, and Vigliano had just stuck a toe over one.

"Not for us to worry about, Quartermaster," Post said with just a hint of edge. "Not for us to make judgements on the captain... whoever that might be. Our skipper's got his style, and our XO has his. Best not call it into question too casually."

Mug nodded and cleared his throat, "Sorry, sir... I didn't mean to make that sound like a dig or nothin'."

Post shrugged, "I know, Mug... but whatever is going on and whoever's in the big chair, so to speak, we owe him our respect, dedication, and support. And we owe it to him and to ourselves not to second guess him. You read?"

"I do, sir," said Vigliano, accepting the mild rebuke without resentment. "Our XO has more than proven himself, too… I guess I was just thinkin' about the captain. I got a big mouth, everybody says so."

"Can't argue that, pally," Post chuckled. Wiping seawater from his eyes, he reached out and depressed the bridge transmitter button. "Radar, bridge… full combat sweep on both units."

The SD air search radar would probably not return much of anything, Post knew. The storm was dense enough that it would muddy the global return. When Steve Radcliff, radarman of the watch, reported no contacts and a fuzzy return, Post nodded.

"*Bridge, radar… uhm…*" the young sailor striking for electrician sounded dubious and Post briefly wished Balkley were on the set. But even the A-team had to sleep sometime.

"What is it, Radcliff?" Post asked. "Just make your report."

A throat cleared, "*Yessir… I thought I got a faint contact, sir… but the rain's sort of breaking it up, I guess…*"

Post exchanged a look with Vigliano and said, "We don't do guesses on *Bull Shark*, sailor. Give me what you've got."

"*Aye, sir… doubtful contact bearing zero-three-five… range nineteen… no twenty thousand yards, sir,*" the nervous striker reported.

Post frowned as he pondered. For some reason, a vivid picture of his new wife, April, flashed behind his eyes. She stood there in a pretty, floral sun dress, her mane of blonde hair flying and a smile brightening up her pretty face. For some reason, though, the image… usually so comforting… left Post cold and uneasy. There was no reason for it, but it persisted until another bucket full of water slapped him in the face.

He coughed and swiped uselessly at his face with his rain and seawater-soaked sleeve. He grumbled something dark and pushed the button, "Radar, bridge, concentrate sweep from zero-one-five to zero-five-zero. Watch that contact and get me better numbers, including heading and speed."

"*Aye-aye, bridge… you want I should notify the XO… I mean the skipper, sir?*" asked Radcliff.

Post was about to pass that along to the junior officer of the deck. In this case, it was Chief Weiss. With the captain gone and Porter Hazard deceased, the boat was down two officers from her usually reduced compliment. At minimum, the *Balao*-class should have eight officers. With only five, and with Williams's decision to have every one of them, including Skaggs, standing watch as OOD, the boat's chiefs were taking turns standing in as JOOD as well.

"*Skipper has the word, Radar,*" came William's voice. "*Continue sweep. How is it up there, Andy?*"

Vigliano snorted but said nothing. Post grinned and replied, "Very refreshing, Elmer. Little moist, though. Thought you were at breakfast, Skipper."

"*Just finished. Andouille omelet with green peppers and onions... mm, mm, mmm... figured I'd post myself at navigation and see how things were shaping up.*"

"Be happy to trade ya'," Post quipped. "Me and Mug are hungry enough to eat powdered eggs."

"*One more hour, kids... What's your assessment on contact, Bridge?*" asked the acting captain with a chuckle.

"Unknown as yet, sir... I have a hunch but would rather have more data before I make a call."

"*Bridge, radar... contact appears CBDR... speed fourteen knots,*" Radcliff said. "*Still unclear but appears fairly large, sir.*"

Post frowned and preempted Williams's question, "Control, bridge... assess enemy vessel headed for Timor. Supply ship maybe? Recommend we investigate."

Williams chuckled, "*Roger that, bridge. How's about our visibility on top?*"

Post frowned at that. Vigliano's earlier question had come up at last, and now it was Post who was to make the call. He glanced around at the situation. The light off the starboard quarter was growing, but still dark gray and diffuse. In all likelihood, the boat wouldn't be seen unless the enemy was very close. If he turned toward them, the combined speed of twenty-five knots... *Bull Shark* was making a sluggish ten in the heavy weather... would bring them into visual range in five minutes.

Post pressed the button, "I think conditions are favorable to stay on top, sir... but if we're gonna I.D., line up, and plot a solution..."

"Then we'd be better off taking our time and letting it get lighter, too… very well, bridge. Let's button her up."

"Hallelujah…" Vigliano sighed.

"Clear the bridge!" Post ordered and sounded the dive alarm twice. He pressed the button once more. "Diving officer, bridge… take her to radar depth. Maneuvering, standby to answer bells on batteries. JOOD… sound general quarters."

The lookouts were already scrambling down and beginning to drop down the now open conning tower hatch. Vigliano went next, followed by Post. Post hit the hatch release and Vigliano dogged it as the OOD went down.

"Main induction closed!" Weiss called from below. "Pressure in the boat!"

"Rig out dive planes," Post ordered. "Helm, all ahead two-thirds. Flood safety and negative tanks. Open main ballast tank vents."

The orders were carried out smartly and within seconds, Weiss was giving his orders to the diving planesmen to angle down five degrees.

Post and Vigliano shed their rain gear and let the coats and hats drop through the open hatch to the control room. Someone down there would hang them up in the pump room along with the lookouts' gear and harnesses. A second later, Eddie Carlson popped up through the hatch with a pair of towels and a moment later, two hot mugs of coffee.

"Bless you, Eddie," Post said.

"I love you, Ed," Vigliano added.

"My pleasure, fellas," Carlson said and dropped out of sight.

"Okay, sound, you're up, too," said Post, shivering a bit as the hot coffee went down. "Get a bead on them. Radcliff, get me that heading ASAP. Skipper, do you wish to take the deck?"

Williams popped up through the hatch, the IsWas hanging around his neck, "I'll handle the approach, you handle the pickles, Andy."

Post grinned, "Aye-aye, sir. Torpedo, please have the forward room open their outer doors."

"Both rooms," Williams's disembodied voice said from below. "Just in case."

Joe Dutch spoke into the sound-powered telephone. As he quickly relayed orders to the two torpedo rooms, Chet Rivers and Ted Balkley jumped up through the hatch and slid into their stations. Although Radcliff and Eckhart, manning the radar and sonar stacks respectively, stayed in position. The tower was overcrowded and quickly growing warm.

"Enemy course is one-five-five," Radcliff reported.

"JP is a bit muddy so shallow, sir," Eckhart said.

Post nodded, "Switch to the JK, then. You get all that, XO?"

"Roger," said Williams and after a brief delay. "Helm, come to course three-four-five. Make turns for three knots."

"Coming right," Oscar Dolsworth, striking for machinist's mate and helmsman of the watch reported. He was something of a pudgy man, and the back of his thick neck was beaded with sweat that Post accurately assessed had little to do with the eighty-three-degree temperature. "Maneuvering answering three knots, sir."

"Range is now fourteen thousand yards, Mr. Post," Radcliff said. "Decreasing at sixteen knots."

"Estimating seven minutes to visual range," Post reported. "Torpedo, set speed to high for now."

"All ready in both rooms, Andy," Dutch reported.

The minutes crawled by. After only a few, Wiliams ordered the boat to periscope depth so that their radar masts wouldn't be seen now that it was growing lighter, if not clearer, above.

"Estimated range now five thousand yards, OOD," Williams said. "See if you can get an observation."

"Up search scope," Post ordered.

Radcliff, acting as periscope assistant now that the boat was no longer able to use her radars, activated the periscope motors. The familiar mechanical whine of the servos sent a little thrill through everyone who heard.

Post flipped the handles down and pressed his face to the eyepiece. The charcoal gray of false dawn had lightened some. Now there was a definite distinction between sky and sea. Both depressing shades of slate, but with the darker and lumpier one rolling sickeningly past the lens. More than once, large waves completely covered the scope and Post had to wait a moment for the foam to clear.

With only a few feet sticking up above the surface, the search periscope's horizon was hardly more than two miles. It took nearly a minute for Post to finally locate something that was angular enough to be artificial, in spite of being the same shadowy gray in the early morning light as the sea.

"Contact," he said. "Surface vessel bearing off starboard bow. I'm seeing a mast and maybe a stack… possibly a tower, too, but we're still too far away."

"Helm, come to course due north," Williams ordered. "Maintain speed."

Bull Shark turned to starboard, temporarily putting the enemy vessel directly in front of them. However, as the as-yet unidentified bogie was moving slightly east of south, she was beginning to slide away, forcing Post to slowly rotate to keep her in view.

"Looks like a seaplane tender," Post said after another minute and the two ships were within a mile of one another. He moved to look through the ONI-208J ship recognition manual and tapped the silhouette. "Yes! *Kamikawa Maru*-class freighters converted to seaplane tender… sixty-eight hundred tons, 475 feet long… draft of twenty-seven. Don't know which one, XO, but definitely one of them. Joe, have the rooms set depth to thirteen feet. Down search, up attack. Gonna do a first observation."

The scopes swapped and Post centered his wire on the enemy ship, now partly hull-up on the starboard bow, "Bearing… mark."

"Zero-zero-eight," said Radcliff.

"Range… mark."

"One-seven-five-zero yards."

"Angle on the bow is starboard ten," Post said. "Down scope."

"JP new contact!" Eckhart blurted. "Negative… two new contacts separating from target bearing, sir… light fast screws!"

"Assess destroyers," Rivers added and touched the fireman on the shoulder as a calming influence.

"Uh-huh…," said Post. "The fangs come out at last, eh?"

"Sonar, give me individual bearings when you can," Williams said. "Andy, I'm designating primary target as Master-1."

Post looked at his watch and grimaced at the laborious swing of his

DECEMBER 23, 1942 - 0630 SHIP'S TIME

second hand. When it came around at last, he ordered the scope up and a second observation taken.

"Okay, Joe... bearing, mark!"

"Zero-one-three," Radcliff enthused.

Post fiddled with his stadimeter. The bulky freighter turned seaplane tender was hull-up now and close enough that the assistant engineer could easily make out detail, including the float planes clustered on deck.

"Range... mark."

"One-two-eight-five yards!"

"Angle on the bow is starboard fifteen," Post said. "Down scope. What range, sir?"

"One thousand yards, Andy," Williams replied. "How about it, sonar?"

"Uhm..." Eckhart fiddled with his controls and gripped the right earcup of his headphones. "Bearings separating... looks like one is coming port and the other slightly starboard, sir."

"Assess destroyers breaking off for a circular sonar scan, XO," Rivers added.

"Order of tubes is one, two, three," Post said.

"Joe, tell Tommy I want those tubes reloaded as fast as he can," Williams added.

Dutch worked the torpedo data computer quickly, the machine's quiet hum joined by the faint clicking and clackings as its incomprehensible internal circuitry mechanically calculated the exact firing angle for all three tubes. Finally, Dutch turned to face the junior officer.

"We have a solution, Andy. Shoot anytime."

"Range?" Post asked.

"One-zero-five-zero," Williams said. "Give it a few seconds and then let her rip, Andy."

If the seconds between observations crawled, then these last few dragged themselves over blistering asphalt. Now that the ships were closer, their closing rate was decreasing. As *Bull Shark* headed north and the seaplane tender headed more south, southeast, their vectors began to open, and the range decreased slowly.

Post internally calculated the rate to be about fifteen yards per second. He counted to five and then, unable to wait any longer, said: "Fire one!"

The ship shuddered as 3,300 pounds of torpedo was shoved into the sea by a blast of compressed air. Its alcohol-fueled steam turbine whined up to full power and every man aboard heard the faint whistle as their first weapon screeched away.

Post counted to six and then ordered: "Fire two!"

"Trim tank valve malfunction!" someone bleated from below. Post didn't hear who, but he heard the chorus of swears that accompanied the announcement.

For a brief instant, the young officer recalled one of the boat's first torpedo attacks. He'd been assistant diving officer and responsible for the ship's trim.

When a submarine fired a torpedo, the ship became instantly lighter by a ton and a half. While that might not seem like much against her submerged weight of 2,600 tons, even that small amount could upset the delicately balanced trim or levelness of the boat. When running at only sixty-five feet, even a small up or down angle could cause the ship to breech the surface, making her visible to an enemy.

Which is what was happening now.

The bow rose by nearly ten degrees. Somewhere in one of the tanks used to shunt water back and forth to keep the ship level, a transfer valve must have jammed open. *Bull Shark's* bow was suddenly lighter by three tons, and she was bucking toward the surface like a desperate sealion.

"Helm, all back full!" Post snapped. "Diving officer, flood negative tank! Joe, fire three!"

Fighting to keep the ship from becoming visible, Post hadn't forgotten about his opportunity and his readied fish. However, this only made the bow lighter once again.

The submarine's four GM electric motors whined as they tried to reverse her forward progress, slowing her forward attainment and hopefully keeping her nose below the waves. As water rushed into the negative tank, the boat's neutral buoyancy became negative, adding to the resistance.

DECEMBER 23, 1942 - 0630 SHIP'S TIME

But it was too little, too late for the ship being so shallow. In spite of their efforts, the submarine's bow broke the surface, smashing through ten-foot waves and throwing up huge sheets of spray.

Then the bull nose vanished, pulled below by reverse thrust and greater weight. Post cursed, his face beet red with the shame of it and the shame of his much earlier error.

Williams popped up through the hatch, "XO has the con! It's okay, Andy... not your fault this time."

Post nodded but the heat in his face did not diminish, "Thanks, Elmer... permission to go below?"

Williams squeezed his shoulder, "Only to take over the plot, Andy. Not to hide in shame."

"Yessir..." Post mumbled and went down the ladder.

"Time to impact?" Williams asked.

"Twenty-two seconds, Elmer," Joe Dutch said.

"Fish running hot, straight, and normal, sir," Rivers reported.

"Helm, all ahead two-thirds," Williams ordered. "Blow negative to the mark, Chief. Get us down to two hundred feet and make it snappy."

"Aye-aye!" Weiss said. "Planesmen, twenty down two-double-oh."

Frank Nichols was in the control room at the master gyro compass table with Hernandez and Leroy Potts. Since it was still Post's and Weiss's watch, the chief engineer and diving officer did not take over his usual station.

"Welcome to the party, Andy," Nichols said and offered a reassuring look. "Sticky pump valve. Not your fault. Not like last time... okay?"

Post nodded and sighed, "Sure. What've we got?"

Nichols pointed at a pair of Xs on the chart and almost as if the gesture was the impetus, a sharp *thwack-booom* reverberated through the steel hull of the submarine.

"A hit!" Radcliff whooped from above. "Second fish passing through target bearing in—"

Another distinct torpex explosion and then a few seconds later, another. All three of Post's fish had struck. The men in the control room and the tower whooped and cheered.

"Silence about the decks!" Williams and Post seemed to roar in unison.

There were chagrined faces, but not one lost its smile.

"Rig for silent running," came the acting captain's order. "Rig for depth charge… plot, designate the other two targets as Masters two and three… it's about to get interesting."

11

"Phone talker, after room... get the outer doors closed," Williams ordered. "Helm, right full rudder. Steady up on... zero-four-zero."

"Right under the sinking ship, sir?" Post asked wryly.

"That's the plan, Andy," Williams looked from the young officer to the slightly older Nichols. "Think you fellas can get that trim tank valve squared away?"

"Of course, Elmer," Nichols said and looked to Post. "It's three-baker, Andy."

"I'm on it," said Post and called up through the hatch to the conning tower. "Eckhart, you're with me."

Just then Joe Dutch slid down the ladder, "Want me to take up DCO, Elmer?"

Williams frowned. He really could use a couple more officers, "No, Joe... better take over the plot. I need an XO. Andy, once you're done with that valve, take the DCO station, huh?"

"Aye-aye, Skipper," Post said and led Horris Eckhart aft.

"Now passing one-five-zero feet," Nichols said.

"Sonar, where are those remaining contacts?" Dutch asked.

"Bearings are port beam for Master-2 and starboard bow between zero-three-zero and zero-five-zero for Master-3, sir," Rivers said. "They're going active. Estimated range is a little over a thousand yards for Master-2 and... maybe a little less for Master-3."

"Helm, increase to four knots," Williams ordered.

"Maneuvering answering four knots, sir," Dolsworth called out. "Sir, my course is zero-four-zero."

"Very well," said Williams, trying to sound big, bold, and confident.

This was hardly his first depth charge attack, but they never really got easier. Williams always secretly hosted a squadron of butterflies in his stomach and just as secretly chided himself for it. The captain shouldn't be afraid, right? Shouldn't be worried every time some Jap wants to drop an ashcan on him?

Of course, Elmer Williams was no fool. He knew that a man could be scared and fight through it. That a man could appear outwardly calm... had to when he was in command... and that by reassuring others, he was reassuring himself. Yet recently, his own captain's strange behavior and what must be something of a depression had affected him in ways he was just now beginning to understand.

Turner's coldness, his anger, and his seeming single-minded desire to come to personal grips with the enemy had shaken Williams to his foundation. The executive officer hadn't realized just how much of his own self-assurance had been linked to Art Turner and his larger-than-life presence. And now that this emotional bedrock had been torn away, both physically and psychologically... the acting captain felt as if he'd had a piece of him torn out, too. That piece that held all that he'd learned over the past year, or so it felt. Leaving behind a man who, at least a little, couldn't shake the dark feeling that he was once again that new XO on his first mission... and would he screw it up?

"Two bills, Elmer."

Williams blinked, smiled to cover it, and pulled a pack of Lucky Strikes from his blouse. He'd never really been a brand-loyal man, and something about the popular brand and that Turner himself smoked them gave Williams a tiny flicker of comfort.

He lit up and nodded, "Very well. Can you handle the trim issue, Frank?"

Nichols nodded, "I've compensated by putting a bubble in the after MBT. I can keep her level until Andy gets that valve sorted. You all right, Elmer?"

Williams's mouth flicked upward ever so slightly, causing the tip of his cigarette to bob, "I'm swell, Frank. Just got a couple of Nip tin cans up there want to kill me. Why worry?"

Nichols's square, handsome face looked good with a smile on it. The juxtaposition of his gold-rimmed cheaters gave him the look of some Hollywood actor playing the part of a scientist or college professor. His usually calm demeanor worked wonders on crew morale, even in tense situations.

"Worried about the skipper?" Nichols asked quietly.

Williams harrumphed, "Frank, if I want a shrink on board, I'll requisition one… I'm fine. Thanks."

Nichols nodded in understanding. Either his friend didn't want to talk, or it wasn't the time. Both, most likely.

"Aspect changes on Master one and two," Rivers called out. "Bearings are steadying down, sir. Assess they're converging."

Dutch and his team marked the chart, and the acting XO looked up. He'd overheard the exchange with Nichols, of course, and knew better than to try to talk to Williams just then. However, the meaningful look in his eyes wasn't lost on the acting captain.

"They're gonna try to get us in a pincer," Dutch opined.

"Yup," Williams said.

"Think that Yamata guy or maybe Pageant or Lanser or whatever his name is is up there?"

"Dunno."

"Guess you're not in a talkative mood this morning."

"Nope."

The two men chuckled softly and cocked an ear. As if from a great distance and from a realm where the gauzy veil between life and the afterlife had begun to fray, a low, mournful cry reached out and caressed *Bull Shark's* cold, steel skin. Only with the boat running silent could it be heard, but no one aboard who heard it took it for anything other than what it was.

If it was a spirit… and now it was joined by another… then it was a restless spirit seeking only one thing. To reach out and touch an American submarine and draw it down into the inky blackness from which no man may return.

* * *

The multiplicity of tanks, lines, and valves that allowed a fleet submarine to operate were dizzying in number and scope. Their locations, operation, and potential problems were essential for any crewmember to understand before getting their dolphins. As assistant engineer and as a fireman, Post and Eckhart were intimately familiar with every component aboard, but especially those involving the mechanics of pushing water around.

On some ships, there would be a great deal of difference between the skillsets of a fireman, machinist, motor machinist, or even an electrician. On a submarine however, a man might be many things, but he was invariably a mechanic who understood everything from pumps to circuit breakers to valve lineups.

So it appeared very straight forward to the two men as they yanked open the deck hatch in the mess and dropped down into the dimly-lit and downward curving section of *Bull Shark's* hull. Down there below the platform deck, forward of the massive bank of 126 battery cells, the Navy had contrived to squeeze in the freezer and refrigerator used to feed a hundred men for more than two months along with a reinforced magazine and pyrotechnics rooms containing shells, flares, small arms, and their ammunition as well as a variety of other odds and ends used in the art of locating and the subsequent blowing to hell of enemy property.

Amid all of this were electrical conduits, bilgeways, bilge sumps, drain and pump lines, air lines, and colorfully-labeled valves for all of this as well as the myriad of hydraulic lines used to control *Bull Shark's* moveable surfaces from a distance… leaving hardly enough room for a pair of men to squeeze in with drop lights and a toolbox to locate and repair any minor or major casualty.

"Here… hook that light onto this frame…" Post groaned as he

angled his body to squeeze between the forward bulkhead of the battery compartment and the inner portside hull. "Yeah… yeah…"

Eckhart snapped the squeeze clamp of the drop light on a bit of overhead framing and switched it on, pointing the beam in the general direction Post was looking, "I see it, sir. Looks like the valve failed and is partially closed."

"Yeah…" Post grunted as he reached out, bracing his back and taking hold of the four-inch orange manual valve handle. He tried to move it and got only a fractional response. "Damn! It's stuck! Might be corrosion… back pressure, maybe?"

Eckhart withdrew a long pair of vice grips from the toolbox and eased in beside his officer. The two men were belly to belly and nearly touching in the confined space, "See if some leverage will help, sir… gotta watch out, though. Half-open valve like this, could be back-pressure like you say. Learned that workin' in my daddy's garage… ought to de-pressurize the trim system."

Post snorted, "Yeah, that'd be the smart thing… we'll just ask the Jap up there if he wouldn't mind twiddling his thumbs a few minutes."

Eckhart chuckled, "War sure is inconvenient, ain't its, sir?"

Post laughed, "Yeah… much rather be jitterbuggin'… okay… let's give 'er a whirl…"

Post gripped the long handles of the grips. It was at that moment, unfortunately, that the first four depth charges launched by Master-2 reached their set depth and exploded. Although set a bit shallow, the 1,400 pounds of TNT exploded within fifty feet of the submarine, setting up a concussive effect that hammered the boat from port to starboard and then back again in two successive jolts that caused the lights to flicker, loose objects to skitter off flat surfaces… thankfully almost none… and for every man aboard to be heaved this way and that in a most uncomfortable manner.

There was no damage, and even as the charges plunged into the dark sea, the XO ordered Nichols to take them down to 300 feet at a steep thirty-degree angle. This combined with the shaking effect to set up an unlikely but not impossible series of events.

As the ship was slammed side to side, Post gripped the plyers with fear-fueled strength. Eckhart, pushed halfway into the space and halfway between vertical and horizontal, braced his feet and gripped Post with the same resigned strength. As the ship surged and angled down, the two men's weights placed several hundred pounds of lateral force onto the valve.

Normally this wouldn't be a problem, as submarine equipment was remarkably robust, considering what it was called upon to do. However, this valve had been damaged and the connection to either side weakened by an as-yet undetected galvanic current leak exacerbated by the fact that *Bull Shark* had not been degaussed in far too long. The force weakened the valve further and it burst, tearing free on one side and allowing pressurized water to blast into the small space, battering the men and slamming their heads together before flinging them sideways and flat onto their backs, where brilliant lights flickered behind their eyes just before deep blackness swaddled them in its warm embrace.

There both Andy Post and Horris Eckhart lay, unconscious, as a steady jet of seawater poured over them, failing to rouse them, and slowly accumulated in the lower space. Thanks to the rumble of explosions and other activity aboard, no one heard any of this and took no notice for some time.

* * *

"Master-1 crossing to starboard, sir!" Rivers announced. "Here comes his buddy…"

Above and now slightly behind, the eerie echoes of the Japanese echo location had now become the sharp, insistent pings of high-powered sonic blasts. Mixing with these in a sickening cocktail of aggression and heralding potential death was the incessant shooshing of propellers biting and chewing up the ocean.

"Now passing two-five-zero feet," Nichols said.

"How far to the sinking ship, Joe?" Williams asked, one arm wrapped around the attack periscope barrel.

"Not far… maybe a hundred, hundred and fifty yards," Dutch said.

Radcliff, who had moved to the sonar station and taken up the JP stack adjusted his headphones and his gain. Rivers had moved to the JK system in order to track the targets by their sonar returns.

"I'm getting breaking up noises, sir," Radcliff said. "Directly ahead... pops, metal groaning... can't tell how deep she is yet, though."

"Let's hope it's enough..." Williams said.

From the chart desk, Vigliano was making rapid notes and calculations. He frowned, "Sir, if she's foundered... we could be—"

"I know, Mug," Williams said, "but I'm counting on two things, here... three if necessary. One that the Nips won't depth bomb near any potential survivors, and a seaplane tender'll have plenty. Second that we can use the sounds of the ship going down to mask us... and if necessary, find a halocline."

Vigliano nodded, knowing that the captain had spoken for the benefit of everyone, not just himself. However, his math was worrying him and he said, "Captain... if she's breaking up, she's under... we're moving at two yards a second and she's sinking at more than that, I'd guess. What with three holes in her, if she's not blasted apart."

"Which means we could sail over the top... or beneath... or run right into her," Williams said. "Chance we'll have to take. Keep your ears sharp, sonar."

"Splashes!" Radcliff gulped. "Four... six... ah, geez..."

"Three hundred feet, Captain," Nichols reported. "Sir... I'm losing trim down here. Getting a slight up angle..."

Williams bit back the string of filthy oaths that went against his nature but were so eager to burst forth, "Never rains... what's the cause, Frank?"

"Can't tell yet... but my guess is we've got water coming in someplace."

"Phone talker, all compartments," Williams ordered. "From forward aft... check for flooding below the platform and report to the diving officer. Helm, all ahead full. Make turns for six knots."

"Twenty seconds..." Vigliano counted, mostly to himself.

Depth charges descended at about seven feet per second. It would take one forty-five seconds or so to come level with the submarine. Everyone else who heard began their own internal clocks.

In that same time, *Bull Shark* would have nearly reached the wreck of the seaplane tender. That was awfully close for the enemy to lay depth charges. Even at 150 yards, underwater concussions could injure or even kill men in the water.

"Master-3 is coming forward to port, sir," Rivers announced. "Master-2 coming forward to starboard, sir. Assess they're circling."

"Probably guessing where we're going and want to intercept us, Elmer," Dutch said from below.

"Concur," Williams said. "All stop, helm! Frank, flood safety and negative tanks as well as auxiliaries. Let's see if we can't find a halocline."

The electric motors shut down. Although their whine was faint, especially with hatches and flappers closed, there was a low vibration that everyone could feel through their shoes. Once it ceased, although minute, the men were gripped by a silence that seemed far deeper than it ought to.

"Negative buoyancy," Nichols said calmly.

"Mr. Nichols! After battery!" the control room phone talker almost squeaked. "Flooding below the platform deck, sir! Sir! Mr. Post and Eckhart are down there!"

"I'm on it, Elm!" Dutch said even as Williams swung his foot into the hatchway.

The acting captain swore under his breath. He, like the rest of his men, must now play the waiting game. Wait for the Japs to find them, wait to see if his next gamble would work... and wait to find out the fate of his ship and his men.

* * *

"What the hell's going on in here?" Dutch shouted as he half-dove through the hatchway.

A group of men were gathered around the open deck grating, including Martin and Borshowski, his assistant cook, and the two men normally assigned to assist Hoffman. Now that the pharmacist's mate was gone, they were on the front lines of any medical care that was required.

"Make way!" a voice boomed from aft and there was no mistaking the urgency and command of the chief of the boat. "Make way, God *dammit!*"

"Mr. Post and Eckhart are down there, sir!" Paul Baxter said, an electrical toolkit in hand. "Bernie Fetlock was the first one down and—"

"Somebody gimme a hand down here!" came a frightened voice over the sound of rushing water.

Dutch shoved men aside and swung himself down the hatch, plunging into darkness and knee-deep water. From the lights above, a pair of compartment lights and a drop light clipped to a frame, he could see the hideous tongue of silvery seawater shooting in at a forty-five-degree angle. It splashed off Fetlock, a burly young man from engineering and the two prone men floating amid a pool of water. Their faces were ashen, and they didn't move.

"Stand from under!" roared Rogers as he jumped down, eschewing the ladder for the direct approach. The big sailor splashed down, took in the scene in an instant and moved in.

"Fetlock!" Dutch shouted as he pushed the man aside, leaping over the bodies and lifting Post's head out of the water. "Get topside! Tell Mr. Nichols we need the trim lines shut down! Tell him we got water in here and to drain it. Have Martin and Borshowski send down a stretcher, too!"

"With straps!" Rogers snapped, cradling Eckhart's head in his lap. "On the double!"

"But they ain't breathin'!" Fetlock blurted, standing and clutching the rungs of the ladder but not moving.

"Standin' there with your yapper hangin' loose ain't gonna fix it!" the COB thundered. "Now *MOVE YOUR ASS!*"

"He's right, Buck," Dutch said, feeling around on Post's neck with his middle and index finger. "And I'm not gettin' a pulse."

Rogers's eyes were hard, "Men have been drowning in ships ever since they invented the ocean, sir… and we ain't givin' up yet."

12

ABOARD LIGHT CRUISER AGANO

"It would appear, Teacher, that the round eyes have taken the bait."

Hitake Yamata, The Sensei, stood a meter or so away from the speaker and eyed him with an expression kept carefully neutral. Beside him, the German pilot, submarine commander, and spy Friedrich Lanser was not so restrained and offered a light chuckle only Yamata could hear over the fresh breeze.

The three men stood on the signal bridge of the new light cruiser *Agano,* very recently seconded to what was being called the "shark hunt." The ongoing plan to locate, trap, and destroy the American submarine USS *Bull Shark* and her commander, Arthur Turner. The plan had become something of an obsession of Admiral Yamamoto's, and had drawn Yamata in, along with Lanser, who'd been with Yamata since flinging himself overboard from the very hunted submarine several months earlier.

So far, the attempt had yielded several lost destroyers and a heavily damaged light cruiser, *Hammerhead,* which was still undergoing repairs at Rabaul. In order to continue the mission, Yamamoto had drawn in The Sensei, Japan's top anti-submarine warfare instructor, the German spy and two pilots and submariners of his own. The four had been placed at the head of the task force to locate the particular vessel and remove that particular irritating thorn from Japan's side.

Ryu Osaka and Hideki Omata were not currently aboard with Yamata and Lanser. They were on another assignment and were supposed to rejoin their comrades with further information. In the meantime, the newly commissioned *Agano* had been shifted to this hunt, much to the frustration of her captain, Kenji Nashiri, the third man on the bridge.

Almost as soon as *Agano* and her escorts had left Truk, Nashiri had begun exercising his authority. Of the same rank as Yamata, Nashiri had the added leverage of being the ship's posted captain and lorded this fact over Yamata at every opportunity. He'd even gone so far as to cut off any communication with Truk that wasn't personally authorized by himself.

In short, Nashiri had pulled the rug out from under Yamata and was visibly enjoying it.

"As we knew they would," stated Yamata.

Nashiri, a somewhat ill-tempered who had been unfortunate in the receipt of his physical attributes. Short, even by Japanese standards, portly and who's countenance made even the most seasoned geisha wince.

The effect was enhanced, if one could use that term, by a jagged scar that ran from his hairline down the right side of his face to just under the right side of his mouth. A hideous, white thing with multiple branches that had been received in battle with the Chinese when he was a young man. Combined with the perpetual frowns, scowls, and sneers Nashiri wore, the scars lent the man a foreboding presence. Something with which he was fully aware and wore proudly.

The smile he directed at his old rival was ghastly in the pale moonlight, "Yes… fortunate that Japan has lost yet *another* vessel to this holy quest of yours, Hitake. A ship, several aircraft and perhaps several men. No doubt they feel fortunate in dying for the cause, eh?"

"The ship was scheduled to be scrapped," Yamata said, still maintaining his passivity, about the only weapon he had against Nashiri and one that usually worked. "The aircraft damaged beyond repair and the skeleton crew has been prepared."

"Indeed," observed Nashiri, raising his binoculars to his eyes once more and staring out at the horizon before him. "Let us hope they remain grateful for your favor. What do you say, Herr Lanser? No doubt the Fatherland is equally pleased by your efforts so far away from home?"

Friedrich Lanser did not have Yamata's aplomb. The blonde-haired, blue-eyed German was too much like Nashiri to have developed this talent. Too arrogant, too ego driven. Yet Lanser was not a cruel man by nature, which at least gave him some redeeming qualities.

"No doubt, Mein Kapitän," said Lanser with a smile that Yamata did not need to see to know reached no higher than his upper lip. "Some sacrifices have to be made, Ja?"

That nearly broke Yamata's carefully crafted stoicism. Since coming aboard and immediately pegging the ship's captain as what Lanser interchangeably labeled *der arschficker* or *der arschloch*… ass fucker or asshole, respectively. He'd also taken to utilizing a thick, almost comically overblown German accent when speaking to Nashiri in English. He did not deign to use Japanese or German around the man. It amused Yamata, but it also reminded him to be wary of Lanser himself.

After all… the Nazis, like the Japanese, had certain views about who it was who constituted members of the master race. And these views did not align. One must be cautious, as always.

Nashiri made a non-committal noise, "But how much sacrifice is required? Six or seven ships? This seems a high price to pay for one be-shitted Yankee submarine, no matter how much you might *fear* her captain."

"You might think differently if you knew the man Mein Herr," Lanser said.

Nashiri offered a derisive little laugh, "I doubt that. And I must ask, gentlemen… what makes you think that the boat that just torpedoed our little diversion is even your precious *Bull Shark?* The Ame-cohs have many of them… as do we."

"There *is* no guarantee," Yamata said, purposefully avoiding any honorary mention of rank or title. "But we have instituted events and have access to intelligence sources in Australia that lead us to believe there is a one in four chance. After what happened not far from here a few weeks back… we believe Captain Turner will be most aggressively seeking revenge."

"Psychological warfare with an invisible opponent…," Nashiri shook his head. "Your bailiwick, I suppose, Teacher?"

"All submarine versus surface warfare is psychological, Nashiri," Yamata said. "You would be wise to remember that."

"Ja, he tells truth," said Lanser and his eyes did crinkle this time.

Nashiri grunted but said nothing. That was, at least, one thing in Yamata's favor. Nashiri's supply of wit was rather limited.

"Sir!" a messenger darted out of the starboard hatchway and bowed. "Radio message from Mongoose-1. They and Mongoose-2 have lost the target. Estimated near the sinking at a depth of one hundred and thirty meters."

Nashiri nodded, "Very well. Order the helm to proceed, as planned. All ahead full. Alert Mongoose three and four to widen their separation."

Nashiri had his own plan to encircle and locate the hiding submarine. He had not consulted either of the two men Yamamoto had put aboard his ship for this very purpose. It rankled, of course, but the man was at least a fair squadron commander. The net he was casting was predictable, but had the advantage of five ships, at least.

Lanser withdrew a pair of Golden Bats from a pack and passed one to his compatriot, "The game is afoot, eh, *Mein Freund?*"

Yamata harrumphed and offered a wisp of a smile, "Hmm…"

* * *

With some effort, Dutch and Rogers guided the heads of each stretcher out of the lower compartment. Two pairs of hands above eased them out of the hatchway and laid them on deck. The two from below came up, after ensuring that the spray of water had trickled down and stopped, indicating that Nichols had diverted the pressure. By that time, water was above their knees.

Without hesitation or even a hint of self-consciousness, Martin had taken over. While the Navy didn't see fit to put anyone with more medical training than a pharmacist's mate aboard a submarine, they did at least provide him with good equipment, medications, and help.

Martin, Borshowski, Potts, and even Eddie Carlson had received a good deal of training from Hoffman. They often assisted in procedures and cared for injured men when they went to retrieve them from where they'd been injured. Now, Martin and Borshowski were unstrapping the two sopping men from the stretchers.

Neither Post nor Eckhart looked good. Their skin was a pasty blue and they were not breathing.

"How long?" Dutch asked. "Do you think you can revive them, Henrie?"

"We're workin' on dat, you hear?" Martain said, paying only marginal attention. "Billy, get him on his side... like dis, and pump dem leg..."

"What can we do?" Rogers asked.

"Get these men back to their stations and the hell out of our way!" Borshowski snapped.

"Back to stations!" Rogers barked as he came up. "Give the men some room, for *Christ!*"

Everyone who wasn't assigned to the after battery compartment took off, going forward or aft as required. Hatches were opened and shut quietly and the forward end of the compartment, where the galley and mess were situated, took on a thick, heavy silence.

"Mr. Dutch, brought me dem ventilator bag from the locker," Martin ordered as he pumped Post's legs. Trickles of water splashed from the still man's mouth. "Hurry up, now!"

No one balked at Martin's commanding tone. Not the COB nor the acting XO. This was Martin's command now, and no one dared question him.

Dutch unlocked the medical cabinet and found what the cook had asked for. It was a rubber bag with a mask at one end and a pair of handles on the other. He threw it to Rogers who caught it deftly and knelt on the other side of Post.

"What else?" Dutch asked.

"Two syringes and adrenaline," Martin said. "One for each. Okay, Chief, you put you two hand ri'cheer..."

Martin placed Rogers's hands one atop the other on Post's chest, just above the tip of the breastbone. He then made sure the officer was lying flat on his back before fitting the mask over his face.

"Now, I gonna pump dis bag four or tree time," Martain said, his thick Cajun-Creole Louisiana accent in no way diminishing the enormous authority his knowledge and position gave him. "When I'm done, you start compressin', you hear? Fifteen time, nice and steady and not too strong to hurt."

"Okay…" Rogers said quietly.

Dutch came over with the needles and a bottle of alcohol and a couple of swabs, "Where?"

"Let's see if we need dem," Martin said. "You go help Billy, sir."

Dutch moved aft to where Borshowski was pumping Eckhart's legs like mad. The assistant cook looked up at Dutch, his face shining with sweat and grave.

"What can I do?" asked Dutch.

"Let's roll him prone, sir," Borshowski said. "Get the last of the water out."

They did so and Borshowski started compressions once they'd gotten a bit more water out. They could hear rogers counting aloud and the soft whoosh of the Hoger Neilsen bag as Martin pumped air into Post's lungs.

"Need another one of them things," Dutch bemoaned.

"No argument here, sir," Borshowski carped. "Especially on a submarine… lotta water around here, y'know… check for a pulse, sir."

"Nothin'…" Dutch hated to say. "How long until…"

"Mr. Dutch!" Martin ordered. "Open up his mouth, put yours on it so it seals and blow three breath into him."

Dutch's face flushed red, "What? Hey, I ain't no—"

"Do it!" Martin snapped, his voice a crack of thunder in the nearly empty compartment.

"It's okay, sir," Borshowski said, managing a slight smile. "Mr. Hoffman read an article on this. An experimental way to do CPR, sir. It don't make you a sissy."

Dutch wanted to laugh, except that the sodden corpse of one of his men lay touching his knees. The scene robbed the situation of any attempt at levity. Resigning himself, Dutch formed Eckhart's lips into a rough O and placed his own over them, using his hand to help the seal. He inhaled deeply through his nose and immediately blew air into the fireman. He did it again, feeling slightly lightheaded as he did so.

"It's working!" said the assistant cook. "His chest is inflated, sir… okay, here we go… one, two, three…"

For what might have been two minutes or two hours, Dutch was unable to tell, he and Borshowski took turns breathing and compressing. On their fifth go round… or fiftieth… Dutch heard a watery cough from his left and then another. This was followed immediately by whoops from Rogers and Martin.

He was just bending down to Eckhart again when the man coughed, spluttered, coughed again, and his eyes fluttered open. They were unfocused at first, but after a few blinks, locked onto Dutch's gaze only inches away.

"Sir…?" muttered Eckhart. "What…? Where…?"

"Martin!" Dutch shouted and then more gently. "Lie easy, Horris. You're okay."

Borshowski sat back and made room for Martin, who slid in next to Eckhart and placed his stethoscope on the man's bared chest, "How you feelin', *mon ami?*"

"Ugh…" Eckhart said. "Wet, cold, thirsty and… and my head smarts… oh, Christ… somebody hit me with a sledge in the ribs, or what?"

Martin grinned, "No, dat were bill, gettin' you all tender for supper."

"How's Andy?" Dutch asked.

"Feel like a blivit, sir…" Post said, being helped to sit up by Rogers. "What the sweet *Christ…?*"

"Easy, sir," Rogers soothed. "don't think you should be getting up just yet."

"That's for true, da' both of you," Martin said authoritatively. "You probably got a concussion. We gon' make you all comfy right here."

"Sir… the pipes down below…" Eckhart mumbled.

"We know, kid, we know," Dutch patted him on the shoulder.

"Been taken care of. You rest now. Need me for anything else, Henrie?"

"No, sir," said the cook. "But we ain't got no DCO now…"

"I'll stay," Rogers said. "You go on forward, sir. Skipper needs you."

Dutch rose, patting Eckhart, Martin. and Borshowski. He then smiled at Rogers, patting him and Post too. "Thanks, COB. You take her easy now, Andy. Permission to gold brick."

Post managed a pain-filled smile, "Finally… get to be just like you, Joe…"

"You can say this for this tub, Buck," Rogers chuckled. "You just can't knock the wise ass out of her."

"What's going on, Joe?" Williams asked as a damp Dutch re-entered the control room. "Men okay?"

"They will be… had to revive them," Dutch said, running a hand through his moist hair. "Christ, Elmer… I actually breathed life into a man…"

The XO's brows rose, "That's a report I wanna read."

"How are *we* doing?"

"Now passing four-five-zero feet," Nichols said. "I've got the portside fore and aft lines blocked off, Skipper, Joe… and have cross-connected to the drain pumps, so we can use either one. Water's coming out of the after battery bilges now."

"Good work, Frank," Dutch said and smiled at Bill Borshowski when he stepped through the hatch with a tray of coffees.

"We've lost contact with our friends up there," Williams grumbled. "Turned our rudder full right and then let us drift. Think we're clear of the sinking ship… but the tin cans must've stopped their screws."

Dutch groaned, "So it's a cat and mouse game, huh?"

Nichols snorted, "More like blind man's bluff."

Chief Clancy Weiss made a note on the chart and moved over to the three officers, "More like men in a pitch-black room jabbing at each other with knives, this is. But who am I to kvetch?"

Williams aimed a crooked smile at his chief yeoman, "Kvetch?"

"Means complain," Weiss shrugged. "What can I say? I'm from Long Island."

"So what's the plan?" Dutch asked. "Do we sit around with our thumbs twiddling for the rest of our lives or what?"

Williams held his hands out to his sides, "I'm open to suggestions, XO."

"Five centuries, Elmer," Nichols said.

"And no salt layer yet..." Weiss said, glancing up at the bathythermograph above the chart table.

"Best guess, Clance," Dutch said, moving over to glance at the chart for himself. "Where would you say Masters one and two are?"

"Lost their screw sounds about five minutes back," Weiss said, tapping the chart. "I'd say no more than a mile off to port and starboard from our original bearing. We're..."

He looked at the compass and nodded, "We're facing eighty degrees now, so figure Master-4 is a point or two abaft the port beam and Master-3 a point or two forward of the starboard beam."

"Just sitting out there and waiting..." Williams mused.

"Waiting for us to make a sound?" Dutch asked rhetorically.

Williams frowned, "Maybe..."

"Or is it something else, sir?" Weiss asked and then smiled sheepishly. "Sorry, didn't mean to kibitz."

"Means offer unasked for advice, Elmer," Nichols said wryly.

"I don't mind, Clance... you may be on to something," Williams said, rubbing his chin. "Maybe they're waiting for friends."

"Skipper... doubtful contact on JP!" Radcliff said excitedly. "Faint engine noises coming from the north, sir... possible multiple screws. All fast, least as far as I can tell."

"Well, well..." Dutch muttered.

"Why do I have the uneasy feeling," said the acting captain unhappily, "that we just stepped in something."

"A trap?" Nichols asked. "Or a pile of shit."

"Both..." muttered Vigliano.

"XO... Captain... confirm multiple new contacts." It was River's this time. "Three distinct targets, sir. Diverging and at long range, but their signal strength is growing."

"What now, Skipper?" Nichols asked.

Williams drew in a breath, "Pray."

13
EAST TIMOR

"First light," a soft British voice said from the darkness.

Art Turner groaned slightly as he came awake in his bedroll. It lay atop a moldering pile of hay, or some Timor equivalent, but was still somewhat uncomfortable. After the night they'd had, though, sleep had come quickly, but it was dying a slow death now.

"What time is it?" muttered the submarine captain.

"Zero-six-thirty," Archer said. "Bit of a storm in the offing. How do you feel?"

"Like I slept outdoors in a dank barn," turner said, extracting himself and stretching. "The men?"

"The youngster and medico are still corking away in the truck," Archer said. "I've got Swooping Hawk out on a short-range patrol. Your electrician there is preparing a bite of breakfast."

Turner blinked. The light inside the old sway-backed barn they'd found on the deserted farm they'd also found was lit only by a faint, infernal red light coming from behind a dividing wall in the rear. Through the closed doors ahead of the truck, dark gray lines glowed through spaces above, between and below the doors.

"What's the plan?" turner asked.

Archer snorted, "Shall I tell you? Or will you just do whatever you feel like regardless?"

"Do we have a problem, Colonel?"

Archer leaned in close, "Your bloody right we do! I thought we had an understanding, Captain. That once ashore, it's *me* who's in charge. That means that *you* follow *my* orders, what? I told you and Hoffman to stay with the gear… but you deliberately disobeyed and came running."

"I thought you might need help."

"Bollocks! You saw an opportunity to do a bit of damage. You couldn't stand sitting by and came in to fight."

"And what if I did?" Turner asked. "I didn't come on this little jaunt to sit back on my hands, Colonel."

"No… you came to get *revenge*," Archer snapped, keeping his voice to a harsh whisper. "I saw the look in your eye after you murdered that Jap, Arthur… I know why you came."

"Murder?" Turner growled. "Since when is it *murder* to kill the enemy, Colonel?"

"Since a man throws down his weapon and squeezes the life out of another with his bare fucking hands, that's when," Archer replied. "We're here to do a job, damn you, not to indulge in your need to extract a pound of flesh from old Hirohito! In order to do that, we must maintain the chain of command. We must remain professional, eh? There are other men counting on us, and this is not the time for… for any cowboy nonsense!"

Turner's anger from the previous night flared behind his eyes. A thick, hot, and heavy fury that wanted to pummel the arrogant shit for questioning him. However, his intellect won out… barely… and he forced himself to remain calm.

Turner unclenched his jaw and said: "You're right, Colonel. I guess I… guess I've got a lot going on inside."

Archer laid a hand on Turner's shoulder and squeezed, "Then we're agreed that we'll conduct ourselves like proper soldiers and not vigilantes? That you will follow my orders so that your men follow them too?"

Turner nodded. The man's point was inarguable, "All right, Colonel. Reprimand received."

The hand loosened a bit but remained on the shoulder. Turner couldn't see Archer's eyes, but the glint of teeth showed him a moderate smile.

"Now see here, Old Boy," said the Brit in a friendlier tone. "I understand. I truly do. I share your desire to crush the lives out of these yellow bastards. And we will… before this is over, we'll get our pound of flesh and then some. Dammit, Arthur, I don't need to lecture you on the chain of command. You're a bloody ship's captain, for God's sake. You know this better than anyone. I need your obedience, and I also need your trust… and that of your lads. If you and I aren't together…"

"Then the unit falls apart; I know," Turner said, genuinely contrite now. "I'm sorry, Colonel."

"Good man," Archer patted Turner's shoulder and let his hand fall. "Look here, Old Man… I know it's difficult for us to be friends under these circumstances… but would you at least call me Percy for all love? Long as we're not on duty at any rate?"

Turner returned the smile, "As you wish, Colonel."

Percy chuckled, "That's the spirit! Now let's have a bite, eh? Feels like my belly button is sticking to my backbone."

The two men strode to the rear of the decrepit old barn and saw that Tank had set up a small cooking fire and had several items laid out on a nearby workbench. He looked up from his skillet and grinned, his face lurid in the firelight and his smile tinged in crimson.

"You look like the devil," Turner tossed off.

"Spot on as usual, sir," Tank said. "Welcome to Tank's, gentlemen. We have a scrumptious repast planned for you this morning. A delicate filet of Spam, instant coffee, and canned peaches."

"Proper flats we must look having forgotten our ties, then," Archer joked.

"Smells damned good, Tank," Turner said.

"You *must* be hungry, sir," Tank said, plating a couple of Spam slices on the men's kits that he'd set up on the table. "If you mighty officers would dig in, I'll go and wake the gold brickers."

"I'm a bit surprised by this," Turner said, nodding his head at the barn's interior. "So far what I've seen of south Pacific living isn't this… advanced."

Archer bolted down a slice of Spam and washed it down with coffee, "Oh… bloody Christ… needs a bit of sugar… well, Timor is a bit of a different animal, Art. Many of the people here are of Portuguese and Dutch descent. Been here several centuries, you know. Mixed with the Malay population such that there are few true bloods left, as it were. Europeans brought modern farming techniques and natives brought a knowledge of their land. A good deal of the island is mountainous and unfit for agriculture… but there are forests and fertile land. Mostly coffee, rice, corn, beans, and coconut plantations, some bamboo… but as you've seen here, many farms are now defunct since the Jap landed. There must have been livestock here. Perhaps swine and poultry… even beef. But the Jap came in, stripped it bare to the bone, and left the owners to fend for themselves… or worse."

"They're like locusts," Turner said darkly. "Despoiling everything they touch."

Archer grunted around a mouthful of peach, "Just so, Old Boy. Why our mission is so vital. Without my lads get this radio kit we're lugging about… they're isolated. Completely cut off. A losing proposition. However, should we reattach that link to the mainland, they can then receive intelligence, set up supply deliveries, and get important people away from here and back to Australia. Then, and *only* then, can a coordinated and effective resistance be set up. Set going in preparation for the inevitable invasion. West Timor is held by the Dutch and is holding out… but the people on this side of the Laclo Rivers are up the proverbial creek, I'm afraid."

"They're neutral Portuguese, right?"

A snort of bitter derision, "As much as they can be. But you've been to the Solomons, mate. You've seen what allying with the Nip gets one. Neutrality is all the worse."

Turner grunted.

"Now, we're not going as far as the North and South Laclo… they're close to and are often used as the borders between east and west," Archer explained. "But my lads are hiding in the middle hills not far from here. The major difficulty we face is locating them. They are, naturally, doing their upmost to remain undetected."

Wayts and Hoffman stumbled over, appearing bleary-eyed and less well-rested than Turner would like. Evidently bunking down in the bed of the truck wasn't any better than on the hard-packed hay. As they began to eat, Swooping Hawk arrived, almost magically appearing in the firelight. Turner marveled at how he hadn't even heard the barn door open.

"We should have a guard posted," he said, eyeing the Indian. "If you'd been a Jap…"

"No Jap moves like a Navajo, sir," said the young man.

"Anything to report, Petty Officer?" asked Archer with only a hint of formality.

"No sign of the Jap, sir," Swooping Hawk said, accepting his mess kit now full. "Went a mile or two up the road in both directions. No sign of anyone, not even locals. It's sort of… eerie. Did see some tracks, wild animals, possibly loose livestock. Should be able to forage some fresh meat if we need to, sir."

"Anything from the coffee plantation?" Archer asked.

Swooping Hawk shook his head, "Not that I could see, sir. I didn't go quite that far… even though we're maybe three miles away. No sign of Jap patrols out looking for their missing men or truck… yet."

"You can bet they will," Turner said. "Now that it's getting light."

"Pretty nasty storm coming in from the north, though, Captain," Swooping Hawk said. "Might make it tough on them."

"And us…" Wayts grumbled around a mouthful of spam.

"Good cover for our next move," Archer stated.

"What is our next move, Colonel? You don't mind me asking?" Hoffman asked. He set down his mess kit and dug several small foil packs out of his utility blouse pocket. He began to pass them out. "Atropine. I know this isn't Guadalcanal… but we can't afford to get malaria or dengue or some other mosquito-borne illness."

"Just so," said Archer, opening and swallowing his pill. "And I don't, Doc. This is not a random journey, lads. I know where we're going. As I was explaining to your skipper here, my men are hidden quite well in the high country. Doubtless they're making hit and run raids down into the more populated areas when they can… yet they're working blind. Rather than poking about fruitlessly, I intend to make contact with one or more locals whom I know. One in particular is a woman who's remarkably connected. She lives not far from here, perhaps a day's travel and across one of the rivers hereabouts. Part way between here and Dili, on the Banda coast. She'll know how to get in touch with my 2ICs."

"Who is this woman?" Turner asked.

Between the light of the fire and the slightly brighter but still diffuse gray light leaking between the cracks, Archer's expression was visible enough to accurately show his reserve. It appeared to Turner that he was being careful, although the captain couldn't figure out why.

"She's… a cook and housekeeper," Archer said. "She's connected to the Portuguese government. Let us say… she has a very *special* connection to Manuel Ferreira de Carvalho. He's the governor of East Timor."

"Mistress?" Tank asked.

Archer's eyes blazed and the look he levelled on the big electrician could've drawn blood, "That'll do, Petty Officer."

Tank blinked, cleared his throat and mumbled, "Aye-aye, sir…"

Archer composed himself and let a sigh escape, "I beg pardon, lads… she's a friend. She's a fine woman and has been forced to adapt to terrible circumstances. But yes, Broderick… she may indeed have a relationship with the governor. At any rate, she knows things and is also connected to my lads. She'll know how to get in touch. I can only hope we find her at home…"

Turner thought he understood, or at least partially. He thought that the lady might in fact be the mistress of one of the leaders of Archer's Second Independent Commandos. And he was worried about her.

"Sounds Jake to me," Turner said. "The locals always know the score. Of course, we need to…"

He trailed off, not wishing to stomp on the man's toes again. To his relief, though, Archer offered a conciliatory smile.

"Be cautious. Of course. Come, lads, let's finish up and get underway. If we can cross the river before the weather lets up, we ought to be able to get into the high country straight away."

Hoffman stayed behind to help Tank pack up the gear and extinguish the fire. There was little to do, but while Wayts and Swooping Hawk got the truck bed settled, including letting the Navajo catch a few Zs, and the officers conferred in the cab, the two seasoned sailors had a few precious moments to speak openly.

"I don't like this, Tank," Hoffman forewent any preamble. "There's something… off… about this whole show."

Tank sighed as he kicked dirt over the fire and poured water from a pail he'd left out in the now heavy rain, "I read, pally. I don't trust Archer. I ain't sayin' he's pullin' a grift… but I think there's more under his hood, if you know what I'm sayin'."

Hoffman nodded, "And the skipper? There's something off with him, Tank. He's got his own agenda, too."

Tank sighed, "You see the look in his eyes after he took out that Jap? I ain't never seen that look before, Hank… not from him. Not after any of the shit we been through. Not even on The Canal."

"It was murder," Hoffman said, swallowing. "Murderous rage, anyway."

Tank cursed, "I ain't judgin' him, Hank. Don't get me wrong. After what them slants done from that downed bird… fuck 'em all, I say."

"Yeah, but to choke a man to death like that…" Hofman muttered. "Beatin' his head against a truck…"

"We's all gonna have things to answer for when this is over," Tank said. "Ain't a man in this war is gonna come out with a clean soul, on any side. Maybe that's the worst part of war, y'know? It's what the survivors gotta live with. When we're watching our kids and grandkids grow up… grow up safe… we'll know what we done to make that happen. But only we'll know how much had to be paid for that. You, me, Freddy, Lee… the guys back on the boat… we'll have enough to keep us second guessing until we're in the home. Just imagine what men like Archer or our captain gotta live with."

Hoffman nodded slowly, "Yeah… but I still say we gotta keep a weather eye on this."

Tank smiled and thunked him on the shoulder, "Never a truer word, chum. Now let's get this peanut grift on the road, huh?"

* * *

The rain that rolled in from the slate gray wool that spat it down was so heavy that even several hours after sunup a man could hardly see more than a hundred feet in front of him. The solid blanket above cast the sodden world below in dull shades of gloomy steel, only broken occasionally by brilliant forks of actinic blue flame.

The going was also slowed. The roads, muddiest near the end of the rainy season, were now deep, rutted slurries that the six-wheeled truck had to negotiate at hardly more than a walking speed. More than once, Archer lost the road and had to swerve into fields or sparse trees in order to avoid being swamped.

After the first hour, the moldy canvas over the bed began to drip in several spots. The men in back shuffled about, finding drier places and hunkering down. At first, it was actually pleasant. Two days before Christmas, even the tropics were somewhat moderate in their swelter and the heavy storm had sapped much of the warmth and left behind a cool damp that hovered below eighty. However, as the storm went on, its own damp seeped into the men's bones with the same slow but inexorable progress it made in locating and saturating the canvas until there seemed to be more leaks than dry spots.

Finally, perhaps three hours after leaving the barn, the British soldier pulled the truck into a stand of leafy trees and killed the engine. With the added cover, the leaks in the canvas slackened and the damp men in back lowered the tailgate, allowing more of the four inches of rainwater inside to sluff away.

"What's on?" Turner asked.

"Just around that bend," Archer said, "is a bridge we must cross."

"Do we need to?" Turner asked. "Is there a ford or another way up the river or stream?"

He couldn't see, but if there was a bridge, then there must be a substantial water course ahead. All Turner could really see outside were trees. An open space where the narrow road cut between them and more trees on the other side.

"Indeed, we must," said Archer. "There's a trail that leads up into the hills on that side. However… there is also a village on the far side of this river and if the old intelligence I possess remains accurate… a Jap outpost there. Which means…"

"Which means they control the bridge," Turner cranked. "Swell. How far is it?"

"Hundred yards around that bend," Archer pointed.

"Well," said Turner, hefting his Thompson. "Let's roll in and give them a surprise, Colonel."

Archer smiled wryly, "That eager, eh? I think perhaps a bit more caution is required here."

Turner shrugged, "We're in a Jap truck, it's raining cats and dogs… and they'll be wet, miserable, and inattentive. Sounds like a perfect time to strike to me, Percy."

The soldier smiled, "Indeed. However, I feel we should have ourselves a bit of a look-see first, what? Which one of your poor lads do you think we can con into taking a stroll in the wet?"

Turner snorted, "Being wet is nothing new to a sailor, Percy. But I'll volunteer this sailor for one."

Archer eyed him sidelong for a long moment and then nodded slowly, "You've got an experienced eye… all right, then. Take young Wayts with you."

Turner cocked an eyebrow, "Wayts? I was thinking of our Navajo."

"Yes, quite… but however… young Wayts strikes me as a bit of a tenderfoot as yet," Archer explained. "I think he could use more experience. And being at his captain's side will lend him a bit more bottom, I should think."

Turner frowned, his desire to go with a more experienced combat veteran pushing him to argue. However, he had been given an order, couched though it was as advice… and the Brit had a point, after all.

Turner nodded and opened the door, leaping down to the damp ground. The Isuzu type-94 was a quality truck, and the submarine captain hoped they could hold onto it for a while. Its rugged design and high clearance made it a good choice for the terrain. However, he wished there was a sliding back window that opened directly into the cargo bed.

By the time Turner jumped up and into the dubious cover of the canvas personnel area, he was nearly as soaked as his men, overhead tree cover notwithstanding.

"Welcome to Shangri-La, sir," Tank offered.

"You fellas okay back here?" Turner asked.

"We're alive, sir," Hoffman grinned. "A bit moist, though."

The captain harrumphed, "Well, one of you is gonna get a lot damper. Colonel tells me there's a Jap-held bridge up ahead and me and a lucky scout are gonna go up there and lay our peepers on it."

"I'm in, sir," said Swooping Hawk without hesitation.

"Me too," said Wayts, though sounding far less enthusiastic.

Turner held up a hand to quell any more gung-ho replies, "At ease. Wayts is coming. You could use the experience, Lee, and I could use a strong young fella with me. Leave your pack, just take your sidearm and coffee grinder with extra ammo. And a radio."

Wayts nodded. He'd already shoved his pack under the wooden bench and had his SMG in hand, "Ready to go, sir."

A figure materialized out of the rain and scrambled up into the bed, "God help us! Who'd be a soldier on a day like this, eh, lads?"

"We're ready," Turner said.

Archer scrubbed a hand across his damp face, "Very good. Quick, simple and quiet now, Captain. Sneak about, get a good look without being seen, and report back. No heroics, no getting too close. Just radio in and we'll decide what to do next, right?"

"Yes, sir," Wayts said, nervous but eager.

Turner nodded, "Roger that, Colonel."

"Good luck and God speed, then," said Archer and removed a dry pack of Viceroys from his pocket, "Meantime, I'll treat the lads here to a fag. Good hunting, Art… and be careful, eh?"

"Always," said Turner and then he and Wayts leapt out into the rain.

14

At first, Turner and Wayts made no pretense at stealth. They simply ran up the road, trying to avoid the ruts or deep potholes as best they could. The storm was a doozy and showed no signs of stopping even after more than four hours. As such, the landscape was awash, and the road was anything from three to ten inches deep in places.

Once they reached the bend, however, things improved somewhat. The road bent through dense collections of Candlenuts, Betelnuts, Australian pines, and conifers and began to descend. No doubt the river valley was lower than the land on which they'd been traveling.

Timor was shaped something like an arched chicken leg. A bit more than 300 miles long, it thickened to sixty-five miles in West Timor and narrowed to only ten miles wide in the far eastern region where Archer and his team had come ashore. Much of the island was mountainous, with the agricultural sections huddled along the rivers that flowed both north and south and, as Turner had seen, near the East Timor Coast.

However, all that day's drive, they'd seen land rising and less and less farming. It was no surprise, therefore, that the two scouts found that after the road bent through the trees, it angled down rather sharply and descended more than a hundred feet into the river valley.

"One advantage we've got," Turner said as the two men stood near the top of the ridge that looked down toward the river, "is that if we can't see more than a hundred feet away, neither can the slopes."

Wayts looked over at his captain, silvery rivulets of water flowing off the bill of his cover and smiled thinly. A wise crack danced on the tip of his tongue, but he checked himself. He didn't know the skipper well, and he knew enough about Navy life and how things seemed to be aboard *Bull Shark* that an E2 didn't joke with the captain.

He simply said, "Yessir."

Turner frowned, reading the young man's mind, "I know, lucky us, right? Well, from here on in, we try to hug the side of the road and walk down. I can't see the bridge or the river yet, but I think that's a good thing. We'll move cautiously until details start to materialize."

"Should we split up, sir? Each take a side?"

Turner frowned. In spite of his eagerness to fight, he had to do things intelligently.

He was a little worried about Wayts. Not that the kid had given him any reason, but Turner had allowed the young striker to be volunteered for a mission that was far out of his experience. Yes, he'd been a sheriff's deputy for a year... yet the Navy, either intentionally or not, had ignored that. Rather than putting him with the SPs, they'd made him a steersman on a submarine. And yet here was Wayts, running around a tropical jungle gunning for Nips.

Turner was even a little worried about himself. Not that his skills weren't up to the job. He'd gotten plenty of on the job training on Guadalcanal. He'd also had an experienced Marine officer, Al Decker, to watch and to guide him.

Yet Turner was no fool and he was introspective enough to understand that he'd been letting the whole business with losing Hazard and the other men eat away at him. So much so that he burned with a desire to kill Japs... and in ways that were far more intimate than just getting one in his iron sights.

Deep down, Turner could admit to himself that what had happened the night before had been almost sexually gratifying. That squeezing the life from that Jap had felt so good... so *right*... and yet, even minutes afterward, it'd unsettled him.

Hell... be honest with yourself, Art... it'd scared him. Scared him how much he enjoyed it and how that emotion wasn't balanced with his sense of ethics and repugnance at taking another life that way.

Would that continue? With every new kill would Art Turner descend into darkness? Would he de-evolve or even morph into a true, cold killer who reveled in the letting of another's blood? And if so... would the line between right and wrong be smudged out... in blood?

And what kind of man would come home to Joanie and Arty and Dotty? Would their husband and father be replaced by a monster?

"Sir?"

Turner blinked and shook himself out of his dark thoughts, "No, I think we'll stick together, Lee. Better, especially in this soup. Besides, you've got the only walkie. C'mon, let's get this show on the road."

They slogged another half mile or so, being careful not to slide down the muddy hillside. Although the grade of the land allowed the water to flow and left far fewer puddles, it did turn the road slick.

Soon enough, the trees began to thin and the land grew flatter, more arable land came into view. The land ended at what was obviously a water course, although the far side was invisible through the rain.

What was visible was the bridge. As the two Navy men moved cautiously closer, its framework came into view. From what they could see, the bridge was of wooden construction. Rough-hewn planks laid over a log framework that gently rose toward its center. Not a very high rise, probably only high enough to allow small boats to pass beneath. The wood was stained a dark gray by the rain and the structure was only wide enough for a single vehicle to pass. At its foot, two decorative stone columns rose, each topped by an iron cross, thus providing some clue as to the Catholics who'd probably built it.

Also visible, made spectral by the downpour, was the bulky shape of another Isuzu truck. The vehicle was parked facing the approaching sailors. There may or may not be one or two enemy soldiers standing huddled against the pillars, Turner couldn't tell. If he had to guess, however, he would assume the guards were settled into the cab of the truck and staying dry.

"Uh-oh…" Wayts said, crouching low behind some scraggly brush near the road's edge. "Wonder how many guys are in that truck, sir?"

"Yeah…" Turner said. "At least two, I'd have to think. Maybe more in the back… but what concerns me is what's on the other side of the bridge. Colonel says there's a village there… so probably a lot more Japs."

Wayts pointed, "See that, sir? That's a dipole radio aerial sticking up from the truck. Probably gives them a couple of miles of extra range."

Turner harrumphed, "Yeah… not to mention they're monitoring. All right, Lee, gimme the blower."

Wayts handed over the bulky SCR-536 hand-held and Turner extended the forty-inch antenna, which activated the unit. He and Archer had already worked out their radio procedures. They'd start on channel one and walk up the odd frequencies until forty-nine. Then they'd go back and start counting by fives and then twos and then go back to the odds again.

"Red, Blue… Red, Blue… do you copy?"

A blast of squelch and then Archer replied: "*We read, Blue, proceed.*"

Turner gathered his thoughts, "Have eyes on objective. Approx. one-half klick whiskey your twenty. Sugar fox over."

Sugar fox or SF was shorthand for switch frequencies. Turner unlocked the frequency hold, tuned the radio to channel three, and locked it again.

"*Blue, Red… I read,*" said Archer. "*Sitrep?*"

"One enemy vehicle at foot of bridge, no sign enemy units… suspect under cover, over."

A pause and then, "*Understood. Recommendation?*"

"Sugar fox."

Now on channel five, Archer once again acknowledged.

"Enemy has portable aerial," Turner advised. "Suspect listening as well as bridge Obo Peter. Over."

Another pause, "*Roger… possible you can deactivate, over?*"

Turner frowned and looked at Wayts who wore a similar expression, "We could try to sneak up and attack the truck... but it's too open."

The young sailor appeared relieved and nodded.

Turner thumbed the button, "Negative, Red. Open terrain. Suggest... suggest you drive up and get stopped. Should expose enemy units and then we can surprise, over."

"*Very good. Oboe Tare Whiskey. Be prepared as best you can. Out.*"

Turner slid the antenna down and handed the unit back to Wayts, "Well, they're on the way, Lee. Let's see how close we can get. These bushes and a couple of trees get pretty close. Let's see if we can't shorten the range."

Wayts nodded, "About sixty yards now, sir. If I had a good deer rifle..."

Turner chuffed, "We could plink at them easy... if we could *see* them. But these Tommy guns are only good to about twice that range, and I'd prefer to be as close as possible. Let's move. Stay behind me and do exactly what I do."

Turner rose and began to slink through the line of brush and toward the nearest tree. Wayts, who'd been chosen for this mission partly due to his hunting background, was impressed at how the captain moved. Turner was quiet, fast but not hurried. He used natural cover and stayed low. Wayts wondered if the man had been an avid back woodsman too.

They'd gotten another fifteen yards closer and huddled together behind a pair of thin slash pines. Both men were panting. In spite of the cool rain and the short distance, the efforts of slinking about took a lot more energy than it appeared.

"Wow, sir... you a hunter?" Wayts puffed quietly.

Turner grinned, "No, grew up in South Florida. We moved down from Pennsylvania after Flagler got the railroad started into the keys. When we first got to Miami, it was little more than a fishing village with some rich folks... by the time I was in junior high... well, we *had* a junior high and the city was really becoming a city. The construction of route one really helped that. So, I grew up on the water. Beach, back-country... fishing and like that."

Wayts was shocked at how much he'd just learned about his captain, "Wow... so how'd you get so good at this jungle stuff?"

Turner harrumphed, "Spent some time with the Marine Raiders on Guadalcanal before and during the invasion."

"Holy cow..." Wayts muttered.

Turner held up a hand for silence, "I think this is as close as we're gonna get. I don't think they've seen us, but we're pushing it... listen... here comes the cavalry."

* * *

"And we're off," Archer said, handing the radio to Broderick. "Be a good fellow and let the lads in back know to be ready with their submachine guns would you, Broderick?"

Tank set the radio onto the floorboards and asked, "Plan, sir?"

Archer cocked an eyebrow, "We shall, as you Jonathans say, wing it. I'm going to roll up beside the other truck. Someone will get out to inspect us... and at that point..."

Archer pulled his colt 1911 and racked the slide, setting the gun between his legs, "We open fire. Quick, clean, and efficient. At that point, the lads in back will exit and get round to the rear of the other Lorry. Surprise and, I dearly hope, limited noise."

Tank frowned and nodded, "Aye, sir... want me to stay with them?"

"No... I'll have you crouch behind the dash. You exit and fire across the bonnet. Let's go now, chop, chop."

Tank vanished into the rain and in less than two minutes, had returned, still soaking and with his face set into hard lines, "Good to go, Colonel."

"Then we're off!" enthused Archer and put the truck into gear.

Tank, a big man who was ill-suited to hiding in the cab did his best to do so. He had his own sidearm out and laying on the seat. As the six-by-six whirred and jounced along the muddy road and began to angle downward, the electrician prayed that the Japs wouldn't simply start shooting on sight.

After all, two of their vehicles had been attacked at the joy house the night before. Surely by now the word must be out. The hope was that the guards at the checkpoint wouldn't shoot first and ask questions later.

However, should that prove to be the case, then Hoffman and Swooping Hawk were instructed to jump out and return the favor. Theoretically, Archer and Tank would be protected inside the cab. At least long enough to bail out of the passenger door. Further, based on the captain's report, the bridge would be narrow enough to deal with who or whatever might trundle across once the shit hit the fan.

"Bit of a gully washer, this," Archer mused as he guided the truck into the valley. "Bloody tropics… and here I thought England was damp."

Tank, having nothing to add to this observation, only chuckled.

"Here we are…" Archer said, suddenly tensing in his seat. "Be ready, Broderick… I see the Jap Lorry at the foot of the bridge. As your skipper indicated, no Nips about… hello… I believe we've been noticed. Yes… the driver's door is opening, and a man is stepping out with a pistol… another on the passenger side."

"Can they see you, sir?" Tank asked from his crumpled position.

"I think not… no wipers you know," said Archer. "They're having me stop. They appear none too pleased about being out in the wet… no worries, lads… won't trouble you long…"

Archer stopped the truck and over the idling engine, Tank heard the faint and muffled shouts of men calling to them in Japanese. Tank risked a peek over the dash and gulped.

They'd stopped no more than five feet from the other truck and perhaps twenty from the bridge. The man on the passenger side of the other truck was pointing an Arisaka at them and the man from the driver's side was stepping closer, shouting.

"Damned fool… he's blocking his mate's shot… go, Broderick!"

Tank yanked the handle and tumbled out, his Colt 1911 clutched in his right hand. Instantly, the rain slashed at him, filling his nostrils with the ozone scent of clouds and the slight mustiness of a large fresh water source not far away. Even as he got his footing under him, several thunderous reports boomed from inside the truck.

Tank had no time to see what was happening. He slammed the

door shut and slouched to the front right tire, peeking up over the hood and leading with his pistol. The man who'd come to the window was gone and as he lined up on the riflemen fifteen feet away, the man's chest exploded in a nimbus of dark vermillion.

"The back! The back!" someone, possibly the Navajo shouted, as Tank moved forward, launching himself toward the open driver's door of the guard's vehicle. There was no one else inside, of course. Not much room for more than two men.

"Watch it, Tank!" That was definitely Swooping Hawk, calling out from behind.

Tank didn't pause, didn't hesitate. He flung himself down, rolling half under the running boards of the guards' truck as a Tommy gun began chattering its guttural war cry.

More screams, more American shouts... more rounds.

Loud... too loud... Tank thought even as he got onto his knees and tried to discern just what in the hell was happening.

He saw the Navajo engineman standing six feet away, hosing down the canvas covered bed of the Jap truck with his Thompson. The gun spat flame and growled as its .45 rounds plunged through the fabric and ripped into whatever was inside.

More blurs, another figure on the other side, angling his shots to duplicate Swooping Hawk's assault without hitting him in the crossfire.

"Cease fire!" Archer called. "Cease fire!"

Tank blinked and looked around, his heart hammering at his ribs. The world was a gray, misty collage of odd images. A pair of trucks, a narrow wooden bridge bordered by rough stone pillars with... crosses on them? Several men stood by or moved back and forth and...

"Got two more back here!" called Hoffman who was apparently in the bed of the shot-up truck.

"Tank, you all right?"

The electrician blinked again, seeing his captain standing by, his weapon at port arms and his blue eyes studying him, "Uhm... yeah, fine, sir. You and Lee okay?"

Turner nodded, "Four-oh. Two guys in the cab and two in the bed. Could've been ugly."

"It still can be, Old Boy," Archer appeared, casting an eye at Tank. "Broderick, help the lads load these two buggers into the bed of their truck, will you? There's a good fellow."

Tank bent to help pick up the man who'd made the mistake of coming too close to Archer's window. He met Swooping Hawk's gaze as they lifted the dead man. A dirty business, they both seemed to tell one another.

"My hope is that the shots weren't overheard due to the rain," Archer was saying. "We may yet have a grace period. We should get across the bridge forthwith."

"Agreed," said Turner. "But I also think we can take the bridge out, at least for a while."

"Blow it?" Archer asked.

"No... not unless it's really necessary. Just blockade it."

"But how... oh, yes, of course!" Archer chuckled. "We'll need a volunteer."

"Got one," Turner said.

"And a helper," Archer stated. "Two men to handle the truck and then they'll have to follow us on foot. I'd rather not risk you, however, Arthur."

"I've got to do something," Turner said. "I'm not just here to look beautiful."

"I'll stay with the skipper, sir," Tank volunteered as he exited the other truck. "Thinking we park the Jap truck on the bridge and then blow the engine, Skipper?"

Turner nodded, "Exactly. Let's load up whatever we can take out of the Nip wagon and put it in ours. Let's also hope we don't have to fight our way through the next checkpoint."

"Shouldn't be necessary," Archer supplied. "We'll be coming from the bridge and the Nips on that side will believe we've passed muster... at least for a time."

Turner nodded and looked at Tank, "You up for this, Tank?"

"I was born ready, Captain."

15

Turner and Tank parked the truck between the two pillars with its engine compartment on the bridge. They then let the air out of all six tires and even the two spares mounted to the sides of the truck.

Finally, Turner popped the hood and Tank stood ready as the captain edged around the front. The electrician pulled the pin on a hand grenade, dropped it into the engine compartment and shouted, "Fire in the hole!"

They ran like hell.

Rain still poured down, masking the far end of the bridge and whatever might be up or down stream. When the grenade exploded, the sound was muffled, dull, and watery. However, the two sailors still flung themselves down on the rough logs and, as the wooden bridge vibrated, creaked and groaned, prayed it wouldn't tumble into the swiftly moving waters below.

"Think they heard that across the way?" Tank asked as he and Turner got to their feet.

"Hell, if they didn't hear the racket we made a few minutes ago… we might be safe," Turner replied. "Let's double-time it. Got a feeling the shit's about to hit the fan."

"Skipper…" Tank began and then faltered. He was unsure of himself, especially in light of Turner's recent behavior. In times past, he might have dared to broach a sensitive subject, but now…

"Something on your mind, Tank?" Turner asked as they jogged toward the center and up the slight incline to the peak.

In fact, Tank had a *lot* on his mind, but only said, "No, sir."

Turner glanced over at the big electrician and with an accurate flash of insight, realized that there was something bothering Tank. Probably several somethings. Turner didn't have to puzzle that out too long to figure it had something to do with Archer… and himself.

For the first time in a long while… since the day the Japanese sea plane had landed, Turner experienced a real stab of… what? Remorse? Guilt? Perhaps even… shame?

He knew he'd changed and had become distant. He knew that this had hurt unit cohesion aboard his boat. He also knew that more than one man, officer and enlisted alike, had felt or was feeling a sharp pang of hurt over it. Maybe even something deeper.

Well, if happy go lucky Anvil Art Turner wasn't around so much right now, then that was their tough shit, wasn't it? He wasn't their goddamned mother. He had his own problems, too…

Yet now that it had been awakened, that little voice in the back of his mind couldn't be so easily dismissed. It whispered chastisements that he didn't want to hear but worried he wouldn't be able to ignore.

Whatever might have been said didn't get the chance to be expressed. From ahead, out of the gray gloom of the misty rain, dull, regular reports thudded through the heavy atmosphere. Gunfire from the other side of the river.

The two men paused just over the peak of the bridge's deck and listened. From that position, neither bank was visible. Their world was swirling black water below a nearly black ribbon of wood. Looking over, the sailors observed foaming water writhing around the dark piles, illustrating the river's response to the raging storm. In front and behind, as it was to either side, the world slowly dissolved into gray nothingness. It was a strange and rather unpleasant sensation… as if they were trapped and at any moment, something hideous would materialize out of the gloom, ravening for their blood.

"Sounds like trouble," Turner said when more cracks thumped out of the pounding tempest.

There was a louder report that made the men jump and break into a dead run. Tank shouted, "Grenade or a mortar, sir!"

The heavy rain battered at them, masking their heavy boot falls as their own feet pounded over the wooden planks. After a few moments, dark shapes began to coalesce from the curtain of rain. Turner held up a hand and the two sailors slowed to a fast walk, their breath coming in heavy gasps as they huffed on the watery atmosphere.

The two men had long since become inured to the rain. They were soaked through to the skin and had been for so long it no longer mattered. The rain was cool, but not cold, and it actually made the air temperature comfortable. However, Turner was vaguely aware that there might be danger from inhaling so much moisture. At some point soon, he and his men would need warm, dry shelter, or they might risk getting sick… perhaps even getting pneumonia, or so he thought.

Yet this concern became a mild one when the shapes of the upcoming riverbank and the battle ahead came into focus. More shots and perhaps even muzzle flashes were coming out of the gloom.

They could see the far end of the bridge now. Like the other side, there were two pillars topped with crosses. Ahead, a loose collection of low buildings huddled under the low, dark sky. Behind them, a line of trees marked the edge of the village.

Between the trees and buildings, muzzles flashed as men exchanged fire. The truck was parked off to the left, behind a low, brick structure that Turner couldn't identify. There were several other vehicles parked on the other side of the road near another, larger building and around this, shadowy figures fired at what must be Archer and his team across the road.

"Shit," Turner growled. "Looks like they have our guys pinned down."

"That was fast,"

"Must've been waiting. Either they heard the ruckus we made across the river, or they were warned. Jig's definitely up now. Come on, we'll take cover behind those pillars and see if we can't take the pressure off."

***

Percy Archer gripped the wheel with white-knuckled intensity. To either side, the flimsy railings of the bridge sped by faster and faster as he pressed down on the accelerator. Sitting beside him, Fred Swooping Hawk held his Thompson at the ready but contrived to keep one eye on the British commando.

He didn't like the look on Archer's face. There was something bestial about it. Hard lines, flushed cheeks, pursed lips, and flinty eyes drilled through the windshield as if they were radar sets desperately seeking targets. The death grip the man had on the wheel and the way he rammed the gear shift when upshifting all combined to give Swooping Hawk the distinct impression that he was observing a predator.

A predator who slathered to clamp its jaws around the throats of his enemy. A more than professional desire to grapple with the Japanese. It was the same look Turner had in his eyes when he'd throttled the soldier the night before.

The Navajo knew the desire to kill when he saw it. And not the desire of the hunter to take down a deer or even a soldier to shoot another enemy soldier. This was much darker and much more akin to the yearning to murder than to defeat.

Yes, the captain had expressed a similar look… but it had come as a lightning flash in a storm. What the Navajo saw on Archer's face appeared as if it had already taken up semi-permanent residence.

"We gonna slow for the checkpoint, sir?" Swooping Hawk asked.

Archer harrumphed, "Just be ready, lad."

Swooping Hawk repressed a groan and cranked his window down. He rested the barrel of the Tommy gun on the sill and waited for targets to appear. He knew without a shadow of a doubt that Archer intended to go in blazing. There would be no pretense as there had been the last time.

The mechanic reached back and rapped his knuckles on the rear wall of the cabin. Three hard, loud bangs and then went back to steadying his gun. He tried not to look at the uprights and horizontal rails as they blurred past their flimsy construction would in no way impede the truck if Archer lost control.

"What was that?" asked the colonel.

"Signal, sir. Letting Lee and Hank know we're going in hot."

"Smashing…," said the colonel. "Get ready, here we are…"

Out of the gloom ahead, fuzzy shapes emerged, took form, and finally substance. Two more pillars, buildings beyond and what might be trees and even hills beyond that… and several soldiers standing at the foot of the bridge holding rifles and waving.

The truck was doing forty and showed no sign of stopping. Swooping Hawk leaned on his door, turned his barrel forward, and pressed the trigger. The SMG clattered and spat flame as its big rounds leapt toward the two hapless Japanese soldiers.

Swooping Hawk didn't know if he'd hit, or they'd dived out of the way. The truck roared at them, passing between the columns and thumping crazily as it hit and leapt over several lumpy forms on the last planks of the bridge. Swooping Hawk tried not to think about that as he angled his barrel toward the right and began firing again at more scrambling shapes in light khaki.

Archer wheeled the truck to the left, the engine whining in protest and the tires spitting mud and debris as they left the wooden bridge. More than one round slapped the framework of the truck with a gonging whine and Swooping Hawk was thrown hard into the door as the vehicle nearly spun to the left.

He wondered how the two men in the back were, when a pair of Thompsons began to chatter, adding their voice to the chaos. Hoffman and Wayts were still with them.

"Headed for cover!" Archer hollered over the roaring motor, thundering rain and whining bullets. "Be prepared to bail out!"

Swooping Hawk saw why. With frightening speed, a squat gray building loomed up out of the rain and appeared to leap at them. Archer spun the wheel, slewing the truck around the rear and stomping the brake. The six-by actually slid several yards and even began to fishtail as the Brit muscled it to a stop.

"Move!" he shouted even as he hurled himself out the door.

Swooping Hawk followed suit and plastered himself against the cold stone of the building's outer edge. Leading with his barrel, he edged toward the corner that would let him view the bridge and the building and men across the road.

"They're coming!" Archer shouted. "Bloody platoon or two! Take them out, man!"

What the hell did the crazy bastard think he was doing?

Then Swooping Hawk saw Hoffman and Wayts moving toward the colonel. He reached the edge of the wall and turned back.

"Hank! Over here! Lee, see if you can get into this building through that door and find a window to shoot through!"

"It's got a lock on it!" the kid shouted.

"Then shoot the bugger, man!" Archer shouted and opened fire.

"Freddy, what the—" Hoffman huffed.

"Just stay behind me, Hank," Swooping Hawk said. "If Lee gets that door open, you follow him in. Find a murder hole and put that Chicago typewriter to some good use! Building's brick or something, should be safe."

"I'm not here to be safe," said the pharmacist's mate, although clearly unconvinced.

The Navajo chuckled, "You're too valuable to risk. You can help fire from inside… just be careful, huh?"

"Jesus, Freddy… this guy's Nutsy Fagan!" Hoffman jerked his head toward the screaming Archer, who was busily emptying a magazine at the onrushing Japanese.

Swooping Hawk chuffed, "And how… okay, he's got it, now beat it already!"

Swooping Hawk eased around the corner, saw four Japs low-running toward him and opened fire. With resolute control, the Indian walked his tracers through the mud, kicking up tiny geysers until the rounds found the first man… and kicked up a geyser of another kind. Sprays of blood that showed black in the rain and gray light jetted from his chest and gut as the man fell. His three comrades went the same way, almost running directly into the American's line of fire. Only the last one managed to dodge, flinging himself sideways and rolling into the mud.

That's when Swooping Hawk's bolt locked open. He cursed and

released the magazine, fumbling for another even as the surviving fourth Japanese soldier got to his knees and levelled his gun. He never made his shot, however. From inside the building, a cacophony of fire exploded as two men opened up, burning through full magazines in the same instant that the Navajo got his new one home, and his weapon charged.

At least some of those rounds cut into the Jap, almost blasting him in two as the .45 slugs tore into his torso, billowing his guts out in macabre streamers and tearing his left arm away at the elbow.

"Conserve your ammo, *dammit!*" Archer thundered.

There were shouts now from across the road. Somebody was laying on a truck horn and several heavy somethings flew through the air and landed near the building. Throaty cracks shook the ground as 20mm knee-mortar shells exploded near the stone wall. Swooping Hawk cringed, hoping that Hoffman and Wayts, neither one of whom was really a ground-pounding soldier, had the wherewithal to clear the windows while reloading.

"More coming!" Archer shouted. "I'm on my third magazine!"

"Second!" Swooping Hawk shouted.

"Second! Second!" came two muffled voices from the other side of the stone wall against which Swooping Hawk pressed himself.

"Bloody Christ!" Archer cursed. "At least two dozen men taking up positions near that large structure! Damn them all to the fiery pits of hell!"

Swooping Hawk cursed. Without reconning the place, without any intel of any kind, Archer had led four men into a heavily guarded outpost with solid cover. Now they were outnumbered and who knew what reinforcements might be coming. The only consolation was that they wouldn't be coming from the bridge, at least.

The Indian nearly vomited when two automatic weapons added their angry chatter to the din from the direction of the columns that braced the bridge's foot.

Of course, a second later, the Indian knew that this must be Tank and the skipper and grinned as he shouted, "Reinforcements, Colonel!"

"Won't be enough!" Archer shouted and then with true alarm. "Lads! Get out of there! Now... *NOW!*"

Swooping Hawk didn't like the sound of that. On instinct, he back-pedaled, distancing himself from the corner and the building even as Wayts and Hoffman hurled themselves out of the door. A second later, a thundering blast blotted out the pounding of the rain as a heavy explosion roared from within.

From the door that the two sailors had just vacated, a dragon's breath of oily flame belched out, as if the building had begun to vomit fire. All the windows on either side did the same, a bilious exhalation of super-heated gas, jagged flying debris and thick smoke rocketing into the storm.

What had struck the building had either pierced the far wall or blasted it away completely.

"Bloody field gun!" Archer rasped. "Fifty or sixty millimeter!"

Swooping Hawk cursed. How the hell would they fight *that?*

The answer came in the form of multiple weapons firing from off to the west, to their left. The fusillade was accompanied by cries of surprise, fear, and agony from the Japs. Another volley confirmed this, and Swooping Hawk ran to where Archer still crouched low by his corner.

"Sir, what...?"

"Well, I'm damned!" shouted Archer and then laughed out loud. "It's my lads! It's the 2ICs!"

Swooping Hawk peeked. Sure enough, from the mist and rain, dark shapes materialized, their ghostly forms punctuated by bright flashes. Men appeared from behind houses, trees, and several vehicles, firing rifles and even a light machine gun. Swooping Hawk counted no less than two dozen, two of which were laying it on with grenade launchers.

"Colonel!" This was a shout from off to their right. From Turner. "Swooping Hawk! Wayts! Hoffman! You fellas alive over there?"

"We're here, sir!" Wayts shouted from where he crouched under the bed of the truck. "The Nips got a howitzer!"

"And we've got company!" Tank shouted. "Men coming out of the storm!"

"Friendlies!" Swooping Hawk called.

Several large cracks and then a whumping great rush as something or several explosive somethings caught and detonated. More screams and cheers.

"They have a howitzer no longer, ha-ha-HAA!" Archer whooped.

From behind the partially wrecked building that protected them, Swooping Hawk heard half a dozen or more Japanese voices crying out in unison. He didn't know what they were saying, but based on the frantic nature and the repetition, he thought they might be surrendering.

This was confirmed a moment later when an Australian voice shouted, "You there, behind that building! Identify yourself and show yourselves immediately!"

"Colonel Percival Archer! That you, Gus?"

"Colonel?" the man asked in shock. "Crikey! Is that truly you, sir?"

"Indeed, it is, Captain!" Archer called back. "What's the situation?"

"We're securing the village now, sir," said the Australian named Gus. "You might come out now, Colonel. You and your lads. Got quite a bit of catching up to do, eh?"

"Yeah…" Turner mumbled, suddenly he and Tank were standing close by. "Ain't that the understatement of the century."

16

LIGHT CRUISER AGANO

"All stop," Nashiri ordered the messenger of the watch who'd been posted in the hatchway to relay orders to the helm. "All of our assets are positioned, Captain," the messenger said when he returned, adjusting his sound-powered telephone set. "Orders?"

"Stand by," said Nashiri. "We are playing the waiting game. What do you think, Teacher?"

Yamata glanced about him, attempting to locate the dark shapes of destroyers that now surrounded the cruiser. The flagship herself was now nearly at the position of where the seaplane tender had been torpedoed. Positioned at four cardinal points approximately two kilometers out were the four destroyers assigned to *Agano*. They too had shut down their engines and had their hydrophones tuned into what sounds might be coming from deep below the surface.

It was Lanser who responded, "Classic distribution of assets, Mein Kapitän… but what we must remember is that if this *is Bull Shark,* her captain is devilishly clever, tenacious, and experienced. We must also remember that this boat has dived to over 240 meters."

"There is bound to be a salt layer for them to hide in," Yamata added.

Nashiri smiled and the sight was irritating. The man's arrogance evidently knew no bounds. Even Lanser wondered where he had acquired such self-confidence.

"Which is why *my* plan is more complex," said Nashiri. "Every sixty seconds, exactly timed, the four destroyers will sound an active echo location pulse. The submarine will be unable to discern their locations. Every few minutes, *we* will send out one as well. And they *will* know where we are."

"The staked goat," Lanser said and nodded.

"You hope this will corral them," said Yamata. "Clever… but what of the halocline?"

"Walk with me, gentlemen," said the captain and moved back through the pilothouse, navigation bridge and aft to the nearest companion. Once down on the main deck, he led the other two officers to the stern. There, aft of the ship's depth charge throwers and between the two seaplane catapults, a group of sailors were clustered around the taff rail, where a pair of winches had been installed on the fantail. One of these winches had two gauges mounted to its control area. The other had a separate console equipped with a set of headphones.

"Portable listening station?" Lanser asked. "What's the other cable for?"

"Depth and temperature gauge?" Yamata surmised.

Nashiri smiled and once again, it gleamed with arrogant pride, "Very good, gentlemen. We lower the starboard cable which provides temperature and depth. With this data, we can predict a salt layer and thus predict where the submarine may be hiding. Then, we lower the quad-bell hydrophone and listen for transient sounds. Because there are four hydrophones, we can determine a general direction."

"And then drop charges," Lanser said appreciatively. He then smiled thinly. "So long as no one moves… a clever solution, Mein Kapitän."

"Yes," Yamata observed. "Certainly worth a try, however."

Nashri scoffed, obviously disconcerted by the two men's dismissal of his creativity, "I should think that the two of you, of all men, would be eager to try this. After all... is it not the two of you who seek revenge on this Turner and his boat more than any other?"

Lanser shrugged, "Perhaps... but I hold no *personal* grudge, Herr Nashiri. If anything, it might be that Turner holds one against me."

"This is war," Yamata offered, lighting a cigarette. "Should we be angry because our enemy fights back? Should we become vengeful because he does not roll over and die at our convenience?"

Nashiri shook his head and lit his own smoke, "Our grand admiral seems to hold a grudge. Is that not good enough?"

Yamata sighed, "Admiral Yamamoto wishes to remove an enemy who has proven to be both persistent and effective. Natural enough... but I doubt there is any real *hate* there."

The task force commander chuckled and shook his head, "Perhaps there should be, Teacher. This is not your classroom. This is not a tactical exercise. This is a *hunt*. A hunt for a deadly predator... and I, unlike the two of you and your friends Osaka and Hideki, intend to have his *head* mounted on my cabin wall. Lower the sensor!"

USS BULL SHARK

"Six hundred feet, Murph!" newly assigned Torpedoman-1 Chester Bolz said quietly. He glanced away from the pressure gauge mounted between the torpedo tubes to cast a rueful look at the after room's leader. "I ain't never been that deep before..."

"I ain't never been on a submarine before," complained another new man, Lawrence Tate, who sat in a folding chair off to one side absently dandling a Y-wrench on his knee. "Listen to that... them sounds..."

"Take it easy, fellas," Walter "Murph" Murphy said as he slowly and carefully rolled a bit of his family's home-grown tobacco into a paper. "We been down way deeper'n this, ain't that right, Smitty?"

Jack "Smitty" Smith smiled and tapped his new chevron, indicating him as a petty officer third-class, "How I earned this little squiggle, here. But yeah... ole *Sharky* here been down to eight-oh-five one time. You believe that?"

"Yup," said Murph. "And that on a boat with an official test depth of 400 feet. Pretty crazy, huh? Ask ole Bobby here, he knows a little about crazy, don't 'cha?"

Bobby Barrett, who had started out cantankerous and had come around, had seen a few things in his short few months aboard. He nodded sagely but said nothing, his eyes cast toward the stern but not really seeing anything.

"What's with him?" Tate asked. He was a genial young man who'd grown up fishing on the Missouri river and never missed a chance to tell a story.

"Yeah, we smell or somethin', pally?" Bolz needled good-naturedly. Bolz was a farmer from Tennessee with a penchant for gangster movies. Although he spoke with a southern accent, he often tried to sound like a hard-boiled mobster.

"Just got a lot on my mind," Barrett offered.

"Worried about Horris and Mr. Post is all," Murph said, finishing his cigarette and flicking a Zippo at it. "We all are."

"Yeah, hope they're okay," said Tate. "Nice guy, that Eckhart. Mr. Post is tops, too."

"He's an officer," Smitty tossed off. "Gets the best treatment, don't you worry your pretty little heads none."

"Come on, Smitty," Murph chided gently. "That ain't respectful. I know how you feel about officers and the like… but we been lucky aboard. Mostly."

Smitty snorted, "Yeah, 'cept them two wrong Gs we had back in May. But yeah… our high and mighties is pretty okay. Sad we lost one recently, too…"

The hatch from maneuvering opened and Tony Skaggs stepped in. As the junior most officer aboard, he'd taken over Andy Post's battle station in the maneuvering room. He often went between the last two compartments, as during any situation, either battle or damage, he was in charge of damage control in those areas.

He'd overheard Smitty's remarks, although he pretended not to have. It was common for the ratings to grumble about the officers. Their privilege, really. So long as it didn't go too far, most officers turned a deaf ear to it.

When Skaggs caught Murphy's eye and got a slight nod, he knew that even for Smitty, a dyed in the wool enlisted man, there was nothing behind the talk.

"Welcome to purgatory, sir," Murph said. "Come to boost our morale, have ya'?"

"Figured you fellas just gettin' a look at how handsome I am would do that," Skaggs joked, fumbling a cigarette from a nearly empty pack in his blouse pocket. He flicked his lighter, found it to be out of fluid and frowned.

Murph laughed and held out a flame for him, "Got you covered, Mr. Skaggs… and yeah, it's enough to make half of us want to turn into sissies."

"Speak for yourself, Murph," Tate replied and in a passable James Cagney said, "I'm into dames, see… yeah… good-lookin broads, see…"

"Gotta be somethin' in the air in here," Skaggs shook his head.

"How's Horris and Mr. Post, sir?" Smitty asked.

Skaggs sighed, "Seem okay… they came around, which was a helluva thing, way I heard it. Still Hank says they probably have a concussion and is keepin' 'em awake."

"There's a fine howdy-do," Bolz mused. "Got a darky for a medic. Ain't the world a funny place."

"Yep…" Tate mused. "One day they're pickin' cotton, next they're doctorin' up the White folk. Will wonders never cease, huh?"

"Belay that kinda talk, fellas," Murph said. The words sounded casual, but there was carbon steel behind them. "Hank Martin is a fine man. Great cook, helluva gunner, and dedicated a sailor as they make 'em. You lay off them fellas."

Tate and Bolz exchanged a knowing glance but said nothing. Their smiles were conciliatory, but Skaggs sensed that they were as flimsy as dried leaves.

The two men had come out to the Pacific together after meeting in basic. They'd served on the same destroyer and had contrived to get assigned to the same submarine. They were obviously sympatico, and Skaggs only hoped there wouldn't be any problems.

"All in hand back here, Murph?" Skaggs asked just as a tremendous click and wang echoed through the compartment. Murph didn't even flinch, but the new men did, looking about with evident alarm.

"Just settlin' in, boys," said the room leader and then glanced at Skaggs. "We're all fine back here, sir."

"All right... check on you in a bit," Skaggs said and closed the hatch.

"What're we doin', Danny?" Steve Radcliff asked from his seat beside the maneuvering room chief.

"Whateva the officiz' tell me to do, Stevie," said Pentakkus around his Pall Mall. "And you do whateva I tell *you* to do."

From the main breaker panel, Paul Baxter chuckled. Doug Ingram flashed a smile at him from the auxiliary panel and IC distribution panel as well.

"Naw, I mean we ain't movin'... just sinking slowly down," Radcliff said. "And listen to the boat... are we too deep?"

"Not to worry, Radcliff," Skaggs said. "We've been deeper. Skipper's just lettin' us go down and find a salt layer. Then we can creep out from under these Japs."

Radcliff looked a bit green. Skaggs couldn't blame the man. The creaks, groans, and occasional pops that sounded more like rifle reports than metal flexing could start to wear on any man's nerves. Even a man who'd spent years in submarines.

"It's gonna be okay, Radcliff," Skaggs reiterated as he went forward toward the hatch to the after engine room. "Our XO, now the skipper, knows his business. We're in good hands and we're gonna show them Japs, just you wait and see."

"Ayuh," Pentakkus said kindly. "You just listen to Mista Skaggs theya."

Radcliff frowned and nodded. Of course, as Skaggs opened the hatch and moved forward, the first set of simultaneous echo locations sounded. From seemingly everywhere at once, a low, spectral whine began to grow and then rapidly rose to a crescendo and echoed away into nothing.

"Oh, geez..." Radcliff gulped, mopping sweat from his brow. "Where'd that come from?"

"Well... I'm just a simple Down Easta... but off hand... I'd say the Japs," Pentakkus drawled.

"From all around us," Baxter said glumly. "Must be a couple of tin cans up there... and not far off, either."

Radcliff began to breathe heavier, his face now glistening in the incandescent light from the overhead fixtures. The pits of his T-shirt were dark with sweat as well, and another stain was forming on his chest.

"Let's don't speculate heya," Pentakkus said, tossing a withering glare at Baxter.

"Yeah, and so what anyways," Ingram added. "If they knew where we were, they wouldn't be playin' tricks. Just breathe, Stevie. Gonna be fine."

"Yeah," said Baxter, flashing a smile he didn't feel. "Probably end up paintin' three or four meatballs on the tower and the battle flag when we're done, pal."

"How you fellas doin' back here?" Skaggs asked as he closed the hatch, grateful that the new men aboard had seasoned veterans to guide them.

Chief Mike Duncan leaned against a workbench and ashed a cigarette, "Pretty dull, sir. No need for my rock crushers down here. So we're just sittin' around with our thumbs parked, waitin' to surface or to go aft and help reload."

"Not everybody's relaxin', Mr. Skaggs," said Oscar Dolsworth as he carefully removed a filter from the number two lubrication pump. "Chief wants us to swap out filters and scrubbers for the lube, fuel oil, and the AC unit back here."

"Good," said Skaggs and grinned at Duncan. "Can't be a vacation *every* day back here, huh, Chief?"

Duncan snorted, "Like livin' at the Royal most days, sir."

When the ghostly screech of enemy sonar passed, Dolsworth looked to Skaggs with wide eyes, "Sir... we gonna be okay? I mean... we're deep and that sonar..."

"Just the Japs screwing around, Dolsworth," Skaggs said. "Don't you worry. You just listen to the chief here."

Skaggs made his way forward and into the forward engine room, where a group of men were also replacing filters and doing some odd cleaning jobs. At a workbench on the port side near the number two evaporator, Wilbur Dockerty and Bernie Fetlock were filing and sanding something. Skaggs moved over to check on their progress.

"Almost got her, sir," Dockerty said. "Just scraping away the flashing and she'll be ready to install in maybe five or ten minutes."

Skaggs picked up the broken valve that had ruptured and nearly killed Post and Eckhart. The two motor machinists were using it as a guide to ready a replacement. The replacement was similar, but a few minor adaptations had to be made to get it to fit the old lines.

"Fine job, men," Skaggs said, eyeing the shiny new valve fitting. "What the hell happened, anyway?"

"My guess'd be galvanic leakage, sir," Fetlock said sourly. "Someplace aboard we've got a loose connection or electrical bleed and the feed line that ruptured carried it forward. Metal and seawater make a good conductor, sir."

"Probably some dock turkey screwed something up," Dockerty grumped. "Like that time we had to replace the main power cable to the after battery."

Skaggs harrumphed, "Yeah… and we didn't degauss at Fremantle… when this is over, our boat's gonna need a real overhaul."

"Here's that tap and dye you asked for, Will," said a young sailor who'd come aboard at Fremantle named Mitch Headly. Headly was a wiry kid from East Texas who was working on an oil rig before joining up. "Mr. Skaggs…"

Skaggs smiled at the twenty-year old sailor, "I'll tell you what I've been tellin' everybody, Headly. We're gonna be fine. You're on the best boat in the fleet."

Headly, no stranger to dangerous and high-stress environments, nodded, "Yes, sir. Thank you, sir."

"Carry on, fellas," Skaggs said and moved forward once more.

By the time Skaggs had reached the crew's mess, another ghostly wine sang through the dark sea and caressed the hull. This time, however, it was weaker and seemed to come from forward of the port beam.

"How're our sickies, Hank?" Skaggs asked as he looked at the two mess tables where Post and Eckhart had been laid out with blankets and pillows.

"Awake, sir," Eckhart said.

"Oh, they doin' jus' fine, Mr. Skaggs, sir," said Martin, strapping a blood pressure cuff on Post's arm. "Need to keep my eye on dem for a little while, though."

"We're right here, guys," Post grumped.

"Thinking a concussion?" Skaggs asked.

"That's for true," Martin said. "A man hit his noggin hard enough to knock him unconscious… gotta be a bit of bruisin' on dem brain."

"He gar-run-tees," Borshowski jibed.

"Hello?" Eckhart asked pettishly.

"Sounds right to me," Skaggs mused, trying to hide a smile. "What I'll report to the skipper when I go forward."

"How about letting us get back on duty?" Post asked.

"I'll bet they'd like to get back to work," Skaggs said to Martin, as if he hadn't heard.

"You're not funny, Tony," growled Post.

In spite of this declaration, Skaggs, Martin, and Borshowski laughed. Eckhart scowled but the look slowly began to morph into a thin smile.

"Nothin' doin, sir," Martin said to Post. "Bes' you two goin' do is go to you racks for a while. Don't need no trouble."

"Phooey," Post cranked.

Another surrounding sonar blast. Borshowski's broad face looked pinched, especially when the sound was joined by a series of bangs, groans, and a distant squeal.

"Jesus…" Post sighed. "How deep are we anyway?"

"I'd say close to seven fat ones," Skaggs said casually. "I'm headed forward to find that very thing out."

"Now passing seven-zero-zero feet, Elmer," was the first thing Skaggs heard when he ducked through the forward hatch and passed the radio room.

The next thing he heard were no fewer than half a dozen men swearing, blaspheming, and muttering under their breath. He understood how they felt. The ship was now down past her marked test depth and headed to those crushing depths where even previous dives were no guarantee of safety.

"All's well, I trust, Tony?" Williams asked.

"So far, so good, Skipper," Skaggs reported. "Men's morale is a bit shaky, though."

"Could be worse," observed Rogers.

"Yeah, we could be under ash can attack," Dutch mused and then crossed himself.

"What *is* going on, sir?" Skaggs asked.

Williams sighed, "Best we can tell, there are four Jap destroyers spaced out up there around a central cruiser. The cruiser's pinging as if to let us know *exactly* where they are… and the four tin cans are sending simultaneous blasts out."

"So we can't pinpoint their locations," Dutch grumbled.

"And to let us know we're surrounded," Rogers intoned bitterly.

Skaggs looked to the smoky card and stylus mounted over the master gyro compass table. He asked the question, even though he already knew the answer. Perhaps just out of pure hope, "And we've found no layer yet?"

"We have not," Nichols said stonily.

"It's anybody's game at this point," Williams said. "Blind man's bluff… puss in the corner… hide and go seek. But if I had to pick one… I'd say red light, green light."

"Meaning," Dutch added, lighting a pill, "that the first one who moves… makes a sound… could get caught."

"And the clock is ticking," said Williams. "The Jap has all the time in the world. We do not. Finite air, finite electricity… and finite patience, too."

17
LIGHT CRUISER AGANO
0130 – DECEMBER 24, 1942

"I'm surprised to find you awake, Hitake," Friedrich Lanser said quietly as he strode up to the cruiser's taffrail.

Yamata sipped from a steaming mug of tea and gazed absently out at the horizon, "Are you, Friedrich?"

The German smiled thinly, hoisting a cup of his own. He preferred coffee and detested the Japanese obsession with tea. Especially the green variety. To his mind, it was an insipid brew. A drink so synonymous with the Limies and their high-nosed diffidence that the German couldn't help but make unfortunate associations.

To the mind of the average German, especially those in the party, the English were little better than prancing sissies. Yet in spite of this view, the damned Brits could stiffen their upper lips and resist as well as fight back with astonishing tenacity.

Then there were the Japanese. Small by German standards, slight and proper in decorum and conservative in nature. Such a mild-mannered people… and yet they could become unutterably fierce in battle. How strange that was to Lanser.

He could more easily understand the Americans. They were a bit more German in their comportment. Large in stature and personality, bold, aggressive, and often loud. Boisterous people who, in spite of their desire to keep the world at peace, reveled in the fight. Then again, why not? The Americans were made up of the rest of the world, weren't they?

"And what of you, Herr Lanser?" Yamata asked. "What brings you out of your comfortable bunk on this cold Christmas Eve?"

Lanser chuckled, "Indeed it is. At least here. Back home, it's still the twenty-third. How strange, eh? I suppose I'm up for the same reason you are, my friend. We're here to catch a predator... not ample Zs. How long has it been now?"

"Since *Bull Shark* dived or since we've been listening?" Yamata asked.

Lanser sighed, "Both, I suppose. She's been down since just after first light yesterday. Eighteen hours."

"And sixteen since Nashiri dropped his probes," Yamata said, stifling a yawn. "And we have heard nothing... definitive, at least."

"It's possible for that class of boat to stay down for three days," Lanser said.

Yamata harrumphed, "Technically, that's true. And if they are down there, and haven't slipped away in the night, then they haven't used much battery power. Not sitting still. However... eighty men breathing all of that oxygen is certainly going to become a problem for them sooner or later."

"Much as I hate to admit it," Lanser said, swallowing another gulp of green tea, "Nashiri's plan does appear to be working. His thermometer has not detected a temperature change, indicating that down to at least 250 meters the water below us is isothermal. And the four destroyers constantly pinging has perhaps corralled Art Turner."

Yamata offered a non-committal grunt, "For how long? We've begun to drift, and we have no idea of the currents at great depths. For all we know, the American might have simply drifted away and is even now a dozen miles outside of our little cordon."

Lanser frowned, "Perhaps... but I don't think so. Art Turner would not give up so easily."

Yamata chuckled, "Are you saying that faced with four enemy warships, he would engage us? That would hardly be prudent. As aggressive a submarine commander as Turner is, Friedrich, he's still cautious by nature. As any good submarine captain must be. Given the choice, Turner would slink away to fight another day rather than turn and attack out of some sense of vengeance."

Lanser frowned, "Fair enough. As a submariner myself, I cannot argue. Yet… yet we did something to him, I think. That ambush would have affected Turner, especially if our men managed to take out a few of his own."

"We don't know that, however," Yamata retorted. "The last report from those doomed flyers was that they'd opened fire on the submarine."

"And *possibly* hit several men on deck," Lanser reminded him. "To a man like Turner… remember, I *know* him… a man who felt honor bound to help his enemy… and then was betrayed by them… he would take it personally. It would enrage him, to be sure."

Yamata scowled and glanced at the two technicians and the instruments they monitored, "I cannot be convinced of this, Friedrich. It simply flies in the face of all we know… and even if Turner is massaging a vendetta… would he not be more likely to make it a cold one?"

Lanser shrugged, "Perhaps… perhaps… but my gut instinct says that Turner will turn and attack, especially if cornered too long."

Yamata nodded, "Of that, I'm sure. Perhaps we might—"

"*Captain Yamata, Commander Lanser, please report to the radio booth.*"

This announcement over the ship's PA drew an arched look from the two men. They moved forward quickly, climbing up to the command level and entering the small radio room aft of the navigation bridge.

To their surprise, Captain Nashiri was already there, scanning a hand-written missive passed to him by the comm officer of the watch. *Agano's* skipper glanced up and nodded at the two newcomers. Without a word, he bent down, scribbled something onto a loose sheet of paper and handed it to the ensign in charge.

"See that this is encoded and broadcast to Truk," said Nashiri. "No doubt the admiral will want to hear of this upon waking. Come, gentlemen, let us retire to the chart table."

Nashiri went out, moved forward on the catwalk and entered the navigation bridge. At that late hour, the compartment was quiet. The officer of the deck stood between the chart table and the helmsman's post in the pilothouse and several other sailors went about their duties in near silence.

"Captain on the bridge!" noted the chief of the watch, albeit sedately.

"Sir!" the OOD snapped to attention. "What may I—"

Nashiri waved the man off, "At ease, Lieutenant. My guests and I have some information to review. Please do not let us disturb you."

The young officer bowed and turned back to his duties, occasionally cocking an ear and casting a glance aft at the senior officers.

"I wish to get your opinions," Nashiri said, tapping the chart where their position was marked. He then tapped another spot fifty or so miles to the southeast, a point off East Timor in the Timor Sea. "Do you recognize these positions?"

"Ours," Lanser said immediately, indicating the multiple Xs the captain had first tapped.

"And this one?" Yamata asked, pointing to the distant mark. "Is this where the patrol trawler was lost?"

Nashiri nodded, "Very good, gentlemen. That spot is indeed where we lost a boat several nights ago. Indicating an enemy vessel in the area. A vessel that attacked with guns rather than torpedoes, or so the trawler reported before we lost contact. It was dismissed as either a night attack by an aircraft out of Darwin… or an Australian or American destroyer having overtaken the patrol."

"But now, based on our situation and the loss of the seaplane carrier," Yamata said, "*we* believe that a submarine attacked using deck guns."

"And that such an attack executed so quickly indicates a considerable topside armament," Lanser added.

Now Nashiri smiled, "Just so. My compliments on your perspicacity, sirs. Any ideas?"

"Certainly," said Lanser. "The USS *Bull Shark* is unique, at least thus far, as having *two* deck guns. One forward and one aft of the conning tower. Further, they are five-inch... 125 millimeters. Quite heavy. She also boasts a quad barrel Bofors 40mm AA gun as well as the standard twin-barreled Oerlikon."

"More than a match for poor *Ragusai*," Nashiri stated. "And we now have something else to ponder... please study this, Teacher."

Yamata took the message and scanned it. His brows rose, then sunk as he scanned it again. He looked up with a bemused expression. Lanser looked between the two men.

"There have been a series of attacks," Yamata explained, interpreting the Japanese codes for Lanser. "On the eastern portion of Timor. Several trucks with men on liberty failed to report in the other night... a bridge some thirty miles to the west was attacked and the village on the western bank as well."

"That village was a command outpost for a half-company of the Army," Nashiri explained and then smirked. "No wonder it was taken so easily. The Army does tend to get careless, especially during inclement weather. Reports are that some Allied soldiers stole a truck and ambushed the guards, in spite of being prepared. They might have prevailed, except that a platoon of Australians... no doubt the commandos left behind... joined the fray and overwhelmed the outpost. Communication was lost shortly after this report."

"What does this have to do with us?" Lanser asked.

Yamata thought he knew, "*Bull Shark?* They set men ashore?"

"Did you notice the source of this message, Yamata?" Nashiri asked.

Yamata glanced at the page again and nodded, "The flagship... it also says that an asset in Fremantle indicated that a two-gunned submarine was seen in the harbor and left several days earlier. There is also the possibility that a British commando, possibly an SAS Colonel, went aboard. Interesting...."

"Interesting it might be," Lanser said, some irritation at feeling out of the loop creeping in. "But I fear I'm not quite up to speed."

Nashiri's smile was broad, and he took evident pleasure in being ahead of the German and the Sensei as well, "It would indicate that it is *indeed Bull Shark* we're facing. And that they delivered men ashore several nights ago. And perhaps... just perhaps... some of her own men, as there was no indication from our spy that any other commandos went aboard."

"Leverage," said Yamata and smiled. "I believe I should like to make a call at first light, Captain. I have some friends who may wish to hear this."

BULL SHARK

"How we doing up here, fellas?" Joe Dutch asked quietly as he stepped through the hatchway.

The lights were low in the forward torpedo room. As it was the middle of the middle watch, men not on duty were snoozing in their racks. Hours before, Williams had taken the ship off general quarters as well as secured from depth charge and silent running. The understanding was that said conditions may begin at any moment and quiet was still to be observed.

"Lot better now that we don't have to heave around, sir," Perry Wilkes, petty officer in charge of the room while Tommy Perkins slept, said quietly and flashed a grin. "Hotter'n a snake's ass in a wagon rut, though... pardon my French, sir."

Dutch snorted, involuntarily wiping at his damp brow, "Yeah, humidity's up and in spite of the depth, we're over eighty-five."

"Somethin' official we can do for ya', sir?" Bob Jones asked, snapping a Zippo under a smoke and failing to get a flame. "Shit..."

Dutch moved forward so that he was between the breeches and closer to the two men, "Yeah... want to be sure we're okay up here, what with this long dunk and heavy humidity. About ninety-five percent says the meter. Skipper might call for a basketful of fish and I want we should be able to oblige him."

"We done reloaded, sir," Jones said. "All six got WSL tags as you can see."

The red tag that hung from the inner torpedo tube breech wheel stood for war shot loaded. Dutch nodded and smiled.

"I know I'm mother henning, fellas... but we're in a pinch here and can't afford any snafus," Dutch explained. "If we get a shot... one is all we're likely to get."

Wilkes nodded, "I see what you mean, sir… with all due respect… what the hell's goin' on? We ain't had a meal in eighteen hours outside sandwiches and pastries. Been buttoned up silent as the grave and every minute or two, them Japs pings the stuffin' out of us."

"As you were, Perry," came a soft voice from the gloom near the starboard bulkhead. A dark figure slid out from a bunk and materialized under the lone bulb near the control panel and revealed itself to be Tommy Perkins. "Mr. Dutch don't need no insubordination papers on top of everything else he's gotta do."

Perkins had been placed in charge of the room while Walter "Sparky" Sparks was on leave. His laid-back demeanor and California surfer accent gave the man a gregarious and irresistible air. However, when push came to shove and the chips were down, Perkins was as serious and demanded… and *got*… as much respect as Sparky.

"I don't mean to lip off or nothin', sir…" Wilkes said.

Dutch held up a hand, "No offense taken, Perry. Honestly, we're not sure what's goin' on either. Sort of why I'm takin' a turn through the boat. Not just as gunnery officer but as XO. Want to put my finger on the pulse of the crew and give you guys a heads up. So far as we know, there's five Jap ships up top, arranged in a cross. Four tin cans and a cruiser at the center. We're close to the center. It stopped right about where we tagged that seaplane tender."

"So they're bangin' away trying to find us?" Jones asked.

"Let the man talk, Jonesy," Perkins urged.

Dutch smiled, "Exactly. Way we figure it, and its mine and Chet Rivers's personal opinion, that each tin can is about a thousand yards away from the center. They're all going active at once to let us know we're surrounded but so's we can't pinpoint 'em."

"Clever slants…" Wilkes said. "And the center guy does it, so we know he's right up there? But sir… pressure gauge says we're at 815… boat sounds like an old man's knees and…"

"How long can we last like this?" Dutch asked and sighed. "Nobody knows. We're pushing it, that's for sure. Already got a foot in the bilgeways and we can't risk the pumps. But I think the skipper's had it and is ready to try something."

"We'll be ready, sir," Perkins said. "We'll get the gang up and double-check all connections if you want."

"I appreciate that, Perry," Dutch said and sighed. "Give the boys until 0230, though. I'll send a runner when I think it's time."

"You got it, sir... XO," Wilkes said and smiled.

"Yeah, thanks for cluing us in, sir," said Jones.

Thirty minutes later, Joe Dutch was back in the control room with a towel slung around his neck. While the temperature in the boat was warm going on uncomfortable, the temperature in the sea at over 800 feet, even in the tropics, was hardly more than fifty degrees. Yet this was causing its own problems in the form of rampant condensation throughout the boat.

Where there was still good cork insulation, the bulkheads remained dry. However, where it'd come off during the depth charging and where it ended for the purposes of fittings, pipes, hinges, and the like, the hot air in the boat was turning the exposed metal slick with heavy dew.

"How we doing, Joey?" Williams asked. He leaned against the ladder, sipping coffee and appearing as ragged as Dutch felt. The acting executive officer couldn't help but notice the heavy dark circles under the acting captain's eyes and wondered how much longer they could stand the strain.

Not one of the officers or chiefs had slept since they'd first sighted the seaplane tender the previous morning. Several of them had been on watch and had now been awake for over twenty hours. The men, the officers, and the boat herself were beginning to buckle under the tension.

"Hanging on by fingernails, Elmer," Dutch said. "We don't figure something out... and someone or something is gonna crack. We've got condensation and actual leaks from a dozen through hulls and its getting worse. At some point, we're gonna have to shit or get off the pot."

"I'm open to suggestions," Williams said, his voice taut with frustration.

"What would the captain do?" Nichols asked.

"I dunno, Frank!?" Williams snapped, turning on the haggard

engineer. "How the hell should I know? What would you do? How about that?"

Nichols blinked in surprise and cast a glance at Dutch and Skaggs, who stood by the gyro table with uncertain looks on their faces, "Elmer… sir… I…"

Williams closed his eyes and rubbed at them with the heels of both hands, "Aw hell… I'm sorry, Frank. I guess it's getting to me, too. To be honest, I wish Art Turner were here. I'm sure he'd know what to do. Between being dog-tired and lacking information…"

"The captain wouldn't give up, sir," Buck Rogers said. "And nobody else is gonna either. He ain't here but this ain't nothin' you can't handle, Mr. Williams… Captain. There's a way out of any trap."

"A trap…" Williams sighed. "That's what we're in, aren't we? Caught at the bottom of a well just waiting for the ash cans to fall on us."

"Or stuck in the center of a web… waiting for the spider to climb down and sink her fangs in," Dutch sighed.

A silence as weighty as the 344 pounds per square inch that the Banda Sea was currently exerting on the ship's hull. The analogies had done nothing for morale, and indeed, seemed to pile more depression on. At least until their temporary captain's eyes glowed with the light of an idea.

"Yeah… the bottom… the center…" Williams said. "The Japs *know* we're down here. And either they can't find us or are waiting us out. They know our air and juice can't last forever… and at some point, we've got to make a run for it."

"Why they're bein' so quiet, too," Rogers opined.

"Because they *expect* us to be deep," Williams said. "To have found a salt layer to hide in and to escape with…"

"But we haven't found one yet," Nichols said.

"No… which is interesting, isn't it?" Williams asked, warming to his subject and the animation in his face and voice energizing the others too, even the enlisted men listening quietly at their stations. "After all this time? Why haven't they bugged out?"

"Because… they know there isn't a layer?" Dutch asked.

Williams nodded, "Maybe somebody has a thermometer or saline meter or something up there… maybe even a hydrophone. Point is… they know… or *think* they know… that we're down deep. Maybe as deep as we are."

"So do you have a plan, Elmer?" Dutch asked.

Williams's face slowly morphed as a wry smile began to grow, "Y'know, XO… I think I might… think I just might at that…"

18

EAST TIMOR

DECEMBER 23, 1942

"Captain Arthur Turner, Captain Gus Cooper, Second Independent Commandos," Archer introduced.

"Blimey! A Yank? Army or Marines, Cobber?" Cooper asked, smiling and holding out a hand to Turner.

The submarine captain smiled crookedly, unsure of what to make of the ebullient Australian, "U.S. Navy, Captain. Commander of the submarine *Bull Shark*. At your service."

Cooper's mouth dropped open, "Navy? Submarine? What the bloody *hell*... er... begging your pardon, sir, it's..."

Archer grinned, "Anvil Art they call him, Gus. He was kind enough to give me a lift and provide me with a few of his lads as an escort. The captain and these men here have had some experience fighting in the jungle."

"Crikey!" Cooper emoted, glancing around at the sopping wet and muddy sailors and their Thompsons. "Well, for our part, lads, we're glad to have a few more men... with SMGs to boot! Welcome to Timor. Not to sound ungrateful, Colonel... but what in the name of Great Caesar's ghost are you doing here?"

Archer harrumphed, "Think I'd leave my boys out in the cold, Gus? Rot! I've come with gifts. In the back of our truck here. A radio set and a few odds and ends. I trust you've set up a command post nearby? How many of you are there?"

Cooper sighed, looking about him as his men went about the job of securing each building in the village. The Japanese that were still alive had been herded into the half-wrecked building behind which the newcomers had taken shelter. Villagers were being either released or coming out from hiding.

"Me and this platoon, sir," Cooper said. "Lieutenant Smithers and his lads are with me as well. They've taken up a patrol between our post and Dili, however. It's rather advantageous you lot have arrived, actually. We've selected a rather choice target for our next raid, Colonel."

Archer nodded, "Excellent. And Captain… Gus… what of Ananda?"

Turner watched as the two men's eyes met. Something passed between them that he couldn't decipher but that put him on edge. He couldn't have said why just then. Perhaps it was the softness and worry in Archer's tone… but something began to worry at the back of his mind like a dog at a rope toy.

"She's all right, sir," Cooper said, smiling. "In fact… she's back at the CP. She'll be tickled to see you, sir."

Turner stepped forward, "Who's Ananda?"

Archer appeared relieved, "Remember the lady I mentioned who had a connection to the Portuguese governor?"

Turner nodded, "You know her personally, then."

"That I do," said Archer and looked to Cooper. "We'd best be about it, Captain. No doubt the Nips will be sending in scouts to determine why they lost contact here. We've got trucks now, and—"

"With respect, sir," said Cooper, "they won't be of much use, at least not for long. Roads are poor on this island, and our path back is straight up into the hills. That and it might be better for us did the Jap begin aerial reconnoitering not to be seen in stolen vehicles."

Turner heard Tank groan from behind him and endeavored to hide a smile, "Makes sense. But we do have a rather heavy crate, Captain."

"Oh, no worries, mate… er… sir," Cooper grinned. "My lads'll be happy to take a turn at muling. Along with yours. What say you, lads? Captain Cooper at your service. And you all?"

Turner introduced his men, ending with Hoffman, "Our pharmacist's mate, Captain. Closest a submarine can come to a doctor. If you have any medical issues, Hank here may be able to lend a hand."

"That's bloody great!" enthused Cooper. "Well, sirs, if you'll indulge me a moment… bit of business to attend to… Sergeant Vickers!"

This last was bawled into the rain and a moment later, a tall, lean man in his early thirties appeared. His dress, like the rest of Cooper and his men, was somewhat the worse for wear. Permanently stained, torn in more than one place, and missing several buttons on the fatigue blouse. He stopped, came to attention, and saluted.

"Sergeant Wallace Vickers reporting as ordered, *SIR!*"

Cooper grinned, "Bag it, Sarge. Look who's come a 'callin'."

Vickers blinked, "Colonel Archer, sir? Well, I'll be buggered!"

Archer nodded, "Sergeant. Glad to see you well."

"Vickers, this fellow is a genuine American submarine commander, and these four lads are with him," Archer explained. "They've brought us a few bits and could use a hand unloading and getting acquainted with our ways. Take them in hand, will you?"

"Yes, sir," Vickers said. He stared at Turner. "Submarine, sir?"

Turner nodded, "That's right, Captain. With some shore combat experience. Was with the Marines on Guadalcanal."

"By Jove…" Vickers said and then turned to Turner's men. "Well, fellows, show me the way and I'll fill you in. Any guts from Aus, then?"

Tank blinked, "Guts?"

"That's Digger slang, mate," Vickers said, correctly identifying Tank as the senior rating. "Means information. News as it were."

Turner couldn't help but grin as Vickers and his men moved off toward their pilfered truck. He was compelled to comment, "Your men are in good spirits, Captain."

Cooper shrugged, "This sort of rot is what we're trained for, sir… oh, one moment… that the lot, Peters?"

Cooper called over to a trio of his men who were escorting half a dozen villagers toward them. One of the Aussies, Peters, apparently, waved a hand.

"Yes, sir! Near as we can tell!" said the soldier.

"Very good," said Cooper and at first, Turner didn't take note of the change in the man's demeanor. He'd turned cold and stony in the blink of an eye. "Line 'em up, then."

The six confused and bedraggled villagers, perhaps Portuguese or perhaps Malay, Turner couldn't tell, were lined up side by side. They looked around in confusion as the three soldiers backed away and formed another line facing them from a distance of perhaps six yards.

"What the *hell?*" Turner stepped toward them but was stopped by an iron-fingered grip on his shoulder.

"At ease, Arthur," Turner turned to see that Archer's eyes were as icy as his tone had been.

Turner looked back in time to witness the second volley of three shots from Peters's and his two companions' rifles. He saw three villagers crumble into a heap beside the three already bleeding out in the mud.

"What's the meaning of this?" Turner snapped, yanking free of Archer's grip and rounding on him and Cooper.

Cooper's eyes, too, were chips of glacial ice. Completely gone was the gregarious man he'd just met and, in his place, a stone-cold killer. Turner was as sure of that as he was that it was still raining.

"Collaborators," Cooper worked his mouth around the word as if it were edged in shattered glass. "They were found in comfortable housing. No doubt a privilege of helping the little yellow bastards. Proceed, Peters!"

The three Aussie soldiers turned and lined up in front of the blasted-out wall of the structure that had so recently been the Americans' cover. They raised their rifles and fired. Three quick, efficient volleys. Nine shots.

There had been nine Japs sequestered inside the building.

Turner felt sick. He stared in horror at the evidently casual brutality. Although he wasn't particularly sorry for the Japs… he was mildly surprised to find a bit of sympathy for them. Something about being gunned down when you were tied up and helpless…

"Don't tell me you object to that, Arthur?" Archer asked, smiling and waving a hand at the scene twenty yards away.

Turner swallowed, and found his voice, "It's a bit… cold, isn't it?"

Cooper snorted, "Been rather unpleasant here since the Sparrows left, Captain. I've lost good men to these slant fuckers. More because of cowardly little shit collaborators buying their freedom with Australian blood. So I don't apologize for being harsh."

"I see," said Turner, intellectually understanding but finding his emotions oddly mixed.

"The good captain here recently saw a similar situation," Archer explained. "Stopped to help some down Nip flyers and they bushwhacked him. Killed four of his men, including his torpedo officer."

"Hard luck, mate," Cooper said. "Been no bloody picnic on this rock either. No support, Nips everywhere… people you thought you could trust turning on you. Bad business, this."

Archer smiled then, breaking the tension, or at least trying, "Art here is just sorry you didn't let him pull the trigger, Gus. Took out a Nip barehanded last night."

"Good on ya', sir," Cooper said. "Well, if you'll excuse me… we'll get the lads organized and put this balls up behind us."

At the rear of the stolen truck, Tank stepped closer to Vickers after seeing at least part of the execution, "What the fuck was all that, Sarge?"

"All what, mate?" Vickers asked, eyeballing the crate inside the truck's covered bed.

"Your boys just gunning down those locals," Tank asked.

Vickers glanced at the big sailor and at the frowns on the other three Americans' faces, "Collaborators, mate. Bloody sympathizers who bargain for special treatment at the expense of others. Notably tossing some of our men to the dogs. Bloody Portuguese niggers aren't worth a cunt full of cold piss."

"Maybe they don't have any choice, Sarge," Swooping Hawk said, his frown turning to a scowl. "Japs come in and hold a gun to their head, what're they supposed to do?"

"Keep their fucking mouths shut, that's what," Vickers snapped.

He eyed Swooping Hawk for a long moment, noting his square features and the slight tinge of red in his skin. "You aren't quite White, are you, lad?"

Swooping Hawk's amber eyes narrowed, "No… I'm an Indian. A Navajo."

Vickers actually grinned, "Ah! An aborigine, then! Smashing. Got hordes of them back in Aus. Black fellas, though. Bloody good bushman. Glad to know you, Cobber."

That took Swooping Hawk aback, "Uhm… thanks… same here…"

"Now look, lads," Vickers said. "I know you're used to submarines and all that rot. But I also here some of you have shore experience. This sort of war… the sort we're fighting… Guerilla warfare, don't you know. It's… a bit different than the usual round. We're not just fighting the enemy. We're fighting to survive."

"Seems like shooting natives is going beyond the line," Hoffman said.

Tank drew in a breath and held up a hand, "Let's not judge, fellas. Sergeant Vickers is right. Shore warfare can be a dirty business."

"Good on ya', mate," Vickers said. My friend's call me Wally… or just Wall. "Now… let's see about getting this box out and being on our way, eh?"

* * *

The journey into the hills was fairly easy at first. A series of raids and paths led into forested areas that slowly climbed up the hills and toward the craggy peaks that separated the center of the island and were the source of the South and North Laclo rivers. The rain stopped sometime after noon and the men slowly began to dry out, although with the cooling effect of the storm gone, the remaining moisture and tropical warmth soon replaced water with sweat.

Also, in spite of the sky clearing, the going became difficult, as the troop had to stay away from anything that might be a settlement or a well-used path. On one occasion, during the middle of that afternoon, one of the forward scouts reported a group of six Japanese soldiers bathing in a stream high up in the hills. Archer elected to circumvent them rather than engage, simply so that the area wouldn't be suspected by the enemy as a guerilla location.

Near sunset, the troop topped a hill and found a small valley between the hills and the true jagged mountains. The valley was small, with a placid lake perhaps four or five acres in size and a set of grassy fields not much larger. In these fields and ambling in and out of a ramshackle barn were a loose herd of sheep going about their business, which amounted to grazing, creating fertilizer, and baying incessantly.

Here and there, a native man wandered among them, his crooked staff at the ready and doing little more than keeping an eye on their charges. When the two men saw the two dozen soldiers wander out of the forest, neither one appeared alarmed. Indeed, they both waved and received waves in return.

"With your permission, sir," Vickers said as the group paused by what might generously be called a rutted track that lead to the two-story farmhouse. "I'll get the lads squared away and this gear set up, shall I?"

"Yes, do, Sergeant," Archer said. "Show our Yank friends where we bunk down and see that they're given food and a chance to clean up. I'll go up to the house and call on our hostess."

"Very good, sir," Vickers said and turned to the men, specifically making eye contact with Tank. "Come along, lads. Been a trying day, eh? Let's have ourselves a bit of a cork."

Tank glanced over at Turner, "Sir?"

"Go ahead, Tank," Turner said. "See that the sergeant gets his radio set up and you and the fellas relax a bit. I'll recon the sitch here."

"Aye-aye," said Tank and reached down to heave up one end of the crate.

"Well trained lads," Archer noted. "Come along, Old Boy. I want you to meet a friend of mine. Assuming she's in, in course."

The farmhouse appeared somewhat odd to Turner. He'd gotten used to the building style and lifestyle he'd seen on Guadalcanal. Grass and bamboo huts and people who lived little differently than they had for thousands of years, probably. On Timor, he'd seen some of that but the influence of western culture and probably eastern, had penetrated more deeply.

The house might have come right out of any mid-western farm region or perhaps even an English country manor. Two floors with a pitched roof and even several dormers that the captain could see. The front of the house featured a full-width porch on the front. The place was situated so that its rear faced the lake behind. Turner guessed the place had at least four or five bedrooms on the second floor.

"Not too shabby, eh?" Archer asked as they left the rutted track that ambled around the left side of the house and onto a flagstone walk leading to the three porch steps. "Governor's mountain place, you know. Hoity-toity."

"And his... uhm... Ananda? She has the use of it, I take it?" Turner asked.

Archer harrumphed, "It's actually *hers*, Old Boy. Been in her family for several generations. She's of Malay and European blood, Ananda. Lovely, sweet and kind. Too good for that cowardly fool she entertains now and again."

Turner heard the distinct flare of bitterness, even anger, in the man's voice. He was beginning to get a better picture of just who this Ananda woman was.

However, when the front door opened and a figure appeared in it, cried out with joy and flew down the steps, arms wide, Turner's picture came into much sharper focus.

Ananda, if that's who it was, was a tall, slim woman in her late twenties. She had the sunkissed skin of a Malay and flowing raven hair to match. However, her face was lean and her nose small, with large blue eyes that bespoke her Portuguese heritage.

"Percy!" Ananda all but shrieked with joy. "Jesus and Mary!"

Ananda's light cotton shift billowed about her as she flew into Archer's arms. His filth seemed in no way to discommode her as she wrapped her arms around him and kissed him with a passion and intensity that nearly caused Turner to blush.

The picture was crystal clear now.

Archer returned her fervor with his own. After a moment, the pair broke apart, breathless and flushed. Archer grinned and cleared his throat, "Ahem... Ananda Ribeiro, allow me to introduce you to a friend of mine. Captain Arthur Turner, USS *Bull Shark*."

"Ma'am," Turner said, reaching up to tip his dirty cover to her.

"American?" she asked in bewilderment and then. "A ship?"

"Submarine," Turner said. "I brought Percy here with a few supplies for his men."

She stepped forward and held out her hands to him, a brilliant smile lighting up what was a very pretty face, "And so I owe you a debt, sir. You brought my Percy back to me. I'm very pleased to meet you."

"Sir, I've seen to the... oh, Ananda, hello," Gus Cooper said as he rounded the side of the house. He too tipped his cap.

"Gus, you found them!" Ananda said.

"Yes, ma'am."

Ananda chuckled and then stepped back, looking at the three bedraggled officers, "You boys look like you've been in a tumble or three. =Good lord!"

"Been a bit of a day or two, love," Archer said, offering a wry smile.

Ananda placed her hands on her hips, "Well, this simply won't do. Come, gentlemen. Let's get you out of those filthy clothes and see that they're cleaned up. No doubt those packs are a burden as well."

"We don't want to impose, ma'am," Turner said. "I'm happy to go and see to my men..."

"Nonsense!" Ananda insisted. "We have power and running water here, Captain. All the luxuries of home. Please, let me offer you the hospitality of my house."

The inside of the home matched the outside and drew Turner even further out of time and space. Quality furniture, if a bit more on the function than form side adorned the front parlor and dining room. A variety of pleasing bits of art and knick-knacks hung on the walls and decorated the mantlepiece. The atmosphere was homey and warm... and it filled Turner with indescribable sadness and loneliness.

He missed Joan and the kiddos something awful. Standing there, surrounded by warm, still air redolent with old hardwood, freshly cut flowers and cinnamon drew out an aching in his heart he could hardly bear.

Before his mind's eye, Turner saw the smiling faces of Arty and Dotty, the brilliant and mischievous smile of his lovely wife... and then he saw ghosts. Sailors that had died under his command. He saw Joe Hadley, lying on deck in a spreading pool of his own blood... he saw Porter Hazard's eyes, frozen in surprise by the cold hand of death... Milt Zagler's pallid and bloated face swam up toward him, the black and dead eyes accusatory...

"Art..."

Turner flinched, tearing himself from his reverie and turning to face Archer, "Colonel... yes?"

"You all right, Old Man?"

"Just swell."

"Good... shower's available, if you're keen for a scrub down. Ananda's got some spare togs we can wear until the laundry's done."

Turner scoffed, "Hot shower... how about our men?"

"Same for them," Archer said. "Bunk house has facilities. Well and a diesel genny. Come on, man... take what you can while you can. You all right?"

Turner sighed, "Are any of us?"

After his much needed and astonishingly welcome shower, Turner donned a pair of duck trousers and a pullover made from sheep's wool. His fatigues and boots were gone, and instead he found a pair of sandals that were a close enough fit to do.

The house was quiet, as if it were some fortress against reality, keeping out the war and the suffering that seemed to coat the Earth. Turner ambled down the hall and downstairs, neither hearing or seeing anyone. A waft of something mouth-watering filled the downstairs and he fought down the urge to peak into the kitchen. Instead, he moved to the back porch to have a smoke and try and figure out what the hell to do next.

The submarine captain was mildly surprised to find Gus Cooper already there, puffing on a pipe and sipping, of all things, a Foster's. Like Turner, he was dressed in loose white duck trousers and a blue woolen pullover.

"Evening, Skipper," said the genial Australian. He waved Turner into a chair beside him and to a large and unopened can of beer next to his own. "Have a sit and enjoy a sipper on me. Church key's right there."

"Thanks," said Turner, poking two holes in the can and sipping. "Ahhh… any chance our boys can get a few of these?"

"Many as they can, sir," Cooper said. "Don't worry yourself about that, Captain. Sergeant Vickers will see to them. Lovely evening, eh? Now that the sun's gone down, might be in the seventies."

Turner lit a Lucky Strike and settled back, "Hard to believe we're two days from Christmas."

Cooper grinned, "Maybe for you lot. Down under its summertime. No white Christmases here, I fear. White June, though."

"Sitting here like this… hard to imagine there's a war raging out there," Turner waved his smoke vaguely at the mountains behind the lake.

"Yeah… well, we don't get many chances to forget around here," Cooper said. "Indeed, by this time tomorrow… we might be in a real rarey show."

Turner glanced over, "How's that?"

"Me and Smithers… that's the lieutenant in charge of our other platoon… only officer I've got other than myself these days… anyway, we've located a prime target for a real hard raid. Give the Jap what-for and bloody his yellow nose."

"Oh?"

"Little village called Mindelo, Cooper said. "Other side of the mountains. Bloody Nips been using it as a supply and communication depot. Got half a company there, at least at times."

"And you want to hit this place with one platoon?" Turner asked.

"Two. Smithers should join us. Forty men… a few more if you and the colonel and your lads join us. Surprise attack, swift, hard, and final. Go a long way in making the Jap think twice. Also eliminates a listening station so we can use that kit you brought in more safety."

"I didn't bring my men here to fight a war," Turner said. "At least, not here."

Cooper eyed him sidelong and drained his beer, "Way I

understand it, Captain… you've got a score to settle with Tojo. Be a grand chance, eh?"

Turner harrumphed, "And a good chance to get my men killed where they have no business being. Besides… is Colonel Archer behind this plan?"

Cooper's open expression seemed to fold in on itself. He cast a furtive glance upward toward the house's second floor, "I'm sure he will… if he can divert enough attention to the problem."

Turner nodded in understanding, "They seem to have… a close relationship."

Cooper chuckled, "That's puttin' it lightly. Wasn't for her, why…"

Turner couldn't let that go. He flicked his ash and leaned in, spearing Cooper with a hard glare, "Wasn't for her, *what*, Captain?"

Cooper shrugged and offered a weak smile, "Not for me to say, sir."

"To hell with *that*," Turner snapped. "My men and I risked life and limb to get here, Cooper. Brought you and your men a radio set because your colonel believes it'll help you in this conflict here. Now if there's more to this, I need to know… those are *my* men out there being put at risk and—"

"I've got bloody men, too!" Cooper snapped, his anger roaring up like a gas-fueled blaze. "And they number twenty less now! Twenty less thanks to this goddamned *conflict!* A conflict we've no business fighting. Not with so few. Most of our regulars buggered off and left us behind to stand on our own two… well, that's just what we've done."

"Including Archer?" Turner asked. "I had to bring him back… he *did* come back for all of that."

Cooper harrumphed, "Yeah… I don't blame him for having to go, you understand. Was the correct thing… he's a fine officer, fine soldier… but make no mistake, Captain Turner. He's not here for you, me, or our men."

Now Turner glanced up at the second-floor windows, behind which Archer and Ananda were no doubt making up for lost time. He looked down slowly and met Cooper's gaze again.

"Are you telling me all this was to get back to *her?*"

Cooper sighed, "I'm not saying anything along the lines that the colonel doesn't believe in this goal. He trained us, after all. But I *will* say that... that beating the Jap isn't his primary motivation."

"Son of a bitch..." Turner whispered and would've said more, except that an unexpected swell of guilt kept him silent.

Was he any better? Hadn't he volunteered... forced himself was more like it... for this mission for personal reasons? Sure, the welfare of Tank, Freddy, Hank, and Lee was important to him... but what was *really* important?

The vivid image of strangling the Jap soldier the night before bloomed onto Turner's mental movie screen in full technicolor and refused to be batted away.

"Son of a bitch..." his whisper was swallowed by the oncoming night.

19

Turner stepped from a dark hallway and into a cavernous, high-ceiling place nearly as shadowy. For although there were tall, stained-glass windows to either side of the long space… little of the sunshine outside bled through.

It was a church, of that Turner was certain. A double row of orderly pews marched forward toward an altar whose detail was swallowed by the heavy gloom. Silhouettes stuck up from the backs of the pews… broad masculine ones, slimmer feminine ones, and low round ones that must be the heads of children. None of the inky figures moved, yet low murmurs hovered in the air like the wisps of sea fog.

Whatever had drawn people into this chapel, it certainly wasn't a happy occasion.

"Welcome to the party, Art."

Turner froze, solidified by the ice water now pounding through his veins. After a time, he found he was able to move, albeit slowly… dragging himself around through thick fuel oil. He desperately did not want to see the speaker… would give anything not to confirm what he damned well knew… yet he was forced to by titanic compulsion.

Standing just a few feet behind the last pew were a group of men dressed all in black from head to foot, save their crisp white dress shirts, the pearly cuffs neatly extending beyond their jackets, and a touch of gold on their ties. An iron fist of pain and guilt crushed Turner's heart at the sight of Porter Hazard, standing at the head of the group.

"Port..." Turner heard his own voice from far down in a hollow valley. "What...?"

"Paying our respects, sir," said Wendel Freeman.

Marty Janslotter was there, too, standing beside Milt Zagler, Joe Hadley, and Jimmy Snyder... there were others as well. Vague, pale faces whose features eluded Turner but whose identities he was certain he knew. He thought that Tom Begley and Burt Pendergast might even be among them. A crowd of tenebrous figures who all had one thing in common.

They shared the waxwork pallor and sunken eyed stare of corpses.

Turner reached out to his friend, desperate to touch the man but terrified by what he'd feel when he did, "Port... I... respects for what?"

"It's a funeral, Art," said Hazard. "For them... for us; it's an initiation."

That was confusing.... or at least, Turner wanted it to be. Deep down he somehow knew the significance of what Hazard had said. He would've asked, except three new figures stepped out of the cave-like entry hall. And in spite of the strangle hold the shadows held over the church, the three newcomers stood out in sharp, brilliant relief.

"Joan!" Turner exclaimed, his heart thundering as it leapt for joy. "Arty! Dotty!"

They didn't seem to hear him. They stopped, but did not turn their heads his way. That's when he took note of their clothing. All black... Joan and Dorothy in black dresses and young Arthur Jr. in a black suit and tie.

The soaring of his heart was abruptly jerked back down toward despair by the frigid, steel claws of terror that now clutched it.

"Joanie..." Turner pleaded, reaching out, longing to feel her hand... yearning to hear her voice. "Joanie!"

She did turn then. Her lovely blue eyes met his and for a single heartbeat, the fear was gone and the joy held sway... until she spoke, and Turner's world spiraled into horror.

"Hello, Art," said Joan somberly.

"Joanie... what're you doing here? What is this?"

"What do you mean? This is for you, Art, honey."

The truth loomed up behind him like a scythe-wielding specter, but Turner still ran from it, "For me? I don't understand... where are you going? Stay here with me."

Joan's smile was lovely but the sadness in her eyes made his belly ache, "I'm sorry, Art... we can't. You made your choice."

"Why, Daddy?" Dotty asked.

"Yeah, Pop... why?" Arty added.

"I don't understand... of *course* I want to be with you! You three are my choice! Joan, please... why?"

"Because you're *dead*, Arthur Turner!" Joan's angry words and the twisted expression of bitter rage on her face were a hot knife in his belly. She pointed an accusatory finger at the illusory figures nearby. "*They're* more important, so now you can be with *them... forever!*"

Joan whirled around and hurried toward the altar. Art reached out and clutched at her sleeve, but his fingers passed through nothing.

"No..." he pleaded, his words strangled by despair.

Then multiple pairs of cold hands settled on his arms and shoulders. Eerie voices from the past spoke to him, the low soothing tones carrying an undercurrent of malevolent glee.

"You're always welcome with us, Art," said Hazard.

"Yeah... part of us, now, sir..." Janslotter said.

"Forever and ever..." another muttered.

They laughed, softly and quietly as blackness overtook him.

"No!" Turner thrashed and couldn't break their grip. "*NOOOO!*"

The church, the men, the cold dead hands were gone. He lay in a soft bed, the sheets damp with his sweat. A rectangle of pale moonlight spilled through the open window to splash upon a hardwood floor and onto the foot of the bed. Outside, a trio of crickets sang to one another while a distant owl hooted its ethereal song.

Turner's heart raced and his breath was short. He wiped a hand across his eyes and drew it back again, damp with tears. Taking several long, slow breaths, he calmed himself and got to his feet, groping outside the moonbeam for his trousers and shirt.

The glowing hands of his watch said it was a few minutes after midnight. Christmas Eve... Christmas Eve and he was four thousand miles from the warmth and love of his family. In a strange house in a strange land doing an even stranger job.

"Jesus..." muttered the captain and he padded out into the hall, moving silently toward the dark staircase.

The entire evening had been replete with a sense of wrongness for Turner. In spite of the friendly talk, the hearty meal of lamb stew, roasted potatoes, and fresh vegetables, it'd all seemed oddly disjointed to Turner. Watching Archer and Ananda together was the icing on the cake. The idea that all of this had only been to get Archer back to his lover was becoming ever clearer.

Yes, they'd delivered a teleradio set to Cooper along with some ammunition and a few sundries... but was that worth the potential lives of his men?

As he crept out onto the back porch, lighter and cigarettes in hand, the message from his terrible and vivid dream was not lost on Turner. He'd been dead... perhaps killed on Timor and reunited with his lost men. But at what cost? The eternal separation from those he loved most?

"What the hell am I *doing* out here?"

He'd told himself back aboard *Bull Shark* that he was there to watch over Tank and the others. That after what happened to Hazard and Freeman and the other men on that terrible day in the Indian Ocean... he couldn't just send them off on another man's errand. A fool's errand, it was looking like.

"Skipper...?"

The soft inquiry out of the dark came from a shadowy figure framed by Eldridge moonlight. For a frightening instant, Turner was gripped by horror. It hadn't been a dream... and they were coming for him after all...

"Tank?" Turner asked, hoping the quaver in his voice was masked by the whisper.

"Yes, sir... talk to you a minute?"

"Pull up a chair," Turner said, lighting a Lucky with unsteady hands. "Kinda late, ain't it? Figured you fellas would be crashed out by now."

"Yeah..." said Tank, sitting down in the creaky ratan chair Cooper had used when they'd first arrived. "They are. Guess I couldn't sleep. Lot on my mind, sir."

"You and me both..." Turner mused. "How're the guys, Tank? =They take care of you? Get the radio set squared away and all that?"

Tank muscled a crumpled pack of Pall Malls from his pocket and lit one from a box of kitchen matches on the cocktail table between the two men, "Got plenty of chow, showered up... got the blower goin'... lot of Jap talk out there, sir."

Turner nodded, "I'll bet. So what's on your mind, Tank? You didn't come out here at half past midnight to chew the fat."

Tank sighed, a ghostly wisp of smoke arcing into the moonlight, "Sir... Captain... you know what these Aussies got planned for tomorrow... today?"

"Yeah," Turner said, flicking an ash. "Yeah. Archer wants... or maybe Cooper wants... to hit some village called Mindelo. Guess the Nips are using it as an OP on the other side of the mountains."

"Yeah, ten miles away," Tank muttered. "Through rough country and then down toward the North Laclo. Maybe a third of the way to Dili. Wants to hit it hard... wants *us* to help... and raise the joint."

Turner shrugged, "Probably a good plan, considering their situation and that they've got a radio. Place that close could probably Huff-duff it in a few minutes."

"So... it's your thinkin' that this is a good idea? Us all goin' in, I mean, sir?"

Turner sighed and thought for a long moment. The chair he was on, the mate to Tank's, was a rocker. He began to rock.

"Tank... you got somethin' on your mind?"

The petty officer shrugged, the chasm between officer and enlisted suddenly yawning between them in a way it usually didn't at sea, "Well, sir... I guess... guess I'm just wonderin' what to tell the fellas."

Turner sighed, "Tank... let's drop the rank and the tradition and the bullshit for a minute, huh? You got somethin' on your mind… then out with it. Man to man."

"Straight goods?" asked the electrician.

"My word on it."

Tank fluttered his lips, rocked back and forth half a dozen times and then slapped a hand on the arm of the chair, "What the hell's the matter with you, Art?"

"Damn," Turner cocked his head. "Both barrels, huh?"

"You're fucked up and I think you're fuckin' us up, too… sir."

Turner met the other man's gaze and though he couldn't see it in the low lighting, he could easily visualize the purple flush on the big man's face, "I said tell it, friend. No rank, no barriers."

Tank stood and took to pacing, "Ever since that day the Jap gunned down our boys, you been acting loopy. Touched, you might say. You ain't yourself, Art. You're short with the men, with the officers… you're angry, pinched off, and irritable. And worse'n that… you're takin' stupid fuckin' risks with your life, with mine, and with them men out there in the bunkhouse."

"How do you figure?" Turner asked, anger growing but he wasn't going to pull rank. Couldn't now.

Tank stopped and aimed a finger at his captain, "What the *hell* are we *doin'* here, Art? We ain't in the fuckin' Army. We ain't *Marines*. We're sailors, for Christ! You got an electrician, a mechanic, a steersman, and a friggin' medic out here and now we're gonna fight with these guerillas and their war?"

"We're here to help," Turner offered.

"Help? Art… what the hell are *you* doin' here? This is a ridiculous mission. All we had to do was put that nutjob ashore and row back to the ship. But that wasn't enough, huh? You got the captain, the submarine's *only* doc and a couple of guys trained for sea duty running around a jungle and attacking villages like the friggin' Raiders!"

"We've got the best experience."

"That ain't the *point!* God *dammit!* We ain't soldiers, Art! They got enough of them in the other branches. They sure as shit don't need the likes of us to fight this way. So again, I ask ya'… why the hell are we here?"

"I'm here to make sure you guys are done right by," Turner snapped.

"Oh, yeah? And what about the boat? What about Mr. Williams out there someplace? Suppose there's a casualty and they need me to fix it. Suppose Mike needs Freddy on an engine... or suppose somebody's hurt aboard. Hurt bad."

Turner felt his face turning crimson now, "Henrie can—"

"Henrie's the fuckin' *cook!*" Tank managed to thunder while still speaking in just over a whisper. "That's *Hank's* job. Point is... and I hope I ain't so far past the line I can never get back... but the point is, you're here to do what you done the other night. To take out your mad on every Jap you can find. You want to hurt 'em... kill 'em... until you spill enough blood to make up for Mr. Hazard and Wendel and Marty and Joey."

"And what's *wrong* with that?" Turner shot to his feet, whisper-shouting his fury. "What's wrong with getting some good, old-fashioned revenge, Tank!?"

The two men were toe to toe now and the pause between them crackled with electric potential, "There's an old sayin', Art. A man seeks revenge should dig two graves... one for his enemy... and one for hisself. Problem is, your desire for vengeance is likely to dig a helluva lot more'n two."

Tank framed the theme of Turner's dream so accurately the captain's flushed face went tingly as the blood drained. He sighed and it was as if somebody had popped his anger with a pin. His shoulders slumped and he looked away.

"Meaning I'm being an asshole and gonna get us all fragged for nothing... Buck said just about the same thing couple nights ago..."

Tank's own anger deflated, and he went so far as to put a fraternal hand on the other man's shoulder, "Aw, hell... all's I'm sayin' is it's *possible*, Art."

"Horseshit," Turner drummed up a paper-thin smile. "I asked you to give it to me straight, Tank, don't stop now. You think we oughta bail and get the hell outta here? Get back to the LZ and blow?"

Tank sighed and went back to his chair, "Ain't my place, Skipper."

Turner frowned, sensing the freedom about to slam down on

them, "For this operation, Tank, you're my top shirt. Give it to me straight. Won't hold it against ya'."

"This ain't our business," Tank said and then glanced upward. "And it's pretty obvious what Archer's really about. You're here to punish the Jap, which is at least in line with what we're doin'… he's here for that frail."

"Yeah…," said Turner, "my thought, too."

"Thing of it is," Tank plowed on. "These guys… these Second Indies… they're decent enough. = Been through a ration of shit and then some. And their plan to attack that village is a good one… sort of rankles to leave them to it. On account of we're here now and all."

"It does at that," Turner sighed and settled back, retrieving his half-smoked pill from the ashtray. "All right then… we give them a Christmas present and help them take down the Jap OP. Then we high tail it back to where we left the raft… using that radio to get *Bull Shark* to meet us and get us the hell outta here. Go back to what we do best… bein' sharks. Think the guys will be keen on that?"

Tank nodded, "I think they will. Hank's more about taking care of the sick and wounded… got a few here. Lee is just a scared kid making his bones out here. Freddy's a gamer, we all know that."

"But we gotta make sure we don't get pulled in too deep," Turner said. "This isn't our war… not our part of it, anyway."

"One more thing, sir," Tank said, lowering his voice to barely audible. "Be watchful of the colonel. I don't trust him… and I don't think I'm alone. Been some whispers among the Aussies… probably unfounded… but let's just say the circumstances surrounding his retiring from the field have been questioned… even by the two remaining officers."

"Uh-huh…," Turner said. "I read you, Tank. I read you."

20

In the end, what decided Turner in favor of helping the 2ICs with their raid was practicality. For one, it was believed that Mindelo had equipment that could be seized and taken back to the lake house. This gear, once added to what they'd brought, would equip the Aussies to set up a true command post. Radio equipment of several types and possibly other vital electrical and mechanical items could be brought back.

Second, due to the nature of the island's terrain, the distance from Mindelo back to where they'd come ashore was actually shorter than going back the way they'd come. No doubt safer as well, as that route was probably being heavily patrolled by then.

It came to pass, therefore, that all that Christmas Eve day, Art Turner and his sailors accompanied Archer, Cooper, and their platoon on the ten mile trek to their rally point above Mindelo. A fire team had been left behind to guard the house, naturally, leaving a total of thirty men.

As the *Bull Sharks* were the only ones equipped with automatic weapons, they were split between the three squads. Red squad, led by Archer, featured Tank as their SMG man. Blue squad, Cooper's, exchanged Swooping Hawk's Tommy gun for Cooper's Enfield Pattern

1914 rifle. Swooping Hawk was then assigned as forward scout along with a wiry Black Australian called Jim. Turner was put in charge of the reserve squad, white, which was smaller and subsidized by Wayts and Hoffman.

As part of the care package, Archer had brought several hundred rounds of the British .303 for the bolt-action Enfields. There were three-dozen grenades as well, giving each man exactly one. Over the course of the last few months, the 2ICs had run very low on supplies. They'd taken to capturing Japanese Arisakas, as the weapons were plentiful, and the enemy had ammunition for them. More than half of the Australian soldiers now sported Japanese rather than British weapons.

They would travel light, each man's pack loaded with as little as necessary. Rations for two days, a full canteen, minimal camping gear and as many stripper clips as they could carry in pockets and packs along with each man's single pineapple.

The ammo situation for the Tommy guns was scant. Due to the fighting the previous day, each of the men from *Bull Shark* had what remained in their magazines and two full replacements. The Tommy guns were to be used sparingly and from a much closer range so as not to waste bullets. Each man was also entreated to keep the weapon in single-fire mode.

The hike through the mountains wasn't overly grueling, but it was slow. The trails and paths the men had to follow to avoid climbing the highest peaks were often narrow, winding and treacherous. Although Mindelo was hardly more than eighteen kilometers or about eleven miles from Ananda's house, it took the platoon the better part of the day to cross the barren mountains and begin to descend into the hills on the other side.

What they saw there reminded Turner of several of the observation points they'd used on Guadalcanal in those first early days with Decker's Raiders. The hills rolled down toward the plains that bordered the sea, and the North Laclo River quickly widened and dug its way through a wide watershed on its inexorable rush toward the Banda Sea. The hills between the proper granite mountain crags and the fertile plains and forest below were laid out like terraces and offered a long-range view of the northern parts of East Timor.

When the scouts called back that they'd spotted the village, Archer ordered a halt in a temperate forest above the town. From the edge of the gently rolling hill onto which the forest clung, Turner could see down into a small valley and then the land seemed to drop away shortly after a collection of buildings beside the river. Beyond this, the land sprawled out for miles and became a series of farms and patches of trees before vanishing over the horizon.

"We'll set up here," Archer said, indicating a clearing in the forest a few dozen yards from its edge. "Bed down here for the night and attack at first light."

"Plan?" Turner asked. "What do we know about this Mindelo?"

"Lads?" Archer turned to Swooping Hawk and Jim, who came forward and sat on the ground and swept an area clear of pine needles. Jim began to draw a crude map in the dust as the officers, Sergeant Vickers and Tank gathered around.

"It's on the bank of the river," Jim said, his heavy Aussie drawl coming in strange contrast to his aboriginal appearance. "It's on a plateau about fifty feet higher than the next row of hills. Waterfall there, too. A road leads out to the east and we thought we saw another running down and paralleling the river."

"There are a few fields to the east and a few trees to the north, between us and them," the Navajo continued. "The village itself looks pretty modern, at least from a distance. Don't think they have electrical power, not as we do, but there are a few dozen houses, a central area with a couple of larger buildings… and near one of these, maybe a governmental facility, we saw two Jap six-bys parked and a couple of tall radio aerials mounted."

"Bloody neutrals…" Cooper cranked.

Archer harrumphed, "Lord save us from the *neutrals…*"

"What's our best approach, Freddy?" Turner asked.

"I'd say a squad from the trees and another from the fields," Swooping Hawk said. "Looks like grain, so it should be high enough to offer concealment.

"Pity we don't have any boats," said Jim. "Could hit 'em from the river… but I wouldn't recommend it otherwise. Bloody crocs are all about."

"You've seen them?" asked Cooper.

"Nah… but they leave their mark, for those who know what to look for, Captain," said Jim, eliciting a nod from Swooping Hawk.

"Too bad we couldn't train the buggers to go after Japs only," Cooper mused.

"What about your Lieutenant Smithers?" Turner asked.

"We don't have any way to contact him," Archer said. "They've got a few hand-held radios and a backpack set, but we've had no word for over twenty-four hours."

Turner almost asked how the hell Archer would know, having spent most of the previous day in his lady's bedroom. However, he refrained and waited.

"He may be about, however," Cooper said. "If so, and they're in range… they'll come toward the fighting."

"Fred, give us a layout, will you?" Turner asked.

The Indian and the native Australian drew a series of small squares and circles into the map. They indicated where the houses were and the central buildings.

"Plan?" Turner asked again.

"What say you, Sarge?" Cooper asked Vickers.

"I think two squads placed like the lads say," said the sergeant. "Synchronize watches and all that rot, then we strike at a preset time from two angles. Rush in, take out as many yellow devils as we can and secure the central building with the radio equipment."

"What about us?" Turner asked.

"Way I see it," said Cooper, pointing to the dirt map, "is that when we attack from the south, we do it at the eastern end, so that both squads are aiming for the center of town. White squad can hit the village from the western side, where most of the houses are. You can sweep them and close in. By the time you do, we should have the main objective secured."

"Any idea of numbers, fellas?" Tank asked.

The two scouts shook their heads. Swooping Hawk said, "We

counted maybe a dozen, moving in and out of buildings... but there's bound to be more."

"Soon as we attack," Turner said. "They'll radio for backup. We'll never be able to hold this position."

"Doesn't matter," Archer said coldly. "Not our objective. Be careful we don't damage the vehicles, however. They'll be handy. Right! Let's get settled in and set a watch, Captain. Make sure the lads get a good rest... tomorrow will be quite a hullabaloo."

No fires were lit so as not to reveal their position to the nearby enemy. Cold canned rations were eaten without complaint and when the breeze, what little of it penetrated the trees, shifted around to the north, the men were allowed a smoke. Half of them no longer had any cigarettes and were forced to share out the Golden Bats they'd taken from dead Japanese soldiers. The Americans shared out what they had, too, which endeared them more than a little to the Aussies.

While Tank and Vickers and the other noncoms were getting prepared and setting the watch, Henry Hoffman found a private area and joined Wayts and Swooping Hawk there for a smoke as well. The three Americans said little at first, yet they each sensed a tension in the air. A question that wanted asking. Finally, the youngest and newest man did so.

"What're we doing, Doc?" Wayts asked. "I mean... why are we here about to attack a village?"

Hoffman sighed, "Dunno, Lee... seems I keep hearing rumors there's a war on."

Wayts sighed and cursed under his breath. Swooping Hawk grinned and patted him on the shoulder, "He's just foolin', Lee."

"Yeah, well this ain't foolin' around," Wayts waved a hand at the now dark clearing where faintly visible shapes of men moved quietly about. "I thought we was just droppin' this Archer guy off and going back to the ship."

Hoffman shrugged, "Hey, I'm just a pharmacist's mate, chum. What do I know from nothin'?"

"You're senior," Wayts said.

Hoffman chuckled, "Tank's the senior noncom for us. More combat experience."

"We don't have a choice, Lee," Hoffman said. "It's not like the boat's just waiting off the beach for us to get back. We all knew this would be a long run ashore."

"Yeah but... but this ain't our job," Wayts went on. "And the skipper don't seem too enthused, either. It just seems like we been pulled into these fellas' racket and now we're risking our necks. And for what?"

Hoffman sighed, "Lee... we don't have a choice. How could we sit back and stay comfy at that lake house while these guys go off and fight? For my part, I can be of some help, anybody gets wounded. We got Tommy guns and if this goes well, we might be able to take some of that radio gear back and maybe even make contact with Fremantle. Hell, maybe we can get in touch with the ship. Tell them to come and get us."

Wayts settled into glum silence.

"Look, Lee," Swooping Hawk said. "These Aussies saved our bacon back there at the foot of that bridge. Took us in, gave us a place to bed down and clean up... least we can do is return the favor. Besides... this is a simple hit and run. We got numbers and surprise. Should be easy enough. Then we can head back to the house, make arrangements, and get the hell off this rock, huh, Hank?"

"Sounds good to me," Hoffman said.

"So it's an easy one, then?" Wayts asked.

"Oh, sure," Hoffman offered a smile. "Walk in the park, kid."

"Like bustin' up a reefer den back home, "Swooping Hawk grinned.

Wayts snorted, "Yeah, well lemme tell ya'... you get two cops bustin' into some joint where six, eight fellas and dames been puffin' jujus... it's all goofy smiles and puffy eyes 'til you try and stop their fun. Then it's Katie bar the door."

"Well... the Japs drink their tea... don't roll it into sticks," Hoffman said.

* * *

Down in the village of Mindelo, the Japanese were not as unaware as the Australians and Americans believed. They had been forewarned and reinforced. A radio transmission from a light cruiser out in the Banda sea alerted the local command in East Timor that an American assault team was likely ashore. The locals rightly assumed that they were there to assist the remaining Australians.

In a further turn of bad luck, a Japanese patrol had intercepted a squad from Lieutenant Smithers's unit and wiped out all but three men. These were captured, tortured, and although they held out admirably, eventually let it slip that Mindelo was likely the next target for a heavy guerilla assault.

As such, the three squads of IJA regulars in the town were ready and, after dark, had begun taking up strategic positions. Further, a platoon of Riekusentai from Dili had been dispatched and were even at that moment moving along the road from the capital toward the mountain road that led into Mindelo. By midnight, these soldiers would themselves be bivouacked less than a half mile from town and would come in once the fighting started and catch the enemy in a pincer.

Lastly, all of these men were instructed that should any Americans be captured, they should be brought to headquarters immediately for interrogation. Indeed, any enemy should be, but there was a special desire and even reward for Ame-cohs.

As Christmas Eve gave onto Christmas morning, a thick fog rolled in from the sea. The heavy damp air spread its fingers far and wide across the land, even climbing up into the hills and nearly blotting out the light of the bloated moon arcing gracefully across the sky.

As dawn approached and both sides readied for what they believed would be an easy fight, the weighty air vibrated with tension and expectancy.

* * *

"Fog," Turner said when he was gently shaken awake.

"Sure enough, Old Boy," Archer said from the dark. "Might prove a blessing... or a curse."

Turner was awake and instantly alert, "Time to go?"

"That it is," said Archer. "I've got my lads organized, as does Cooper. I'm giving you the Indian chap, as he knows his way about in the dark. My unit will go into the fields with Jim, and Gus will flank you on the right. Quiet is the order of the day. Faster we get into position, quieter we can set up... the more rapid this shall all be, what?"

"When's H-hour?" Turner asked.

"Well... this bloody fog certainly complicates matters. Pea soup doesn't signify... but I believe first light. We'll all three have a radio and I'll give the word."

"As I've got your man Broderick," Archer went on. "I'll let you have Vickers. Good man, solid noncom, knows his business. With him, plus your lads Hoffman, Wayts, and Swooping Hawk, which gives you a properly bloated fire team."

"Seems a bit light," Turner said. "Not even half of red and blue squads."

"Necessary, Old Boy," Archer explained. "As you're on the fringe, my guess is you won't need as many men. Your job will be to begin clearing houses. If that can be done in silence... so much to the good. Once Cooper and I start in, we'll draw the Nips attention, eh? Just keep your radio tuned and the volume low and you'll be all right, mate."

Turner frowned, "It's not *me* I'm worried about, Colonel. I've done this before, you know. We're a unit, are we not?"

"Of course, Art!" Archer said, patting him on the back. "And you're my ace in the hole, to quote a Yank expression. Now, let's synchronize watches then... I have zero-four-hundred... now."

"Check," said Turner, adjusting his watch. "All right, then... let's get underway."

The makeshift camp was broken down in a matter of no more than three minutes. Men were gathered, assembled into their units, and sent off with what guides were available.

Red squad was the first, being led to the east and then down toward the fields by Jim. Next went Cooper, with no guide. His job was the easiest, as he only had to move down their hill, cross a bit of waste ground and then assemble in the trees just to the south of town. Finally, Turner and his five men moved closer to the river, with Swooping Hawk guiding them expertly toward their position.

With the fog masking most of the light, only a ghostly pale glow from the moon filtered down to allow the men to tell open ground from cover. In order that they didn't lose their way, every man took hold of the next man's pack until they got where they needed to be.

Although quiet, the thirty-odd men did make a small amount of noise. Had they known that on more than one occasion, they passed within whispering distance of Japanese soldiers, the situation might have devolved into chaos immediately.

However, for good or ill, both sides dismissed any sound they heard as their own men moving into position. Without realizing it, almost fifty men were intermingled so closely that turner could've passed a whispered message from his place near the southwestern corner of the town to Archer's in a wheat field on the south side of the road almost half a mile away.

The minutes crawled by in heavy silence. In the dark, crouching, listening, and waiting, human predators tensed for the moment that they could strike out at their prey… none of them knowing that they were both the hunter and the hunted alike.

21

LIGHT CRUISER AGANO
DECEMBER 24, 1942

"Where *is* this damned boat!?" Captain Nashiri snapped, his outburst breaking what had been a protracted silence.

After the meeting in the radio booth, Nashiri and his two guests had gone back to the fantail. That had lasted only a few minutes before the growing impatience of the cruiser captain propelled him back up to the bridge. Yamata and Lanser followed in silence.

"Maybe he's gone," Lanser offered, drawing a faint smirk from Yamata.

"Gone?" Nashiri snapped. "No... no! He's down there... he *must* be."

"Perhaps it is time to change our strategy," Yamata said.

Nashiri spun and speared The Sensei with a steely glare, "Are you questioning me, Teacher?"

Yamata did not flinch away and met the man's steel with his own, "I am suggesting that if a strategy has brought no results for an extended period, it is necessary to adopt another."

"Herr Kapitan," Lanser added, "we have penned the boat in... of that we can be reasonably sure."

"So we wait him out," Nashiri said.

"Or we increase the pressure," Yamata said and smiled thinly. "Not to pun... but it might be possible to draw him out."

Nashiri frowned, "We have only so many depth charges, and they are likely unable to reach such depths, Yamata."

"I do not suggest we roar at him," Yamata said, his serenity digging at Nashiri's irritation as Lanser's earlier suggestion had. "Perhaps, it is time we use a different weapon."

"Silence," Lanser said and smiled. "We've penned him in with asdic... now we remove even that input."

"And simply let him slip away?" Nashiri asked.

"No," said Yamata. "We cease all active echo location. We order the destroyers to begin circling. Slowly, perhaps no more than five knots. Everyone listens, including our deep hydrophone. It's likely that Turner will either assume we're moving on or make an attempt to flee without fear of being located."

"And the moment we hear something," Lanser was smiling now. "We have him! Let him attempt to crawl away. We triangulate and then pounce!"

"He's going to have to try it anyway," Yamata said. "Why not force his hand?"

Nashiri frowned and looked out at the horizon where several of the dark, angular silhouettes of his escorts could be seen roughly two kilometers away. At last, he drew in a deep breath and slowly nodded.

"Very well, gentlemen," said Nashiri. "I am dubious... but perhaps it is time to change our plans. You have my permission, Captain, to execute your new strategy. Please see to it, gentlemen."

"I must admit I'm a bit surprised," Lanser said as he and Yamata moved aft toward the radio booth.

Yamata grunted, "You may be an excellent pilot and submariner, Friedrich... but I'm afraid when it comes to politics, you lack a bit of something."

Lanser raised his eyebrows, "How's that?"

Yamata placed his hand on the knob to the radio booth hatch and turned to smile thinly at his companion, "Nashiri isn't doing us a favor. He has little faith in this plan. However, since it's our idea... *my* idea… it's likely failure will fall upon me. If it succeeds, as he believes it won't, then he can claim that he ordered us to initiate it."

Lanser sighed, "This sort of thing never ends, does it. I suppose I prefer a much more straight-forward war. One in which you know who your enemy is."

"And don't have to fight among your friends… yes, I empathize," Yamata sighed and pulled the hatch open.

BULL SHARK

"Skipper, something's going on topside," Chet Rivers called from the conning tower.

Williams went up the ladder, followed by Dutch. Ever since his announcement of a few moments before, the men had been given a vital boost to their morale, even if temporary. The expectation in the control room and conning tower was palpable, and it was even then spreading throughout the ship.

"What've you got, Chet?" Williams asked.

"Echo location seems to have stopped," Rivers said. "From all five contacts. Been almost four minutes now."

"What're those crafty slants up to…?" Dutch muttered.

"Oh… and I think…" Rivers fiddled with his gear and pressed his headphones harder against his skull. "I think I hear screws, sir… hard to tell how many… but more than one set."

Although Williams had said that he might have a plan, it'd been a generous admission. He had only a few loose kernels he still wasn't sure what to do with. Yet the excitement that permeated the boat had reflected back at him, and the captain pro tem felt as if his fatigue had, if not vanished, backed off considerably.

"Hmm… I can't believe they're bugging out," Williams observed.

"No… they're giving us an opening."

"Luring us into thinking we can escape?" Dutch asked. "Then when we try, they lock down our position and nail us?"

"Yeah…," said Williams. "And they know we're deep… think they know we're deep… Frank, what's our battery sitch?"

"Seventy percent," said Nichols. "Been over eighteen hours, but all we've done is sit here."

"And you've got us balanced for the extra water we're carrying in the bilges?" Williams asked.

"Of course... oh..." Nichols's face appeared in the hatchway, looking up at Williams and grinning. "You want me to pump it out?"

"Yeah," said Williams. "And while you do that, helm, I want a reverse bell. One knot only. And set the rudder to twenty-degrees left. On my mark, Frank you engage the drain pump and helm, you engage the telegraphs."

"Sir, my helm is two-zero degrees port," said Mug Vigliano, once more taking up his familiar post at the wheel.

"You're gonna confuse their listening gear and spiral slowly topside," Dutch said. "And then what?"

"As we spiral," Williams said, "we'll open the circle and slowly move away from the central ship, that cruiser. Then when we're shallow... we'll see."

"Drain pump coming online... now," Nichols said.

"Sir, maneuvering answerin' all back one-third... one knot," Vigliano reported.

After what seemed like an eternity, the silent hunter uncoiled herself and began to move. It was more like a crawl at first, the sternway barely putting enough water across the rudder to turn her, but it did. Slowly, ever so slowly, *Bull Shark* began to execute a wide, spiraling turn.

At the same time, the whirr of the drain pump, silenced as much as was possible, began shunting the bilge water out to sea, making the boat lighter by several tons. As slowly as she was backing off, she began to rise through the water column.

"Positive buoyancy," Nichols announced. "Now passing eight-one-zero feet... ascension one foot per minute."

Williams frowned, "That won't do... add the safety tank to the pump-out, Frank. Get me as close to ten feet per as you can. Add the negative, auxiliaries, and trim tanks if you have to. If we start to get squirrely, assemble a trim party. Phone talker, pass the word to all compartments. Battle stations torpedo. Silent stations."

"Orders, Elmer?" Dutch asked, settling into his seat at the torpedo data computer.

"Yeah… order both rooms to set speed to high and depth on all tubes to four feet," Williams said. "And when the pressure gauges read fifty PSI… open all outer doors."

That drew nervous smiles from the men in the conning tower. Their XO turned captain wasn't just going to try and run. He was going to fight.

He was going to pull an Art Turner.

* * *

"Helm, all ahead one-third," Nashiri ordered after stepping through the hatch from the signal bridge. "Quartermaster, engage circular course inside the ring of our destroyers. Four knots."

Yamata and Lanser hurried in after him, the former making a concerted effort to remain neutral. The Nazi, on the other hand, cared little for appearances. He found the entire concept of "face" to be rather ludicrously over-indulged in by his Asian allies.

"No!" said Lanser. "We must remain at the center—"

Nashiri glared back at him, "Contain yourself, Commander! This is *my* bridge, my ship, and my task force."

Yamata placed a hand on Lanser's shoulder, "Be easy, my friend…"

"Captain, fantail!" the navigation bridge phone talker exclaimed. "Technicians report faint audio signature, sir!"

"What of the echo location booth?" Nashiri snapped.

The young man repeated the question, waited and then nodded, "They are uncertain… too much interference topside, sir."

"You see?" Lanser pressed. "If we begin to move, Captain, we'll have to reel in your hydrophones."

"Not with 265 meters of cable out," Nashiri said. "Thus, the sedate speed. Do not tell me—"

"Captain," said Yamata serenely. "Perhaps Commander Lanser and I could go to the sonar booth and assist."

Nashiri frowned and then nodded, a smirk settling in, "Yes,

Teacher. Do. No doubt you and our esteemed advisor can be of the most use there... rather than on my bridge."

Lanser flushed, his blue eyes flashing and his square jaw clenching. Yamata saw the storm clouds gathering and took hold of the German by the elbow, "Come, my friend. We have a shark to hunt."

On the catwalk, Yamata glanced up at Lanser, "It does not do to antagonize him, Friedrich."

Lanser harrumphed, "Rather let him antagonize *me* instead?"

"It is his ship."

"Fuck his ship," snapped Lanser and then smiled thinly. "Fortunate for us that I have you to reign in my Aryan tendencies, eh?"

"Come," said Yamata, moving to the nearest ladder that would allow them to descend to the central sonar room.

Once there and ensconced in the small, dark and smoke-filled chamber, the two officers felt more at ease. It was something familiar to them both. The stacks of listening gear and sound projector controls and their technicians was an environment which spoke to their warriors' hearts. For Yamata, it was to the crafty destroyer captain hunting for a mysterious and elusive enemy down in the darkness. For Lanser, it was avoiding detection and searching for an opening to turn back and strike.

"What have you found, Petty Officer?" Yamata asked the sailor in command of the two sound technicians sitting attentively at their consoles.

"There was a faint sound, Captain," said the man only slightly older than the two seamen, and yet possessed of a confidence beyond his years. "Hydrophones are somewhat muddled now by the screw noise of our companions. And now our own."

"Can we slave the output from the stern gear into this room?" Lanser asked.

"I have already done so, sir," replied the petty officer. "It's crude, just a line plugged into the auxiliary jack on the hydrophone... but you may listen in at those headphones there on the desk."

Yamata nodded to Lanser who immediately sat and slid the bulky headset over his ears. He reached out and turned the gain knob to full on the small control panel into which they were plugged. He wore a mask of fierce intensity, as if by sheer force of will alone he could detect their foe. Finally, the German's eyes narrowed, and he slowly nodded.

"Anything?" Yamata asked, leaning in.

"Something… it's barely audible, however… but it sounds electrical," Lanser said. "A low hum not unlike that of those new fluorescent lamps…"

"An electrical motor?" Yamata asked.

Lanser nodded, "Yes… certainly… but at a low level… could be propulsion or a pump."

"So…" Yamata mused, "our prey *is* still with us. And he's doing *something*…"

"I'm losing it," Lanser frowned and pressed his headphones tighter. "It's fading… gone. *Scheiße!*"

"Because we are *moving*…" Yamata growled. "Sonarman! Give me a full power active echo location now!"

The petty officer turned to him, "But sir, we—"

"Do it," Yamata said calmly. His order was underscored by the iron foundation of rank, authority, and fame.

"Hai,' the petty officer bowed at the shoulders and gave the order.

A single, echoing pulse blasted down from the ship's projector. There was no definitive contact made, but the technician on the passive hydrophones flinched ever so slightly.

"Something?" the petty officer demanded, clutching the back of the sailor's chair.

"I… no… but perhaps…" the sailor prevaricated.

"Well, which is it?" the petty officer snapped.

The sailor frowned and shook his head, "I thought for a moment there might have been a return… but it is far too faint, sir."

Yamata rubbed his chin thoughtfully, "He's down there… and perhaps we are not the only thing moving. Keep listening."

* * *

"The cruiser's definitely moving now," Rivers said. "Four light screws, sir. It's hard to track, though, we're so deep. Whoa!"

"What?" Williams asked but the spectral whine that lanced through the black sea was all the answer he needed.

"Sounded fairly close," Dutch said, leaving his TDC and slipping into the seat beside Rivers. He slipped the headphones for the WCA stack over his ears. "A shot in the dark, I'd say."

"Now passing seven-eight-zero feet," Nichols reported. "We're dry, Captain. Deactivating drain pump."

The faint whirr that was hardly audible inside the ship vanished. Only the low, deep hum of the four GE motors running at low power still underlined the light whirr of other equipment. With the air conditioning and ventilators off, the boat was tomb silent.

"Frank... pass the word for all compartments to open the hatches," Williams said. "Leave the flappers closed, but at least get some air flow in here. Smoking lamp is out, too."

"They're circling the wagons up there, Elmer," Dutch said. "I can hear the twin DD screws... can't pinpoint them... how about you, Chet?"

"No, sir," Rivers said, watching the bug on his bearing indicator rotating. With hydraulic power still shut down, the men in the forward torpedo room were now manually sweeping the sound heads. "I can tell there are five of them... but it's hard to track any. I concur, though... they're circling. And... and maybe the big boy is, too? Her screws are going, so..."

Williams glanced at the gyro compass repeater above Vigliano's engine enunciators. It now pointed at one-two-zero. Before they'd been moving, the boat had been pointing roughly east, northeast. He tried to calculate the size of their circle and found it impossible. Too many variables and no point of reference.

"Mug... full left rudder," Williams ordered. "Let's see what happens..."

After several minutes, Williams timed the movement of the needle on the compass. Just about ten degrees per minute. The boat was now facing southeast.

"Foot and a half per second... divided by the angle..." Williams muttered.

"We're moving outward at about a quarter knot, sir," Hernandez said from the chart desk. "Twenty yards per minute away from our original position… at least now. I'd say we've already gone a hundred yards from that point… assuming we and the Japs drifted at the same rate, sir."

"Geeze, Hotrod," Williams grinned.

"Yeah… not too shabby, pal," Ted Balkley said.

"I'm not just another pretty face, *mijo*," observed Hotrod.

"And how," said Balkley.

"*Pinche gringo…*" muttered Hotrod.

"What's that mean?" asked Balkley.

"Means you're a real swell fella," Vigliano tossed off and chuckled to himself.

"Yeah," said Balkley proudly. "I really *am* a peachy grincoat."

22

LIGHT CRUISER AGANO
DECEMBER 24, 1942

"I've got it again!" Lanser blurted after long minutes of silence.

Yamata stepped closer, "The electrical motor?"

"Yes... yes... very faint, as before... although perhaps slightly louder," Lanser wore a frown of concentration. "Growing... we're getting closer, no doubt of that... no, wait... it's fading again!"

"Shall I go active, sir?" the sonar petty officer asked.

Yamata frowned. A picture was forming in his mind. Vague, shapeless but insistent enough to nag at him incessantly.

"No..." he said finally. "No... not just yet."

"I'm losing it, Hitake!" Lanser warned.

"Petty Officer, note the time, compass course, and... Friedrich, if you had to give the sound an intensity, on a scale of one to ten...," Yamata asked.

Lanser rolled his eyes toward the overhead, "Hmm... perhaps a two. It was slightly louder, or perhaps I only *think* it was..."

"No..." Yamata said, shaking his head. "No... I believe you're right. If we were not *moving*... ah, well. Petty Officer, please have your men pay special attention as well. Their equipment should pick up the sound next time."

"Will there be a next time?" the man asked.

Yamata permitted himself a half-smile, "Oh... I think so."

BULL SHARK

"Now passing six-five-zero feet," Nichols reported. "Don't mind saying I feel a lot better easing the pressure on our lady, Elmer."

Williams harrumphed from his place near the hatchway, "Oh, there's gonna be a heck of a lot more pressure soon, Frank."

"What's the game plan, Elmer?" Dutch asked.

Williams fluttered his lips, "Prayer for one, XO. We're gonna do pretty much the only thing we can. Get topside, fire a full spread, and then run on all four as fast as we can."

"*Ay Dios mio...*" Hotrod muttered.

"You mean... on the surface?" Nichols asked from below.

"Unless you've fixed our snorkel," Williams said. "Buck, you down there?"

Rogers appeared in the circle of the hatchway and came up the ladder until he was halfway into the conning tower, "Skipper?"

"Buck, I want you to pass the word to the deck gun crews," Williams ordered. "Quietly, of course. Have them standing by to go topside and prep 'em for firing. As soon as we dump our fish, I want them assembled."

"What about reloads?" Dutch asked.

Williams shook his head, "This is a one-shot deal. If we do have to fire off the guns, that means we've been spotted. My idea is to use them to dissuade any uppity Nips before we put some distance between us and dive again. *Then* we can reload. I know it's a lot to ask and the men are gonna have to shift around... but it's our only shot."

"Aye-aye," Rogers said. "I'll let 'em know, sir."

Williams looked at the compass again. The boat was now facing due south. He crossed his fingers and said a silent prayer.

"Now passing six-zero-zero feet," Nichols reported.

The hull popped several times and groaned, as if in relief. Men swiped at their brow, enjoying the same sense, at least for a moment. They were rising out of the crushing depths, but they were rising toward a deadly foe.

It was said that aboard a warship like a submarine, much of the time consisted of boredom broken by short moments of terror. That was mostly true… except that the terrifying moments were rarely so short.

When enemy warships prowled the surface, intent on the boat's destruction, those moments could stretch into long, tense hours that could easily break a man. Being closed in, blind and cornered touched off one of the deepest-rooted fears of the Homo sapien. The horrifying knowledge that at any moment, death could swoop in and take you… and there was nowhere left to run.

"Five-zero-zero feet…" Nichols reported, his voice grew quieter with each announcement.

"Sir, my helm is two-tree-zero…" Vigliano said softly.

"All stop," Williams ordered. "Rudder amidships… standby, Mug."

* * *

"Got him!" Lanser clapped his hands. "Machinery signals growing, Hitake! A four this time. Suggest we haul in the hydrophone a bit. He's coming up!"

Yamata nodded, "Yes… he's spiraling up toward us. Moving in a circle to try and throw off our sound gear. Most clever… but it will not avail him. Petty Officer, go to active echo location. Search frequency."

The lower frequency active sonar pulses reached down into the dark waters, probing for their enemy. The ship, however, kept moving. Yamata was reaching for the phone on the bulkhead when it buzzed.

He snatched it, "Yamata."

"*What is going on?*" It was Nashiri, sounding none too pleased. "*Why have you gone active?*"

"We have detected the submarine," Yamata explained. "He is spiraling up toward the surface. Also, recommend hauling in trailing hydrophone by one-half. Captain, I also suggest we either stop or change course. Our movements are too predictable, as are the destroyers."

"*You question me?*"

Yamata's fist squeezed the phone as he tried to reign in his temper, "I'm trying to destroy our enemy, *Captain*."

"*By giving our position away,*" Nashiri mocked. "*Very clever. And where is this enemy going, Teacher?*"

Yamata seriously considered telling the man to go to hell. Let the submarine escape and let Nashiri take the blame rather than himself. However, his sense of duty to his Navy and his country were too deeply ingrained.

And the question was a critical one. Which way *would* Turner go? Eventually, he'd pick a direction and try to skulk away. What would he do? Run north, further into the Banda Sea and away from Japanese occupied Timor?

No. If Turner was known for doing anything, it was the unexpected.

"He will run south," Yamata said and looked to Lanser, who glanced over and nodded and smiled, showing his solidarity.

Nashiri laughed, "*Toward Timor? Toward us? I think not, Teacher. If he runs anywhere… it will be to more open sea. To escape, especially after so much time. No, we will maintain our turn… but keep echoing. Perhaps you'll get lucky. Bridge out.*"

Yamata slammed the phone back into its cradle and shook a Golden Bat from a nearly empty pack. As he lit the cigarette, his hands shook. The rage inside him was a huge and ugly thing, and his self-control was beginning to crumble.

How he wished he were aboard a destroyer again. Or commanding a squadron of them. How pleasant it would be to stand before a class of DD skippers once more, imparting his knowledge, experience, and wisdom. Teaching those who were eager to learn and who held him in high regard. How he wished to be anywhere but aboard another man's ship… where he could be relegated to uselessness and mocked all the while.

Yamata began hoping that the *Bull Shark* did get away. He began hoping that she'd attack and send *Agano* and Nashiri to the bottom.

* * *

"Active sonar!" Dutch exclaimed. "Search frequency! Bearing... one-one-zero to one-three-zero, Elmer!"

"They can hear us," Williams surmised. "Somebody just passed over us, heard the motors and tried to ping."

"Four screws, sir," Rivers said. "Definitely Master-1."

"Helm, all ahead two-thirds," Williams said. "Make turns for four knots. Frank, give me a twenty-degree up-bubble."

"Oh, *madone*..." Vigliano said as he carried out his orders. "Maneuverin' ansiz' four knots, sir."

"Now passing four-zero-zero feet," Nichols said. "Rising fast, Elmer."

"Estimate time to surface?" Williams asked.

"Two minutes," Nichols said.

"Very well," Williams managed to say evenly in spite of the maelstrom now raging in his belly. "Stand by to blow the MBTs, Diving officer. Buck, your guys told off?"

"Aye-aye, sir," Rogers said. "On your word...rigging for red throughout the boat, sir!"

"Joe, take the TDC," Williams ordered. "Balkley, you take the WCA gear. Joe, I want a ten-degree spread from both rooms."

"We're gonna shotgun 'em?" Dutch asked, slipping into the seat at the computer and slipping the sound-powered telephone around his neck.

"Exactly," Williams said. "Maybe we'll scare them into maneuvering away... and who knows? Maybe we'll get lucky."

"Now passing three-zero-zero feet," Nichol's voice was now growing *louder* with each update.

"Forward room, after room, conning tower," Dutch spoke. "Ten degree spread. This will be a rapid-fire evolution. I want two men on the triggers. In... thirty seconds, begin opening the doors."

"The jig's up now... Frank, put hydraulics back online," Wiliams said. "Open flappers. Joe, let the boys know they don't have to use Y-wrenches on this one."

'They'll be glad to hear that, sir," Dutch grinned.

"I'm getting distinct signatures now, sir," Rivers said. "There's a tin can off our starboard beam and another off the port bow. I'd say they're circling counterclockwise, Captain."

"How about Master-1?" Williams asked.

"Got him, too!" Rivers pumped his fist. "Port quarter… traveling in the same direction."

"Any guess on ranges?" asked the Skipper.

Rivers shrugged, "I'd say no more than a thousand yards for Master-1, based on what we've heard. The two DDs… maybe even closer. Hard to tell, sir."

"Goin' for broke…" Williams muttered. "Diving officer, blow main ballast tanks! Alert maneuvering to standby to answer bells on diesels. Gun crews prepare to go topside!"

Bull Shark echoed with the sound of high-pressure air blasting hundreds of tons of water from her ballast tanks. Immediately, the boat surged upward, and Nichols had to compensate by reducing the up angle on his stern planes. Still, after so much waiting and skulking, the definitive maneuvers once more jolted the men with a surge of adrenaline.

They'd need it.

* * *

"No contacts," reported the technician at the active projector.

Yamata was not surprised. However, when Lanser slammed his fist on the console before him and let fly with an exultant string of German, The Sensei almost jumped.

"Contact!" Lanser declared. "Transient noise in the water column. Near-field effect…"

"What is it?" Yamata asked.

"A hiss… they're blowing their main ballast tanks!" Lanser exclaimed, his face pale with shock and awe. "*Mein Gott!* He's *surfacing!*"

"Come on!" Yamata said, yanking the hatch open. "A phone call will not do for this!"

The two men ran for the bridge. When they burst into the control center a few moments later, puffing and sweating, Nashiri laughed at them.

"So excited!" sneered the captain. "What is—"

"He's surfacing!" Lanser snapped, pointing a finger toward the starboard beam. "He's that way!"

"Running south," Yamata said, his glare boring into Nashiri's own. "I suggest we alter course."

"Sonar has reported nothing," said Nashiri. "You are grasping at straws."

"You are a damned fool!" Lanser spat, stepping forward and clenching his fists. "Our enemy is ripe for the plucking and at each step, you have—"

"Boatswain!" Nashiri snapped. "Alert the master at arms! We have a—"

"Captain! Captain!" a sailor shouted from the after end of the compartment where the air search radar monitoring station was situated. "New contact on radar! Range six hundred meters!"

"What is the bearing!?" Nashiri demanded.

He made the same mistake many commanders made who were not yet familiar with radar and how it worked. Japan was behind the United States in radar technology, only having the system installed on a fraction of their ships. The one on *Agano* was of the air-search type. A globally-broadcast radio beam that could only return range but not direction.

"To the *south*, you fool!" Lanser barked.

* * *

"All outer doors open!" Dutch reported. "Speed is high, depth set to four feet. Depth and speed spindles removed."

"Twenty feet... ten... breeching!" Nichols called.

The placid ocean was torn asunder as a huge steel shark pushed her nose up into the early morning air. She cast aside great sheets of spray and even before her hatches were opened, the main induction valves slammed open, and her exhaust ports coughed as her four mighty General Motors diesels growled out of their slumber.

Williams was up the ladder and pushing the bridge hatch open, a silvery cascade of cool Banda Sea soaking him to his waist. Rather than regret this, however, the captain whooped as the cool water and refreshing air blew into the dank heat of the conning tower.

"Contacts on sugar jig!" Ted Balkley, back at his own station, shouted, his excitement bursting out of him just as his ship had burst from the sea a moment before. "Bearings... three-five-zero... zero-seven-zero... one-niner-zero—"

"That's enough!" Williams shouted. "Ranges on those three?"

The temporary captain knew which ships they were. The two circling destroyers and the cruiser behind. He vaulted up and onto the bridge with Hernandez hot on his heels. Even as they did so, the forward torpedo room and galley hatches banged open and men poured up onto the deck, chattering and calling out orders and responses. Three lookouts shot from the bridge hatch and swarmed into the shears like spider monkeys.

"*Bridge, radar... first is six-five-zero yards... second is one-three-five-zero yards... and the third... six-three-five yards and opening, sir!*" Balkley's report came over the bridge speaker now.

"Helm, all ahead standard," Williams ordered.

He cast about and blinked as his night vision returned. Even though the interior of the boat had been red lit for several minutes, it still took time.

Then he saw them. Angular shapes extruding up from the black sea against the starry sky of early morning. And behind, a larger shape with its starboard flank turned toward them.

"Fire control, bridge!" Williams's voice was pitching up with fear and eagerness. "Weapons free! Fire all tubes! Repeat, fire all tubes!"

It was up to Dutch now. Rather than ordering each individual shot, Williams had given the torpedo officer permission to fire at will and at his own pace. Generally, each shot was set up with a six or seven second delay. This allowed for men to prepare, poppet valves to be operated, and impulse air to be readied. It also prevented one torpedoes' wake from pushing the next off course. However, with fully loaded torpedoes and a fully ready crew, this could be shortened.

The ship shuddered as the first of her forward torpedoes was expelled and the first of her stern torpedoes was expelled almost simultaneously. Mere seconds later, two more fish screamed away. *Bull Shark* quivered as if in ecstasy at finally being able to strike out at her prey.

"Fire control, close outer doors!" Williams ordered. "Hotrod, flank speed!"

"Helm, bridge, all ahead flank!" Hotrod thumbed the speaker.

Joe Dutch popped up through the hatch, his face sweaty and his smile big, "All tubes fired electrically, Elmer! Hot, straight, and normal! It's in God's hands now."

"Great, Joe," Williams said, "now get my damned guns ready!"

"Number one ready, sir!" shouted Eddie Carlson from forward. He was now gun captain since Tommy Perkins was still in the torpedo room.

"Number two ready, sir!" That was Leroy Potts, taking a break from his baking to obliterate a few Japs.

"*Bendix log indicates twenty-knots!*" Tony Skaggs said, having come up to take a position in the conning tower. Even as he reported, the search periscope rose.

"Do we fire, Elmer?" Dutch asked, pointing to the destroyer now almost directly before them.

"Not yet, Joe... they haven't seen us yet," Williams said. "Let's not tip our hand."

* * *

Frantic shouts rose from outside. Nashir, Lanser, and Yamata broke from their positions, the staring contest at an end now. Because some lookouts were reporting sighting something off to starboard.

The officers bolted for the signal bridge, pushing past lookouts and the ship's executive officer to get a better view. At first, nothing could be seen. The darkness and the silhouettes of other ships obscured the low profile of a surfaced submarine.

"There!" Lanser shouted, pointing at the faint and glowing foam trail just forward of their beam. "A wake! There she is!"

"Helm!" Nashiri turned and roared into the pilothouse. "Full right rudder! All ahead flank! Alert gun and torpedo crews to stand by!"

"No!" Lanser shouted, seizing the Japanese captain. "Maintain your course!"

"Get your hands off of me, you German *pig!*" Nashiri roared. "I'll have you in irons!"

"He's right, Nashiri!" Yamata said. "They have stern tubes!"

But the Japanese Captain would hear nothing. His blood was up, and his patience was at an end, "Yakuin! Order all gun crews to sight in and fire! And get the Master at Arms up here instantly! I want this Nazi placed under arrest!"

Yamata surged forward, blocking Nashiri's path, "Captain, don't let your emotions get the better of you! You're playing into Turner's hands."

"Get out of my way unless you want to join your Nazi friend in the brig," Nashiri's tone was as brittle as dried bones.

"He's right," Yamata said quietly but forcefully. "You are a fool and be damned with you!"

He spun away, took hold of Lanser's arm and propelled him toward the after end of the navigation bridge. Stunned by this bizarre turn of events, the German couldn't find his voice but allowed himself to be drawn away.

"Come, unless you want to be tossed in the brig for the two minutes of life this ship has left," Yamata said, and they ran.

Yet there was nowhere to run to, and no time left to do so. As the two men hurried along the portside catwalk, the sea and the clouds above bloomed into bright relief as a titanic white flash illuminated the world for miles around.

Instinctively, they turned and saw that where a ship had been moving nearly a mile off their starboard bow, a brilliant white-orange cloud of incandescent death now roiled. Both men gaped in horror, each knowing the terrible truth of what they saw.

Multiple torpedoes had struck the flank of the destroyer, ripping her open, igniting fuel and munitions and setting off even more cataclysmic explosions as magazines blew apart in a display of unforgiving physics. Her guts had detonated and blew themselves outward, rending the vessel's steel flesh like rice paper.

"We have failed," said The Sensei, knowing what must come next.

In their last moments, Lanser reached out and took the man's hand in his own, "It was a good fight and an honor, Captain."

Like the destroyer escorting her, *Agano* was struck by multiple warheads. Nashiri had turned the ship directly into their path, allowing three of *Bull Shark's* four torpedoes to strike her below her armor belt.

Although even at that late time of 1942, the mark XIV torpedo was still suffering problems, the men of *Bull Shark* had modified their fish. The magnetic exploder had been removed and an impact igniter used instead. Her captain aimed the fish shallow, since they ran too deep. These modifications combined with hard-won experience paid off.

The light cruiser lurched as if batted by a giant's fist. Men were thrown off their feet, light fixtures and electrical equipment sparked, sizzled, and ruptured. Tons of ocean water blasted into the ship, igniting boilers, setting off explosions that ignited magazines, and dealt a swift and terrible end.

Like the destroyer, the light cruiser was engulfed in super-heated fire even as she dissolved into her constituent components and a swirling cloud of molten shrapnel.

Death was mercifully swift. There would be no survivors, as what organic flesh remained was blasted into shreds and those shreds cooked to ashes.

* * *

"Sweet Jesus…" Joe Dutch breathed, as the heat from both ships roared over the boat's decks like the breath of some angry volcano.

A wind like that from a blast furnace roared past from both ends of the ship, buffeting her and causing men to clutch at whatever came to hand. So bright were the explosions that nothing else could be seen that wasn't in their direct light.

Williams had to swallow twice to find his voice, "Hotrod... ring me up an emergency bell."

The shaken quartermaster did as asked, looked at the still burning sea ahead of them, and then back at his commander, "Shall I turn us, sir?"

"Negative," Williams said. "We're gonna go right behind that explosion."

Beneath them, the mighty submarine's diesel voice roared to a fevered pitch, her powerful engines pushing more than five million watts into the generators and thence back to her four motors. The fleeing boat strained, racing across the sea at more than twenty-two knots.

"We're making smoke, sir!" a man from the after gun shouted.

"Yeah, well we ain't the only ones!" another hooted with unrestrained elation.

Williams crossed his fingers. The destroyer ahead had been barely more than 500 yards away when the two torpedoes struck her. At twenty-two knots, *Bull Shark* would cover that distance in less than a minute. No doubt the remaining ships were even then altering course and putting on speed.

What would they do? Would they chase the submarine, which they would see for a short time thanks to the fires on the sea's surface? Or would they hunt for survivors... or send one to do each job?

The burning slick of fuel oil and whatever might remain of the destroyer was leaping toward them rapidly. It was just slightly to the right of the boat's bull nose.

"Hotrod, five degrees port," said Williams.

The order was given and acknowledged. With agonizing slowness, the fireball crept to the right ever so slightly. It was huge now, covering five or six hundred feet and with writhing, raging tentacles of plasma a hundred feet high. There could be no survivors.

"Standby to stop starboard engine," Williams said, pressing the button himself. "Frank, alert maneuvering we'll be going to batteries again soon."

The steady hush of the sea parting before the speeding submarine was drowned out by the nightmarish voice of the flames. As the fire breathed, pulling in oxygen, it exhaled a terrifying wail and moan, as if some huge creature were crying out in its death agonies. It might have been the combined wailing of the hundreds of souls the men of *Bull Shark* had just consigned to their fate.

Everyone on deck shivered, even as the temperature around them rose to over 125 degrees.

"Stop starboard engine!" Williams shouted over the din. "Hard right rudder!"

With the ship's great speed, she wouldn't turn on a dime. However, with one engine stopped and the other remaining to push along with the rudder, *Bull Shark* began to swing around. Slow at first… maddeningly slow. Yet the turn became faster, tighter, and the great ball of the Japanese destroyer's death pyre rotated to starboard, appearing to be circling the boat.

"Secure the guns and everyone below!" Williams shouted. "Hotrod, hold this course! All ahead full!"

The fleeing submarine straightened, angling to the southwest… a direction no one would expect her to go, or so her skipper hoped. With admirable swiftness, the guns were secured and the men filed below decks. Once the hatches were closed, Williams pulled the diving alarm twice and every last man on deck hustled below.

The diesels were stopped, and the vessel's great speed allowed her to pound down beneath the waves in seconds, leaving behind a rapidly dissipating furrow of foam… and a sea that burned and lit up the scattered clouds above.

"Four-five feet!" Nichols reported.

"Blow negative to the mark," Williams said, wiping his brow. "Diving officer, make your depth two hundred feet, smartly. Helm, all ahead two-thirds. Make turns for four knots… and give me ten degrees left rudder."

"Putting us back toward the south again, Elmer?" Dutch asked.

"Last place the Japs would expect us to go, XO," Williams said and sagged against the ladder. "Let's get the hell outta here…"

"Hey," Joe Dutch grinned, "Merry Christmas, huh?"

23
VILLAGE OF MINDELO
EAST TIMOR
DECEMBER 24, 1942

Turner and his team had just crossed the little band of open land and were about to enter the woods to the south of town when Fred Swooping Hawk held up a fist. He was in the lead, his tracking skills making him the obvious choice for point man.

Five yards back, walking side by side, Turner and Vickers stopped as well. Directly behind them were Hoffman and Wayts. At Vickers's instruction, the four of them stood an arm's length apart and arm's length behind in a perfect square. This was a classic fire-team formation and gave them open lines of fire and cover… provided they didn't start shooting at their scout.

Swooping Hawk eased back to the two senior men and spoke in a whisper hardly more audible than the distant hiss of the waterfall, "Somebody's in there, sir… Sarge."

Vickers glanced at Turner and then at the Navajo, "A guess, mate?"

"No," said Swooping Hawk. "I can sense them… smell them maybe. Can't quite tell you how I know… but I *know*, Captain."

"All right," Turner said. "Recommendation?"

"Split," said Swooping Hawk. "I'll go straight in, the two of you break ten yards to the right and left. Go in slow and low, hand guns or

DECEMBER 24, 1942

knives only. Don't know how many, but I know there's at least one in the woods directly in front of us."

"Might be a good idea to report this," Turner said. "Might not be a lone occurrence."

Vickers shook his head, "Too noisy... let's be sure first, sir."

Turner frowned, "All right... you fellas heard? We separate, count to twenty, and then go in."

Wayts was behind him and Hoffman behind Vickers. Each man reached out and tapped the two senior men's shoulders once.

The men quickly slung their Thompsons and pulled out their Marine Corps issue KA-bars. Their Colt 1911s were in their holsters and already chambered for action. Vickers and Turner nodded, and each man took ten sideways steps away from one another, their partners following.

By the time they'd separated by sixty feet, they couldn't see through the fog. Even Swooping Hawk was only a ghostly figure a shade darker than the eerily glowing mist. Then he vanished. As instantly and completely as if he were indeed an other-worldly spirit.

"Sixteen... seventeen..." Turner muttered, tensing his muscles and feeling the body heat of Wayts almost touching him. "Nineteen... go."

Swooping Hawk melted into the trees. The small band of woods wasn't particularly thick, and it was a temperate wood, too. Pines, eucalyptus, oak, and even some Candlenuts. Ground cover was sparse, a few bushes here and there but nothing like the tropical foliage near the coasts. Nothing like what he'd had to contend with on New Ireland.

So it was easy to locate his target in what amounted to near pitch black. The trees and their canopy blocked most of the moonlight and the dense fog, a little lighter in the trees, did the rest.

Yet for the Indian, who'd grown up in the deserts and on the forested Colorado Plateau of Arizona, it was like being home. His hunting and tracking instincts, honed by countless generations of his ancestors, allowed the young man to move like a wisp and straight toward the unsuspecting Japanese soldier who crouched behind a trio of pepper trees.

All humans had this instinctive capacity. The Native American tribes who'd lived in North America since the last ice age had no special power… it was only that they used these instincts and the skills they helped to hone regularly. It was no surprise to Swooping Hawk, therefore, that at the last moment before he struck, the Jap tensed, sensing danger nearby.

The warning came too late, however. Before the man could react, a rough hand slipped over his mouth and a razor-sharp black blade slid between his ribs and into his heart. The soldier spasmed, jerked, and twitched as his heart burst, but made no sound.

When the man was still and dead, Swooping Hawk let his body fall. He wiped his blade on the man's tunic and said a quick prayer for his spirit. He didn't like killing this way… it was dishonorable. Except that the Jap and his friends had planned just such a thing, so all was fair in war.

Turner's experience thirty feet to the east was almost opposite. He sensed the lone attacker almost too late. However, he had some experience with this type of fighting, and he had another advantage that the Jap didn't take into account.

The soldier leapt from behind his cover, silent as a wraith, bayonet in hand. Turner flung himself sideways and down, tucking and rolling to gain distance. The soldier stumbled, wheeled clumsily toward Turner and raised his blade for a killing stroke.

That's when Wayts jumped on his back, driving the man to his knees. The rugged sailor then began pounding his fist into the smaller man's face, the blows and *umphs* like dull reports in the fog.

Turner came in then and drove the point of his KA bar up under the man's chin, through his tongue and soft pallet and into his brain. The ease with which the steel penetrated the flesh almost made Turner puke.

Wayts let the dead soldier fall and gawked at the nearly invisible silhouette of his captain. The younger man was breathing hard, almost hyper-ventilating with fright and horror. Turner moved close and put his hands on Wayts's shoulders.

"Easy…" he whispered only inches from the man's ear. "Get your breath back… breathe easy, Lee…"

"Sir..." Wayts pleaded, not knowing how to frame what was in his mind.

"I know... I know... c'mon."

The five men came together at the far end of the hundred feet or so of woods, near the far corner of the village. Once reassembled, Swooping Hawk spoke first.

"I think there were only two," he said. "Skipper and I got one each."

"No resistance for our part," Vickers said. "But you can be sure there are more yellow bastards further along... and in those fields. I certainly hope the captain and colonel fair all right."

"We could still warn them," turner said.

Vickers frowned, "My fear is that our transmission would make a sound and give them away. Bad luck, I'm afraid."

A quarter of a mile away, Archer and Tank led their twelve men into the far end of a field of wheat. The rows, perhaps a hundred yards long, had been planted perpendicular to the road. Not ideal, but still useful.

Archer moved all the way down to the far end of the row and peeked out. He studied what little could be seen for a moment and moved back to the small group of men.

"All right, lads," he whispered as they huddled as close together as they could. "These vegetables run right up to the edge of town. Across the street there is a line of trees. Not very thick, I should say, as the edge of the plateau is likely near."

"Shall we simply break through right up to it, sir?" a man Tank didn't know asked.

"Something like that," said Archer. "However, I'd like a team to parallel us from across the way. Send rounds into the rows if the need should arise. Sound like a job you might manage, Tank Old Boy?"

"Yes, sir," said Tank, wondering if he could even see across the road in the fog.

"Splendid... Wallace, Evers, Bridgeton, you're with our submariner here, "Archer said. "Go across and attempt to stay in the tree line, Broderick. Move toward town at a regular pace. Not too swiftly, now.

We'll be pushing through eye-high stalks, so the going will be slow. Any questions? No? Right, let's be about it, then."

Tank and his men peeled off from the squad and moved quickly and silently out of the wheat fields and across the rough track and to the line of trees beyond. Even in the open ground, the visibility was terrible. For although the fog glowed with the ethereal light of the bloated moon above, this meager light offered perhaps fifteen or twenty feet of visibility.

It reminded Tank of some sort of amusement park fun house. A hall of mirrors or smoked glass where anything could appear around any corner. In this case, however, that might mean an angry Jap and his razor-sharp bayonet rushing at you from the mist.

It went well, for a while. Archer and his men spread out in teams of two and began picking their way forward. They pressed as quietly as they could through each row, scanning up and down the lanes between plants, and moved on again. They were spaced as far apart as possible while still maintaining at least a partial view of each pair. This meant that Archer and his partner were no more than twenty-five yards away from the other end of his line.

It was something of a surprise, therefore, when the colonel pushed through perhaps the twentieth or thirtieth row of grain that a dark, crouching figure was already waiting just a few yards to his left. In the gloom of the fog, realization took an extra second or two, and fortunately for the colonel, his teammate came to it first.

The young Australian slammed into his boss, driving both men to the ground as the shadowy figure let out a startled little cry, brought up a long-barreled rifle… and ended any hope of a stealthy approach.

The shot was dull, watery, and swallowed up by the heavy mist. But it was enough to alert the rest of the enemy hiding in the wheat… and two crouching behind trees right in Tank's path.

The man who'd fired first had missed, his shot going wild and wide. Archer, regaining himself with admirable speed, rolled and pumped a round into the man's chest, eliciting another cry and toppling the soldier over.

Archer's partner moved in, quickly stripping the man of extra ammo and a grenade. He showed it to the colonel who nodded.

December 24, 1942

"Throw it, far as you can, Culver," instructed the Commando leader.

"But the Nip, sir?" protested the young soldier.

Already, several shouts and hurled Japanese curses could be heard from further ahead. Although oddly distorted by the fog, there was no doubt that the jig was up.

"What's done is done," Archer shrugged.

The 2IC soldier pulled the pin and hurled the grenade toward the town. A few seconds later, the fog nearby lit with a smokey glow, and a dull, throaty report pushed through the wheat.

This elicited another set of alarmed shouts. No screams of pain, however. But the Jap was now on notice that they were under attack.

"Charge!" Archer shouted down the line. "Staggered attainment, lads! Five seconds and for God's sake… be careful what you shoot at!"

Tank heard the ruckus, of course. Heard the dull thud of the Arisaka's report and the follow-up from Archer's weapon. The much larger .45 slug from the Thompson distinctive even in the heavy, damp air. When the grenade went off twenty seconds later, Tank cursed Archer's name.

"What the bloody *hell*…?" Wallace blurted.

"Cards are on the table now!" Tank exclaimed. "Let's double time it and keep low! Who knows where the shots'll come from."

Good advice, but advice that Tank's men didn't need. They were Second Independent Commandos. Well-trained for counter insurgency and, over the past few months, had gained experience no classroom or instruction could ever impart.

Tank had hardly taken more than a dozen jogging steps when the trees exploded before them. A pair of khaki-clad wraiths came shrieking out of the darkness and fog, leading with killing blades at the end of their rifles.

All that saved Tank was his size, instinct, and no small amount of luck. His opponent simply appeared before him, the sharp blade driving for his chest. Tank's Thompson was shouldered, ready to find a target and he was able to swing the weapon out, batting the killing thrust aside so that it only tore through his tunic and skittered along his ribcage just under his left arm.

There was a nearby shot… another… and the wild eyes of Tank's opponent, now only inches from his own as the two men collided, froze at their widest aperture as a sharp blade was driven into his neck from Tank's right.

The electrician saw the pale face of Bridgeton, a lean wiry man from Sydney who fancied himself a shark hunter. The soldier, about Tank's age, grinned at him.

"Got the blighter, mate! You all right?"

Evers and Wallace had already dispatched the other Jap and were stripping both bodies as Tank took stock of himself. His tunic was torn, and a warm trickle slithered down his body from beneath his armpit. He reached through the tear and felt the raised welt and linear slice in his skin. It was maybe three or four inches long, but not deep. His fingers did come away sticky, however.

"Just knicked me," Tank said. "C'mon, fellas… let's get movin'. Something tells me it's been easy so far."

When the shots, grenade, and more shots and shouts batted their way through the fog, Captain Cooper and his men were already in position. However, they would not find that the battle began easily.

For an equal number of Japanese regulars had melded into the woods south of town in preparation for an attack. Although they were not surprised when signs of one began, they were rather nonplussed when they came out of concealment in the shadowy wood and found that they were not alone.

The squad of Australians was equally alarmed by the sudden appearance of spectral figures in the dark and seemingly from every direction at once.

Two dozen hearts took to pounding with adrenaline-fueled terror. Terror at the shock and at the even more horrifying realization that it was too dark to tell friend from foe. The main difference was that most of the Australians were larger than the Japanese, but that couldn't be determined until the men were within grappling distance.

An eerie and blood-curdling cry of "Banzai!" rose from the Japanese soldiers, momentarily distinguishing them from their enemy. With lightning speed, Cooper and his men slung their rifles, most of which were Arisakas like their counterparts, and drove in toward the nearest enemy, ducking low and launching themselves upward.

"Fuck you, Tojo!" Cooper cried, and his men followed suit.

What followed was a grunting, shouting, and heaving melee of warm bodies smashing into one another. Clawed hands lashed out, reaching for throats, eyes, and genitals. Weapons were dropped and more than one man fumbled out a blade.

At first, though, the fighting was fists, feet, and even teeth. The commandos, having trained for such close-quarters chaos, had a method for determining friend from foe.

"Kanga!" a man would shout into the vague face of his opponent.

Should the other man answer with "roo," then the two would know that they were friends. Should that not occur, then holds were no longer barred.

As Cooper and his men grappled with the writhing forms of mostly invisible opponents, therefore, a strange cacophony of kanga and roo were lifted into the foggy night. On at least two occasions, two Australians found that they were grappling with their friends and turned to locate other targets.

As soon as Allies and Japanese were paired off, however, the fight devolved into something bloodier and far more deadly. Knives appeared. KA-bars, clasp knives, and IJA issue combat blades as well. Rifles were lost and pistols useless, so men went for each other with mortal intent.

Not a single man escaped some injury, be it a bloody nose, a slash across a limb, or a puncture to the torso. As this madness ensued, a writhing, grunting, screaming hullabaloo, the battle in the fields grew in intensity as Archer's men met a squad of IJA regulars and a deadly game of hide and seek began.

The only thing that perhaps saved Cooper's men and their opponents from total destruction were shouted calls from the town in Japanese. Evidently, this was a rallying cry because upon shaking loose from their Australian foes, the remaining Japanese retreated into the darkness and to the north.

"Sound off, lads!" Cooper shouted, tossing a dead soldier away from him and struggling to his feet, the soldier's blade still protruding from his right buttock. "Who's left?"

Men called out their names. Cooper counted eight, where there had been a dozen just five minutes earlier. He yanked the blade from his backside and cringed as a flood of hot blood spilled down his trouser leg. He fumbled on the ground and found his radio.

"Someone get a light and get me an accurate count!" he ordered as he turned the unit on. "Blue, all! Repeat, blue, all! Have met enemy force at position! Have wounded! White squad, can you send your medic?"

There was a brief pause and then Turner's voice came out of the speaker, "*Blue, White... Roger. What's your position, over?*"

"Position two," Cooper said, indicating that he was roughly where he had planned to set up. "We'll watch for your man. Be advised, White, there are enemy units in here."

A snort, "*Roger that, Blue... have eliminated several. Standby.*"

Cooper turned to try and make sense of his situation. It was still too shadowy and foggy to tell much. However, his men were busy getting themselves in hand as well as stripping the bodies... of both sides... of essential equipment. The captain tried not to think about that.

"Red, blue... what's your status, over?" he asked.

There was no response, even when he repeated the call. However, the increasing frequency of shots from the east gave him a pretty good idea of what was happening.

"White, Blue... proceed with objective," Cooper said.

"*Roger.*"

"And Captain... burn what you complete," Cooper said. It sounded like an order, which he had no right to give, regardless. The submarine captain outranked him and may or may not comply.

"*Say again, Blue?*"

Cooper smiled thinly, "We're here to raze this place, White... leave no retreat for enemy units. Out."

Turner didn't respond, and Cooper was left to wonder what the man would do. He could tell that the submarine captain, although formidable, was a man who still held some ideals. This in spite of the story Archer told about Turner strangling a Jap several nights earlier.

That was a flash in the pan to what Cooper, Smithers, and their men had been through over the past five months. How they'd had to live off the land, hitting Japanese outposts and patrols when they could and then melting back into the bush. How they'd had to trust locals, sometimes to their peril. How they'd had to become cold, calculating killers in order to survive... and how perhaps much of their humanity had been stripped down to bare, savage bones.

Turner might be angry at the Japanese, but he wasn't anywhere near that level. Even the fight Cooper and his men had just fought was welcome to them. A savage, tooth and nail scrap that rent flesh and smashed bones. A pure, unadulterated slugfest up close and personal with their hated foe.

Rustling and crashing came from the foliage to the west. Two figures appeared out of the darkness, tracking the torches now being used to scan the clearing, where ten dead men lay in a psychotic impressionist painter's nightmare of blood.

"Jesus Christ!" Henry Hoffman blurted as he slid to a stop near Cooper. Young Wayts was beside him. "What the hell happened here?"

"War, mate," growled Cooper. "Look after my men, will you?"

Hoffman saw the dark stain on Cooper's leg in the brief beam of a flash as it swept by, "You've got a wound there, Captain. I should—"

"My men first, Doc," Cooper's voice was tempered steel. "I'll do for the time being. What's on with your skipper?"

"He and the Sarge and Freddy are moving into town," Wayts said.

"And we shall follow," Cooper said. "You two men are all right tending to the wounded?"

"Got three I can treat... one okay for duty, two that'll have to hang back," Hoffman said after quickly inspecting the men still on their feet. "Four fatalities, sir... I'm sorry."

Cooper sighed, "It's war, mate. Hard luck."

Cooper's radio crackled, "*All units! All units, Red! We've got new arrivals to the ball, lads! Two trucks coming up the road from the east! Possible reserve troops, the slanty-eyed buggers! May be as many as thirty or forty! Be advised... we are surrounded!*"

Wayts's eyes were huge in the dim glow of multiple flashlights, "What does that mean, sir? What do we do?"

Cooper met the younger man's fearful gaze, "We stop mucking about, lad."

24

"Oh, you gotta be puttin' me on!" Tank grumped when he heard the faint but growing whine of engines.

"What is it, Cobber?" asked Evers.

Tank moved to the edge of the trees, and swore, "Can't see shit through this pea soup... but it sounds like trucks. Like them Jap six-by-sixes comin' up the road."

"Crikey!" Wallace griped. "It's *two* of the blighters!"

"So much for hitting the town..." Tank said, turning east. "Let's make tracks, fellas!"

"Bloody *what?*" asked Evers. "There must be a whole platoon back there!"

"Yeah, and they're driving right up our friend's asses!" Tank barked. "So we're gonna make 'em think twice! You boys with me or do I have to win this fuckin' war all by myself?"

"Blimey!" Bridgeton guffawed. "You oughta come and work with us, Tank!"

Tank scoffed, "Run around in the jungles all day like this? That's crazy."

"You spend all day locked into a sewer pipe, mate," Evers pointed out as the men began jogging through the tree line.

"Good point!" quipped Tank, crashing through brush and not caring about noise.

Evers had been right, though. Tank could hear two distinct engines now. The fog still obscured the vehicles, and its thickness was probably giving a false impression of closeness. However, if Tank couldn't see the Jap, then the Jap couldn't see him.

"No headlights!" Wallace observed.

"They're stopping…" Evers noted.

The man was right. The roar of the trucks' motors fell off into a low purr. Tank thought that they'd stopped short of the edge of the wheat field but couldn't be certain. When multiple shouts arose from the fog, shouts in Japanese, there was no doubt that a significant number of men were organizing to fight.

"Sons of bitches knew we were comin'," Tank muttered as he slowed and brought up his SMG. "Somebody tipped them off."

"Locals maybe," Bridgeton surmised. "It's hit or miss with these Portagees."

"Or some of your men were captured," Tank said. "Don't you have a squad out on patrol or somethin'?"

"Platoon," Wallace said and spat. "But Lieutenant Smithers wouldn't give the game away, mate. Not him. Not for all the prawns in Perth."

"Any man can be tortured," Tank said darkly. "Even the toughest of us can be broken, fellas… but that don't matter now… I think I see the first truck."

"What's the plan?" Evers asked.

"This," said Tank, setting his Thompson to full auto.

He moved forward a few more paces, leaned against a tree and sighted in. He lined up and squeezed the trigger. The Tommy gun clattered; its heavy caliber fire impressive even dulled by the heavy air.

.45 slugs ripped into the engine compartment of the truck, shattered the windscreen and hurried the driver into death. Tank then swept the weapon to the left, hoping to hit any men who would naturally be sheltering between the first truck and the trees.

"Bloody *hell!*" Bridgeton blurted and then laughed as he too stepped forward and searched for targets. "They always said you Yanks were daft!"

"You know they'll come for us now, right?" Wallace asked as he lined up.

"Let 'em… the slant-eyed bastards!" Evers said. "We've got cover, fog, and dark. Four against thirty is good odds, eh?"

"Hit and move," Bridgeton advised as Tank swapped out his empty magazine. "And single shots only, Cobber!"

"Already ahead of ya'," Tank said, moving closer through the trees. "Let's hope somebody returns this favor!"

* * *

Turner, Vickers, and Swooping Hawk darted from the woods and made a beeline for the closest house. The town of Mindelo wasn't organized like any modern American town Turner knew. There were no streets and delineated yards. In spite of the somewhat more modern and western construction methods, Mindelo was still an island village. The homes were arranged in a haphazard semi-circle around the centralized structures. They were laid out with comfortable spaces in between them, with some even having erected makeshift fences to segregate their property from their neighbors.

There were perhaps two dozen houses south of the center of town, a few more near the fields, and several others on the far side of town between the square, for lack of a better term, and the rough cliff of the plateau. Evidently there was more open land along the river's edge used as communal space.

The strangest part to Turner was how there had yet to be any outcry from the residents. One would assume that once the shooting started, especially early in the morning, that lights would come on and alarmed voices would call out.

Yet the town was as silent as the grave. The only auditory clues of occupancy were the occasional squawk of a chicken, the bleat of alarmed sheep and goats, and the clipped, guttural crack of a Japanese voice.

"Bloody ghost town," Vickers mused as they neared the first home.

"Maybe the people took to the hills when trouble was sniffed out," Swooping Hawk suggested.

"I hope so," Turner said, slinging his Thompson and pulling his .45. "Not keen on barging into innocent people's homes and doing them harm."

Vickers scoffed, "They're letting Tojo use their village as an outpost, sir. Nothing innocent about these blighters."

"Easy to say when some slant isn't holding a pistol to your baby's head, Sergeant," Turner growled.

Vickers scoffed, "Believe me, sir… it doesn't take near that much."

Turner grunted as he went up the two steps to the front door of what might be a two- or three-room house. The structure was perhaps seven or eight hundred square feet, with a pitched shingled roof and rough siding. There were even glass windows. With only a little imagination, the submarine captain could imagine a turn of the century midwestern farmhouse. Perhaps even finding a young Laura Ingles Wilder within, painstakingly penning her *Little House on the Prairie* series that his own daughter loved so much…

Turner tried the knob. Locked, of course. He stepped back on the small landing and aimed his pistol.

"One moment, sir!" said Vickers, bounding up and brushing past Turner as he raised his right leg and slammed the heel of his boot into the doorknob.

The door flew inward, and Vickers dropped to his back. Turner was momentarily confused until the dark shadowy form leapt out, a Banzai war cry splitting the night air.

The Japanese soldier drove his bayonet toward his target and was almost comically surprised to find none. His momentum carried him forward, where Vicker's left boot connected with the man's midsection, carried him over the prone commando, and sent him diving over the stairs, Arisaka spinning and war cry disintegrating into a shriek of agony as Swooping Hawk's pistol round smashed his breastbone.

"Christ!" Turner exclaimed, even as he dove through the open doorway and threw himself sideways and into a crouch.

The door opened into a large room, with homemade furniture in the middle and a small kitchen to the right. A separate doorway led into what might be a bedroom. The captain swung his pistol back and forth, searching for a target in the nearly pitch black house.

Vickers was there, crab-walking into the door and followed by Swooping Hawk, who knelt down with his pistol at the ready.

"Clear in here!" Turner said, moving toward the kitchen and on his feet again.

"Hang on, sir!" Vickers said. "Let's check this area…"

Vickers dashed to the bedroom door and swung in, leading with his pistol. After a moment, he leaned his head back out, "All clear. Everyone all—"

There were three windows facing more or less east. One in the bedroom, one in the parlor, and a smaller one in the kitchen. All three exploded, heralding the not so distant but fog-muffled crack of multiple rifles.

"Down!" Swooping Hawk said, flinging himself forward and moving toward the living room window, being careful not to slice himself on broken glass.

"Bloody yellow bastards!" Vickers cranked as he got low.

The exterior wall of the house was smacked by several more shots. Although dark inside, there was just enough light coming through the windows to reveal puffs of dust blooming into little vanishing nimbuses as they caught a tiny shard of moonlight. Turner noticed and swore.

"What the hell're these houses made of? Plaster? Out!" he barked, getting as low as he could and making for the front door.

Vickers was doing the same, half-crawling across the wooden floor. Swooping Hawk shouted in triumph, alarming Turner at first.

"Freddy?" asked the captain. "You hit?"

"Nah!" whooped the Navajo, hoisting something dark and tubular. "Found a souvenir, sir!"

The three men leapt out of the front door as more rounds peppered the house, punching through the thin walls and shattering more glass, tinging off invisible somethings and clunking into wooden furniture.

Once outside in the dim glow of the fog, Swooping Hawk held up his prize again, "20mm knee mortar, Captain... Sarge... and four shells!"

"Smashing!" Vickers said. "Think you can give those buggers in the next house what for, mate?"

"I can try," said Swooping Hawk confidently.

"Nix that, lad," Vickers said, slinging his rifle and holding out his hands. "You and the skipper go to either side and send a few of those heavy rounds their way, give them pause. I'll set up back here. Have some experience with these fellows. Call out range and effect, all right?"

"Got it," Turner said and slid around the far wall while Swooping Hawk slid around the other.

There were apparently three Japs in the next house, perhaps thirty yards away from the back of the first. Turner slid along the wall, eased his barrel around and peaked in time to see a trio of muzzle flashes coming through the open windows of the next house. Even at that distance, the fog was thick enough that the scene was blurry and indistinct, at least until the Arisakas lit up the fog with little tongues of flame.

"Thirty yards!" Swooping Hawk shouted, then ducked back as several rounds splintered the corner near where he'd been.

Turner leaned out, shouldered his Thompson, and sent half his magazine into the next house. He had no idea if he'd hit anything, yet if the 7.7mm rounds from the Japanese rifles could penetrate the walls, then his .45 caliber rounds, more than half again as heavy, would do so easily.

Turner never heard the thump of the knee mortar going off. Yet when the shell struck just in front of the house and flashed in a thundering crack that lit up the fog like some Hollywood special effect, he felt the impact in his bones.

He ducked back as several more rounds zipped past, at least two of the Japs inside the house having survived his onslaught. As more Thompson rounds from Swooping Hawk's weapon tore the night open, Turner bellowed back toward the other side of the house.

"Good line up! Five yards short!"

Crack! Crack! Crack!

"Argh! Shit!"

That'd been Swooping Hawk. Turner's shout was drowned as yet another mortar round exploded. This time, it hit the mark.

Vickers's round went straight through the middle window of the house. The explosion was muffled by walls and by the wet air. Yet the screams of agony and the crackle and crumble as the house's rear wall was disassembled by the concussion told the tale.

Turner bolted, rounding the backside of his house and racing across, exposed to the threat from the other house and not caring. Of course, that threat hardly seemed a viable one. The house had half collapsed and was already smoking as yellow flames licked at the windows and reached their incandescent talons for the roof.

"Again!" shouted the submarine captain as he slid around the corner and nearly went tumbling over his engineman's body.

Turner slid to his knees and reached for the young man, "Swooping Hawk! Freddy!"

Another rumble, another series of cracks, and then the steady, sizzle and pop and the heady campfire tang as Vickers's third round ignited the next house and whoever might still be within.

"Sir…?" the Indian gasped, blinking up at Turner with wide amber eyes and a pallid, sweaty face.

"How bad?" Turner asked. "Where are you hit?"

"I… I think my chest, sir…" Swooping Hawk gasped.

Vickers appeared and took up a defensive position, kneeling beside the two men, "How bad, sir?"

"Chest, he says," Turner rolled the Navajo onto his back and tried to look closer. The light inside the fog was now brighter, the burning house only a hundred feet away imbuing the mist with a hellish crimson glow. In that glow, Turner saw a dark red splotch spreading on the left side of the young man's blouse.

"You're gonna be okay, Freddy," Turner reassured. "It's high up, near the shoulder. Doesn't look too bad."

"White man speak with forked tongue…" Swooping Hawk coughed and then grinned. "Feels like somebody stuck a damned marling spike in there, sir."

"I'll bet," said Turner, lifting the man's left hand. "Can you squeeze that?"

"Yeah... *shit!* Yeah, I can..."

"Good sign, that," Vickers said and smiled down at the Navajo. "Get a purple heart for this, mate. Be a hero. All the sheilas in Perth will be fighting over you."

"So... what else is new?" groaned the Indian.

Vickers's and Turner's laughs were cut short as multiple dark figures swarmed out of the fog, their rifles crackling. The three men had beaten back one attack only to draw another.

"Christ, this never ends..." Turner growled as he readied his weapon.

"Skipper!" shouted a familiar voice.

"Blimey!" Vickers cheered. "It's our lads! Good on ya', mates!"

Men ran, some behind and some in front of the burning house, their weapons flashing and angry battle cries and shouts splitting open the night. As Cooper's men advanced, more than one Mindelo residence responded as more concealed Japs poked from their hidey-holes and returned fire.

The battle was joined, and evidently, the enemy had foreseen trouble. Yet they were holed up. Stationary. Identifiable. Cooper and his remaining men were mobile, aggressive, and coming out of the dark.

One of them split off and angled for Turner, fumbling to remove his pack even as his silhouette resolved into the tall, handsome form of Henry Hoffman.

"Good timing, Doc!" Turner enthused. "Freddy's been hit. Where's Wayts? How goes Blue squad?"

Hoffman was huffing as he dug through his pack, "We ran into a squad of Nips hiding in the woods... hand to hand... bloody. Cooper lost four men, three more wounded but able to fight. Damndest thing, sir... can one of you hold this light, please?"

Turner did so, "Where's Wayts?"

"With the captain," Hoffman said, bending close to examine the wound. "Oh, yeah... got you in the meat, pal. Gonna have to cut your tunic away."

Swooping Hawk scoffed, "It's my best outfit… but okay."

"Captain, Sarge… can we get him someplace?" Hoffman asked.

Turner and Vickers exchanged a glance and Turner replied, "This house is intact. Some broken glass, but it might have a decent bed."

"Okay… if you can help me, I'll get to work," Hoffman said. "You can leave us, sir. No doubt Captain Cooper could use two more good hands."

"Bugger…" Vickers grumped. "Can't leave you undefended with a wounded man, mate."

"Won't have to, Sergeant," said a new figure. He and a companion hobbled out of the night. "It's Corporal Stephens, Sarge. Mathews and I can stand watch over these blokes. Use this house as a makeshift hospital, eh?"

"Can you shoot?" Vickers asked the wounded men.

"Aye, that we can," said Mathews. "Me and Willy here's got leg wounds, so we're a bit hobbled… but can aim a rifle certain sure."

"Captain?" Vickers asked Turner.

Turner bit his lip. He didn't relish leaving his men again, especially with one wounded. However, the situation demanded it, "All right… if you're sure, Hank."

"We'll be all right, sir," said the pharmacist's mate.

"Go get 'em, Skipper," Swooping Hawk added.

Turner rose to his feet and gritted his teeth, "C'mon, Sarge… let's get this *done*."

25

They were halfway to the town and already Archer had lost four men. The Japanese were hidden seemingly everywhere in the dense wheat rows. At every other one, in spite of their best efforts to be cautious, one of the little yellow sons of bitches would appear and let go with a shrill Banzai and a full clip down the row.

When the new threat came in from the east, Archer considered falling back. He had already cleared several hundred yards of field, and with his remaining men, he could line up along the rows and ambush the Japanese platoon no doubt forming up to attack from his rear.

There had been no further radio communication once the announcement was made that two trucks were coming in. He had no idea what was happening with Red and White squads. Although when automatic weapons' fire and several dull explosions rippled through the fog from the direction of town, he could well imagine.

No doubt both Turner and Cooper had joined the enemy in battle. Of Cooper's skill, Archer had no doubts. The past five months on Timor had hardened the new commando into a deadly blade of war. For Turner's part, Archer had no doubt of the man's courage or tenacity. However, he worried that the submariner's inexperience or his anger might lead him into folly.

Of course, Archer wasn't much better off. With Broderick and three men gone and the four he'd lost; Archer was down to but five commandos and himself. Yes, they'd taken out more than twice as many enemy… but attrition was still taking its toll. Who knew how many more Japanese lay concealed in the wheat. Or what surprises they might have had time to prepare.

He could press on or fall back and try to link up with Broderick. With the two fire teams and good concealment, they might stand a chance even if there was indeed an entire Japanese platoon coming in.

He needed a third option. Archer knew that he couldn't simply turn away. The Japanese lying in wait for him would figure that out eventually and then come after them. A large and well-organized force to his front… a stealthy enemy in his rear…

When the clatter of a Tommy gun rippled from a few hundred yards to the northeast, Archer knew that Tank had made up *his* mind as to what to do. A bold move, but eventually foolhardy.

Then it came to him. Archer let out a shrill double-horse whistle and waited as his remaining men pulled back to join him. In that time, he yanked several wheat stalks up by their roots and laid them into the next row so that they connected the two groups of plants. Once done, he pulled out his trusty Zippo and applied the flame to the foliage before him.

The air was heavy with moisture, but the crop was somewhat dry. He could only hope that the flame would take and that the faint breeze might carry it to the west.

"Bloody *hell*…" Archer cranked as the little tongue of flame succeeded only in sizzling against the base of a wheat stalk.

"Here, let me, sir," said a dark figure who moved to squat beside him. Something rustled and then gurgled.

"What's that, Blomfield?" Archer asked.

The soldier's grin appeared ghostly in the gloom. "Bit of sippin' medicine, sir."

"Liquor?" Archer asked, indignant at first but then smiling himself. "You could be disciplined for that, man."

"A court martial would mean I get out of this mess, sir…" said the man, finishing soaking a rag in the acrid booze. "Be Fiddler's Green by comparison… try it now, Colonel."

The rag caught, whooshed, and a foot-high tongue of fire licked at the wheat. At first, the damp plant sizzled and hissed, but then began to blacken, crackle, and the tongue grew into a pillar.

"Jolly good!" enthused Archer. "Let the slants deal with *that!* Come on, lads! The Nips think they've got the drop on us… let's repay the favor, eh?"

"From the sounds of it, sir…" Blomfield huffed as they crashed through the wheat in the direction they'd come, "that daft sailor's already begun!"

"And God bless him for it!" another man cackled.

* * *

"Well, this is a fine kettle of fish!" Evers groused as another two dozen lead bees sizzled through the leaves, smacked into tree trunks, and vanished into the fog.

"Thought you boys liked to fight!" Tank exclaimed as he belly crawled toward the base of a Candlenut tree at the edge of the road.

"Yeah, a fair fight!" Wallace complained. "Not being shot at by two dozen squint-eyes, mate!"

Tank leaned around the base of the tree and squeezed his trigger. The last dozen rounds from his Thompson's magazine sped downrange toward the first truck. He couldn't really look, simply poking his barrel out and firing, but thought he heard at least two screams of pain.

Tank then hurled himself back to the left as more than a dozen Arisaka rounds pattered into his tree, sending a cloud of razor-sharp splinters spinning into the night.

"Now there's twenty-two!" he declared, scuttling sideways and ejecting his magazine. He fumbled with the next, nearly dropped it, and seated it home. It was his last.

"Are all Yanks as daft as you?" Bridgeton asked.

"Nah… I'm considered to be pretty tame," Tank lied.

That drew laughs from the other three men even as more round's pitter-pattered through the foliage. Now the reports from the individual weapons could be heard.

"Think they're gettin' closer!" Evers shouted.

"Yeah... probably figured out we're just four mental cases out on a lark!" Tank jeered. "Let's move!"

The big American began to low-crawl through the trees, and nowhere but to the east. The three Australians gawked but followed dutifully.

"That's not a bloody retreat!" Evers noted.

"What the bloody Christ...?" Wallace seconded.

"He's goin' for 'em! Right for 'em!" Bridgeton exclaimed, half admiring and half in disbelief. "Out of his bleedin' mind, he is!"

"I can hear you guys!" Tank said. "Move your asses already!"

Evers was right, though. Tank could now hear Japanese shouts and orders over the rifle cracks. They might be moving forward, perhaps even taking up firing positions in the field across the road. Only one truck engine was still running, at least. No doubt his rounds had killed the leading vehicle's engine. Although that would make it difficult for the second truck to move toward town, it also created a fairly solid bit of cover for the enemy.

"Hey... what's that smell?" Tank whispered as the men found a new position.

"Me... I've gone and shat my bloomers..." Wallace chuckled.

"Nah... that's smoke... did somebody—"

That's when two much heavier projectiles crashed through the trees and exploded, shaking several large trunks, bringing down a hailstorm of limbs, pinecones, and leaves, and throwing up a pall of dust that hovered on the thick air and spread like a cloud of pesticide.

The mortars had landed not far from where the four men had been just a few minutes before. Had Tank not moved... they'd have been torn into bloody rags.

"Shit..." Bridgeton hissed as the four men huddled together, covering their mouths to keep the dust out.

A heavy silence fell. A palpable tension floating on the heavy fog. And then a Japanese voice spoke, its arrogance echoing slightly through the humidity.

"Hey! Hey, Kangaroos!" the man heckled. "You come out! You give up and we be friends! We make you nice cup of tea!"

Men laughed. A *lot* of men. Tank couldn't tell how many, but he accurately guessed it was more than twenty-two.

"Why you not answer?" the Jap sneered. "You scared, Kangaroos? We kill crocodile! Throw him on barbie just for you! No? You no want crocodile? All sand groper and gum sucker like crocodile! You come out, now!"

"Little bloody bastard…" Bridgeton's knuckles were white on his rifle.

"And all slants like *this!*" a voice shouted from the south and several rifles began to crackle, maintaining a volley fire.

"Jesus Christ!" Evers blurted. "It's the colonel!"

"Let's not give them any air, fellas!" Tank got up and into a crouch. He shuffled forward until he could see through the trees and began sending rounds at the dark shapes ahead in the fog.

The other men joined in and combined with the men across the road in the fields, they began to push the Japanese back. However, they were still outnumbered more than three to one, and when mortars began to fly and a heavy, throaty chatter tore the fog open, the Australians and their British and American friend began to doubt their bravado.

And then, from behind and to the east, the woods in which Tank and his team were sequestered rattled and rustled as many large forms crashed through them. In a heart-stopping instant, the four men knew they were lost as more than two dozen silhouettes materialized out of the foggy gloom.

"G'day!" an Australian voice shouted cheerfully. "Could you lads use a hand?"

"Lieutenant Smithers!" Wallace shouted and whooped in joy. "By God!"

The woods, the fields and the road came alive with snapping, chattering, and roaring ordnance as the now three dozen strong Commando unit surrounded and cut the Japanese down. With no more cover than the trucks they'd come in, more than a few of the enemy soldier's broke rank and made a mad dash to the east. In spite of the shouts and curses of their officers and sergeants, ten men tried in vain to vanish into the fog.

But Smithers had set his men up well and they were spread out along a thirty-yard line. Even in the darkness and fog, the routed Japanese were cut down in less than ten seconds.

Just like that, the tables had been turned and turned again. The Commandos surged out of the forest and fields and met near the front of the shot-up truck. Archer and Smithers shook hands, men pounded each other on the backs, and Tank and his team were enveloped into the fold.

"God bless my soul!" Archer said, shaking his head. "Taking on a bloody nip platoon, Petty Officer! What would your captain say?"

"With all due respect, sir… I'd like to go and find out," Tank grinned.

***

They were spreading out. Moving from house to house, each new structure and each new victory a brawl of lead and steel.

Although Turner didn't like it, he had to accept the willful arson by the Commandos. Cooper and his men, upon clearing a house, set it ablaze. With each new fire, the battle scene at least became more and more lighted.

Turner's and Vickers's first assault was fast and brutal. They cleared the next house over from the one Hoffman was now using as an aid station and Vickers set fire to the place. The next one to the north was turned a bit and from one of the windows, a Japanese sniper nearly did them in.

A round slammed into the corner of the house mere inches from Vickers, who jerked back, nearly knocking turner off his feet.

"Blimey!" snapped Vickers. "Captain! If you can lay down suppressive fire, I'll dash across and surprise him, eh?"

"It's gotta be twenty yards!" Turner shouted over the snaps and pops of multiple weapons fire. The sound was swallowed by the fog and regurgitated in echoes that seemed to come from everywhere at once.

"Can't have it too easy, now can we, sir?" Vickers said. "Hang on…"

Another five crackles as the Jap in the next house emptied his clip at the two partially exposed Allies.

"Now!" Vickers shouted.

Not waiting for a response or to see if Turner was ready, the Australian sergeant took off at top speed, ducking low and chewing up ground. Turner swore and sighted in, squeezing his trigger and sending four controlled bursts at the next house. He walked his tracers along the bottom of the three windows. The heavy rounds splintered wood and plaster and sent a galaxy of glittering glass shards vomiting into the house. More than one man screamed, their flesh torn open by thousands of jagged shards.

Turner's bolt locked open. As if that had been a switch, he saw a shadowy figure rise near the house and a voice shouted.

"Fire in the hole, you yellow butt-fuckers!"

The three black squares that yawned in the house's face like some tri-cloptic monster lit from within. Blackness turned to bright white, and more screams were heard, even as part of the wall blew outward, burning and leaving licking flame behind.

"Bloody hell!" Vickers yipped.

Turner was already running. He fumbled with the magazine release and let the empty fall unheeded to the damp earth. He fumbled in his pockets and could not find a replacement.

He was nearly to Vickers when two ghouls right out of a nightmare hurled themselves from the blasted open house. The figures flew into the night, their hair and limbs dancing with yellow flame as they bellowed an inhuman nightmare screech.

Turner threw himself to the left, involuntarily squeezing his trigger as the phantoms plummeted to the earth, still writhing in agony as death roasted them.

"Good God!" Vickers shouted. "Must've been half a dozen in there… poor buggers."

Turner gaped. Gaped at the two cooking soldiers now lying still on the wet grass and mud. Gaped at the twisted and bloody forms inside as they too began to sizzle and pop as the flames roasted their flesh.

"Oh, Jesus…" muttered the Captain. "Oh, sweet Jesus…"

"That'll learn 'em, eh?" Vickers's grin was as inhuman as the charred skulls of the burning corpses at their feet. "Pay the devils back a bit, sir… well done. Crikey! Smells like a pig roast, eh?"

Turner's gorge rose and it took all of his will not to let it spew out in an acidic jet. Vickers's face was a glistening pale demon's in the firelight.

Turner looked, looked deep… but no matter where he turned, he couldn't find the blind, merciless rage that had held his soul in its clutches for three weeks. He couldn't look at the dead men and crow over their destruction. All he saw now were young men whose lives had been brutally taken from them by the pitiless lust of World War.

"*White, Blue! White, Blue! Do you read, over?*"

Turner blinked in surprise as he fumbled the radio from his belt. Shocked that it was still there and transmitting.

"Blue… White… we read…" To his own ears, Turner sounded dull, lethargic… worn down.

"*We've done it, mate!*" Cooper enthused. "*The village is ours! I'm at the command center and Colonel Archer is inbound… request you rendezvous there immediately.*"

Vickers's smile was so broad his teeth reflected the flickering flames of the half dozen or more burning houses. Turner raised the radio to his lips and said, "Roger that. By the way… my medic is caring for your wounded. If you're interested."

Not more than five minutes later, Lieutenant Smithers along with what remained of Red squad and Tank's fire team converged in the center of town. Cooper had half a dozen Japanese prisoners corralled with their hands tied behind their back. The captain was all smiles when the officers joined him.

"Well done, sir!" Cooper said to both Turner and Archer.

"Likewise, Gus," said Archer and looked to Turner. "Feels right good, doesn't it, Arthur?"

Turner only looked at Tank, "You all right?"

Tank smiled, "Fit as a fiddle, sir."

"Oh, by the by," Cooper said to Archer. "I've got a couple of lads inside holding a Nip officer for you, Colonel. He says he has information for you."

"Such as?" Archer couldn't repress his enthusiasm at this victory.

"He asked who was in charge and said that he must deliver the message directly to you, sir," said Cooper with a shrug.

"Then let's not keep the bugger waiting," said Archer and grinned at Turner. "Like to join me, Old Boy?"

Turner was pleased to see that in the town's main building, some sort of municipal center or other, Wayts was one of the men holding a pistol on the Japanese officer. The man was middle-aged, and Turner thought his rank to be that of major.

Archer confirmed this when he stepped close to the man, "Well, Major. I'm Colonel Percival Archer. My man here says you have some information for me?"

The major smiled and it sent a little unpleasant tickle up Turner's spine. There was something unsettling in that smile… and perhaps something unsettling that wasn't.

"Oh, I know you, Colonel," said the Japanese major. "I know you quite well. I congratulate you on your victory today. Well played."

"Indeed?" Archer was clearly enjoying lording it over the enemy.

The major's words only served to deepen Turner's concern, however. The man was too conciliatory, too pleasant… something was wrong. There was another shoe, and it was about to drop.

"Yes… but alas, war and victory are such fleeting things, are they not?" asked the major, a little derision creeping in now.

Archer caught it now and the gloat that had been roosting on his face crumbled before Turner's eyes, "Yes… just so… what are you driving at, sir?"

The major laughed, his veneer of pleasantness bubbled away and, in its place, a cold, hateful sneer, "You may have won this battle… but your lady friend, Ananda, has lost the war."

And there it was. The other shoe… studded with spikes and caked in horror. The implications struck like a freight train. And the transformation that seized Archer hit with equal power.

The Brit let out an anguished cry without form or reason. He leapt forward, took hold of the major by his throat and lifted him bodily out of the chair. He slammed the man down, squeezing until the yellow face turned purple.

"What... what... what have you *DONE?!*"

"Sir!" the new officer, a rugged, blonde lieutenant moved in, trying to grapple with Archer. "Sir, we need to—"

Vickers and Turner moved in, hauling Archer away and allowing the major to breathe. A tiny part of Turner's mind marveled at how just a few nights before, it'd been him being hauled off after throttling a man to death.

"Answer me!" Archer thrashed, a mindless animal whose fury had dashed his self-control to a handful of gravel. He calmed, or appeared to, and the men let him go.

The major coughed, spluttered, and smiled cruelly at the British soldier, "Everything comes at a price, round eye! And by now, the governor's *whore* shall have paid your fee! I sincerely hope that—"

The shot exploded and its echo drifted on the air, echoing slowly into eternity. Turner saw Cooper, pistol held in a two-handed grip, barrel smoking. His face a twisted mask of rage equal to Archer's own.

"Fuck you... fuck your entire race..."

26

"Raze the village," Archer snarled as he exited the building and stood before the prisoners. His eyes were wild. Their depths reflecting what fires had already been set like windows onto hell itself, "Every last building… every last crop."

"What about the prisoners, sir?" asked Lieutenant Smithers.

Archer glared, his face a lurid mask of hate. Without a word, he ejected his magazine, inserted another, and stepped forward.

"Colonel, what are—" Turner's question had hardly formed before he got his answer.

With quick but methodical accuracy, Archer pumped a round into each of the Japanese soldiers before him. Each a head shot. Each instantly fatal. Each having as much effect on the Englishman as if he were watching a family of ducks gliding over a pond.

"There's a working truck?" Archer's voice was a flat, bottomless rasp.

"Yes… sir…" Smithers, who had himself been calloused by the hardships he'd endured on Timor was pale and shaken. "It's still parked near the end of the field."

"Good," said Archer. "I'll leave the village to you, Lieutenant. I have business. See that nothing remains, do you hear? Nothing.

Cooper, Turner... gather a squad and come with me. We've got to get back to the lake house."

"Archer," Turner stepped in and tried to reason with the man. "We can't just—"

Archer whirled on the submarine captain and seized him by the front of his blouse. The man's eyes were wild saucers and even in the darkness, Turner could see that they weren't quite stable, "I said we have *business*, damn you! You heard what that yellow fucker said!"

Turner met his gaze and in an even tone that barely hung onto calm said, "Get your hands off me."

"Then stay here for all I give a damn!" Archer said. "She's in trouble, Captain! We tried raising her... no response! We've got to go!"

Archer was going, Turner knew it. He either went with him or stayed and watched the commandos burn down the entire town. What was better? Stay and watch one horror or go and possibly prevent another?

"Let's move!" Turner shouted. "Tank, Wayts, double-time it to the truck. Bring it back here and load up the wounded."

Archer whirled around, "We don't have time for all that rot! Ananda's—"

Turner stepped in and lowered his voice, "Those are my men in that house, Archer. Yours, too. We *will not* leave them. Attempt to do so and so help me *God*... I'll shoot you where you stand."

Once more the two men were locked face to face. Fury and tension crackled between them with enough palpable force to do Smithers's work for him. They stayed that way for long seconds. Long enough for Tank and Wayts to jog off into the night.

"They may already have her, Arthur..." Archer's fury instantly became fear. "My God... what if...?"

"We'll go," Turner said, "together and in force. There's a way to drive back I take it?"

"Yes, sir," Cooper stepped forward. "The road here connects to a mountain road. With a working truck, we can be there in less than an hour."

Archer barely had enough of his frayed self-control left to endure the few minutes it took to load the wounded into the back of the truck. Hoffman rode back there with them, and Fred Swooping Hawk, now on his feet, treated Turner to a smile when the captain asked how he was.

Cooper Rode up front. Turner was happy to get into the back with his men and with the eight men that could be spared. Smithers said that he'd finish up and make his way through the mountains and rendezvous at Ananda's house that evening.

Dawn was breaking when Cooper drove the truck around a bend in the forest road and along the lake. A thick, snake-like coil of smoke rose over the trees and the heady tang of wood ash reached them before they could see the property. It was too strong and from too far away. Turner's heart sank when the truck suddenly jolted to a stop.

"Move out!" Archer shouted as he bailed from the cab. "Form up!"

Cooper, Archer, and Turner had several men each. Swooping Hawk and Hoffman stayed with the truck and the wounded commandos. Sergeant Vickers stayed with Turner, Tank, and Wayts.

The three fire teams jogged down the road and when they finally saw the source of the smoke, they knew that they were too late.

The lake house was ablaze. Oily smoke poured from every window and bright yellow flames licked up the walls like some hideous ivy.

"Ananda!" Archer's cry was long, anguished, and echoed across the lake only to bounce back with magnified despair.

There was no longer any hope of stealth. Nor was there any hope of stopping the man. His fear, fury, and horror were more than any spirit could have borne.

Archer took off running straight for the house. Admirably, his men kept pace. Cooper glanced at Turner, a haunted look of resignation in his eyes and he took off as well. Cooper, at least broke left to try and come in with some hope of flanking what enemy might still be around.

"Come on," Turner growled.

"Sir, it's too late," Vickers said, his voice low and mournful.

"We have to try," Turner said. "We just… we have to."

So they ran. Between them all, there were only three magazines for the Thompson's left. Turner, Tank, and Wayts had a single load.

Vickers carried a Japanese rifle with bayonet affixed like the rest of the 2ICs. It hardly seemed enough, but it would have to be.

The house was a total loss. That was clear even from the truck a quarter mile away. The barn and barracks, however, appeared intact as the three teams converged across the too-open ground. It was intact and occupied.

Multiple rifles began crackling from within, sending rounds across the intervening ground in volleys of four. The men took what cover they could, including simply throwing themselves to the ground. They were not alone.

Lying between the house's back porch and the barn a hundred yards away were more than two dozen bodies. Some wore olive green fatigues and were clearly White men. Some wore the khaki of the Japanese Army, and a few wore civilian clothes. But all were broken, bent, and bloody. None would ever rise.

A fierce battle had been fought here, that much was obvious. Men had grappled and come into close quarters. Most of the dead enemies were close together. Bullet wounds and blades still buried in one another's flesh told the grisly tale.

Although the Japanese had prevailed… surprise and night assisting them… there was little left of them to gloat. What remained were five soldiers holed up in the barn. They made a valiant attempt to defend themselves but were quickly overwhelmed by the fire teams and their various angles of attack.

One by one, the Japanese snipers were picked off. Finally, after wounding two of the Australians and possibly running out of ammo, the remaining two surrendered. With the last rifle silenced, the heavy horror of the event could at last swoop in and settle over the scene. A scene made all the more nightmarish by the wisps of fog that still hugged the land.

Archer had gone into the barracks first and the sound that came out of the building as Turner approached froze his blood and jolted him to a stop. It was an animal sound. A wordless, thoughtless, and indescribable cry that was barely human… except for the anguish it conveyed.

Tank's, Wayts's, and even Vickers's faces were pallid masks in the early morning light. Without asking or wanting to… they appeared to understand what Turner could not deny.

"Come on," the submarine captain croaked, his voice as reluctant as he was. "We've got to go in there. Tank… you and Wayts… get the radio warmed up. Try to get in touch with Fremantle and get us a ride. Get us the hell off this rock."

Turner found Archer and Cooper in the bunk room. They, along with several of their men, held two Japanese soldiers prisoner. Yet Archer wasn't focused on them… his attentions were directed to a small, crumpled figure lying in a pool of vermillion on the wooden floor.

The commando held the limp body of Ananda Ribeiro in his arms, the blood that coated the front of her dress staining his hands, forearms, and tunic. The woman was dead, of that there was no doubt. Her throat had been cut from ear to ear and bled her to the color of bleached bones.

Archer's tears poured down his face, leaving pink streaks in the blood that had been smeared there. The man simply sat there, rocking his dead lover and sobbing. Over and over, he shook his head and whispered, "No… God no… please God no…"

It was heartbreaking and Turner felt his own eyes grow hot. Heartbreak hardly seemed an adequate description of the raw emotion Turner witnessed… or what dragged at his own soul.

Ananda was just the latest casualty in a string of heartbreaks. Men fought; men died… civilians lost their homes… the world threatened to tear itself to shreds. And fickle, feckless, and unstoppable fate ground it all under merciless treads. No pain, no suffering… and no man's torment could slow its progress. Not a submarine captain who'd lost friends… not a soldier who'd found something precious in the midst of a great horror and then had it ripped away. It seemed that all one could do was to cling to the threads of one's soul and hope for better times to come.

"Colonel," Turner said. "Percy… it's time to go."

"Go…" Archer whispered dreamily. "Go… time to go…? Go where? Why?"

"Come along, sir..." Cooper urged. "We've got to take care of the lads outside... and... and we can do right by the lady as well."

Archer looked up at the two officers, his eyes red-rimmed and vacant. They stared up from a deep well. A well of torture that sent a shiver up the captain's spine.

"Yes..." Archer intoned, gently easing Ananda's body to the floor and rising slowly to his feet. He shuffled forward, a broken husk of a man barely able to generate enough power to move under the tonnage of his anguish.

Turner wished there were some words he could use... some comfort he could offer the broken man. The only balm for a tormented soul, as he well knew, was time.

It all happened with remarkable speed. Archer's lethargy lulled them all, so that when his pistol appeared in his hand, it took several swollen seconds for the men to understand.

The Colt 1911 held eight rounds in its magazine. Generally, a round would be jacked into the chamber and another loaded into the magazine so that the shooter had nine ready to go.

Archer's eight shots thundered in the long bunkroom. The flashes from the barrel casting lightning flashes of white and shadow around the room. His face never moved, never twitched. There was no smile nor a grimace. Just a cold, granite sculpture of a human visage.

The Japanese prisoners roared in agony as .45 slugs smashed knees, elbows, and ravaged their guts. Their agony didn't last long... although it was in no way due to mercy... because each one received a final shot between their eyes.

"Do right by her," Archer muttered.

He smiled then, and it nearly forced Turner to take a step back. It was the smile of a death's head.

It was Cooper who comprehended first. Archer had fired only eight shots. There was one more bullet... and Archer used it.

He turned the barrel around, placed the muzzle under his chin and pulled the trigger. Black hair, bits of skull, and gelatinous lumps of brain fountained out the back of the man's head. Percival Archer toppled back, falling almost gracefully like a felled tree. The body landed with a hollow, terrible thunk that Turner would experience over and over in nightmares yet to come. Archer's head lay perfectly positioned in Ananda's lap. The two lovers united by the horrors of war were now joined forever in the cold embrace of death.

"Sir... oh, my sweet Christ..." Sherman Broderick gasped as he entered the room. He glanced about at the faces of Turner, Cooper, and the three soldiers standing over the bodies. "What... what the hell...?"

Turner simply turned and walked outside. He didn't want to see anymore. He didn't want to smell the acrid tang of cordite hanging in the air... or the rank coppery odor of death.

"Something to report, Tank?" Turner asked, lighting a cigarette that tasted like it'd been stored in an urn.

Tank swallowed, "I... yes, sir... I got in touch with Fremantle. They said *Bull Shark* was able to pick us up. Tomorrow night, same place. Should I tell them we'll be there, sir?"

Turner snorted, "Yeah, Tank... yeah. It's time to leave."

The two men said nothing for a long few moments. The heavy scent of the burning house floated about the property, mixing with the fog now being burned away by a cheerful rising sun. It was horrific in its pleasantness.

"It's Christmas," Tank said flatly. "Believe that, sir? Christmas morning."

Turner chuckled. If he hadn't, he thought he might have cried, "Peace on Earth and good will toward men... wonder where that might be true today?"

Perhaps it was because of Christmas, perhaps it was simply dumb luck. But Cooper and several men conducted Turner east toward their landing zone. They drove much of the way before having to hide the truck and finish the job on foot. It took the better part of the next day and by sunset on the twenty-sixth, the Australians and the Americans parted.

With little conversation, the men of *Bull Shark* pushed their raft out onto the dark, peaceful little bay and rode toward the sea. When the large, dark shape of a submarine rose before them, their spirits lifted but weren't quite ready yet to soar.

Elmer Williams noted the five returning men and instantly grasped the situation, even as he shook Turner and the other men's hands.

"I take it the colonel elected to stay, Art?"

Turner did not smile when he said, "That's one way of putting it, Elmer. How's my boat? Do we need to put in?"

"We've had a few shakes, but nothing to write home about," Williams downplayed. "We've got plenty of fuel but we're down thirteen fish. We can put in at Exmouth for both, though. Before we continue on with our mission… if that's what we're gonna do."

Turner nodded, "Why we're out here, Elmer. Faster we beat the Jap, faster we wake up from this bad dream and go home."

Williams cast a look at the bedraggled men and then back at his captain, "How are you, Art?"

"Tired, Elmer," Turner said and then drew in a deep breath of salt air. He even managed a little smile. "But nothing a good night's sleep and some sea air won't cure. Acting Captain Williams… shape us a course for Exmouth Gulf. And don't spare the whip."

Williams watched his captain descend into the conning tower. A man in torn battle fatigues forever stained with mud and dried blood. And perhaps a soul beneath in a similar condition.

He knew Turner wasn't ready to talk about the mission yet… but he thought that he would be soon. Thought that Turner would talk about the mission and about other things.

Without knowing why, Elmer Williams felt as if Turner had experienced a cleansing on Timor. Not the way in which fresh water can clean a wound… but perhaps in the way that blood can. He shuddered, turned back to the bridge and gave his orders.

Bull Shark turned her head to sea, revved up her engines, and drove for the horizon.

BEFORE YOU GO

One chapter ends and yet another looms on the horizon. And yes, I most certainly will deliver Pat Jarvis's and *Megalodon's* story soon. War is a hard and messy business… and your scribe needs to clear his pallet before diving back in. A quick breath and no more, though!

Thank you for reading. Your dedication is what keeps our characters alive. In this series and in all my others.

Please rate and review this work. Your feedback is always appreciated. Also, please visit my website and sign up for the free, no spam email list. There are discounts and free goodies waiting for you!

www.scottwcook.com

Warmest regards,
Scott W. Cook

OTHER BOOKS BY THIS AUTHOR...

Scott Jarvis, Private Investigator Series
Choices - Book 1
The Ledger - Book 2
Play The Hand You're Dealt - Book 3
Isle of Bones - Book 4
Shadows of Limelight - Book 5
Sins of the Fatherland - Book 6
A Fortune in Blood - Book 7
That Way Lies Madness - Book 8
To Honor We Call You - Book 9
What Lies Beneath - Book 10
Suffer Not Evil - Book 11
He That Covets - Book 12
Whom Predators Fear - Book 13
The Wicked Flee Where None Pursueth - Book 14

* * *

A Florida Action Adventure Bundle - Books 1-3

USS *Bull Shark* – WWII Submarine Thriller Series

Operation Snare Drum - Book 1

Leviathan Rising - Book 2

The Cactus Navy - Book 3

Tokyo Express - Book 4

Behavior Reports - Book 5

Seas of Flame - Book 6

Outta the Frying Pan - Book 7

Blood Warm Waters - Book 8

Dig Two Graves - Book 9

* * *

USS *Enterprise* - Naval Adventure Series

Wings of Destiny - Book 1

Wings of Vengeance - Book 2

Wings of Glory - Book 3

Wings of Valor - Book 4

* * *

Decker's Marine Raiders Series

Pacific Blood - Book 1

Pacific Guts - Book 2

Pacific Grit - Book 3

Pacific Mettle - Book 4

Catherine Cook, an Age of Sail Adventure Series

A Heart of Oak

A Treacherous Wind Blows Foul

* * *

The Immortal Dracula Series

The Dead Travel Fast - Book 1

The Blood is the Life - Book 2

The Sword and the Spirit - Book 3

What a Hell We Would Make - Book 4

* * *

A Collection of Horror Stories

Whispers From the Dark

* * *

Terrors of the Deep

The Crushing Darkness - Book 1

Made in the USA
Middletown, DE
24 May 2025

76025231R00166